BRIEF IN

Natasha stared at the dark-haired stranger, studying his features with eyes that were cautiously critical. He wasn't one of "them." She could tell that by the way he was dressed. Likewise, her ears told her that although he was communicating very well with them, their language was not his. There was something different in the way he said the words. More importantly, she could sense that he did not like them any more than she did. That gave them something in common.

She took a step closer, unafraid of staring. The closer she got to him, the more she liked what she saw. The man had long, dark hair that nearly touched his wide shoulders. His chin was firm and smooth, without the rough beard the Norsemen displayed. His nose was straight and shaped just right to go with the rest of his face. His arms were strong, and even beneath the cloth of his garments she could see that he was muscular with a broad chest, flat belly, and narrow hips. His whole body spoke of strength and power. He was, in fact, handsome, which perhaps was responsible for the strange, unknown sensation that coursed through her as he glanced her way again.

She froze as their eyes met and held for a long, halting moment. His blue eyes mesmerized her. She read compassion in his look, as if he somehow knew how she felt. Both of them stood, unmoving. Suddenly she realized that she had been holding her breath. She let it out in a sigh. He was decidedly pleasing to look upon, and she found herself wishing that if she had to be owned it would be by this man.

Dear Romance Readers,

In July of 1999, we launched the Ballad line with four new series, and each month we present both new and continuing stories set everywhere from medieval England to the American West—the kind of passionate, romantic stories you love best, written by the most gifted authors. At the back of each book, we tell you when you can find subsequent books in the series that have captured your heart.

First up this month is **After the Storm,** the final book in Jo Ann Ferguson's heartfelt *Haven* series. When a mother in search of her children finds them with a man who has become like a father to them, will he become a husband to her, as well? Next, talented Kathryn Hockett introduces us to the third proud hero in her exciting series, *The Vikings.* Raised to be a scholar, he never expected to be an **Explorer**—until the fate of a young woman falls into his hands, and her love burns in his heart.

Men of Honor continues with Kathryn Fox's emotional tale, **The Healing.** Can a desperate woman on the run from her past fall for the mounted police officer who intends to bring her to justice? Finally, Julie Moffett concludes the *MacInness Legacy* with **To Touch the Sky,** the gripping story of a woman born to heal others who discovers the strange legacy that threatens to harm the one man she has come to love.

These are stories we know you'll love! Why not try them all this month?

Kate Duffy
Editorial Director

The Vikings

EXPLORER

Kathryn Hockett

ZEBRA BOOKS
Kensington Publishing Corp.
http://www.kensingtonbooks.com

ZEBRA BOOKS are published by

Kensington Publishing Corp.
850 Third Avenue
New York, NY 10022

First Printing: September 2002
10 9 8 7 6 5 4 3 2 1

Printed in the United States of America

Author's Note

From the time of the first raids and beyond, the Vikings aroused strong passions in those they came in contact with. They were called "fearsome wolves," "stinging hornets," devils, heathens, and ruthless, wrathful pagans. The monasteries of Ireland were one of their prime targets, so it is no wonder that monastic scholars have left us contemporary chronicles with bitter accounts of their misfortune.

The lush, green hills of Ireland were crowned with uncounted monasteries, which were the center of study for all kinds of subjects from astronomy to theology. Indeed, Ireland had the most intellectually advanced culture in the West. Many scholars from Britain and the mainland of Europe traveled to Ireland to study in it's famous monastery schools. The monasteries were devoted to the preservation of higher knowledge, beautifully illustrated manuscripts, and exquisite decorative art.

Ireland soon became an economic and political focal point to the Vikings for provisions, precious goods, livestock, and captives. Thus, the monasteries were raided not because the Vikings were anti-Christian, but because these sites were centers of wealth and were ill protected. They contained ecclesiastical treasures and provisions of wine for mass. Also, the defenseless abbots, monks, and nuns were captured for ransom, and if funds were not available for their return, they were sold as slaves. The slave trade was a thriving business for the Vikings.

Like the Vikings, the Magyars were travelers, wandering from place to place on the eastern steppes and in Russia, taking their women and children with them. Their mode of travel, however, was wagons, not ships. The Ukrainian steppes offered a harsh environment to the Magyars, with hot, dry summers and bitterly cold winters.

The Magyars were derived from tribes loosely named Ugri or Igurs (hence ogre). They had a strong infusion of Hun and Turkish blood but spoke a language closely related to their relatives the Finns. They were hunters and warriors, who fished in winter and, like the Vikings, made a profit from the slave market. When they were captured they were likewise sold into slavery in many of the slave markets of the ancient world, including Ireland and the Russ (Russia), where this story takes place.

Woven into the fabric of these happenings, the search continues to find the last son of Ragnar Longsword, the daring Viking jarl whose name is already legend. To each of his lovers he has given a jewel from his Viking sword to hang around his sons' necks when they are born. Will the last pendant reveal the whereabouts of Ragnar's long-lost son?

In Ireland the third quest begins, linking a man who has been raised in a monastery school with a daring Magyar slave who is determined to escape her circumstances . . . at any price.

Note: The Vikings traveled not only via the seas, but also sailed up navigable rivers such as the Rhine to inland ports. In eastern Europe, Vikings known as Rus pioneered trade routes along the rivers of Russia to the Black and Caspian Seas, giving their name to the Russian state that developed at Novgorod around 862. This became the main trade route between Scandinavia and Constantinople. Kiev, because of its strategic location on the Dniper River, was the most important of all towns of the Rus, and for the Vikings using this trade route.

Portages were found on both inland waterways and on the coast where the Vikings could save sailing time or avoid dangerous headlands by cutting across promontories. Portages formed essential links on the trade route through Russia between the headwaters of the rivers Dvina, Volga, Lovat, and Dnieper and around the rapids on the Dnieper. Transporting the ships in this manner, however, could be dangerous, because at such times they were vulnerable to ambushes by Slavs and Petcheneg raiders. The portages in Russia continued to be used into modern times.

PART ONE
Captive Heart

The Steppes and Eire (Ireland)
Autumn 858

One

The setting sun shimmered through the haze of choking dust stirred by the horses' hooves in the large caravan. The band of Magyars was silhouetted against the horizon as they traveled along the steppes looking for a new settlement. At the head of the caravan, Osip the Tall rode upon a white stallion, towering over the others like an ominous shadow. Acknowledging his leadership, the others of the group followed closely behind.

The men rode haphazardly, side by side, their long sheepskin *subas,* or cloaks, flapping in the wind. Each was obviously trying to outdo the other in horsemanship, proud that they, like the Huns, were unequaled at riding. Next were the wolfhounds and other hunting dogs, spare horses, and horses pulling wagons piled high with household belongings, food, clothing, treasures, seeds for new planting, and even a few crated chickens they had been able to gather, along with their cattle, sheep, and goats. Following this entourage came the women and children, also cloaked in warm subas, trudging along as fast as they could.

A chill breeze whipped through the branches of the few scattered trees, tangling the light-blond hair that cascaded nearly to the knees of the young woman at the back of the caravan. As tradition declared, Natasha had never shorn a single lock of her tresses. Now, cursing softly, she reached up with both hands, grabbed the offending hair, and hurriedly stuffed it down the back of her sheepskin cloak where it would be out of the way.

"I wish we had time. I could braid it for you," a soft voice beside her said.

"Osip wouldn't give us time, Nadia. He herds us as unmercifully as the Khazars do their goats!"

Natasha looked accusingly toward Osip, then blinked. For a moment she could almost see her father in Osip's place, riding astride his saddled white stallion. Unlike Osip, her father had been concerned with the others and not just himself. But her father was gone now, killed along with her brothers in a battle against a tribe of Petchenegs, raiders of the steppes and their enemies. The loss of her loved ones had been the death of her mother. Now it seemed as if the whole world was in turmoil. Natasha had suffered many hardships after losing her entire family. She had no one except her friend, Nadia.

Feeling a surge of affection, she looked over at the young woman who had been her friend since childhood. She and Nadia had each been the youngest child in their families. Their only siblings were brothers who were grown men and too busy to bother with girls. Perhaps that was why the two had so quickly bonded. That and the sense of protectiveness that Natasha had felt right from the first.

Nadia, also blond but darker of hair than Natasha, was like a flower, delicate and fragile, and exceedingly kind of heart. She was not meant for the grueling life, constant traveling, and hard work of scratching out a mean existence that they were forced to endure. Nadia was gentle, like the fawns that lived in the forests. That was why Natasha more often than not did Nadia's share of the work and gave her friend a large portion of her own share of food.

Now there was yet another reason to be concerned.

Nadia had injured her left knee several weeks ago in a fall while trying to hurry along in the caravan, and Natasha was deeply concerned that the injury had left her friend with a permanent limp. Knowing that on the steppes only the strong survived, Natasha had instinctively protected her friend, walking side by side with Nadia at the end of the caravan—something even Nadia's family wouldn't do.

"Osip tries to be a good leader, Tasha, but he is still young. Give him time," Nadia whispered. "I think he wants to be like your father but doesn't know how."

"He will never be like my father! No one could ever be like my father!" Natasha exclaimed.

For a moment the pain of her loss made her choke, and she fought against her tears. She remembered how her father had always ridden up to her in the caravan and spoken her name, "Tasha," in such a soft caressing voice that seemed at odds with his large, muscular frame.

"I just wanted to see your sweet face," he would say, with none of the fierce thunder that could frighten some of the others. "The long ride has jiggled my bones, but your smile always soothes me."

Forgetting for a moment that he was supposed to be stern and unsmiling, he had swept her up in front of him on the horse and ridden with her to the front of the caravan. She had always felt so protected in her father's strong arms. Protected and loved.

"I want them all to see what a beautiful daughter I have. I want them to know how proud I am of you, my little Tasha!"

"Tasha!"

The sound of the voice was harsh and pierced through her reverie. Natasha turned her head, not surprised to find that it was Osip who yelled at her.

"What is it?" She looked up at him defiantly. "Did you ride all the way back here just to startle me?"

"No. I came to give you warning." He reached

down to grip her arm, holding her so tightly that she winced in pain. "You are walking much too slowly. You are forcing the others to slow their pace. I will not have it!"

"It is my fault, not hers." Nadia would not let Natasha take any of the blame. "My leg has been hurting me. Natasha has been kind to give me company as I hobble along."

Osip grunted in irritation. "Pain or no pain, you must walk faster! If you do not, we will leave you behind in the dust."

Nadia paled. "You wouldn't!"

Osip grunted again. "I would!"

"Then you are a pig!" Natasha exclaimed. "My father would have shown Nadia mercy."

"Your father would have gotten us all killed! But I won't. Even if I have to push the tribe until their feet bleed and they are so weary they want to die, I will not put us in the path of danger."

For a moment his shoulders slumped. The arrogance had vanished from his face and he looked older than his twenty-seven years. He heaved a sigh.

"It seems peaceful now, but the steppes are a place of terror as well as beauty." He gestured with his hand. "Its flatness and the luxuriance of its grass make it a pathway of invasion by fierce nomadic tribes from central and eastern Asia who have been pouring into it since the beginning of time. They are always a danger. And you should know that! You of all people."

Natasha winced, remembering her father's death. It was true. There were many dangers from Turks, Volga Bulgars, Alans, Petchenegs and others. Natasha knew that the Avars were said not to use horses or oxen to pull their wagons but instead to yoke up four or five women. The Khazars had taken their place. They were a more enlightened people than their predecessors and were more interested in trade than in plunder and butchery. They permitted the Slavs to pass through their territory, extracting a tax of about one-tenth of their goods. Even so, there were times when they could be treacherous.

More fierce and feared than of any of these, however, were the wandering bands of Norsemen, called "Varangians" by her people, who were warrior-traders. They had searched out the inland water routes from the Baltic to the Black Sea. Natasha shivered at the very thought of them, for their interest was in obtaining wealth, including slaves, by trade where it was possible, and by the sword where it was not.

"Let Nadia ride on one of the spare horses," Natasha suggested, eager to put her friend out of harm's way. "She can ride sidesaddle so that her leg doesn't bother her."

"Let her ride on horseback? A woman?" Osip looked at her as if she had lost her mind. "I would have a rebellion on my hands from the other women. Worse yet, you women would think that riding horseback was your due. No!" He shook his head stubbornly. "No!" he said again. He gave them one final warning. "You had better keep up, or I swear by the bones of the witch Baba Yaga that you will be left behind!" Angrily, he rode off.

"Baba Yaga!" Nadia gasped, afraid of the mythical character who was said to guard the gates between this world and the next.

"I'm not afraid of that hideous old woman, nor am I afraid of Osip," Natasha insisted. Even so, she prodded Nadia along, even putting her arm around her shoulder to help her friend.

As they walked both were silent, concentrating upon keeping up with the others. Natasha's mood was deteriorating footstep by aching footstep. They were always on the move! For just once in her life she wished that they could stop wandering. She longed for a permanent home.

"We have been traveling since I can remember," she whispered to herself.

She thought about how she had clutched the soft wool cape with the beaver collar that her father had given her after his first raid into the urban country further south. She had been excited as she sat next to her mother on the seat of their wagon. Although she had only been five at the time, she had known that they were going into a new territory, the Khazars' territory, to try to live peacefully with them and start a new life.

For a time Natasha and her family had been happy there. Her father and brothers, like the other Magyar men, were superb horsemen, archers, and swordsmen, and much in demand as allies to the Byzantines and others of the Orthodox Christian faith who were fighting the advancing Arabs.

The Magyar tribe had needed someone strong to lead them in war. Not a king or a lord but a strong horseman, for the Magyar men considered themselves equals. Her father was chosen. Her brothers were old enough to sit in council and make plans. If her mother and the other women were often left alone while the men fought, well, so be it. That was the way of things.

But then everything had gone wrong. The Abbassed caliphs of the Turkish Ottoman kingdom had begun to press westward as the Muslim world expanded. People who were in the way were destroyed. Many villages lay in ruins because of so much warfare. Whole tribes of people were destroyed; crops, animals, and buildings torched, including Natasha's own home. The Turkish tribe of Petchenegs had destroyed the Khazar empire and driven the Magyars westward. That had been the beginning of the Magyars' constant push from place to place, migrating from the Ural-Caspian steppes to the lands adjoining the Don, the Dnieper, and the Black Sea.

Natasha was jolted as Nadia stumbled over the hem of her embroidered linen skirt. Luckily, she caught her before she fell. Nadia looked close to tears, but before she had time to succumb to frustrated weeping, Natasha helped her hike up her skirts to resemble the *gatya,* the trousers worn by the men. Then she hiked up her own skirts.

Natasha was tired and miserable, but as she glanced at Osip out of the corner of her eye she knew that they would receive no sympathy. "Even Osip has to tire eventually," she whispered to Nadia, trying to hide her worry that they were falling farther and farther behind. It was dark. Even if the others outdistanced them they would have to stop and make camp.

"Leave me, Tasha. There is no reason for you to suffer because of me." Nadia tried to smile. "I'll be fine. Really."

"Leave you? Never!" Natasha only wished that she were strong enough to carry Nadia on her back. As it was, however, she was growing so weary that she could barely put one foot in front of the other. And all the while Osip kept going, or rather his horse did.

As they traveled, Natasha tried to think of something other than her tired legs and sore feet. Closing her eyes for just a moment, she conjured up her homeland on the Ukrainian steppes. At first there had been few families there, but then other people had begun to arrive. Other Magyars, Khazars, Lithuanians, Volga Bulgars, Danube Bulgars, and, farther east on the steppes, even Turks. All were rushing away from something, that being the Eastern Roman Empire, known as the Byzantines, the Western Frankish Empire, which was pushing from the west, and, of course, the Turks. Natasha and her people had been in between.

Her father had fought furiously along with some others who had formed a brotherhood to preserve and protect their homeland, but they had been pushed over the mountains and onto the plains farther westward.

"Tasha, I can't go any farther."

Turning her head, Natasha was struck by the look of pure agony upon her friend's face. Fearing total collapse, she dragged Nadia over to a large rock, where she could pull off her boots, sit for a short while, and rest.

"It's getting too dark to see it, Nadia, but you can almost smell the rich, black soil of the steppes." It was said that the open country offered no obstruction to the plow; the land was not only rich but also beautiful. "All the way to the Black Sea it is a green virgin wilderness. Never has a plow driven through the long waves of wild growth, and only the horses, hidden in it among the trees of the forest, trample the tall grass. Imagine if you can, Nadia. And know that we will be there soon."

Nadia did imagine. "There is nothing more beautiful in the world. It is like a golden-green ocean, its waves topped by multicolored froth. Close your eyes, Tasha. Share the view with me."

Natasha's mind saw the tall, slender stems of grass mingling with sky-blue, marine, and purple star thistles. Yellow broom thrust up its pyramidal head. Partridges scurried among the thin stalks of the steppe plants, and in the sky hawks hung immobile on their outspread wings, eyes fixed on the ground.

"Look, Tasha!"

Natasha opened her eyes to see that the beauty unfolding before her eyes was even better than her daydream. The nighttime world seemed to erupt with color as the last bright reflection of the sun began to darken. Fragrance from the plants increased: every flower, every blade of grass released its incense, and the whole steppe was bathed in a wild, intoxicating aroma. The daytime music was replaced by a different one as spotted marmots crept out of their holes, rose on their hind legs, and filled the steppe with their whistling. The whir of grasshoppers gradually dominated the other sounds. Like a silver trumpet, the cry of a swan reached them.

Suddenly, Natasha realized that she heard another sound as well: the crunching of boots on the dirt. She started to caution Nadia, but before she could utter a word she was set upon from behind.

Natasha felt a scream start somewhere deep inside and sear its way through her heart, lungs, and up to her throat. "Run, Nadia! Run!"

Hands grabbed her, holding her immobile, but she fought like a wild thing, kicking, biting, and scratching. She could hear them talking in a strange language but didn't understand a word they said. She could only wonder what they were. Bulgar? Khazars? Slavs? Petchenegs? Whatever they were, they were big, bearded, blond, and strong! Natasha's hands were tied behind her back. Like an old sack, she was thrown over her captor's shoulders.

"Nadia!"

At first she was elated to think that her friend had escaped, but then she saw Nadia's silhouette. Just like Natasha, she was being treated like trade goods and not like a human being.

Natasha started to struggle even harder. Somehow, she had to get free so that she could help Nadia. The more she fought, however, the tighter their hold was on her. Hoping to bring help, she made a loud sound deep in her throat that soon became a scream. Osip had to hear her shrieks. She willed him to hear her!

A gag was stuffed in her mouth and knotted tightly, silencing her completely. A large blanket was thrown over her head, and Natasha found herself in total darkness.

Two

The meadows were ablaze with the muted tones of the coming autumn. A myriad of shades covered the hills and valleys. Half of the tree leaves were either a rusty red or burnished gold; the other half were still green. The wild grass and bushes were varied tones of green. As Sean walked down the hill, he thought how the color green seemed to symbolize his beloved land of Eire. There were some who even referred to it as the emerald isle.

"Green and blue . . ." he whispered, pausing to look at the view. "The sapphire blue of the sea and the azure blue of the sky." Against the green and blue was gray, the color of the magnificent cliffs and the stone walls of the monastery of Armagh in Ulster. The monastery was the place that Sean called home.

Sean didn't have any idea who his real parents were, or anything about their fate. All he knew was what the monks had told him: that he had been found bundled up in a blanket lying on a bed of straw in the monastery's stable. Brother Fionan had insisted that right from the first the monks of Armagh had known that Sean was special, that the location where he had been placed had been a sign. That was why they had fostered him out to a childless couple only until he was old enough to walk and talk. As soon as he was of school age, he had lived at the monastery and had been schooled by the brothers.

Sean had never disappointed them. As a boy he had learned almost the whole of Scripture by rote, and there were other things that he had committed to memory. He had learned quickly, spending most of his hours either studying the written word or watching the monks in the scriptorium patiently copying texts for the monastery's library. As soon as Sean was able to read and write he began to work on the manuscripts.

Tall, broad-shouldered, dark-haired, and strikingly handsome, Sean had a thirst for knowledge as well as a joy in all things that were beautiful. His was a quiet strength. Gentle, penetrating blue eyes reflected his inquisitive mind. He had wanted to know everything about everything since he was just a child. It was no wonder, then, that he had so eagerly embraced the opportunity granted him to study at the monastery school and learn the art of transcribing and decorating books.

Creating a book was slow work. First, vellum had to be made from calfskin, then quills made from goose feathers to pen the texts. Brushes to illuminate the manuscript were created with hairs from Sean's head and from the hides of cattle and pigs.

Sean painstakingly pulverized and mixed the minerals and the plants to produce the dyes that would light up a chapter, a paragraph, or a page. Red was from ochre that came from the earth, green from verdigris, yellow from orpiment, golden brown from lichen, and blue from woad. Sean had even learned how to cook fish in such a manner that he could extract oil that would bind his colors, and how to burn the fats that made the inks.

Sitting at his desk, he would pen the words, adding a curve or distinctive pothook to a character. Later he would embellish some of the letters with a crimson stroke of the brush. Each page was arranged in two carefully planned columns. If by chance his calculations went astray, which meant several words had to be slipped in, he would do it as unobtrusively as possible between existing lines.

That was not to say that his life was entirely about reading and writing. There were times when he, like the monks, would withdraw to a cell or to the oratory to meditate or pray alone; times when he busied himself in the necessary tasks of washing garments, or fishing, or cultivating the small garden, or mending and rebuilding things. He was skilled at building and was exceedingly proud of the curragh, or small boat, he had built for the brothers to use when they went fishing.

Sean knew that in these turbulent times he was one of the lucky ones. He had the comradship of the monks, plenty to eat, warm garments to wear, and most important, he was doing what he really loved—learning. The learned men were a distinct class in society. Their skills gave them status. In many ways they were as respected as the warrior.

It was just that sometimes when he looked toward the great ocean he felt strangely unfulfilled, as if he was missing something. Though he had never been on a ship or even knew any seamen, he felt a yearning to sail out and find what lay beyond Eire. He felt in his heart that there were new lands, new peoples just waiting to be found.

The monks believed that the greatest sacrifice they could make was to go into exile for the love of Christ; thus, some of them had traveled to all parts of the world, bringing back with them strange tales of foreign lands. These tales fueled Sean's wanderlust. Someday he too would travel. For the moment, however, he had learned to be content with the life that God had granted him.

Sean reached for the leather pouch that hung from his belt. Inside was a pendant shaped like a wolf. According to one of the older monks, it had been hanging around his neck the night he was found in the stable. So many years ago!

Taking the pendant and silver chain from the pouch, he gazed at it. "The wolf. The amber wolf!" A symbol of cunning and strength to some, evil and savagery to others. What did this wolf mean?

It was placed in the silver setting in such a way that it looked as if the wolf had a shadow. Sean fingered it with a mixture of curiosity and affection. Somehow, it was connected to his parentage, but how, he might never know how.

His fingers traced the form of the wolf. Since he was a boy he had ached to wear it, but because such things were considered pagan, he had been forbidden by the abbot to put it around his neck. Still, he had always been curious. Perhaps one day he would find out its meaning and why it had been placed around his neck. One day!

"As Brother Fionan always says, all things in due time," he said aloud as he started back down the hill.

The monastery appeared on the horizon like a whittler's intricately fashioned handiwork. The stones of the small church had been laid painstakingly one upon the other, without mortar, built by the monks themselves. Nestled by the church's side, around the great quadrangle of the cloister, were the dark monastic buildings that seemed to break the spell and made the viewer realize life was far from frivolous at Armagh. Here were the holy wells, sun dials, the refectory, and the library and scriptorium where Sean spent much of his time now, designing covers for the gospels and other texts, and, of course, the living quarters. The monks lived within a walled enclosure of beehive huts. Those who had not taken such vows yet, including Sean, were outside the walled enclosure. Sean and his fellow students lived two to a hut but spent endless time alone in study or at work.

Sean's eyes touched on the gardens of the cloister.

Now those gardens were bleak, the flowers devoid of petals, its stepping stones slick to walk upon because of the early morning rain, but once there had been brightly hued flowers, carefully tended by Brother Doulagh, despite the warning that he was being frivolous and that gardens should only be used for growing food. The abbot's hut stood apart from the other buildings, just as the abbot seemed to stand apart from all the others who lived in the monastery.

Beyond the church and monastic buildings lay the outbuildings and halls, and the jumble of kitchens with their larders, sculleries, bakehouse, buttery, and brewhouse. Then there were the more somber dwellings: homes for visitors, for they never let anyone looking for food and shelter go without aid; the home for aged monks; the infirmaries, and the house for letting blood. It was a self-contained community. There was a school for novices and a priors' hall; the baths, guest halls, farm buildings, and workmen's huts; a byre and sheepfold; sties and goat sheds; a small stable; henhouses, pigpens, beehives; tanks for fish; several small walled-in gardens; and acres and acres of open fields.

Hurrying his steps, Sean moved forward, not wanting to be late for vespers. The abbot had always been a strict disciplinarian. He ruled his household with an iron hand, expecting those who hovered about him to be just as punctual and obedient as he. There was a contrast between the everlasting confusion, disorganization, and discomfort of ordinary households, where no one knew from day to day what might be in store, and the quiet regularity and authoritarianism of the abbot's staff.

"God has been with you, Sean," Brother Bron called out cheerily. "You are back early this time."

Sean slowed his pace. He could see the light, cream-colored robes of the monks as they ambled about, each engrossed in a task. Unlike the Benedictines, whose robes were dyed black, the monks from Eire chose not to color their garments artificially; thus their robes were the same natural color as the fleece from which they were spun.

Sean always dressed in an ankle-length linen *leine,* a long-sleeved tunic embroidered at the neck, wrists, and hem, which he found very comfortable. On cold days he wore a *brat,* a rectangular woolen cloak fastened with a brooch. Today he had on a light-grayish-blue leine and a dark-gray brat.

"Have you thought any more about joining the order?" Brother Bron inquired, walking along beside him. "We have need of men with your aptitude and ability."

Sean shook his head. "I've thought about it and prayed for an answer, but so far I am not ready to make such an important commitment."

Although he had been brought up in the monastery and truly loved the monks, Sean had resisted their attempts to convince him to join the order. He had found that there was too much seclusion from the outside world in the monastery. He had his reservations about living a solitary, religious way of life where self-deprivation was required. Sean was well aware of the harsh penalties and punishments inflicted upon monks for the slightest transgressions. Sean remembered what Abbot Righifarch had told him: "All things in life must be done mindfully, Sean. This is the spiritual path that all our monks must follow."

"You will be ready soon. I feel it in here." Brother Bron touched his heart.

Sean touched his own heart. "I feel something as well." It was an eerie feeling that hadn't anything to do with the monastery or the monks. It was as if he were waiting for something or someone. . . .

Three

The next few weeks of Natasha's life passed by in a blur of heartache and misery. Though she called upon both Belobog, the white god, god of light and the sky, and Chernobog, the black god, god of darkness and the earth, for help, she and Nadia were not rescued. Not by the gods, not by Osip, not by anyone!

Natasha had no idea where she was or how far she had traveled, or even in what direction they were going. She remembered only bits and pieces of her ordeal. Clutching her suba around her thin shoulders to ward off the autumn night's chill, she had been shoved forward to join a small band of captives.

"What is going to happen to us, Tasha?" Nadia's voice was soft and filled with fear.

Though she was fearful, too, Natasha refused to show it. No matter what their destiny was, she would be strong. "If they were going to kill us they would have killed us by now," she answered, biting her lip to keep from crying. She knew that if she showed even a hint of panic Nadia might break down.

"We are going to be slaves! That's why they spared us. Slaves, Tasha. A fate worse than death." Already Nadia seemed to be bordering on hysteria.

Natasha shuddered at the very thought but hid her feelings from her friend, saying only, "As long as we are alive, there is hope. Remember that, Nadia, and that I am with you. . . ."

Alas, it was the last thing she was able to say to Nadia, because they were soon separated. Due to her injured leg, Nadia was put onto a litter, while Natasha had to walk, burdened with the heavy bundles her captors gave her to carry.

"At least Nadia has been shown a measure of mercy," she whispered, stung by the irony that these captors were in their own way being kinder to her friend than Osip, who shared their blood, had been.

Despite their separation, she kept watch on Nadia from afar, waving to her from time to time with a smile on her face that belied her aches, pains, and feelings of total fatigue. She was tired, bone tired. So weary that she had to concentrate on every step and use all her energy just to put one foot in front of the other. And all the while, the caravan kept moving. They did not stop all day. Nadia supposed that her captors were in a hurry, no doubt anxious to be far away from any who might come to free the captives or bring retribution down upon their heads.

By evening the weary captives were supporting one another in an effort to stay on their feet. A few girls sobbed aloud, but most seemed as determined as Natasha to be brave. Or perhaps they were all in a state of shock. They seemed to form a temporary bond with each other, even sighing in unison as they were at last given a chance to drink from a nearby stream and bed down for the night.

Even though she could finally rest, Natasha felt miserable. Her muscles were so sore that they cramped with pain. A bone-weariness seemed to invade her whole body. Nonetheless, she somehow managed to drag herself to Nadia's side.

"How are they treating you?"

"For the time being they have been kind, but what of you?" Nadia sighed. "My poor, dear Tasha, you have walked the entire way." She shook her head. "Let me talk to them. Maybe they will let us trade places from time to time. That way you can rest and—"

"No!" Natasha hurried to assure Nadia that she was just fine. "A good night's sleep is all I need. Besides, I have a feeling we are close to our destination."

All the captives were given broth and hard bread to eat as well as strong wine, no doubt to calm them so that they would be less trouble. Natasha suspected that the wine might be drugged; thus she drank a lot less than the others. Even with the small amount she did drink, however, Natasha fell asleep immediately.

As if by a miracle, her pain had eased and she felt more relaxed—so relaxed that she seemed to float in and out of a haze. It seemed that there were men all around her, jabbering in their strange tongue. Natasha could see their lips moving but heard nothing. One of the men, however, seemed to be fascinated by her hair. He reached down and touched it not once but several times.

Natasha shuddered, fearful of his intent. She was determined to fight against her hazy limbo and gain back her consciousness. She wouldn't drink any more of the wine; she would feign sleep if need be. Perhaps if she was alert she would be able to find out where she was and what was going to become of them.

Though she had been through an ordeal, she fought sleep, merely dozing off now and again. She was more determined than ever to keep her wits about her so that she would not be taken unawares. No matter what happened, she had to think about survival, hers and Nadia's.

Was it possible to escape? Natasha toyed with that dream. If they were on a well-traveled trade route, she and Nadia might have a chance to find refuge with another caravan, one friendly with her tribe. Until then, she would have to be patient and bide her time until the favorable moment arrived.

* * *

They came to many villages on the long and difficult journey, and passed a lake, where their captors almost lost all their possessions in a violent storm that broke over them in the night. Then they sought refuge in a village ruled over by a woman. In return for her hospitality they presented the woman with gifts of furs, small edible objects called dates, and her choice of one of their new slaves.

Natasha cringed as the woman paused in front of her, fearing that she would be chosen or that Nadia would be picked and thus they would be parted, but the woman chose a male slave to help with manual chores.

"When is this journey going to end, Tasha?" Nadia seemed to have lost heart. There were dark circles under her eyes. She was pale and much thinner than before.

"Tonight!" Natasha told Nadia not to drink any of the wine. "It has something in it to make us docile. Pretend to drink, but keep your wits about you, Nadia. Tonight we are going to escape!"

It was a pledge and a promise that she intended to keep. As soon as it was dark and everyone was abed, Natasha stealthily made her way to the tent where she knew supplies were stored. Fumbling around in the dark, she searched for a weapon to take with her, only to feel a surge of disappointment as she realized that all the weapons had been locked in a large wooden trunk.

"There must be something. . . ."

There was! A small knife had been stashed in a sack of vegetables. Hiding it in her boot, Natasha quickly turned her attention to food, putting what supplies she could find for the journey in a cloth sack. Gathering her courage, she stepped outside.

The moon was shrouded by dark clouds; her only

guide was the light of the fading stars. Nevertheless, she made up her mind to succeed as she moved toward Nadia's sleeping form. Falling to her knees, she gently shook her friend awake.

"Come. . . ." Putting her fingers to her lips, she gestured for Nadia to be silent.

Slowly but surely they worked their way across the campsite, hiding in the shadows. Nadia clutched at Natasha's hand so tightly that she winced. They both shivered, Nadia from fear and Natasha from the chill of the night air.

"It will be all right. . . ." Though her words were reassuring, Natasha wasn't certain that what she said was true. Still, she had to try to get them both to freedom.

Looking behind them several times to make certain they were not being followed, they put as much distance as possible between themselves and their captors. Or at least, so they thought.

"Someone is coming!" Nadia gasped.

Pausing, hiding behind a tree, Natasha thought she perceived the sound of running footsteps behind them. Holding her breath, she listened. It was true. Someone was coming!

"Tasha, let's go back. If we don't we will be punished!"

"Not *we*. Me!" Natasha was determined to take all the blame. "I coerced you. . . ."

"No . . ."

Natasha's eyes swept the dark-gray horizon. Were those distant silhouettes she saw on the hill keeping watch, or were they being followed? She cursed softly as she realized they were being chased. Eight or ten men were running in their direction. There could be no other reason than pursuit.

"Run, Tasha. I will take heart in knowing that at least *you* got away."

"We go together!" Putting her arm around Nadia's

waist, Natasha led her toward the horses. If only they could reach one of them they could ride like the wind to safety. Perhaps somehow, they could even find Osip and the others. They had to try!

The sound of thundering footsteps came closer and closer. The men were gaining on them. Looking over her shoulder, Natasha was prodded on by the desperation of their situation.

Suddenly, she stumbled and fell. She had not seen the large hole that loomed in their path. This time it was Nadia who helped her. Taking her by the hand, she tugged her to her feet.

"Are you all right?"

Natasha nodded, refusing to notice the pain in her ankle. Even so, the injury slowed her down. Now she really did know how Nadia felt, she thought as she hobbled along. All the while, a voice in her head told her that their captors were gaining on them. The reality of the situation could not be denied. They could never escape now. Even so, they tried.

Looming in the darkness in front of the horses was a hulking figure that Natasha recognized. The leader of the men who had captured them stood between them and freedom. His face seemed to be carved in stone. He looked very strong, ominous, and just as determined as Natasha as he stood there staring at them.

Natasha fought against the storm of apprehension that shattered her resolve like an eggshell as he reached out and caught her arm in his strong, long-fingered hand. He jerked her around to face him, mumbling something she wished with all her heart she could understand. Natasha clawed at the imprisoning hand, but it was no use.

Four

Never in all her life had Natasha felt so humiliated. She had been punished for trying to escape. The iron collar and chain she now wore around her neck were a grim reminder that she had attempted to run away but had failed. Now, as she was pushed and pulled along, she wondered what else her captors had in store for her. Alas, as her captors pushed her through a crowd of men herding goats and sheep to market, it appeared that she was going to find out.

Natasha could hear a tone of scorn in the voice of one of her captors as he shoved her through the doorway of a large canvas tent made of colorful cloth. There she was given into the hands of three female slaves, who held firmly to the end of her chain just in case the idea of escape was still firmly implanted in her mind.

Glancing around the room, Natasha assessed her lavish prison. The ground was covered with thick, fancy rugs. Soft cushions were scattered on the floor and on the large, rectangular padded chairs. Oil lamps were abundant and bathed the tent with a bright glow. Curtains hung from the roof of the tent, dividing it into sections. It was what stood in the middle of the tent, however, that filled her with terror. A large metal container filled with water was obviously where the women intended to take her.

"They are going to punish me by drowning. . . ."

She was terrified of water. She had seen several of her people drown in a stream after a terrible rainstorm. Natasha struggled in earnest, kicking and thrashing her arms wildly as she screamed, "No!"

One woman grabbed her by the hair; another pinioned her hands behind her back; the third grabbed her legs. Though Natasha fought for her life, she was outnumbered. Worse yet, they sought to further humiliate her by stripping off her clothes. Naked and trembling, she was hurled into the hot, steaming water, iron collar and all. Then the strongest of the women pushed her head under the water.

They are going to kill me! I don't want to die! I won't die, Natasha vowed, holding her breath as she fought to raise her head above the water. She came up, defiant and sputtering.

Angrily the largest woman scolded her, pushing her head under the water a second time. Again, Natasha fought to raise her head. It was even worse than she thought. The water was hot, and she feared that their intention was to drown her and then boil her.

"Please . . . I won't try and run away again. I promise you . . . please . . ."

One of the female slaves tried another approach. Her voice was soft and soothing as she spoke to Natasha. Reaching out, she gently combed her fingers through her hair to loosen the tangles, then reached up to her own hair as if trying to make Natasha understand that what they were doing had something to do with grooming.

"You aren't going to murder me, are you?"

Though the woman couldn't understand her language, they somehow communicated.

Natasha forced herself to relax. She hadn't noticed it before, but the water smelled like flowers and it made her skin feel soft. On the steppes she had cleaned herself with wet cloths, for water was precious and used only for drinking. These people, however, seemed to have so much water that they could waste it and use it to submerge their whole bodies. A strange and frivolous way of keeping clean, but one that she was learning to appreciate and enjoy.

"Wait until I tell Nadia about this!" She leaned back in the soapy water, closing her eyes as the slave who had shown her kindness put something that lathered on her hair. Next the same foaming substance was put all over her body, including the flesh of her neck beneath the iron collar. Jars of clear warm water were used to rinse the lather away.

Natasha enjoyed the luxury of the warm water for as long as she could, then all too soon she was yanked from the tub and dried with a huge piece of soft cloth. But that was just the beginning. She was massaged with fragrant oils and dressed in a kind of cloth that was bright and sheer and soft against her skin.

"What strange punishment . . ."

The bath and massage made her skin tingle. The brushing of her hair made her sleepy. She eyed the soft cushions on the floor with longing. For the first time in a long while, Natasha felt a sense of contentment. Perhaps being held in captivity wouldn't be all bad. She sighed, feeling a sense of well-being that was cruelly shattered as the curtains of the tent were yanked aside and she found herself looking at one of the largest men she had ever seen. His long, black, droopy mustache quivered as he shouted at the three women, then firmly grasped the chain that was attached to her collar, with a possessiveness that warned her that somehow she belonged to him.

Natasha had never seen so many animals and people crowded into such a small space. There were dogs, horses, camels, goats, pigs, sheep, and even miniature mountain cats that had seemingly been tamed as pets. The cats' collars and chains were a painful reminder of her own, and she reached up to touch it just as the man with the mustache gave her a shove and grumbled at her in such a manner that she knew he wanted her to keep walking.

Natasha pushed through the unsmiling throng of big people, small people, tall people, short people. There were human beings of every shape and size, from fair-skinned Norsemen with blond beards and long hair to men and women whose skin was as dark as the night. There were men dressed in cloaks with neck chains hanging across their chests, men in furs and tall hats, men in helmets carrying large swords, and gaudily dressed men and women garbed in cloth that sparkled. Some wore veils to hide their faces. All of them stared.

It was noisy, so noisy! Putting her hands up to her ears, Natasha tried to block out the sound, but the man who held her in tow, like a leashed dog, forced her to put her hands down at her sides. Well, so be it, she thought, squaring her shoulders and lifting her chin. At least if she was going to be on display she would be proud. Her father had once said that only if one acted like a captive could one truly be enslaved. Freedom, he had always said, was in one's mind and heart.

As she walked, Natasha tried to ascertain where she was, but the city, located on a series of bluffs on the west bank of a river, was truly foreign to her. Had they traveled all the way to Kiev? It was possible. She had heard that city was the destination of many captives who were to be sold as slaves. *Slave.* How she hated the word.

"A slave. Never." She would live by her father's words and therefore would always be free in her heart, she said to herself as she joined the other unfortunate captives on the large wooden platform.

Natasha searched visually for Nadia and saw her standing at the edge of the group of slaves. Sad and downcast, Nadia looked so pale and thin that Natasha was worried. She moved toward her to give her what comfort she could, only to feel an agonizing yank on her chain. Even so, she stared at Nadia until they made eye contact.

"Everything will be all right," she whispered, hoping Nadia could read her lips.

What were the chances that they would be sold to the same owner? Small, she knew. Nevertheless, she held that hope in her heart as the trading for the slaves began.

It was a chaotic scene. Even though it was not the height of the trading season, buyers and sellers swarmed in the streets, haggling in at least a dozen languages.

Though Natasha had been certain that she was prepared for what was about to happen, she was shocked and horrified as the captives were lined up, men and women alike, and stripped nude so that they could be inspected by prospective buyers. Worse yet, they were pinched, prodded, and examined like horses or other animals. Hands, feet, teeth, ears: nothing was overlooked as each captive was appraised. Even their private parts were not left untouched as both buyers and sellers went about this nasty business.

Fretfully Natasha looked toward Nadia and could see that she was clinging to a pole of the pavilion, as if fearful of fainting. Then she was stripped, exposed and vulnerable to all the leering male faces. Hopelessly she tried to hide her shame with her hands. As the prodding began, she started to swoon.

"Nadia!"

Natasha tried to get to her side, but the chain held her back. All she could do was watch as her friend was poked and prodded as tears ran down her cheeks. It was as if everything being done to Nadia was being done to her. She suffered as Nadia was humiliated and dehumanized, then traded to a man who appeared to be one of the hated Rus.

All too soon, it was Natasha's turn. Bravely she endured the rough fingers that ravaged her with brutal force. Her expressionless face hid the venomous hatred that swept over her. Then, thankfully, her ordeal was over and Natasha was tugged off the platform to stand at the side of her new master.

"So, that's the end of it," she sighed.

It wasn't. It was only the beginning.

Natasha was herded to the wharf, where a ship rocked roughly on the waves. As she was led across the long ramp that led to the ship, she realized that the man who had bought her obviously intended to take her far away across the sea.

Unceremoniously, Natasha was hauled aboard, then pushed to land in a crumpled heap on an unfurled sail. Shaken, she struggled to her feet, glaring at the man who had pushed her. As the other men hurriedly boarded and the ship pulled away from the shore, she ran to the side, looking down at the foaming waters.

"Water!" It was the one thing that terrified her.

Every muscle of her body stiffened as she realized the magnitude of her fate. She stared in disbelief at the shoreline as it slowly disappeared, fearing in her heart that she would never see her homeland or Nadia again.

Five

Sean heard the clang of a bell through the haze of his deep sleep, a bell bidding all to arise for the morning mass. His awakening was instantaneous, his mind and body responding quickly to the familiar chiming summons.

"Morning comes much too quickly," he muttered as he rolled over on his side. But never too early for Brian, the young man and fellow student who shared his small hut.

As usual, Brian was already awake, for it was his custom to be up long before dawn to scourge himself, perform penance for imagined offences, and pray. Sean doubted that it would be long before Brian joined the order. Unlike Sean, Brian was certain of his calling and of what he intended to do with the rest of his life.

"Water . . ." Sean rasped, noting that Brian, who was always very methodical in his preparations even for daily matters, was using the water in the pitcher to cleanse each part of himself so that he would be worthily immaculate. "Save me some. . . ."

Brian shrugged, setting the pitcher on the tiny table between the beds. "Forgive my greed," he said in a sarcastic tone that implied that Sean and not he was the one who had transgressed.

Certainly the austerity of the sleeping arrangements was troublesome, Sean thought, wondering what it would be like to be afforded the luxury of a room all to himself. There were times when he truly longed for solitude and privacy. That longing was amplified whenever he was in Brian's presence, for in truth, Brian irritated him.

Though Brian was always agreeable, there was little warmth shown toward anyone. His pious aloofness was irritating, for it was as if he set himself apart from all the others, like someone "chosen." Moreover, with his jaw held high, his long aquiline nose pointed upward, he did not carry himself like a naturally humble man but like someone already acknowledged to be of the abbot's rank.

"Judge not lest ye be . . ." Sean mumbled beneath his breath.

The young man closed his eyes, bending his knee to the hard floor. Somehow, Sean knew the frenzied prayer that Brian whispered was for Sean and not for himself. It only emphasized to him how oddly he fit in here sometimes among such devoutly religious men. *Like a square peg in a round hole,* he thought as he watched Brian walk through the door.

"Bron would insist otherwise. . . ." he mumbled. Brother Bron always saw the good in everyone. He was an optimist, a truly good man and Sean's friend.

Hastening to dress in a dun-colored leine hemmed with embroidery, and brown leather shoes, Sean hurriedly combed his dark hair with his fingers, splashed water from the pitcher on his face, then made his way to the domed chapel. There he took his place, watching as the procession of monks entered to take their positions toward the front. Sean chose a spot toward the back, feeling more comfortable in the shadows where he was not under scrutiny.

It was cold and damp as he knelt before the altar, listening to the chanting voices of the service. Though he tried to pay attention, his thoughts were elsewhere. The time was coming when he would have to make a decision whether to join the brothers or leave and find a vocation elsewhere.

"If I don't stay here, where would I go? What would I do?"

The only life he had ever known was here at the monastery. Although he was hungry to know about the outside world, the only information he had been granted was vicarious, gained through reading and listening about other lands beyond the walls.

"In these troubled times there is also a need for men who wield a sword, not a pen," he whispered to himself.

The opposite was true here at the monastery. Sean knew that his skills were greatly needed. He had many duties in addition to working on his manuscripts. Since he had proved to be skilled with numbers, he managed the abbot's accounts, including receipts, revenues, and payments.

Everything he needed was at the monastery. Except for the times when they were expected to fast, he was well fed. He had a place to sleep, garments to wear, the companionship of those of like mind, and even access to learning. It was a secure, routine style of life with few challenges and fewer surprises. His life was predictable. Perhaps that was the problem. There was a deep yearning inside Sean for the unpredictable. Excitement. Adventure. A chance to explore the undiscovered and unknown.

Standing, kneeling, and sitting in accordance with the ritual, his attention was suddenly drawn to the abbot, undoubtedly because the abbot's attention was riveted on him, as if somehow he had been able to see into Sean's mind and read his thoughts. Despite the fact that the service was agonizingly long, Sean forced himself to hear every remaining word.

Once the final blessing had been pronounced, the abbot turned around, looking directly at Sean as if speaking to him. "You must submit yourself to God's will without reservation, for that is the key to this life and the next." The abbot touched his ear with his index finger. "You must listen, for only then can you see."

As Sean went about his daily duties he followed the abbot's advice. He tried to hear and thus understand what he was to do with his life, but no voice spoke. In disappointment he turned to his thoughts and imagination. Strange, but when he closed his eyes he felt as if he were in a boat. He could almost feel the waves and smell the salt in the air.

"Are you hungry?"

Sean looked up to see Brother Bron standing in front of him, holding a bowl in his hand. "It seems I'm always hungry in one way or another," he answered, taking the vegetables and broth that the kindly monk offered.

"That's because you have a great deal of energy and a quest for learning the likes of which I have seldom seen before." Brother Bron lowered his voice. "I have heard through the grapevine that Abbot Righifarch wishes to speak with you in private."

"To chastise me again?"

Brother Bron shook his head. "No, to the contrary, I think there is something he wishes to ask you."

"Ask me . . ."

Sean's curiosity was aroused, but it wasn't until the end of the day that he was summoned to the abbot's cell. Wondering what the abbot wanted with him, he nonetheless bowed in homage at the door until the abbot appeared and invited him in.

The abbot's gray eyes were piercing. For a long time he was silent, but when he spoke his question was direct and to the point. "Are you at peace here?"

The question took Sean by surprise. "Why . . . why, yes. I am at peace." He was strangely troubled by the abbot's stare. The abbot was waiting for him to say something profound, but it just wasn't there. He hurried to say something. "There is nothing I find as fulfilling as working on my . . . the books."

Sean awaited a strong plea for him to join the order, but no plea came. Instead, the abbot quirked one brow. "Ah, yes. The books." He smiled. "I remember how as a child you were inordinately interested in the story of Michael and his angels fighting Lucifer and his demons."

"Perhaps because I somehow felt as if I were a part of that struggle," Sean explained.

"Hmmm. You have always had an imaginative as well as an inquisitive mind. That is good." He motioned Sean closer. "But there is much more than just reading and writing." He looked Sean directly in the eye. "What if there were no books here? What then?"

"That is a thought too dreadful for words." Sean thought a moment. "But if that were to happen, then I would have to learn in a different way."

"And what if you were forbidden to learn, as some people have been?"

Sean clenched his hands into fists. "Learning is as important to me as breathing!" It was a way to live vicariously and share the adventures of those who had lived before.

The abbot pulled away. "I hear a tone of defiance in your voice that decries the total discipline, faith, and obedience so necessary here no matter what is asked of you."

"I'm sorry if my answers have disappointed you."

"Disappointed me? You haven't." The abbot shook his head. "You have a determination and an inner strength that I would welcome among us, but I can see that your heart is not here."

Sean started to speak, but the abbot silenced him. "Though others would try to lull you into making a commitment before you are ready, I know that you are not ready to aspire to the austere life of a monk. I sense that you would need to experience more of the outside world before you could ever make such an important decision. That is why I am sending you on a mission."

"A mission?" A jolt of excitement swept through Sean's bones. "Where?"

A scowl furled the abbot's brow. He didn't answer Sean's question just yet. Instead he said, "Norsemen."

That word was all that was necessary to conjure up memories and imaginings in Sean's mind. "Those wrathful, pagan murderers." Now they were known throughout Christendom as the Vikings. Plunderers.

The first Norse raid had occurred over fifty years ago, when they had plundered the monastery of Lambay Island, in the Irish Sea. At first they had come in small parties, made surprise attacks on places along the coast, then sailed away with their plunder. Twenty-eight years ago, however, they had changed their tactics and sailed up the rivers to plunder inland places. Places such as Armagh, the great Irish monastery chosen by St. Patrick as the seat of his church and Sean's home.

"They often strike the same places again and again. In truth, two years after we found you they struck Armagh three times in one month." The abbot's entire body stiffened as he remembered. "They plundered her five times in all."

Sean remembered one of those times very vividly, for it had taken place just six years ago. "They are devils! More so because no one knew where they would strike, or when, or in what numbers."

"Some call them the scourge of the civilized world. Then there are others who have seen them as the fulfillment of the words of the Old Testament prophet Jeremiah. 'Out of the north evil shall break forth upon all the inhabitants of the land.' "

"Surely they are the evil ones!" There were many who supposed that because of the Vikings, the Day of Judgment might well be at hand.

The abbot sighed. "A necessary evil, I fear, and one that we must learn to live with." He closed his eyes as if in pain. "Their ships have been sighted on the river again."

"Their ships . . ." There had been a respite from the attacks as the Norsemen had turned their attentions elsewhere. Was the violence at Armagh to begin again?

"The Norsemen have set up bases and have attacked the surrounding countryside from them. They have also begun to stay in Eire during the winter. Even now they are headed to Dubh-Linn to stay for the winter at the mouth of the River Liffey. And I hear that they have also set up a settlement at Larne."

Sean clenched his hands into fists. "Then we are lost, for we cannot fight them, nor can we rely on the provincial kings to give us aid. They are too busy quarreling amongst themselves." Eire lacked the political unity necessary to drive the Vikings away. "What are we going to do?"

"Give them what they want before they use violence to take it," the abbot answered. "I am sending someone with tribute to keep the Vikings away from our shores."

"Bribery?" The thought troubled Sean.

The abbot ignored the censoring expression in Sean's eyes. "I have heard that the Vikings accept tribute in lieu of battle in other lands. We must avert bloodshed at all costs. If it is gold they are after, then we will give them what they want." He paused. "I am sending *you* on the mission to deal with these would-be intruders."

"Me?" It was as if lightning struck him.

"Yes, you."

For a moment Sean was too stunned for words. He was puzzled. At last he found his voice. "Why have you chosen me?"

Unwilling to confide the truth of Sean's heritage to

him just yet, the abbot skillfully averted the question. "As I have said, you are strong, intelligent, articulate, and I sense a courage deep within you, the depth of which perhaps even you are not fully aware."

The abbot was usually miserly with his words of praise; therefore, Sean felt a glow of pride. He would put his feelings of misgivings aside and do as he was asked. "I will not disappoint you in my efforts to convince these heathens to accept our offer, but I am troubled. How can we be certain that we can trust these Norsemen?" What if they killed him on the spot, then raided the monastery anyway?

"We will hope that they are honorable."

"Honorable." Sean's voice held a tone of scorn. "Who ever heard of Viking honor? They are known to be incorrigible!" And dangerous, and threatening and brutal.

The abbot patted him on the shoulder. "We will trust in the Lord."

Sean nodded. He knelt for the blessing, rose, and turned away. He could hear the abbot's voice whisper softly, "May God go with you. . . ."

As he walked outside, Sean reached into the pouch hanging from his belt. He felt the need to clutch his rosary to give him comfort and courage. By mistake he drew forth the pendant with the amber wolf carving instead. Or *was* it by error? Sean had the eerie feeling that somehow the pendant was a sign.

Six

The soft warmth of early morning sunlight caressed Natasha's face as she lay on her straw pallet. Stretching her arms and legs, she shrugged off one of her thick cloth coverlets as she opened her eyes and lazily sat up. She sniffed, relishing the fresh smell of the air. For a moment she almost forgot that she was sailing to a strange new land. But as she caught a glimpse of the carved snake's head of the boat, it all came back to her. Bolting upward in her bed, she remembered that she wasn't in her land—wasn't on land at all, but on a ship taking her far away from her caravan, her people, her beloved steppes, Nadia, and everything else she had ever held dear.

She felt dazed, unsure of anything secure or reliable in her life anymore. Although her initial shock had passed, she felt all alone, drowning in a sea of uneasiness and a dread of the unknown. Not even the warmth of the sun could ease the pain tugging at her heart.

"I can't bear it! I would rather die than go to live among these fair-haired, bearded men who think themselves to be my masters. . . ."

They were crude, rough, grumpy, and ugly. Their harsh voices constantly battered her ears in a barrage of guttural words she couldn't understand despite the similarity to her own language. Worse yet, they were always shouting out orders or pushing their captives around. They had not a pinch of patience, kindness, or understanding. It was obvious that they considered their slaves to be less than human, devoid of feelings or even basic rights.

"To them I am worse than nothing!" It seemed that they viewed their slaves as property and little more. Well, Natasha knew that she was "something." They would never humiliate her and make her feel worthless. She knew differently. She would never lose faith in herself, no matter what happened.

For a long time she sat as unmoving as a statue on the deck, completely motionless, seemingly unaware of the wind that blew across her face and raked its fingers through her hair. She barely took notice of her surroundings until she moved to the cargo hold of the ship to get out from under the view and feet of the fierce bearded men, who were likewise awakening. These men slept where best they could on the ship's deck between the rowing benches. Some had crawled between hides that had been sewn together to make bags. She could hear the loud rasp of some of the men's snores.

Her lips curved upward in a scornful smile. They thought themselves so big and so strong as they relished the safety of their large boat, but they would not last long out on the steppes, where they would soon fall victim to the fierce, nomadic tribes who would take them unawares.

"If only we were back there . . . back on the steppes . . ." Back where there was hope of being rescued. Instead, she was surrounded by turbulent blue and not the shades of brown, tan, and green that she now fondly remembered.

Looking out toward the sea, Natasha remembered how terrified she had been at first by the loud, thrashing waves, certain that she would be swept overboard at any moment. Even now she always made certain to stay far away from the sides of the ship.

It had been a harrowing journey through deep waters with no land in sight. The ship, completely surrounded by water, brought forth an eerie feeling within her, as if she were being swallowed up by the ocean. Nor were the storms at all reassuring. When huge waves lashed out at the ship, Natasha had prepared herself for death, but somehow the bearded giants had managed to keep the ship under control until the fury passed. At times the ship seemed to be such a fragile vessel that she wondered how it kept afloat; at other moments she marveled at the strength it displayed.

Her eyes assessed her floating prison. It was an open boat, its cargo covered by skins, the crew and captives exposed to the elements. The sides of the boat were nicked with small, square holes from which oars protruded. The oar ports were in the front and back parts of the ship, aligned with six rowing benches. Rising from the center was a sturdy, smooth pole that held a red-and-white striped sail and a cross-beam. In the center of the ship her captors had stashed their treasures: an assortment of metal, cloth, stone, and animal pelts plundered from the steppes. There were also round wooden casks of water and something that made her throat burn, bolts of cloth, and leather-bound chests filled with necklaces and other objects decorated with beads that sparkled in the sun.

I wonder which of these items would be enough to buy my freedom, she thought. Freedom. It was a precious word, perhaps even more so now that she had experienced a lack of it. "Slave!" The very word ate at her heart.

Looking up, Natasha's gaze fell upon the carved snake figurehead of the ship. The sight of it gave her hope, for nothing was more prized in a Magyar home than this symbol of good luck. There were even a few boys who kept them as pets. Serpents were closely associated with the thunder god, the deity responsible for creating mountains and for hurling down bolts of lightning. They also launched storms of life-giving rain onto the earth beneath him. The winged snake carried clouds across the sky.

"Please be with me. Help me to be strong," she whispered, glancing back as if she could still see the coasts of her homeland. But the wind-swept dirt and sand, mountains, and beaches were long since gone; and she feared deep in her soul that she would never see them again. "Unless . . ."

Somehow, she had to get away. Escape must be the focus of her existence until her mission was accomplished. She would smile sweetly at her captors, be obedient and docile until the moment came when she could get free of their odious chains.

Natasha's musing was interrupted by one of the yellow-bearded ones, as she referred to them. He was touching first his mouth, then his belly in a gesture she knew to mean food.

"Am I hungry?" She nodded, despite the fact that she hated the hard, dry biscuits and water that were always her breakfast. At first she had stubbornly refused to eat, a decision prompted by the sick feeling in her stomach, but now she was determined to keep up her strength. She would need it to survive.

Food was mainly dried, pickled, salted, or smoked fish and meat with unleavened bread. Hardly what she was used to.

"How much longer will our journey be?" she asked, forgetting for the moment that her words were just as unknown to him as his were to her.

She shivered as a gust of wind swept over the deck. Natasha gazed up at the sail. It was made of some kind of heavy woollike material, its bold stripes embroidered in bright colors.When would they reach land? How much farther was it to the yellow-bearded giants' home?

She listened carefully to their babbling and watched their gestures, hoping for some kind of clue. Mimicking the words she heard, she tried to understand at least a portion of their meaning.

Natasha had studied the men carefully and had come to the realization that they made their way across the sea by looking at the stars. They had a great fascination with the late night sky, in fact, as well as the clouds and the ocean's currents. Grudgingly she had to admit that it took great courage to cross the great water. Courage and cunning. She would need both!

The bearded men stared at her many times as if she and not they were strange, but not one of them had ever touched her. That, at least, made her feel more relaxed, now that she knew these beings were not going to harm her—at least in that way. At least not yet. But what would happen when they reached land? How quickly would she have to get away?

Staring out at the sea again, Natasha wondered where Nadia was, what she was thinking, what she was doing. Was she well? Was she being treated with at least a measure of kindness?

She gazed at the churning waters, fighting against the tears that threatened to fall from her eyelids. No, she wouldn't cry. Tears were a sign of weakness. Though she would be among strangers, she would stand tall, be proud, use wisdom in all facets of her life, and, most important, get free of her captors as soon as she could.

A cold spray of ocean mist splashed into Sean's face as he reached forward to dip the long, thin oars into the waters of the channel. Stroke by stroke, he moved the wicker-frame-and-hide boat closer toward the Viking settlement of Larne, his destination. Though he was headed for danger and the possibility of death, he had never felt more alive.

Strange, he thought, how right it felt to be upon the water. It was as if that was where he belonged.

Putting the oars down for a moment, he put his hand up to his eyes and looked up at the clouds that were moving quickly across the vast blue sky. He would have to be quick. A storm was brewing. It was in his best interest to reach his destination before the waves became too fierce to fight against.

"Hurry," he said aloud. "You must hasten to your fate, whatever that is to be."

As he pulled relentlessly at the oars, Sean tried to sort out his feelings concerning this mission of his. How did he feel? Afraid? Strangely, no. He wasn't afraid of the Vikings and what might happen, though he knew he had reason to be. Instead, he was curious about these destructive but able seamen.

Sean patted the bundle beside him, a bag filled with gold and silver goblets, plates, candlesticks, bells, two sacks of grain, and five small casks of wine. Would the Norseman be calmed by the gifts he was bringing? Would their bloodlust be fed by the bribes? The Vikings were fierce pagans who had no conscience about evil and showed little mercy toward any who were unfortunate enough to get in their way. Would they likewise be ruthless toward him, or would they be too busy fighting among themselves for the spoils to give him much attention? What was going to happen?

"Is it possible to live in peace with them?" The very idea seemed ludicrous despite the abbot's optimism.

Sean remembered the apprehension and, yes, fear, that had welled up in him six years ago, when a band of Vikings pillaged and looted the monastery at Armagh from their base at Annagassan. The Vikings had taken more than gold and silver that day. They had taken five of the monks into captivity to be sold as slaves. To his eternal shame, he had hidden in the bell tower, watching as the Norsemen swarmed the grounds like ants searching for a meal.

I acted like a coward then, but never again. No matter what happened, he would show courage.

Sean's thoughts were agitated as he continued on the journey—nearly as turbulent as the waters of the North Channel that led to Larne. Though he would not have confided his feelings to any living soul, there were times when he wondered at the abbot's wisdom of completely laying down arms. Surely there were times when fighting might be necessary, times when all attempts at reasoning had failed.

He had heard from Bron that some of the heads of the great monasteries had taken to the field to fight against the Vikings in Terryglass and Clonenagh. The deputy abbot of Kildare had been killed fighting the Vikings at the fortress of Dunamase thirteen years ago. Sean knew that he would be willing to fight for the monastery at Armagh if it came to that.

Suddenly the craft was caught by a fierce puff of wind from the west. Its prow slewed sharply to the side. He felt a surge of fire through his veins. Quickly he took charge of the situation, putting down the oars to ride it out on the waves.

Up and down, back and forth, the boat rocked unendingly, but it rode the waves without capsizing. At last the waters became calmer, and it was then that Sean took the time to partake of a little food and water before picking up the oars again.

At last, from far away he could see dwellings of timber, wattle, and daub as the Viking settlement loomed into view. Near the settlement loomed the menacing presence of several Viking ships, their dragon- and serpent-headed prows threatening all who came near. In the curragh, Sean felt like a small fish waiting to be gobbled up.

Suddenly, he had the feeling that he was being watched. He straightened up and could see nothing at first; then, out of the corner of his eye he caught sight of the huge prow of a vessel moving between his boat and the other Viking ships.

He turned his head, staring at the bestial head

carved on the prow, then at the sail, then at the full, terrible length of the ship. Like the dragon of his childhood fantasies, it was covered with scales, or at least from a distance the overlapping shields looked like a monster's scales. The men standing on the ship's deck were unsmiling and ominous. Muscular, hairy men with metal on their heads and swords in their belts.

For a moment Sean questioned the wisdom of his coming here to try to reason with these barbarians. What if the Norsemen took the gifts he brought, then attacked the monastery anyway? What if he had come all this way only to be killed?

Coward! He mentally scourged himself for his twinge of anxiety and for having so little faith. The abbot would never have sent him here if he thought it would mean his death. More importantly, Sean knew he had to trust in the good Lord, who was surely with them here.

Feeling renewed courage, Sean rowed closer to the Viking ship. Pulling alongside, he shouted out that he was looking for Thordis Haraldsson of Norway, an important man at the settlement and one of the few Vikings Abbot Righifarch had known by name.

Though the Norseman who bent over the side of the Viking ship was bold and contemptuous, he nonetheless gave Sean an answer. He was in luck, the Norseman said, for Thordis, also known as "Forkbeard" by some, had just returned from the Bulgar, where he had acquired several slaves to work at the settlement.

"He is on that ship loaded with slaves," the Viking said, nodding in that direction.

"Slaves . . ." Next to murder, Sean loathed enslavement and bondage more than anything perpetrated by mankind. It was a wrong he wanted more than anything to right.

As the tiny boat glided over the water, Sean reflected with pride on his hero, Saint Patrick, a former slave who had transformed Eire into a Christian culture. Though the Christianity based in Rome often turned its face away and ignored the injustice of slavery and human sacrifice, the Celtic Christians based in Eire had viewed slavery and warfare as unthinkable and had done everything in their power to eradicate such suffering.

Guided by Patrick, the people of Eire had flung away the knives of sacrifice and cast aside the chains of slavery. New laws, influenced by the Church, dictated that arms be taken up only for a weighty cause. Sean clenched his jaw, feeling instant sympathy for the unfortunate souls. The thought struck him that instead of using the gold, silver, and wine that he had brought to bribe the Vikings, he would have preferred to buy the freedom of everyone. But he couldn't. The precious items didn't belong to him, nor was it his decision to make. Even so, as he approached Forkbeard's ship and was hoisted aboard and caught a glimpse of the poor wretches, he was stung by compassion.

One slave in particular caught his eye, perhaps because despite the slave collar around her neck she managed to hold her head up with such dignity. In a brief glance Sean noted her beauty, strength, and pride.

Just as Sean noticed Natasha, her eyes were drawn to the tall, dark-haired man whose eyes showed kindness despite his obvious strength. Though she didn't know who he was, she felt certain that somehow he was the one she was looking for—the man who could and would help her.

Seven

The Viking ship looked much like a sea monster as it headed inland. Its square sail was the color of blood, reminding Sean—if he needed any reminding—that he was among dangerous and violent strangers. Although the Norsemen had so far greeted him with no show of malice, he sensed that they could turn upon him like a pack of wild hounds in an instant. He would have to be careful.

A flock of gulls circled and screeched in the sky above, mimicking the sound that resonated in Sean's head as his instincts cried out a warning. In spite of his vow of courage, he felt a shiver go up his spine as he looked at the scarred, dirty, bearded face of Thordis Forkbeard and heard the chants of the Vikings as they dropped the sail and rowed toward the shore.

"O-din, O-din . . ." It was as if the wind took up their pagan chant. "O-din . . ."

Sean watched apprehensively as the Viking ship headed toward the rocks. The ferocious carved dragon head was being covered with a woolen cloth.

"We do not want to frighten the land spirits," the Viking Thordis thundered in a commanding voice.

If fear was the issue, Sean thought but did not say, then it seemed just as necessary for the Vikings to cover up their own fierce-looking faces as well. Truly, with their scars, beards, and frowns they were a frightening lot.

The Viking looked him up and down as if trying to look through him. "You have brought us tribute," Thordis rasped, taking special care to talk slowly so that the Irishman could understand him. "It is to keep us from sacking your monastery again, uh?"

"It is a peace offering. That is what we at Armagh want. Peace."

Thordis grunted as he thrust his hands into the sack, making a quick inventory of what was within. He mumbled his acceptance of the gifts, then turned toward Sean.

"It is good, but there is not enough."

"Not enough?" Every muscle in Sean's body grew rigid as he fought against his annoyance. Apparently the abbot had not realized the Vikings would be so greedy.

Thordis sneered. "Were we to pay your round towers a visit we would get much, much more."

His reference to the round towers gave credence to a past visit, for after the first Viking raids the monks had built round towers without ground-floor entrances in which to hide and stash their wealth. They would climb up rope ladders and then pull up the ropes so that the Vikings had no way into the towers. In the end, however, even that had not deterred the Norsemen.

Sean was cornered and he knew it. He clenched his jaw and forced himself to remain silent as he watched his small boat, tied by a rope to the Viking ship, bob up and down on the water. He had no choice but to agree to the terms, particularly when the future of the monks and the monastery was in his hands. "How much more do you want?"

Thordis shrugged. "Five times more than what you brought with you."

"Five times more?" It was robbery. Sean knew it, and he could tell from his smug expression that Thordis knew that he knew it and gloated at the helplessness of all those within the monastery. Though he tried, Sean could not hide his feelings of loathing toward the Norseman.

"You hesitate." As if he purposely meant to be threatening, Thordis nodded his head in the direction of the slaves. The meaning was clear. If he turned his attentions to Armagh, several monks would join the ranks of the unfortunate slaves who were now huddled together at the back of the Viking ship.

Sean looked at the unfortunate beings out of the corner of his eye, imagining for a moment that he saw Bron, Brian, or several of the others among them. Or perhaps even himself! He reached up to wipe the vision away with his hand. No. Never!

Anger and hatred were two of the sins that Sean had been taught to fight against even at an early age. He had been taught self-discipline, forgiveness, and compassion toward his fellow man. Never, however, had these lessons been so sorely tested as they were now, when he was in the presence of this Viking merchant who made a profit from the misery and ill fortune of other human beings.

The Vikings were the slavers to the world and provided a commodity: human beings. Although the Vikings did not invent the insidious institution of slavery—it had existed since the first days of men on earth—Sean knew that they exploited it on a scale unknown to any other people before them.

"Quite a collection, don't you agree?" Thordis wove in and out among the slaves, assessing them with cold, impersonal aloofness as if they were objects and not people.

There were slaves of every shape, size, and color, including a few Moorish slaves described as "blue men." The slaves were simply dressed in cloth of undyed wool with a cord tied around the waist. The men's hair had been shorn so short that they were almost bald; the women's hair was braided.

"Poor souls . . ." Sean whispered, feeling their misery tug at his heart.

Once again his gaze was drawn to one of the female slaves, whose hair was the lightest shade of blond he had ever seen. Her eyes were blue, her skin flawless, and she was slender but well rounded in the places where a woman was meant to be. Though she was dressed in a most unflattering manner and her hair was pulled severely back from her face in a long braid, her beauty was striking. In just a brief glance, he noted something else as well: a strength and pride in her eyes that made her circumstances all the more terrible.

"Ah, I see that you have eyes for the Slav," Thordis rasped, stepping between the slave girl and Sean.

So, she was from the East, Sean thought, hurriedly looking away. He had heard that the Vikings would take slaves wherever they found them. But their primary source of supply was in the East, where numberless tribes of Slavs, the name from which the word *slave* was derived, were still living as they had in Old Testament times. Undoubtedly, they were easy prey for the raiding parties that swooped down on them in forest or steppe and led them away in long, fettered lines.

"I was studying them all," Sean responded, not wanting to call attention to his interest in the young woman. "I was thinking that each of them must have an interesting story to tell." Though he did not look at the blond slave girl again, he knew that she was looking at him.

"Interesting?" Thordis guffawed. "Hardly that. After all, slaves are like livestock. By law and by custom they are little more than farm animals, fit mostly to spread dung in the fields, dig peat, herd goats, and tend pigs. They can be bought and sold or offered as payment for debts in but the blinking of an eye."

He seemed to be purposefully goading Sean; therefore, despite the emotional turmoil that raged within him, Sean held his silence and did not argue. What good would verbal sparring do? He and Thordis were as different as night and day. They would never see eye to eye.

Natasha stared at the dark-haired stranger, studying his features with eyes that were cautiously critical. He wasn't one of "them." She could tell that by the way he was dressed. Likewise, her ears told her that although he was communicating very well with them, their language was not his. There was something different in the way he said the words. More importantly, she could sense that he did not like them any more than she did. That gave them something in common.

She took a step closer, unafraid of staring. The closer she got to him, the more she liked what she saw. The man had long, dark hair that nearly touched his wide shoulders. His chin was firm and smooth, without the rough beard the Norsemen displayed. His nose was straight and shaped just right to go with the rest of his face. His arms were strong, and even beneath the cloth of his garments she could see that he was muscular with a broad chest, flat belly, and narrow hips. His whole body spoke of strength and power. He was, in fact, handsome, which perhaps was responsible for the strange, unknown sensation that coursed through her as he glanced her way again.

She froze as their eyes met and held for a long, halting moment. His blue eyes mesmerized her. She read compassion in his look, as if he somehow knew how she felt. Both of them stood, unmoving. Suddenly she realized that she had been holding her breath. She let it out in a sigh. He was decidedly pleasing to look upon, and she found herself wishing that if she had to be owned it would be by this man.

"You! Girl. Stand back." Thordis was not blind. He had seen the way the girl looked at the Irishman and the way he had looked back at her. And he didn't like it.

Natasha didn't understand what he said, but his

rough shove translated his meaning. The brute. Oh, how she hated him! Oh, how she hated them all. She squinted her eyes as she watched the verbal exchange between the Norseman and the dark-haired stranger, wishing that she could understand what they were saying. If only she knew just a smattering of the Viking tongue.

Suddenly, her Norse captor turned his attentions back to her, lifting her face to examine it, just as one might do with a goat or a cow. Natasha smelled the maleness of him, the smell of sweat as he moved closer. His hand covered her breasts and cruelly squeezed them as he taunted her with his strength. She seethed inwardly. Her beauty did not disguise her loathing for Thordis. She made the silent vow that she would take no abuse. If he dared to touch her in that way, she would kill either him or herself, preferably the former.

"I had thought to sell this one, but I think I will keep her," Thordis boasted. "She will be mine." He emphasized the word for Sean's benefit. "Mine!"

The coldness of his voice, coupled with the coldness in his expression, sent shivers down Sean's back. He feared for the girl. He knew that females were frequently used for the sexual gratification of their masters. The young woman obviously hated Thordis, which would make the situation all the more unbearable for her.

"How much? What will you take for her?" The words surprised Thordis, but not as much as they stunned Sean himself. He was troubled by the feelings this woman inspired, yet helpless to fight against them. It had been a long time since he had felt an instant attraction to any female. He wondered if it was her beauty or her proud defiance that intrigued him.

"She is not for sale! Not at any price."

Thordis quickly put an end to any musings Sean might have had. So that was the end of the matter.

After today he would never see this woman again. She belonged to Thordis Forkbeard, and though he hated to see anyone enslaved, there was nothing he could do for her. Nothing! It was such a helpless feeling.

Natasha felt the Norseman possessively tighten his arms around her, squeezing her so hard that for a moment she could not breathe. Her arms were useless, trapped between her body and his as his mouth came down on hers, crushing her lips unmercifully.

If only she had access to a knife she would have used it despite the consequences, but she was weaponless. All she had were her teeth, which now came down on his lip.

With a yell, Thordis pulled back and shoved her away from him so violently that she fell against Sean. Her breasts lightly brushed against his hard chest. The heat from his body seemed to envelop her. She felt light-headed.

Again their eyes locked and held for a timeless moment. He squeezed her fingers warmly and whispered in her ear, "Be careful. Do not anger him too much or he will kill you. I'll find some way to help you. . . ." Sean whispered in the Slavic language, hoping that would calm her.

She was surprised that he spoke in the language of those other tribes who roamed the steppes. Though his words were heavy with the accent of a foreigner, she could understand him. She nodded. This time when the Norseman grabbed her, she didn't pull away.

"She looks to be a stubborn one and overly proud. You will have to take her in hand, Thordis."

"I'll beat her if I have to, Svein."

The other Viking shrugged. "She has the look of a runaway and will no doubt try to bolt at the first opportunity."

"Then I will chain her. My slaves earn their keep one way or another, or I dispose of them." The threat was chillingly real. Of that Sean had no doubt.

Though he had intended to give up the tribute and then proceed back to Armagh with great haste, Sean's urgency now cooled. That was why he accepted the offer by Thordis Forkbeard to stay at the settlement for the night and talk about the terms of the tribute and leave first thing in the morning.

Eight

Natasha and the other slaves were unloaded from the ship just like cargo, then marched up the green, grass-covered hill. As they walked, she found it difficult to maneuver her legs because she had been on the ship for so long. Once or twice her knees buckled. She was certain she would collapse in a heap on the ground, and only her determination to be strong overcame her physical weakness. She knew that only the strong would survive.

At last they reached the Norsemen's settlement: dwellings of timber, wattle and daub. The huts had no windows, and the doors were so low that entry required bending down to get through the doorway.

The mooing of several cows and the bleating of goats drew her attention to the animals sheltered at the other end of the building. The animals were separated from the house by a thin partition instead of roaming free. She couldn't help thinking how strange it was that the Norsemen made captives of their animals, too.

As she marched along to a small, crude house, she realized that unless she found a way to escape, this would be her home—or rather, her place of humiliation and confinement. The realization struck her full force as she was shoved inside the small house and the door was slammed shut behind her.

Wistfully she surveyed her surroundings. In the center of the room a cooking pot, suspended by ropes from the roof, hung over a simple stone hearth. The hole in the roof above the fire was the only source of moonlight or sunlight and ventilation. No doubt the small dwelling would be full of smoke whenever a fire was burning.

"Of course, I will have to cook for them," she said to herself, stiffening as her eyes lit on a pile of furs near the cooking area. The furs were obviously a bed, a grim reminder of what else might be expected of her.

She shivered as she remembered the Norseman's brutal kiss. *No. Never.* She would never share his bed, not even if it meant that she must die.

I have to escape!

There was no other alternative. *Escape.* The word pounded in her brain. But how? Vikings were everywhere. She was surrounded by the enemy. If she broke free they would track her down; they would find her.

Not if I am clever.

Sitting down in the middle of the room, Natasha reasoned it all out. The Norsemen would expect that if she escaped she would travel by foot on land, but she would fool them. She would travel by boat. The handsome dark-haired stranger had told her that he would find some way to help her. She would help him do just that.

Natasha remembered that the dark-haired stranger had come by boat and that the boat was tied up to the Norsemen's ship, bobbing up and down in the water like a hooked fish. But soon, probably first thing tomorrow, he would go back to wherever it was that he belonged. When he did, she would be with him. In the meantime, she had to find a way to get free so that she could hide out in the boat until dawn.

She shuddered at the very thought of being on water again, but there was no other way. All the time they were at sea she had made no secret of her fear of the ocean to the Norsemen. She had been terrified of it, certain that somehow she would fall overboard and drown. They would never imagine that she would be so daring as to face up to her greatest fear and use the waters to escape.

But I will. She would somehow force herself to find the courage.

Both the Slavs and the Magyars appreciated the dangerous power of the waters, personified by the sea and river kings in many of their stories. Natasha knew that water was also a sacred force, bringing life to crops as well as humans and animals. The Magyars also knew that when roused to flooding, the streams could be enemies with awesome power. That was why they traditionally made offerings to rivers, seeking to win their favor or avert their fury. The water could both give life and take it.

I have no other choice. It has to be. Otherwise I will be slave to a brutal master forever.

Even so, she trembled at the very thought of what she must do. Closing her eyes, she could almost feel the water rush over her head, into her eyes, ears, mouth, and lungs, engulfing her, choking her. One wrong move, one false step, and that would be her fate.

Sean watched as the Vikings waded through the water to unload the many casks and chests from the ship with far more gentleness than they had shown their slaves. The casks were being carefully carried ashore to make certain that they didn't crack open and spill the wine and ale within. The chests were being lugged through waist-deep water on the backs of strong-looking slaves, or thralls, who were severely thrashed if they let even a corner of the chest slip and touch the water. The Viking Thordis was being extremely careful with his valuables.

The air hummed with the excited voices of the people of the settlement, who seemed to view the Viking with some kind of awe. His ship had brought wealth from the East, it was whispered: furs, wine, ale, oil, and trunks of gold, silver, and jewels. All to be bartered. He had brought slaves as well, all to be immediately put to work securing the settlement for the coming winter.

"And Thordis has brought ivory. . . ." Sean heard one old woman whisper. The woman proudly exclaimed that Thordis sold walrus tusks to ecclesiastics for crucifixes and to warriors for sword grips, among other things.

The people of the settlement were impressed by the wealthy trader in their midst and did not seem to view him as the brutal villain that he was, Sean thought. Perhaps because Thordis was responsible for fulfilling their many needs.

He traveled far beyond the settlement, buying and selling goods. From the north he brought timber for ship-building, iron for making tools and weapons, furs for warm clothing, skins from whales and seals for ship ropes. These he carried to far-flung places and exchanged for local goods. He would return from Britain with wheat, silver, and cloth and bring wine, salt, pottery, and gold back from the Mediterranean.

Strangely enough, as he listened to the people of the settlement talk about Thordis, it was as if his own dream was enfolding. Ironically, brute though he was, Thordis was living the kind of life that Sean had only pursued in his imaginings. He had sailed across the Baltic Sea and upriver into Russia, then continued on foot or camel as far as Constantinople and Jerusalem. In the markets along the way he had haggled over the price of glass, exotic spices, and silks. All the while he had seen the world.

"Thordis has even brought back the horn of a unicorn," the old woman said with a wink.

"Unicorn?" Sean raised his brows in question. He knew from all that he had read that the unicorn was only a fable, a wonderous horselike creature of age-old legend with one horn. The mythical animal had held human imagination in its spell for centuries. "But it doesn't exist!"

The woman laughed, exposing a smile that lacked several teeth. "It does in here." She tapped her head. "The mind. People want to believe in it and so they do! Ah, Thordis . . ." She laughed again, then confided the story to Sean.

It seemed that Thordis and some of the other Vikings had come across a kind of whale or porpoise in their travels they called a narwhal. A part of the large beast's anatomy was used in a common Viking deception. A straight, spirally grooved tusk grew from its upper jaw, extending as far as eight feet, with a nine-inch girth at the base. Thordis made a profit by pawning off the grotesque tusk upon gullible buyers as the horn of a unicorn.

"He's profiting from a lie!" It was but one more sin the thieving, brutal Viking had committed, Sean thought.

The woman shrugged. "Lie? Lie? So what? He gives them what they want. He is happy and they are happy."

"A unicorn's horn," Sean scoffed. "A useless treasure."

"Not so." For some reason the woman seemed anxious to convince him. "The horn in powder form can be used as an aphrodisiac, an antidote for poisons, a cure for the falling sickness, and a remedy for the stomach." Her voice lowered to a whisper as if revealing a precious secret. "A piece of the horn can be used to detect poison in food or to purify water."

"But it is not really the horn of a unicorn."

Couldn't these people see how wrong it was to take advantage of other people, to make a mockery of their belief with a falsehood? Looking at their expressions he could see that they did not see. They were as dishonest as Thordis. All they knew was that the cunning Viking trader found eager, gullible buyers for all the unicorn horns that he could get from the unfortunate arctic narwhal. It made him rich. That was all that mattered. He had no scruples! But then, had Sean thought otherwise?

I've made a bargain with a liar. How could he be certain that Thordis would keep his part of the agreement? How did he know that the Vikings wouldn't take the tribute from the monastery and still attack Armagh? Certainly he hadn't witnessed anything that gave him any optimism about the Viking's character. Indeed, the man had no conscience, no apparent measure of mercy, and no principles. And this was the man who held the fate of Armagh in his hands.

The aroma of cooking food, a tantalizing smell, permeated the air as Sean walked toward the main settlement house. The Vikings were having a feast to celebrate the homecoming of Thordis, and he had been "invited."

As he stepped inside the main structure, he could see that several of the new slaves were busy in the cooking area preparing the food. Other thralls were hurrying about lighting soapstone oil lamps suspended from the ceiling by iron chains. He scanned the room, looking for *her*, but she was nowhere in sight and that troubled him. He worried for her safety.

"Ah, the Christian. Come in, come in. Don't be timid." Thordis, who was standing in a huddle with several of the other Vikings, was dipping his cup in a large vat of mead. He motioned for Sean to join them.

Seeing Thordis relieved Sean's mind. If Thordis was here, then at least he wasn't with the pretty slave girl, so perhaps she was safe—at least for the moment.

"Drink with us!" Thordis's flushed face gave proof that he had already imbibed of the brew.

Though Sean took a cup and dipped it in the mead, he was determined not to drink it. He would need a clear head if he was going to make any decisions concerning the monastery.

Some of the Vikings were involved in drinking contests; others had placed wagers and were gambling with dice. A few had set up a target at the far side of the hall and placed wagers on which of four men hurling axes would hit the mark. Sean wondered if gambling was what the monks would be doing if they trusted this man. Only this time the loser would pay more than money; indeed, they might all pay with their lives. But what was the alternative? Warfare? Tongues of flame glimmered on the shields, axes, and swords hung on the wall, as if to tell Sean that in any battle the Vikings would be the winner.

Huge pine logs flamed in a sunken trough in the center of the room. The air was clouded with drifting veils of smoke as a huge slab of lamb roasted on a spit over the fire. Cauldrons of iron and soapstone were suspended over the flames from a tripod in which bubbled broth and meat stew. Sean coughed as he looked around. He couldn't deny that, as much as he loathed these heathens, he was still fascinated by them as well.

Certainly they seemed to be a happy lot. The air rang with laughter and chatter as they elbowed their way to the wooden tables laden with plates and platters of freshly baked wheat and barley bread, cabbages, peas, onions, slabs of cheese, chunks of meat, and roasted game birds.

Surprised that he didn't really feel like an intruder and that these people were not treating him as one, Sean grabbed a plate and heaped it with barley bread, cheese, and lamb. Forgetful of good manners, he took a seat on one of the benches and ate like a starving man, only to feel guilty afterward when he realized that he had not paused to say a blessing over the food. But then, perhaps it was not the time or place to remember things that were usually in his routine.

Once again Sean thought about the young woman he had seen aboard the Viking ship. Where was she? He suspected that Thordis had her locked up somewhere as a penalty for her actions. Had she eaten? Or was starvation part of the punishment?

He remembered that he had told the slave girl that he would help her. Could he? He wanted to with all his heart, but interfering in the matter threatened to bring the Vikings' wrath down upon more heads than just his. Still, there had to be a way. He couldn't just turn his back on her. The Church encouraged the manumission of slaves as an act of piety, and though they had never condemned the institution itself, Sean was determined to take the matter up with the abbot when he returned.

Drinking horns clanked; spoons and knives scraped across plates as people of the settlement concentrated on eating and drinking; but there came a time when thirst was assuaged and hunger satisfied. The throng was anxious to hear about Thordis's exploits and of the treasures brought back from across the sea.

Sean blended in with the crowd, watching as the Viking held up his hand, gesturing for silence. "Questions, questions, questions. Too many all at one time." He smiled, obviously relishing the attention, then gestured to the skald who picked up his harp. "I'll answer all of your questions in good time, but first let us have music."

The storyteller's nimble fingers moved across the instrument, plucking the muted strings as he sang about the days so long ago and never-forgotten heroes. Proud, adventurous, with a yearning for glory, these men had excelled in battle and scorned death to venerate the very name *Viking*.

The Norsemen banged their tankards upon the table in a steady rhythm. "Thor-dis . . . Thor-dis . . . !" they all chanted, making it known that they were more interested in hearing about his exploits than those of old. Bolting to his feet, Thordis swayed drunkenly. Before he could say a word, however, the door banged open and one of the Vikings swept into the hall.

"The woman . . . the thrall . . . she's gone!"

Nine

Hiding in the safety of the night, Natasha stumbled about as she darted in and out of the trees on the hillside. Shivering, she pulled her overdress about her shoulders as tightly as if it were the goddess Mokosh's magic cloak. Adjusting the dark scarf she had tied around her hair to keep it concealed, she watched from afar as the Vikings bolted out of their big house like a swarm of angry ants.

They have found out that I've escaped! It was a moment for her to savor the ultimate triumph of besting an enemy. *Ha! They thought that they could keep me locked up like their sheep, but I found a way to get free of them.* Well, not entirely free, for she still wore her slave collar.

Natasha reflected how she had worked at the lock of the door of her confinement with no success, then had turned her attention to other ways to break free. After trying ineffectively to dig an escape hole under one of the walls, she had turned her attention to a less obvious escape route: the roof.

She felt smugly proud of herself as she thought about how she had emptied a wooden chest of its treasures, piled it on top of a small table, stood on the very top, and used a silver tankard to chip away at the thin birch-bark roof. As soon as a large piece had broken away, she had used her hands to tear at the thick layer of turf. Though her fingernails were now broken and bleeding, with dirt underneath to remind her of her persistence, well, it was a small price to pay for freedom.

The moon was shrouded by dark clouds; her only guide was the light of the fading stars. Her people saw the stars as mortal souls. Whenever a new one appeared in the sky, a baby was born. Each time a star streaked through the sky and fell to Earth, they knew that a man or woman had died. Natasha prayed to all the gods and goddesses that she would not be one of the shooting stars.

The night exploded with torches as her absence was communicated from Viking to Viking. Though she was just a slave and therefore of little importance, though they had ignored her and secluded her in a faraway hut, the Vikings now acted as if her capture was of primary consequence.

Natasha ran wildly. Looking back several times to make certain that she was not in any danger of being overtaken, she moved one foot in front of the other with such force and exertion that she feared her heart would burst from the strain. All too soon her legs ached and her bare feet were bruised from the rocks. Her breath came in ragged gasps; her heart beat within her breasts like the waves upon the shore. The iron slave collar around her neck felt as if it weighed a ton.

She crept out on a ledge to catch her breath, hiding in the bushes, watching as a large swarm of Vikings searched the area she had just vacated. It had been a close call. She knew only a brief moment of relief when they headed away from the ocean and thereby away from her. Even so, she waited a long time before she set out again, heading in the direction of the Viking ship.

"If I can only make it to the water without being seen . . ." It was a challenge and a necessity.

Natasha calmed her fears by visualizing how surprisingly shallow the water was near that place where the

Viking ship was tethered. Though she had been frantic when the Norsemen shoved her overboard, fearing that she might drown, she had discovered that the water was just up to her waist. That meant that she could practically wade out to the snake ship. From there, however, her escape would become more harrowing.

The dark-haired stranger's boat was tied on the side away from the shore, where the water became much deeper. Since she did not know how to swim and could not swim out to it, Natasha's only hope was to climb aboard the snake ship, make her way to the far side, then climb down one of the oars and drop down into the small boat, being careful not to slip. If she did, and if she landed in the sea and swallowed the water, the gods of the ocean would no doubt lay claim to her.

Hiking up the hem of her tunic, she gritted her teeth and stepped into the cold, frothy water. She took another step, then another. Soon she was in water up to her knees, then her thighs. Careful where she placed her feet so as not to fall in a hole, she gasped as the freezing seawater lapped at her buttocks and the sacred place of her womanhood, then retreated as a wave swept the waters back out to sea.

The closer she got to the ship, the more turbulent those waves became, frightening her anew for fear she might be swept out to sea. Still, she had to push on, putting her fear of the ocean out of her mind and concentrating on her hunger to be free.

Her efforts were soon rewarded when she reached the wooden plank the Vikings had used to transport their ill-gotten goods. Pausing just long enough to make certain that there were no sounds coming from the ship, she climbed aboard and stooped down as she walked so that she would not be seen from the shore.

Shivering, she hurried to the other side of the serpent ship and peered over the side. There was the boat, bobbing up and down in the water as it was slapped by the waves. Natasha took a deep breath to quell her fears. It was so far down! Much farther than she had realized.

Looking over her shoulder, she could see torches all over the hillside lighting up the night. The angry buzz of voices cut through the silence. The sight of those flames and the sound of the furious mumblings gave her courage. She had to do it. There was no other way. To go back meant the death of her newly won freedom, punishment, and the eternal doom of slavery. Far better to let the waters claim her!

"I must make a sacrifice . . . to the waters." But she had nothing to give. Nothing of value. Nothing that she treasured . . . except . . .

Spotting a discarded Viking sword, Natasha picked it up and used it to hurriedly hack off her braid, knowing that her hair was the one thing she had always valued very highly. Throwing it over the ship's side, she watched as it was swept out to sea, hoping that would calm the gods and water spirits.

Taking a deep breath, then another, she cautiously lowered herself over the side of the snake ship and grasped an oar from the underside. For a long, harrowing moment, she hung over the dark water, letting her arms get accustomed to the weight of her body. Then, very carefully she put one hand in front of the other, moving downward toward the boat.

The progress was slow and challenging. The muscles in her fingers and arms cramped with pain. She grimaced as she felt the sting of splinters and then the slickness of blood. She felt certain that she couldn't hold on a second longer. Worse yet, the blood from her blistered hands made the oar slippery as she moved. Only the fear of falling into the water goaded her on despite her agony and feelings of helplessness.

Suddenly, her hand slipped and she found herself

dangling precariously by one hand over the water. Biting her lip, Natasha held back a scream, then miraculously regained her hold. Closing her eyes, she willed her hands to move. Getting a new, firmer grip on the oar, she moved ahead, reminding herself of what would happen if she was caught. It made any pain she might be feeling now pale by comparison.

At last, just when she feared she couldn't move another measure, she felt the wood of the small boat beneath her foot. One misstep and she would be in the water. She had to be careful.

Swinging free, manipulating the oar so that it was over the boat, she visually searched for any trace of the Vikings. She could see their torches dotting the land as the stars dotted the sky. Fear surged in her heart. They were now coming *toward* the ship. She had to hurry, but no, she didn't dare. She had to take her time, secure a firm handhold, and keep her balance.

For a long, agonizing moment, she just hung, suspended, apprehensive about moving, yet dreading to go back. The rhythm of the waters was steady, making a sloshing sound as it slapped against the boat.

So close to freedom . . . So close! Suddenly her hand came loose. In her desperate attempt to hang on, she lost her balance and fell.

Cold, dark water swirled above and around her. In panic, she began flailing her arms around, not knowing which way was the surface. Her lungs were bursting with the effort to keep from breathing. At last she gasped, choking as she swallowed some of the salty water.

Oh, please! She had so much to live for. Trying to control her breathing, to relax despite her fear of the icy ocean, she determined that she would be the victor, not the icy sea.

At last a wave swept her toward the little boat, and her head came out of the water. Before she could grasp the side, however, the undertow pulled her back.

She felt a sense of panic, but as if to give her aid, a third wave moved her closer to the boat. She reached out for it, fighting the strength of the waves, at last succeeding in her struggle.

Exhausted, winded, and trembling from cold and fear, Natasha used one last burst of energy to pull herself out of the ocean. With a gasp she tumbled into the boat, her ears roaring with the sound of the sea.

Thordis's swearing was as loud as thunder. "Where is she? How could one skinny woman outsmart all of you? Uh?" There was a pause before he roared, "Find her!"

Two Norsemen, anxious to obey the furious Viking, collided in the darkness and nearly toppled to the ground.

"Fools!" Thordis shook his head. "All of you. Fools!"

Sean pretended to aid in the search, yet all the time his thoughts were with the young slave girl, praying that she would not be found and that she was well on her way to freedom. He watched as Thordis paced the rocky ground nervously, unable to come to terms with the thought that a woman had managed to escape right out from under his long nose.

"You! Monk!"

Sean stiffened as he realized that Thordis meant him. "I'm not a monk. Not yet!"

"You are the same as a monk to me." Thordis spit on the ground. "Did you help her? Did you set her free?"

How he wished that he had. Perhaps at least then he would have known where she had gone and that she was safe. "No. I had no hand in this."

For a man of such large size, Thordis moved as swiftly as a cat. Before Sean could even react to any danger, the Norseman had the front of Sean's tunic in his grip. Roughly he dragged him forward until they were nose to nose.

"I think you did. What's more, I think you are telling a lie, for I saw the way that you looked at her."

"I felt compassion for her." A surge of anger pushed at Sean's insides like a stormy sea.

"Compassion. Bah! Such feelings are for women or those who, just like them, wear skirts." He looked at Sean with undisguised contempt. "I say again that you helped the slave. By our laws that means that whoever freed her will take her place. You!"

Sean's words came bursting forth with a never-before-experienced animosity. "If you are accusing me, then I tell you that you are wrong." His temper flared as he brought his fists up and struck at Thordis's hands with enough strength to knock them away.

For a long, dangerous moment, the two men stared at each other, their eyes clashing. They didn't even glance away as a tall, skinny Norseman stepped between them.

"He must be telling the truth, Thordis. How could he have helped the slave when he was never out of our sight?"

Thank God for an alibi, Sean thought. It was true. He had been under the Vikings' watchful eyes from the moment he had first arrived.

For a long time Thordis seemed not to hear; then, with a shove he pushed Sean away. "Perhaps he was blameless this time. . . ." As if unable to let the matter rest, he picked up a torch and held it up to Sean's face, studying his expression. "But if there comes a time when you deceive me, you had better think twice, monk."

In spite of Sean's reprieve from retribution, he found himself being shoved and pushed along behind Thordis as he moved back to his hall. In that moment he knew that he must advise the abbot against giving in to Thordis's demands. There had to be another way to keep Armagh safe besides giving in to a man such as this. He would ponder the matter and come up with a plan of action.

"Tomorrow at the first light of the dawn, I will return to my boat and go back." As far as he was concerned, Sean would have been happy if he never had to look upon the face of any Viking again.

Ten

One by one the smoking torches had flickered, hissed, and died. The hearth fires burned down to ash. Darkness engulfed the Vikings' hall. Had it not been for the loud, throaty rumble of drunken snoring, Sean might have been able to pretend that he was alone. As it was, he was reminded of their presence with each gurgling intake and exhalation of breath.

Drunken oafs, he thought as he lay on one of the sleeping benches. His head throbbed, but not from drinking the Vikings' foul-tasting mead. He suspected that he had a headache because he had been so tense and agitated tonight as he watched Thordis lead the search for the pretty slave girl. Had he been experiencing her quest for freedom vicariously? Surely, even if he had been the one on the run he couldn't have felt any more anxiety.

Sean remembered how the Vikings had continued their search late into the night, halting only when their stomachs growled for want of food. Sitting around the table, they had gorged themselves with meat and mead, all the while listening to Thordis as he described the harsh punishment he would dole out to the poor girl once he found her.

May he never find her!

Realizing that he would never be able to fall asleep, Sean rose from his makeshift bed, stumbling over the inert form of one of Thordis's men as he did so. He would have to be careful where he stepped, for the hall was strewn with the bodies of drunken Vikings.

Slowly making his way across the room, stumbling more than a few times over a sleeping Viking, he reached the door and pushed it open. The fresh air hit him in the face and acted as a potion to revive his sagging spirits and aching head.

Lying down on the hard, cold ground, he put his hands behind his head and looked up at the sky, sorting out his thoughts and contemplating his future as he waited for the first streaks of the dawn.

He suspected that part of the reason the abbot had sent him on this mission was so that he could see the seamy side of the world and thus be only too anxious to retreat behind the walls of the monastery. The abbot valued predictability, solitude, and routine. But what of him? Had his brief interlude with the Vikings soured his quest to see more of the world? Or had it strangely whetted his appetite?

"So, I see you have had enough of Thordis's *hospitality* and choose to be alone."

Sitting up and turning his head, Sean saw the silhouetted figure of a tall, muscular Viking. "I'm an outsider here. Your ways are not my ways."

"You speak of the girl."

Sean chose his words carefully. "I speak for all slaves. It is not my belief that one man put chains upon another."

"Nor is it mine."

Sean stood up, curious about the identity of this particular Viking. "Who are you?"

"My name is Wolfram Olafsson. I have a settlement in Dublin. I came to Larne to trade with Thordis for plowing and harvest tools."

"And not slaves," Sean said sarcastically. He was anxious to leave for the longer he stayed in the settlement the more he felt contaminated, as if somehow greed and cruelty were a disease.

"Never for slaves. I was once a slave myself, you see. A slave of the Irish!"

"The Irish?"

Though Sean had chosen to forget, he was forced to remember that slavery had once been extensive in early Eire. Some had been prisoners of war, others the children of the poor sold into slavery in times of famine, while yet others were brought from abroad. Prisoners condemned to death but released to the church, or unwanted children dumped on the church: all had provided a servile population within the great monasteries. Had he been brought to the monastery a few years earlier he might have suffered a like fate.

"Do not judge all of us harshly because of a few. . . ." Just as quickly as he had appeared, the Viking disappeared into the gray mists of the fading night.

The first pink rays of the sun touched the horizon. Sean quickly gathered up his meager possessions and headed toward the sea. It had been a long night. He would waste no more time in Larne now that his mission was fulfilled.

The grimacing dragon head carved on the prow of the Viking ship seemed to be frowning at him as he moved closer. Nonetheless, Sean hastened through the now ankle-high water and climbed aboard. Giving in to a whim, a fantasy, he stood at the steerboard, pretending for a moment that it was his ship.

He could imagine the waves slapping at the wood of the prow as the ship sliced through the water. He could hear the whine of the wind, feel the harsh breath of a storm strike his face with gentle blows, smell the salt water, the kelp, and the fish. Looking at the oars, he could almost see the men bent to their chore of rowing. Only this time they would be listening to his commands.

"What would it be like . . . ?

Closing his eyes, he concentrated on the sound of the waves and the hum of the wind: like some ancient sea chant. He thought about a verse he had heard the Irish bards sing many times concerning their night watches for the Norsemen and their relief when it was stormy.

Bitter is the wind this night,
Which tosses the ocean's hair so white;
The fierce Norse warriors I need not fear,
For they can only cross the Irish Sea when all is clear. . . .

Sean's trance was broken by the sound of gulls shrilling above the wind as if warning him that these were haunted, evil seas. Combing his fingers through his hair, he was brought back to earth with a thud. It was time to return to his own small curragh.

Throwing a rope over the side with which to climb down into the boat, he paused. Strange, but all the oars had been stowed when the Vikings landed, though one oar was hanging from the side of the ship, banging against the side as the wind whistled in the air. Reaching down, he tugged it back and secured it, then climbed down the rope.

Loosening the rope that held his boat to the Viking ship like an umbilical cord, he grabbed the oars and rowed purposefully away from the settlement. He was soothed by the rise and dip of the blades as they slapped the waves.

Natasha lay back in the boat, hiding in the shadows. Shivering, she admitted to herself that she was fearful, yet the farther the boat traveled the more she came to trust the dark-haired man at the oars. That, more than anything else, helped her fight her inner turmoil and bolster her courage.

Up and down, back and forth, the boat rocked unendingly, at last lulling her to sleep. Deep in her dreams she was conscious only of the motion of the boat and the sound of the water. Awakening for a moment, she pulled the folds of a discarded cloak around her body, then hugged herself to keep from shivering. At last as complete exhaustion took control of her, she fell asleep again.

A cold spray of ocean mist splashed into Sean's face. It was cold on the ocean, and though the boat was rounding a corner and would soon be skimming along the waters of the river, he feared it might grow colder. Seeking to warm himself, he loosened his hold on the oars and reached for his hooded brat.

Clutching the woolen cloth with his left hand as he rowed with the right, he tugged and was puzzled when the cloak did not pull free. He tugged again; then, certain that it must be snagged on a broken piece of wicker, he glanced over his shoulder.

"What in the name of . . ." It was she! The slave. Tucked up in the folds of his brat at the far back of the curragh, she was sound asleep.

For a long, lingering moment he gazed down at her in the early morning light, at her curves, her soft breasts rising and falling as she breathed. High-boned cheeks and a finely sculpted nose gave her the look of nobility despite her status as a slave. She looked peaceful lying there, as if she hadn't a care in the world. In that moment she reminded him of a kitten.

He laughed softly. "A kitten who outsmarted Thordis Forkbeard."

Although she had taken a risk that his boat would not be searched, it was nonetheless a brilliant maneuver. All the time the Vikings had searched every rock, cave, and tree on land, she had been curled up in his boat, floating right beside the very ship that had brought her to the place of her enslavement. How could he help but admire her?

Sean had to keep his attention on guiding the boat on the current, so he couldn't stare at the young woman. Every now and then, though, he would glance back to look at her and make certain that she was safe and secure.

"Thank God you escaped," he whispered, watching as she stirred in her sleep. Was he imagining it, or was she smiling?

Suddenly, she opened her eyes, and Sean once again found himself staring into eyes that were a brilliant shade of blue.

"Where are we?" she asked in her own language, forgetting for an instant that she was far from her home.

For a moment Sean was taken aback, trying to ascertain what language she was speaking. Not the Norse tongue, nor Gaelic, nor Slavic. Certainly not Latin. So, she was not a Slav, then. Thordis had been mistaken.

"Where are we?" she asked again, sitting up and looking around her.

Sean could read, write, and speak several languages and had been told that he had an affinity for analyzing and learning languages other than his own; thus, he was at last able to determine that she spoke a language similar to that of the people of Finland. "Where are we going?" Natasha looked all around her, stiffening as she looked at the water. For a moment she feared that the boat might capsize, but relaxed as she remembered her sacrifice to the waters.

Reaching up, she touched her hair, tracing a handful of strands from the roots to where it fell to a length just a little bit below her shoulders. Once it had fallen nearly to her knees. Was it any wonder, then, that she felt somehow naked? Much like a shorn sheep.

"Your hair . . . !" The last time he had seen her, that pale blond hair had been pulled back in a long braid. He wrongly assumed that Thordis was responsible.

She blushed, feeling suddenly very ugly. Reaching for the hood of the cloak, she pulled it up to hide her hair.

"No . . . no . . . you look lovely." The hair framed her face.

She didn't feel lovely. Quite the opposite, in fact. Avoiding his searching gaze, she looked down at her hands.

Reaching out, Sean cupped her face in his hand, raising it up so that she would look at him. "Don't be embarrassed, not by anything. Not with me!" He smiled at her. "You are not only very beautiful, you are very brave."

Natasha felt warmth burning upward from her throat to spread across her face as she blushed again, but instead of looking away she held his gaze. For just a moment it was as if they had reached out and caressed each other. The unique experience made her feel light of heart, as if a sweet singing took hold of her spirit.

The moment was shattered as the curragh suddenly lurched. Sean clutched at the oars. "Hold on to the sides!" he ordered as he fought to regain control of the boat, battling with an ocean that had suddenly become dangerously turbulent.

Natasha had no choice but to do what he said. Gripping the sides, she was determined to be brave, though she did not realize how her courage would be stretched to its limit.

As for Sean, he felt invigorated, vibrantly alive as he fought to keep the curragh afloat. It was almost as if the sea were a living thing with a mind of its own. If so, it was being belligerent and angry, determined to hurl them toward the dark-gray rocks up ahead. It was as if he were facing a battle, a fight for survival, armed not with weapons but with his skill at the oars.

The hull of the curragh scraped and banged over rocks, but somehow he was able to keep the boat from capsizing; then, with the force of determination he kept the boat on a steady path. Then, as quickly as the danger had loomed in their path, it was over and the water grew calm again. Once again the boat skimmed over the water.

Sean looked over his shoulder. He saw a tremor pass over the young woman's slim form. Even so, he was impressed that she had not cried out. Still, there was something very vulnerable about her despite her courage, and he felt a strange compulsion to protect her.

"Protect her!" But how? As the curragh sailed back toward Armagh, Sean was forced to face some important questions. What was he going to do with the young woman, and where was he going to take her?

Eleven

The sun looked like a golden coin, seeming to ignite the sky with fire as it hovered over the blue, shimmering water. The ocean seemed to go on forever, but at last Sean saw the familiar landmark where the river flowed into the ocean. He started to guide the curragh around the rocky bend and enter the swiftly flowing waters, then changed his mind. He would take an alternate route.

"I'll take the girl to Bangor." Unlike Armagh, where only men were welcome, Bangor was a double monastery in which both nuns and monks lived, in separate quarters. Surely the nuns would take her in and be good to her.

Although Sean had never visited the monastery, he had heard favorable things about it. As the largest center of Celtic Christianity, Bangor was able to send out a large number of missionaries who spread all across western and central Europe. Surely there would be a good chance that someone would speak the slave girl's language so that she might eventually feel at home.

"Keeping her with me is out of the question!" he exclaimed as the thought flitted through his mind. He couldn't and he wouldn't! Already he was becoming much too fond of her, and he could tell that she was likewise much too intrigued with him. Better to sever the blossoming emotional ties quickly.

Sean meant to pass out of the young woman's life

as soon as possible; thus, he was curt and silent as they sailed. He knew it would do him no good to get attached to the young woman, for it would only make their parting all the more bitter.

If he was distant, however, Natasha didn't seem to notice. The morning sun lay like a golden haze upon the land, softening the landscape, making it look almost magical. The bright-green hills and valleys rolled up and down, gentle waves in varied shades of vibrant greens, reds, and golds. Greenery was everywhere, in every conceivable shade. In the leaves of the trees, in the grass, and in countless species of foliage that she had never seen before.

The farther they traveled, the greener it seemed to become. The rich, heavy scent of the fresh earth filled Natasha's nostrils. Her eyes were focused on the panorama presented to her view. This region was unbelievably green and lush. Trees and vegetation covered the hills and valleys. Ferns and vines grew abundantly. She thought about her homeland, so very different from this place.

"I like this land of yours," she said, reverting to the Slavic tongue, the only language they held in common. "Your food must be so plentiful that you never grow hungry." Surely here there were no droughts or shortages of food as there had been when she was traveling in the caravan.

Her tone of voice held excitement; her face was animated. As he turned around, Sean was startled by the intensity of her gaze, as if her eyes could pierce right through him. For a moment he forgot his resolve and warmed to her enthusiasm.

"Eire *is* beautiful. I should remember to be more thankful in my prayers."

"And I in mine. Mother Earth is very powerful."

"Yes, she is," he whispered, thinking about Mary. The Celtic Christians retained an affection for the local Celtic past, for they were nature lovers and had assimilated the old ways with the new beliefs, preserving the pagan tradition in a modified form.

"Somehow it seems that she is even more powerful here. It is so green. . . ." Natasha put her hand on his arm. Without thinking, he turned to her, put down the oar, and affectionately touched that hand.

Once again their eyes met and held for just a heartbeat in time. Natasha thought of what her old grandmother had told her: that if one saved another's life, their spirits would be joined for eternity. Had he saved her life? Yes. Surely she would have died if she had been forced to live with the big, ugly Viking. Though she had been instrumental in her own escape, she knew deep in her heart that she had been inspired to gain her freedom because of him.

Will we be together forever? she wondered. She warmed at the thought and knew that was what she wanted above all things. With that thought in mind she softly intoned another of her grandmother's favorite sayings: that when a woman's heart reached out to another, their spirits would be bonded forever.

"No. . . ." Sean heard her murmurings. She was getting too attached to him, and if he admitted it to himself, he to her. It just couldn't be. Once he handed the girl over to the nuns, he would be out of her life, away from the temptation she presented. In short, out of the scene entirely.

Angry with himself for succumbing so easily to the young woman, Sean tried mentally and emotionally to keep his distance from her, but his thoughts kept returning to the sweetness of her smile, the suppleness of her waist, the deep blue of her eyes.

Ah, the girl! Oh, how she fascinated him. He admired her erect posture, the show of pride she had in herself, and yet the unabashed enthusiasm she displayed as she viewed the unfolding world. Though he was intent upon rowing, he found time to look back at her from time to time. Each time he looked back at her, he was reminded of what a lovely woman she was, in face as well as form.

Put her beauty out of your mind. She cannot stay with you. Armagh only welcomes males, and she is obviously very female, he reminded himself.

Having been raised in a monastery since he was just a small boy, he was unused to women's ways, though that was not to say that he had not been drawn to women. But never like this! This young woman had come into his life, threatening to turn his very orderly routine upside down. It complicated everything and made it all the harder to make the decisions he knew he would have to make in the very near future.

Natasha pulled away from the side of the boat and turned her attention to Sean once again. She felt so alive! Just being in his presence was stimulating and at the same time comforting. Even though he was a stranger, she somehow already looked upon him as an important part of her life. She had in fact begun to feel more strongly that her grandmother was right and that somehow their meeting was meant to be.

"What is your name?" she asked, suddenly wanting to know everything about him.

"Sean," he answered.

"Sean." She liked his name. "My name is Natasha," she informed him when he did not ask. "Though I am most often called Tasha."

He wished that she had not told him. Somehow, thinking of her as "the slave girl" made their relationship all the more impersonal.

She saw the way his mouth tightened and she could only wonder why. He didn't look like a happy man, and she wondered what might be troubling him. Reaching out, she put her hand on his arm again in a gesture meant to comfort, but this time Sean shrugged it off, determined to concentrate on the matter at hand. He must get her to the monastery at Bangor and then see to the return of normalcy concerning his own life. The longer he was with her, in fact, the more urgent the matter became.

The high stone walls loomed dark and forebidding against the velvet gray of dusk as Natasha and Sean walked over the crest of the hill after tying up the curragh. For the first time in their journey she was apprehensive, wondering why he was so silent and would not tell her where they were going. Even so, she trusted him. Wherever he was headed, that was where she wanted to go. Even so, as they came closer and closer to the walls, Natasha shivered as a sudden fear of the unknown gripped her heart.

"Are you cold?" It was the first time Sean had addressed her since they had left the boat.

"A—a little." Natasha did not wish to tell him of her alarm. He had told her that he thought she was brave, and she wanted him to keep thinking that she was.

"There are fires up ahead to warm you." Sean felt a bit guilty in his aloofness toward the girl but soothed his conscience by telling himself that what he did was for her own good. She would be well fed here, and clothed and schooled. More importantly, she would be free of her bonds of slavery.

"And food?" She couldn't remember when she had ever been so hungry.

In spite of himself he smiled. "And food." He touched her shoulder. "I'll see that you have a bath and a change of clothes as well." And he would have to see about getting the iron slave collar removed.

Following him through the gate, Natasha looked around her at the tall stone tower that reached toward the sky, the large stone buildings, and the strange stone huts that looked like big beehives. This village was much different from anything she had seen so far. And the people! They were all dressed so drably in various shades of gray. They reminded her of woeful pigeons, for not a one of them smiled.

She put her thoughts into words. "They all seem so sad."

"Not sad, just reflective," he answered, although, looking up, he saw them—strangely—through her eyes. They did all seem to have frowns on their faces. He shook the thought away as they made their way toward the main building.

In silence she followed him up the outer stairway and into the gloomy stone building itself, stiffening at what she beheld. Inside there were even more gray-robed people, who displayed no sign of welcoming them. They were ignored, in fact.

The fact that he, too, wore the drab hooded cloak prompted her to ask, "Is . . . is this your home?"

She was relieved when he whispered, "No."

A large fireplace dancing with flames of red, orange, and blue caught her eye as they walked through a doorway into another room. The floor was covered with fresh rushes, which gave off the smell of herbs. Trestle tables and benches jutted out from the stone walls, awaiting the unsmiling people who seemed poised to take their places. Torches flickered from their positions on the walls, casting a glow on plates and goblets.

Prompted by her hunger, Natasha started to take a seat at the table, but Sean grabbed her by the arm. "No. You must not sit here. This area is only for the monks."

"Monks." Looking closely, she could see that all of those seated looked to be male; thus she supposed that the word *monk* meant male. How strange that they ate segregated from the women and children. No wonder they had such grim looks on their faces. They were missing the sound of children's laughter.

The sound of feminine voices drifted through the great hall, and Natasha turned around to see two gray-clothed ladies staring at her. Suddenly, she wanted to hide from those reproving eyes, but Sean gave her a gentle push in their direction.

"Sisters, please help me. I must find garments for this girl and food for both of us."

The taller of the two stepped forward, eyeing Natasha's scanty attire. "I can see for myself how greatly in need of clothing she is. I will see that she is given proper garments and food. A bit of meat and bread and a clean chemise and undertunic will work wonders to take away the dismay that I read in her eyes."

Sean gave Natasha into the nuns' keeping, refusing to watch as she walked away. Nevertheless, he could see her in his mind's eye and he knew that he would never forget the beautiful girl who had been thrust into his life, nor could he disclaim the ripple of desire that had sparked within him when he was near her—a fire that he must seek to put out.

Twelve

The flames beneath the cooking pot in the women's quarters leaped high, and Natasha found herself mesmerized by their dancing. Breathing in the tantalizing aroma of the cooking broth, she was reminded of how famished she was, for she had not eaten even a morsel all day.

As if reading her thoughts, her companion formed the edges of her mouth into the semblance of a smile. Putting her long-fingered hands upon her slim hips, she strutted toward Natasha, chattering away, obviously asking her questions.

Shrugging, Natasha tried to convey that she didn't understand.

"Are you a mute?" The woman was puzzled by her silence. "I can't guess your needs if you don't declare them, child."

Natasha tried to communicate by rubbing her stomach and saying the word "hungry" in both her own language and Slavic.

"Ah, I thought so. . . ." Moving toward the fire, the nun spooned several portions of meat from the cauldron, then gave Natasha a sly wink. "It will be our secret that I gave you much more than your share. I won't tell the kitchener if you don't."

Smiling her thanks, Natasha sat down on a narrow bench, balancing the bowl in her hand as she ate the meat greedily with her hands and then drank the broth down to the last drop. Whatever kind of meat it was, it was good, though a bit tough.

The woman waited until she had finished eating, then, taking her by the hand, led Natasha down a winding staircase to a large room where women scurried to and fro, bringing buckets of hot and cold water to pour into a wooden tub. She pushed Natasha in that direction.

"No!" Remembering how she had felt as if she were going to be drowned the last time she had been bathed in a tub, Natasha backed away.

"Don't be modest. Come, come, come." Folding her arms across her chest, the woman made it obvious that she was not going to back down.

For a long time it was a battle of wills; then, at last, turning her back, Natasha began to divest herself of her worn and rumpled clothing.

"Now, into the tub before someone else needs use of it."

Natasha was made to sit in the tub upon a stool and shivered as the woman poured water over her body. "C-c-cold." It was not at all as luxurious as her other bath had been.

"Poor child, you look positively miserable, but the next bucketful will be warmer. " She cupped her hands in a box and stroked something on Natasha's skin. The concoction of meat fat, wood ash, and soda was abrasive, but when it was rinsed away she felt her skin tingle. "Now for your hair."

Taking a handful of the shoulder-length golden tresses, she started to lather on some of the same mixture, but Natasha reached up and batted away her hands. Her short hair was still a source of embarrassment, no matter that she had freely sacrificed it.

"What is wrong, child? What is it about your hair that makes you blush so."

Natasha grasped a handful of hair in each hand, tugging at it as if that would somehow make it grow.

"Ah . . . I see." The nun smiled sympathetically, then, lifting the covering on her own hair, revealed to Natasha that her head was shorn.

Natasha stared wide-eyed at the nearly bald head, then out of courtesy looked away. So, this woman was a slave. The shorn hair was proof of that. She clucked her tongue, commiserating with the woman's plight. No doubt that was why no one smiled here. No doubt, they were all slaves.

"I'm a nun. I gave up my hair and all worldly possessions. The priests and monks succumb to the tonsure for the same reason. It is a sign that we dedicate our lives to God."

Though she didn't understand a word of what she was saying, Natasha was soothed by the woman's tone of voice. She relaxed her shoulders and lowered her hands to her sides, allowing the nun to lather her hair. Though her eyes stung, the result was worth the price. Her hair shone like gold. Drying herself on a large piece of linen, Natasha felt refreshed and infinitely more feminine.

"Your hair is a bit lopsided. Let me even it up." Reaching for a strange-looking piece of metal that was bent so that the two blades touched, the nun moved toward her.

Misjudging her intentions, Natasha jumped back. "No!"

"I'm not going to harm you." She held the strange implement up. "Scissors. Very useful. If you will only trust me I will show you."

Again the soothing tone of the woman's voice calmed Natasha's fear, though she was still wary, particularly so as the nun moved toward her. Before Natasha could protest, however, she had clipped one side of her hair.

"There."

Because of the disparity in their sizes, the nun could not lend Natasha any of her garments, but she was able to find the necessaries in one of the storehouses. "I will find you all that you need or my name is not Bridget," she swore, leaving Natasha for a brief period of time, then returning with her bundle. Natasha furrowed her brows. The woman had brought garments that were of the same drab cloth that the others wore. She had no choice but to accept them, however, lest she insult the woman and strain the laws of hospitality. Picking up the gown and outer tunic, Natasha dressed quickly.

Bridget stepped back to assess her charge's appearance, clicking her tongue in approval. "Even our plain gray garments look magnificent upon your curving body, child. You look lovely."

Natasha shook her head, desperately trying to communicate. She didn't want to have escaped the Vikings only to be incarcerated here. Running toward the door, she opened it and searched the hall for Sean, but he was nowhere in sight.

Bridget took her arm and tugged her back inside; then, reaching within her cloak, she pulled forth another bundle: soft shoes cut of stiff fabric. "I believe that perhaps our feet are close to the same size. These are my gift to you. I've only worn them a few times. They're shoes," she answered to Natasha's unasked question. Though an inch too short for her feet, the form-fitting, round-toed shoes finished Natasha's costume.

Turning her back, she closed her eyes as Bridget untangled the strands of her hair with a wooden comb. Though the comb caught in a snarl of Natasha's hair, Bridget quickly untangled it.

"You are fortunate to have a natural curl." She stepped back. "There. Now you look lovely." Taking Natasha by the hand, she led her toward the door. "This is going to be your home now. Let me show you around."

As they walked, Natasha stared wide-eyed at her surroundings: at the altar, the flickering candles, the gold and silver artifacts, the pictures, and the statues. Her eyes rested on the statue of a woman holding a child, and she was struck by the kindness on the woman's face. Who was the woman, she wondered, reaching out to touch the cold stone, fully expecting it to feel warm, like living flesh.

"Mary," Bridget whispered.

Natasha remembered hearing Sean say that name. So this was the goddess he had spoken about. "Mary."

Another statue caught her eye, of a man bound to a tree, a cross. The bearded man was nearly naked, wearing only a loincoth, his bare feet bound together, a crown of thorns upon his head. Poor man, she thought, her eyes misting with tears. She wanted to soothe him, to take away all his pain, to lift him gently from the cross and tend his wounds.

"His name is Jesus."

The look of serenity upon the statue's face mesmerized her. Sean's god was obviously a god of peace. That knowledge made her feel more at ease as she followed the tall, gray clothed woman outside to some kind of rectangular courtyard that was surrounded by several small stone cottages nestled beside the tall stone wall. They walked across a small garden to one of the small, cottage-like stone buildings. Inside was a sleeping room with several beds laid out side by side.

"This is one of the dormitories, child. You will stay here tonight, but I will try to find you quarters near my own so that I can look after you." Patting her hand, she led her to a bed near the door, blew out the light, then took her leave.

Natasha lay down on the cot. She could hear the soft sound of her companions' snoring, but nevertheless she felt all alone. Though she was tired, she was restless. She missed Sean. Where was he? Why had he abandoned her and given her up to the woman? A sudden fear that he might leave without her prompted her to move stealthily toward the door. She had to find him! Even if she had to look in every room or search every stone cottage, she must find out where he had gone.

A bright ray of moonlight danced through the tiny window of the small room, bathing it in a gentle glow. The muted light illuminated Sean sprawled on the bed, as well as Natasha's smaller form lying on a straw pallet nearby. Though it had taken her several hours of exploration, searching all the alcoves, peeking inside a multitude of rooms, at last she had found him and stubbornly informed him that she would not leave. It was an argument that Sean had known in an instant he would not win, so he had given in this time.

"Women can be troublesome," he whispered, "particularly this one."

Though she slept an arm's length away on a woven mat and was now sound asleep, her presence was unsettling. He knew that, were she to be discovered in the men's quarters, it would cause a disturbance and set tongues to wagging all the way to Armagh. Still, he hadn't the heart to wake her, much less to throw her out.

"Troublesome," he said to himself again. *And enticing.* He could well imagine that the very word *temptation* had been coined to describe a woman like her. But he would be strong! He would just pretend that she wasn't there. He had too much on his mind to be bothered with any female and the complications her close proximity would bring. He would close his eyes and get some sleep and deal with all this in the morning.

Lying on his back, staring up at the ceiling, he tried to sort out his thoughts. How was he going to say good-bye? How was he going to explain to her that he couldn't take her with him? Succumbing to a streak of cowardice, he had fully intended to disappear with the first rays of morning sun, but now that she was here that would not be so easy.

He could hear the soft sigh of her breathing and scowled. The night seemed to pass too slowly, giving him more than ample time to refresh in his mind all that had happened: his arrival at the Viking settlement, his first sight of the lovely slave, her escape, the Vikings' desperate search for her, Sean's discovery of the young woman in his boat, then their brief journey together. He had been with her just a short time, but it had been enough time to become strangely attached to her. Now he was reaping the consequences, willing himself not to have feelings for the girl and losing the battle.

Turning his head, he meant only to glance at her, yet she drew his stare as she lay sound asleep on her side. With her head resting on one outflung arm, her golden hair tumbling across her face, she reminded him of an angel, yet he knew that awake, she was full of the devil's own fire. She had discarded her outer garments and slept in a gray leine that hugged her curves. Beneath the hem of the gown peeked her bare feet, exposing to his view her shapely ankles.

Much to his discomfort, she tempted him beyond belief. He wanted to reach out and touch her, to lift her up in his arms and carry her to the bed so that he could hold her in his arms. He shuddered as a sensation he knew to be desire coursed through him. To be beside her soft body all night long, to be so close to her enticing curves, was a torture that even rigorous discipline could not quell.

Sean tried to turn his thoughts to other things, but despite his resolve his eyes kept straying to where the sleeping girl lay. She was a pleasure to behold; he had to admit that. She was graceful, her body enticingly rounded, her legs long, her waist slim. She was a puzzling combination of gentleness and strength. Seemingly shy at times, she had nonetheless had the perseverance and presence of mind to find him.

Sean stared down at her for a long moment, his eyes moving from head to toe and back again, lingering on the rise and fall of her bosom. For a moment he felt an almost overwhelming urge to feel the softness of those young, firm breasts against his naked flesh, but he angrily fought down the desire that coursed through his veins. He would not give in to his body's urgings, he told himself. Even so, he was mesmerized by her loveliness.

"Natasha!"

She looked so vulnerable lying there like that, he thought. She brought out his protective instincts and made him wish that he had the power to protect her from the world's cruelty. Oh, that he could. She'd suffered so much already. Though he had not heard the story of her capture and enslavement, he knew it had been a terrible, frightening blow.

"But it is not my duty to make it up to her. She is not my responsibility," he told himself, trying to harden his heart. *I will not even look at her,* he thought, turning over on his side and facing the wall. That vow was broken, however, as soon as he heard her soft moans.

Thrashing her head from side to side, she seemed to be immersed in a nightmare. Reaching out her hands, she mumbled frantically as if trying to grasp someone or something. Unbidden, a wave of tenderness washed over him as he listened to her tearful, whispered pleading to spare someone named Nadia. Her sister? He supposed it to be.

"Please . . . don't let them hurt her. No . . . no! I have to find a way to escape."

Rolling from his bed, Sean moved to her side, kneeling down beside her. "Shhhh. Quiet, it will be all right," he whispered.

"So many hands . . . touching . . . pinching . . .

I'm human . . . not—not an animal!" Her voice was a choked murmur that would have softened even the hardest of hearts. "What will happen? Oh, Nadia . . ."

Lightly Sean shook the girl, but she continued to sleep, immersed in her tortured dreams. "We're slaves! The Norsemen . . . hideous." A long, shuddering sob tore through her. "A ship . . . water everywhere . . . surrounding me. Nowhere to go . . ."

Smoothing the hair from her brow, he watched as her eyelids fluttered open. "You were having a dream." His fingers were strokes of velvet as he soothed her.

She looked up at him and smiled. *Just a dream, a memory, but you are with me now.*

The hand that gripped her shoulders made her feel warm and tingly inside. Without really thinking, she flung herself against him, instinctively seeking the hard comfort of his naked chest, relishing the muscular strength of him. She'd had so little comfort in her life. Instead, it was always she who gave of her strength to others.

Sean felt the lithe firmness of her body, tight against his bare chest, with a potency that was his undoing. Unwilling, he felt desire stir, a hot ache that coiled inside him despite his effort at self-control. He could not take his eyes from her, nor could he pull away. Then, as she reached out to touch his arm, he was lost. The touch of her hand was the final straw. Before he knew what he was doing, his mouth claimed hers, fastening on her lips, stealing her breath away.

Natasha was entranced by emotions and sensations she had never experienced before. It was her first willing taste of a man's lips, but somehow she knew how to answer the searching of his mouth and tongue with a similar quest of her own.

Sean was lost in the kiss, forgetting for the moment all the reasons he should keep away from her. He only knew that her mouth was every bit as soft as he had thought it would be. He kissed her for a long, exquisite moment, his tongue exploring, claiming her mouth. Intoxicated by her sweetness, he could think of nothing except the hot pounding in his ears, the fire burning in his veins.

"Natasha . . . so sweet," he murmured against her lips. The reaction to her nearness, the soft yielding of her mouth, had brought forth a fierce surge of desire so strong that he trembled. For the first time in Sean's well-ordered life he was totally ruled by his passions, forgetting for the moment where he was.

Natasha's eyes met his and her heart hammered at the glitter of passion she saw in those blue eyes. She had never felt the touch of a man's hand in love, but she was not naive. She knew what was to follow. Was that what she wanted? As she stared in fascination at the face so close to her own, she was confused. A curious flutter in the region of her stomach could not be ignored and told her all too clearly that she was not unwilling. In anticipation she held her breath, yet when his fingers slid up her bare arm, moving toward her breast, she stiffened. She did not know what to do, how to respond. In nervousness she shifted her position slightly, little realizing what the brush of her breasts across his chest would do to him.

Compulsively his hand closed over her breast. The moonlight cast a soft glow, intensifying her beauty. Her lips were parted, beckoning another kiss, yet he knew a kiss would not satisfy the hunger her nearness inspired. She was too tempting, too soft and warm. He wanted much more of her.

Sean hovered above her, his tall, muscled length straining against her softness. Pushing aside the cloth of her gown, he slid his mouth slowly across her chest to the breast he had bared. His tongue caressed the peak, his teeth lightly nibbling. Natasha gasped as the flesh tightened and tingled with an agonizing ache.

For a moment they didn't hear the pealing bell, but

as it continued, its vibrating bong shivered through their embrace, tolling its way into Sean's consciousness. He pulled away, forcing himself back to reason.

He could hear her breath, quick and rasping, echoing his own as he stared blindly down at her, forcing his brain to think coherently. "Dear God! Forgive me. . . ." He was in a monastery, a house of God, surrounded by those who dedicated their lives to fighting against the sins of the flesh.

With stunned surprise he noted the rumpled disarray his questing fingers had wrought on her tunic. Hastily he pulled the cloth up to cover her breast. With an angry oath he pulled away, severely displeased with his show of weakness. He could barely bring himself to look at her. He'd viewed a baser side of his nature tonight. He was nothing but an animal driven solely by his own hunger, with little thought of the young woman and what she might have suffered.

How easily he would have betrayed his own rules, he scoffed. The thought engulfed him with a wave of self-condemnation. So when all was said and done, he was not much better than Thordis or the other Vikings after all.

Natasha watched as he rose slowly, then walked back to his cot, mistakenly thinking his look of revulsion was aimed in her direction. That he would not even look at her only emphasized her misunderstanding. When he did turn her way, his face was so cold, his mouth so grim, that she recoiled inwardly. She wanted to say something to break the increasingly uncomfortable silence between them but didn't quite know what to say.

Sean sat on the edge of the cot, his head in his hands. He wanted to tell her he was sorry, but the words stuck in his throat. Clenching his jaw, he was more determined than ever to set himself free of this girl, more so as he heard the bell toll again. He assumed it to be the bell announcing the early morning service of matins, but as he heard a series of screams he readjusted his thoughts. It was not a bell announcing prayer; it was a warning bell.

Thirteen

"Vikings!"

"Holy Mother of God, they are attacking!"

Startled exclamations, shrieks, and hastily mumbled prayers accompanied the sound of wood splintering and the blood-chilling cry of "Odin!"

Opening the door just a crack, Sean could see that the outer courtyard of the monastery was crawling with Vikings, their swords, axes, and spears drawn as they moved forward. In a quick count, he determined that there were thirty or more. Glancing down the hill, he could see dark-gray whirls of smoke drifting skyward as the village below burned to the ground.

"It must be Thordis. He must have somehow guessed that you were with me and followed us!"

That he might in some way be responsible for this carnage tore at Sean's soul, yet he was determined to stay strong and in some way help the monks and nuns. With that thought in mind, he told Natasha to hide, then ran from one monk's cell to another, issuing orders. Someone had to take command.

"Gather together. Alone we can be picked off like sparrows. Together we can make some kind of show of unity and resistance."

"We cannot and will not fight," a rotund monk exclaimed in response, falling to his knees as he mouthed frantic prayers ending with ". . . *in nomine Patris, et Filii, et Spiritus Sancti.* Amen."

"Better to die than to shed another's blood," said another. "Let us say the Lord's Prayer and then take the precious things to the hiding place. The books. We cannot let them harm the books." The illiterate Vikings often destroyed books by ripping off bejeweled covers for booty.

One by one they crossed themselves exactly as they did a hundred times every day. *"Pater noster, qui es in caelis, sanctificetur nomen tuum. . . ."* The voices were low and steady, the panic and trembling held within them.

"We must come to some sort of civilized agreement with them. We can pray later." Remembering his own negotiations with Thordis, Sean volunteered to meet with the leader of the Vikings and work out some sort of tribute.

"Brother Maidoc tried to reason with them," gasped a tall, gaunt monk. "He offered them gold and silver artifacts!" He shuddered. "Now he lies out in the courtyard. Decapitated."

Hacking, burning, and slashing, the Vikings seemed hell-bent on destruction. It was frustrating and puzzling to Sean. Why had Thordis negotiated with him but not with the monks of Bangor? As the swarm came closer and closer and he was afforded a closer look at them, he knew in an instant. This band of Vikings was not Thordis's band at all, but a ragtag, dark-haired band of rogue Vikings. Who were they? Did it matter?

"If they will not negotiate, you must fight! If you do not, you will end up dead, or worse yet, as slaves. And the women. Vikings show no deference for nuns. They will rape them and carry them off," Sean said bitterly, remembering the raid at Armagh several years ago. The Vikings then had been as fearsome as the heathen gods they worshipped. He had been afraid of the Vikings then and had hidden while several of the monks had been stripped, tortured, then herded off like sheep. He would never hide again, no matter what happened.

"But what can we do? We are no match for their swords."

"And even if we were, we have no weapons."

"Fight with anything you can find. Sticks, stones, kitchen utensils, hot porridge, torches!" Spying a pastoral staff hanging on the wall, he pulled it down. The staff was encased in a rich metal coating that protected it against destruction. It would protect him from the Vikings as well if he used it with courage.

The monks scurried along after Sean in a billowing throng of hoods and gowns, some tripping in their haste, arming themselves with anything they could find. When the Vikings moved inside, they would be in for a surprise.

The final barrier to the courtyard was broken. With a blood-curdling war cry, a dozen men burst through the demolished door and stormed into the sanctuary.

Sean stood by the stairs, legs apart, the staff held firmly in his hand. Hearing a sound behind him, he turned around just as an ax missed him by inches. Strangely, he was unafraid, even when a sword-wielding Viking came at him.

The sword was heavier than the staff, and each blow he encountered was backed by enormous strength. His arm and back ached with the effort as he warded off blow after blow. Shrieks coming from behind him added to his determination. With a strength he had not realized he possessed, he knocked the Norseman's sword aside and wielded blow after blow to his head until the Viking fell with a thud. He kicked him away, readying himself to take on the Viking who took his place.

Once again Sean made a good show of himself, but his stamina was failing and he wondered how long he could go on. Still, the alternative to winning was losing, and losing meant death; thus, he somehow found a renewed strength, lashing out with the staff until, with one powerful downward thrust, the Viking's sword split his staff in two.

Sean stared at the broken weapon in his hand, then looked up just as the Viking moved in for the kill. He dodged the point of the sword just in time. Picking up a statue of Saint Patrick, he swung frantically, grinning triumphantly as the Viking dropped the sword and grabbed his shattered arm. It was at that moment that Sean hefted the stone statue with every ounce of his strength, rendering the Norseman senseless.

Whirling around, he was pleased to see that the monks were making a surprisingly good show of themselves. Facing their opponents, eight monks to one Norseman, they picked, poked, and struck out like hornets attacking a bear. One of the tallest monks was fending off an attacker by gouging at his eyes.

Suddenly, the Viking raised his knife and stabbed the monk in the throat. Another fell, stabbed in the chest.

"Drive them back!" Without thinking, Sean reached over and picked up the discarded sword of a fallen Viking. Some primal instinct, an inner force determining survival, egged him on. The clang of sword against sword echoed in the room as Sean fought wildly.

From her place at the doorway, Natasha watched as the Vikings retreated, moving back in the direction from which they had come. Her heart was thumping so loudly that it sounded like a drum as she looked toward Sean. He was gentle, but he could also be as fierce as any Magyar fighter, she thought.

Turning around, Sean saw her and yelled out, "Tasha, gather up your possessions."

Tasha. He had called her Tasha. That made her smile, for only those who cared about her had ever used that name.

Sean came up beside her, anxious to get safely away now that the danger was over. He couldn't leave her here, not now. Not after this morning. Bangor was too close to the Irish Sea and the North Channel, too vulnerable to the Norsemen's attacks.

"Can you ride horseback?" he inquired, for it was much too risky to travel by boat. Instead, he would borrow two horses from the monastery.

She laughed softly. "I am a Magyar. We are born on horses!" Forgetful of the monks and nuns who were slowly gathering around them, she slipped her arms around his waist, clinging to him tightly. Only when they were approached by the nun named Bridget did she step away.

"Surely you were sent by God to save us this day," Bridget said, looking eye to eye with Sean because of her great height. Holding out her hand, she offered him a leather pouch that he recognized as his own. "In the melee you dropped this."

"Thank you." Opening it up, he feared for a moment that his pendant was gone. Vikings were a thieving lot! He sighed with relief to see that it was still there.

"That pendant!" Bridget looked as if she had seen a ghost. "Who does it belong to?"

"Me!" Taking note of her pallor, he asked, "What is it?"

Though she put her hand to her throat, she didn't answer. She just stood staring as he put the amber wolf back in the pouch. Then, when he looked up and might have questioned, she was gone.

The crisp early morning air was invigorating. Natasha's cheeks glowed pink from the cold whipping her face, and she enjoyed the ride. As Sean rode beside her he thought to himself that the girl had not lied. She did indeed ride a horse as if she had been born to it. He watched as she surged ahead of him, riding like the wind.

Heart beating wildly, Natasha crested the top of a hill. Looking back, she saw his long dark hair ruffling in the breeze as he did his best to keep up with her. She motioned to him, daring him to catch her, then urged her horse onward at a furious pace.

Behind her Natasha could hear the thundering sound of hooves as she led the horse down the hill-side. It was like old times when her father was still alive and they would race each other. The taste of free-dom was like sweet wine to her at that moment, and she knew that she wanted to be free forever.

Sean shouted to her as he followed in hot pursuit. The wind tore at his face and he felt a strange kind of wild excitement, something that he had rarely felt before. It was exciting to be with her.

The woods rustled as frightened birds took to the sky in flight, disturbed by their intrusion. Leaves and branches slapped Natasha in the face. Ruts and rocks threatened to send the horses sprawling.

Sean dug his heels into his horse's side, determined to win the race. Though it was a furious chase and his mount came to within a length of the horse she was on, in the end he was faced with defeat.

"All right, all right. You win!"

Grinning at him victoriously, Natasha let him catch up with her. "My father taught me how to ride. He was the leader of the caravan." Her voice hushed to a whisper, as if someone else might overhear. "Riding horseback was for the men. They fought on horse-back." She was swept back in time as she talked. "My father could even ride standing up in the saddle, all the while wielding a sword."

"How did he die?" He sensed that her father was a bittersweet memory.

"He died protecting us. . . ." She sighed.

"Last night in your dreams you mentioned Nadia. Your sister?"

She shook her head. "I wish she were my sister. We

grew up together and thought of ourselves that way." Nadia's face hovered in her mind's eye. "Nadia hurt her leg. She couldn't keep up with the caravan. I was with her when they captured us."

"Where is she now?"

She shook her head helplessly. "I don't know. . . . Somewhere. They took her to the East, I think." Tears stung her eyes. "I'll never see her again. . . ."

Reaching out, he touched her hand. "You don't know that for sure. God moves in mysterious ways." Just as he had when he had brought the two of them together. Sean could only wonder what the reason was. What lesson was this beautiful young woman supposed to teach him?

Fourteen

The sun shone brightly through the mists of morning. Chirping birds sang a cheerful melody as they flew from tree to tree. The air smelled of flowers, pine, and fresh hay. Winding roads twisted and turned, criss-crossing the countryside and giving it the appearance of a huge chessboard. It was a beautiful area of meandering brooks, rolling hills, and meadows etched by watercourses, woodlands, and pasturelands. Cattle and thickly fleeced sheep grazed peacefully. Tiny cottages were perched on hillsides.

Sean was eager to learn everything he could, not only about Natasha, but about her people and the land she came from far to the east, in the land she called the steppes. A land where men were so skilled at horsemanship that they could ride standing up on the horse's back or play games while they were draped precariously over the saddle.

"Like this," Natasha exclaimed, giving him a dangerous demonstration. "They use a goat's head, like a ball."

With his heart in his throat, he watched as she bent over the horse's back so low that she could nearly touch the ground, then gracefully pulled herself back up to sit astride the horse without even flinching. All the while, she was laughing with the exuberance of a small child.

"You seem happy!"

She sighed. "That's because I *am* happy."

Though he had put it out of his mind, Sean was reminded of the quandary he found himself in once they reached Armagh. What was he going to do with her? He knew for a certainty that the abbot would never agree to let her stay. Women were a distraction, he had always said. That this woman was a pagan made it an even more precarious situation. Where was he to take her, then? It was just one thing that weighed heavily on his mind. The other was the matter of the tribute and whether the monks should give in to Thordis's greed.

The journey back to Armagh was a scenic one, but a grueling journey nonetheless. Sean's backside ached; every muscle in his body throbbed. He had traveled on horseback before, it was true, but not for such a long stretch of time. Now, after over eight hours of clenching his thigh muscles to his horse's ribs, he was in agony, though his manly pride would never have allowed him to make that confession, particularly when the lovely young woman beside him did not seem to be suffering one iota.

"Shall we stop to rest?" he asked hopefully, casting a sideways glance at Natasha, who sat tall and proud in the saddle. She looked as if she could ride forever.

"No. No, I'm enjoying the feel of the wind in my hair and the feel of the horse beneath me."

She purposely ignored the dull ache that spread through her body as she guided her horse at a furious pace. Her bottom was sore, her bare legs chafed from where they touched the horse's flank, and stiff from their outspread position, but she would have died before she would have admitted any weakness—all the more so because he was so strong. She could not forget that he had saved her not once but twice from Vikings. The cuts and bruises he exhibited gave ample proof of his bravery.

Natasha's eyes touched on him longingly as they

rode, noting the way his long, dark hair brushed against the nape of his neck with just a hint of curl. Her eyes were riveted to him as they rode along. Oh, how she wanted to touch that hair and see if it was as soft to the touch as it appeared. And his shoulders. Despite the fact that he was tall and lithe, his shoulders were wide, his body strong. The very thought made her stomach dance with butterflies as she remembered how intimately he had been pressed against her before the bell had warned of the Viking attack and he had been forced to fight.

As she rode, it set her thoughts spiraling through her brain, recalling to mind how quickly her life had changed. She sighed, wondering what Nadia would think of this green land and the dark-haired man who rode at her side. If ever they saw each other again—and she hoped with all her heart that they would—she would have quite a tale to tell. But then, perhaps so would Nadia.

The rhythmic motion of the horse became monotonous as they rode farther and farther. Though they were both exhausted and sore, a mutual stubbornness kept either one from requesting that they rest; thus, they only stopped when a storm caught up with them. Thunder rumbled overhead with the promise of a torrent as dark-gray clouds moved across the sky.

Sean looked over at Natasha, expecting her to be in a hurry to seek shelter, but she gave no sign of wanting to slow down. Instead, she seemed determined to ride through the rain. Didn't anything stop her? She was riding right into the tumult. Clutching his cloak tightly around him, Sean rode in pursuit down the roadway just as the heavens poured forth in a cloudburst.

Natasha was soon soaked to the skin, shivering against a sudden burst of wind, which howled around them. Despite the storm, she was determined not to complain, nor could she had she wanted to, for her teeth were chattering so violently that she was not even certain she could speak a coherent word. In the end it was Sean who sought shelter, guiding his mount to a grove of thickly leafed trees, beside which stood a dilapidated wood hut. By way of explanation, he nodded in the direction of the roadway, which was quickly becoming a quagmire.

Natasha didn't utter a single word as he helped her down from her horse; she was shivering too violently, yet she did sigh appreciatively as he draped his arm over her shoulder, trying to warm her with his body heat. Perhaps if they huddled together they could get warm.

Sean noted that her face was begrimed with mud, rain running in rivulets down her forehead and cheeks, but underneath was such a stunningly pretty face, made even more so when she looked up at him and smiled her gratitude.

"Natasha . . . I . . ." He couldn't seem to find the words to say what was in his heart, or make her understand how torn he was emotionally since meeting her. Instead he said only, "I'll—I'll find some firewood and build a fire. That will soon warm you."

There was not enough dry wood to be found to start a sufficient blaze. Gathering her wet cloak tightly about her, Natasha tried futilely to warm herself, but the shaking of her limbs would not cease. Each quiver, each tremor, was noted by Sean, and he worried about the danger of her catching a chill.

"Natasha . . ." Drops of rain glistened on her thick lashes and brows, and he reached out to wipe them away. His finger moved over her cheek with a gentleness few such masculine men possessed. "Let me keep you warm."

Before she had time to think or to answer he had gathered her into his arms again, his mouth only inches from her own. It was such a sudden embrace that she was stunned. Her heart hammered in her breast, beating in a rhythm with his as she stared up at him mutely, her blue eyes huge. She was giddily conscious of the warmth emanating from his male body, aware of a bewildering, intense tingle in the pit of her stomach. Gone now was her body's chill. The shivering that overtook her was for a far different reason.

"Natasha. Sweet, sweet, Natasha . . ." He was touching her, moving his hand slowly up her arm from elbow to shoulder as he explored, caressed. "There, is that better? Do you feel warmer?"

Silently she nodded.

He arched against her, cupping her face in one hand, forcing her to meet his stare. For a long time he merely gazed at her, then, with an imprecation, bent his head.

"Sean!" Her voice was husky as his lips drew ever closer to her own. He was holding her so tightly that she could not avoid his kiss. But then, she didn't want to.

He claimed her lips in a gentle and strangely chaste kiss, yet one that devastated her senses. Holding her tightly against the strength of his chest, his arms tightened and Natasha was aware of her body as she had never been before. Her breasts tingled with a new sensation, and though she could have denied him, she made not even a token protest as he kissed her again, a kiss that held far more passion than the first.

The tip of his tongue stroked her lips as deftly as his hands caressed her body. In response she moaned, turning her head so that his lips slanted over hers at just the right angle as his tongue sought to part her lips even farther apart. She mimicked the movement of his mouth, reveling in the sensations that flooded over her. She wanted to feel more, to know more about this glorious new experience.

Sheltered together in the hut, they clung to each other, Natasha's slim arms wrapped around Sean's neck. In all her dreams she had never imagined a kiss could be so overpowering. But it was. Twice now she had learned that. With him! Sean ignited a fire in her blood, a hunger that was not for food but was just as important a craving. A yearning that was new to her.

Sean's desire was not any less fierce than hers. His reaction to Natasha's nearness, to the soft, innocent mouth opening to him, trembling beneath the heated encroachment of his lips, was explosive. So much so that he was shaken, giving in to a shiver that was nearly as violent as Natasha's had been. For one moment he nearly lost his head completely. His hands pushed her back slightly as his fingers fumbled at the neckline of her gown, questing for the soft flesh he craved to caress.

"Natasha!"

Her body trembled; her skin was flushed as his fingers moved back and forth, up and down, his hand moving toward the full mound of her breast. Suddenly, a flash of lightning crackled nearby, bringing him instantly and disagreeably back to reality. Reluctantly he lifted his mouth from Natasha's and drew his hand away. Before he gave in to the passionate feelings she inspired, he had to do a lot of thinking, not only about her but about what he wanted to do with his life.

"What is wrong?" For a moment she feared that perhaps there was someone else.

How was he going to make her understand how drastically she had changed his life without making her feel like some kind of burden? "Once we get to our destination many things are going to change. I won't be free to be with you. When we are together we won't be allowed to touch."

"Not allowed?"

He wasn't doing a very good job of explaining. "Where we are going is similar to the place that we left behind, but . . . but . . . women are not welcome."

"Not welcome?" It was difficult for her to imagine such a thing. "But why?"

"Armagh is a place where men devote themselves to God and to learning. Everything else is set aside."

Natasha was troubled by what he was saying. What kind of place insisted that men live such lonely lives without women? And what kind of gods expected such a sacrifice? All she had given up was her hair, but Sean's gods expected him to give up his life.

Sean could sense Natasha's eyes on him. He didn't want to hurt her. She deserved better than that. But was he prepared to throw away everything that was familiar in his life just to keep her by his side?

Natasha gathered what roots, leaves, and berries she could, carrying them in the makeshift pouch she formed with the upturned hem of her long tunic. Taking a leather flask from Sean's saddle, she filled it with water from a nearby spring and offered Sean the first drink.

"Thank you." He held the flask while she drank her fill. His eyes touched on her face, and a strangely potent emotion stirred in him again. Pulling away, he forced himself to concentrate on the fire he had started; then, fashioning a makeshift sling, he went hunting.

Natasha could smell the aroma of the large wild birds he had killed and put on a spit. Impatiently she watched the birds brown over the fire. When at last they were cooked, she knelt by the fire. The flames were soothing, the meat, roots, and berries a balm to her fierce, stabbing hunger. Eagerly she ate her fill, licking her fingers enthusiastically when she came to the end of her portion. Looking up, she realized Sean had been watching her, but instead of being embarrassed she felt at ease.

"Tell me more about yourself, Natasha."

"There is little to tell."

"Do you have brothers? Sisters? Is your mother still alive?" He was curious to know as much about her as he could.

"As I said, my father is dead. He died fighting our enemies." For a moment she could see him in her mind's eye. "Oh, but he was so magnificent, riding ahead of our caravan astride his white stallion."

She told him that the nomadic tribes depended totally upon the horse, and that the white horse was considered the most important creature on earth. Horses were a necessary conveyance for wandering, for transportation while fighting in a war, and as beasts of the field. The white stallion was the most perfect and beautiful incarnation of all. The leaders of the clan always rode on a white steed, she told him. It was a tradition of the Magyar leaders.

"When my father died, his horse was killed and buried with him." The sacred symbol was an object of the most somber sacrifice in the holiest of rituals, she explained, in especially the burial of the chieftain.

"You loved your father very much, didn't you."

She fought against her tears. "Very much."

"What about the rest of your family?"

"My two brothers died also." Her voice was choked; a faraway look came into her eyes as she remembered. "My father's and brothers' deaths killed my mother."

"I'm so sorry. . . ." For just the length of a heartbeat their eyes met and held; then Natasha looked away.

"Osip, a cousin, tried to take over as leader of the tribe, but he will never fill my father's boots. Never!"

She was anxious to turn the talk to other matters. "What of you? Your father and mother?"

He didn't really want to talk about it, but since she had answered his question he did likewise. "I don't know anything about my father and mother. My parentage is a mystery. I was found by the monks, who were very kind to me." He reached for his pouch and drew out the pendant. "This was found around my neck."

"The wolf!" She reached out to touch it in a show of respect.

"I don't know what it means, only that I have been forbidden by the abbot and monks to wear it."

"But why? Such symbols have magical powers to give strength and to protect. Birds of prey, the lion, the snake, the fish, and the wolf are all powerful."

"Not to us. We believe . . ." He started to explain, to tell her about his faith, but realized that now was not the time or the place.

"Maybe you are afraid. The Slavic peoples dread volkodlak?"

"Volkodlak?"

"It is the word for *werewolf,* a man who changes into a wolf when the day changes to night." She explained that the Slavs told many stories of a terrible man-beast that destroyed anything in its path. "It's one of many oborotens. Those whose appearance is changed against their will. A being whom some sorcerer or witch has condemned to inhabit an animal form.

"Have no fear. I am not a . . . a volkodlak," he said with a smile.

"I know, but even if you were I would not be afraid." Turning her back, she concentrated her attention on the night sounds, listening intently to the startling call of an owl and the crackle of night animals in the underbrush. Unfamiliar sounds to her ears.

"What's that . . . ?"

Sean stiffened, hearing the noises, too. Every one of his senses was attuned to the night. He had the unnerving feeling that they were not alone, felt eyes peering at him through the darkness. Human eyes.

"Who is there?" he shouted out.

Reaching for the staff, he hefted it threateningly, preparing to fight the intruder, be it animal or man, only to feel slightly foolish as a long, brown weasel slithered out of the foliage. Feeling more at ease, Sean shrugged his shoulders and settled himself for the night, determined, however, to sleep with one eye open.

Stretched out on his cloak before the dying embers of the fire like a contented cat, he looked at Natasha out of the corner of his eye. She seemed fragile, yet he knew she possessed more than her share of fortitude. He was intrigued by her. Fascinated. There was so much he wanted to know. He remembered what she had said about the wolf amulet, that it was a sacred symbol.

"But a pagan symbol, nonetheless."

Pulling a corner of his mantle over his shoulders, he held the carved amber pendant up, tempted for a moment to cast it into the fire and be done with it. But no! He couldn't. It was all that he had of his childhood, his only link with his parentage. Hurriedly crossing himself, he could only hope that he would not regret keeping it.

Fifteen

Natasha heard the clanging of a bell as they rode toward the monastery at Armagh. The sound chilled her to the bone. and a feeling of foreboding swept over her as she remembered that women were not welcomed here. What was going to happen? What had Sean decided? Would he hide her away and keep her with him, or banish her from his sight so that he could take his place among these strange men who had forsaken all females.

Reining in her horse as the stone buildings of the monastery appeared upon the horizon, she stared at the large quadrangle of the cloister, the dark monastic building, and the oddly shaped beehive huts.

"My quarters are right over there." Riding up behind her, Sean pointed to one of the huts located close to the outer wall.

He made a wide sweeping motion with his hand as he gestured toward the church, monastic buildings, kitchens, bakehouse, buttery, brewhouse, guest halls, farm buildings, workmen's huts, stable, hen houses, pigpens, beehives, gardens, and the acres and acres of open fields.

"It is not as ornate as Bangor, and the buildings are much smaller; but this is the place I have called home for as long as I can remember."

How sad, she thought, conjuring up her own wildly free childhood. What must it have been like for a boy to grow up among these unsmiling gray-cloaked men without the softness, smiles, and love of a mother.

"The monks were very good to me." He sensed her misgivings. "You have nothing to fear."

"I am not afraid of anything when I am with you," Natasha answered. Nonetheless, a shudder ran through her as they slowly rode down the hill.

All along the way, Sean had contemplated various ways that he would deal with Natasha's presence beside him. There was no way that he could hide her, or hope that the monks would mistake her for a boy. Her obvious curves would immediately reveal that she was a woman. Nor did he want her to have to live in the shadows, afraid of her identity being revealed. The truth was the only way. Truth coupled with the monks' own creed of hospitality: that no one looking for food and shelter should go without aid.

Motioning for Natasha to follow him, Sean rode through the gateway to the wall and headed toward the stables. Once they had unsaddled the horses and given them into the hands of a gawking fellow student, he led her to an area that was obviously a workroom. There were hammers, chisels, saws, and a wooden-handled auger that was used to bore holes. Sean used it to unhook the latch that fastened the slave collar around her neck. As it fell to the ground with a plunk, she knew that now she really was free.

"Come, we had best face adversity head-on!" Taking her by the hand, he led her toward the library, where Abbot Righifarch had a small office. Though the library was a hive of activity, Sean was fortunate to find the abbot alone in that area that had been taken over for clerical work. He was sitting behind a desk, his quill furiously moving across a long piece of parchment. He didn't even look up as they entered the room.

"I've returned!"

The abbot turned his head, his eyebrows knitting

together as he studied Natasha with intense gray eyes. At last he said, "It seems you have much to tell."

"It is a long story," Sean said wearily, at last feeling the complete strain of the long week's events. "Before I speak of it I must urge you to remember our rule of hospitality."

"Ah, yes . . . *hospitality.*" Always the perfect host in spite of the circumstances, the abbot drew up a chair for Sean and one for Natasha, treating her with as much deference as if she were an important visitor.

Natasha could not help staring. Despite the many differences in their cultures, the man somehow reminded her of her father. Perhaps because of the way he held himself so tall and strong, as if to announce proudly to the world that he was the person in charge, the tribal leader.

Abbot Righifarch was fair of complexion, with graying red hair that was tonsured in front of a line drawn from ear to ear. His gray eyes were keen and bright, his nose long but well molded, like that of a hawk, she thought. Though he was dressed in gray like the others, he was an unusual man whose very appearance set him apart.

"Are you and the girl hungry or thirsty, Sean?"

Sean nodded.

"I'm certain that there is plenty left over from the early morning meal." He left for just a moment. When he returned he was carrying two flagons filled with cool water from the well. "Was your mission successful?"

Sean paused to soothe his parched throat with a long drink of water, then hurriedly told him about his journey, his meeting with Thordis, and the Viking's demand for more tribute.

Though usually a man who had control of his emotions at all times, the abbot's cool reserve broke down for just a moment. His jaw twitched as he tried to control his anger. "I'm not surprised. After all, the Vikings are little better than pirates."

Sean's jaw tensed as he said, "They *are* pirates and worse, every last one of them. May God forgive me, I cannot help wondering why He created such creatures." He hurriedly crossed himself to atone for his words.

"We dare not question God's reasons," the abbot murmured as he sat back down, "we must only give thanks that you have come back to us safe and sound."

Remembering the turmoil in the Viking camp after Natasha's escape, and the accusations that he might be responsible, he scowled. "For a heartbeat of time my return was questionable, but though Thordis could have taken me prisoner, he didn't. But then, I think perhaps you knew that he wouldn't."

An uncomfortable silence followed his statement. Although the abbot tensed his shoulder and neck muscles, he didn't say a word.

"Why were you so willing to take such a risk?" It was a question that had plagued Sean all the way back to Armagh. "What did you hope to gain by sending me on such a reckless errand?"

"I trusted in God," the abbot replied, "and I wanted you to see . . ."

"See what?"

Rising again, the abbot walked over to Sean and put his hand on his shoulder. "You are torn, my son, between good an evil. I wanted you to see evil close up, and then, perhaps, fully come to realize how desperately you are needed here."

"No," Sean whispered. "There is much more to it than that. What then? What are you and the others hiding from me?"

The abbot stiffened but ignored the question, saying instead, "She is very pretty."

"Yes, she is. . . ." As he had fully intended, the abbot had changed the focus of the discussion. Sean prepared himself for the argument that was to come.

"Who is she?" The words were short and clipped, and his tone disapproving.

"Her name is Natasha." Sean watched as the abbot reached out, traced the telling red mark that still lingered on her neck. The time had come to reveal all, no matter what the consequences. "She is an escaped slave."

"Aha! I thought so." Again his eyes lit on Natasha, assessing her as one might a fine work of art. "What do you plan to do with her?" Before Sean could answer, he put forth a suggestion that she be taken to live with the nuns in a monastery nearby. It was exactly what Sean had been expecting.

"No. Her beliefs are not like ours." His eyes touched gently on Natasha. "She is not a Christian and does not understand our ways. We were at Bangor for only a night, and all the while she was miserable."

"Miserable?" The abbot recoiled as if he had been struck. "Doing God's work is not punishment but a blessing."

"I believe it should be Natasha's choice," Sean whispered, trying to minimize the anxiety their discussion was creating. Although Natasha couldn't understand what was being said, her wide eyes and posture revealed that somehow she knew they were talking about her.

The abbot was contemplative. "What if she wants to stay with you? I can tell by the soft glow in her eyes when she looks at you that this is what she would like."

"She feels grateful because I helped her in a time of need. She doesn't understand so many things." But then, neither did he. At least not now. He had felt the intensity of desire, experienced the excitement of a battle, stood at the prow of a ship and known the longing to sail off into the horizon. It was as if suddenly his life had changed drastically and there was no way he could change it back.

"A week. Seven days. She may stay here that long."

"A week." He had hoped for a longer time.

"Life is about choices, Sean." Though he did not say it, Sean knew the abbot was telling him that he must make a choice between the woman and the life he had known at Armagh—a decision that was binding.

The rushes were fresh, and there was a pleasant smell to the room. The small cot had clean bed linens and blankets stacked by the side of the bed to keep out the cold. From the tiny window there was a view of the gardens and the wall that surrounded the monastery. Leaning out the door, Natasha could smell the potpourri of drying flowers, herbs, and spices from the garden that grew down below, mixed with the tang of fresh autumn air.

Making her way from room to room she explored, anxious to acquaint herself with the place where Sean had grown to manhood. What she found surprised her, for it was not as dark and dreary as Bangor had been. The chambers were painted and there were rows and rows of offices, kitchens, and cellars. The rooms were furnished with items such as chairs, that were considered great luxuries to the always-wandering Magyars. Still, Natasha felt ill at ease, anxious to find a task to do that would make her presence there useful.

Making her way to the large room where Sean had gone, she focused her eyes on him in an attempt to understand what he was doing. He held something in his hand, moving it back and forth with a sweeping motion. As she moved closer, Natasha discovered it was a feather he clutched so tightly. At last, her curiosity got the better of her.

"What are you doing?" She was fascinated by the

figures he was making on a long, thin light-colored object.

"Writing," he answered without really paying much attention to her inquiry.

She reached out tentatively and touched the parchment. "Writing?"

He looked up at her, realizing that what he took for granted was unknown to her. "I am marking words down on this parchment," he said patiently. "Words like the ones I am speaking now. So that I might keep records." His sudden smile altered his face and gave a sudden warmth to his stoic expression.

"Words? Records?" She stared down at the ink marks in awe, realizing by his tone of voice that it must be something of great value. That piqued her interest. "Writing?" It was as mysterious to her as magic.

"Yes, writing." It was a skill he just took for granted, though it had opened a whole new world to him.

"You keep track of all that you say?" Her attention was drawn to his mouth, concentrating on the movement of his lips far more than on what he was saying. She suddenly wished he might kiss her again, but quickly pushed the thought from her mind. Since they had come here he had not shown much interest in her in that way.

"Only the important things."

"What things are important?" She was asking too many questions, she knew, but she wanted to understand.

He was distracted for only a moment as he sharpened his quill with a penknife. "It is a bit like the bards or storytellers. Just as they keep memories stored in their heads, so do I, and those of my profession keep records stored on parchment for others to read."

"I see. . . ." He spoke with such pride in the skill that Natasha was impressed. At that moment she knew what she wanted to do more than anything in the world.

Motioning her closer, he dipped his quill in the ink pot and demonstrated, making several sweeping motions. "There. Now even when I am dead my thoughts will not be lost."

"Please . . . Let me." Eagerly she sat down beside him on the wide wooden chair.

He was amused by her enthusiasm. "All right." As she grasped the quill, their fingers entwined for just a moment and he was jolted by the potency of her touch. Strange that it should always be so. Even the lightest stroke of her fingers had the power to stir him.

"What should I do?" She sat close to him, leaning against his thigh, looking up at him.

For just a moment he glanced at her, his brows drawn together in a frown. The pressure of her body against his mesmerized him, as did she. The large, blue eyes that were now focused on his face were as guiless and frank as a child's, yet he knew all too well that she was a woman. One so very lovely that she nearly made him forget all else. It was as if nothing existed beyond the charmed enclosure of their closeness. Purposefully Sean pulled away, picking up an old parchment that he used to practice his own writing.

"You put the point of this quill in the ink, then move the tip on the parchment, like so." He demonstrated, then let her try, laughing as he saw that it looked more like a chicken's scratching than any words. Natasha joined in, her laughter soft and musical. A happy laugh. She made it obvious that she was enjoying herself, and her delight was infectious.

"Let me try again." This time she moved the quill more slowly, mimicking a letter that Sean had written. Not perfect by any means, but better than her previous effort.

"Good, Natasha. Very good." Though it would be

of no use for her to learn such a skill, he humored her. Matters of letters were not for women. But perhaps it would keep her occupied and out of his way when he was busy. As she bent her head to the task he studied her, feeling a measure of admiration. In many ways he could tell the girl had a good memory. That in itself was of merit.

There was an easy relationship between them as they talked, she questioning and he answering. For a few precious moments Natasha felt close to him, swept up in the wonderful world he was creating. He was like a sorcerer, taking her on a magical journey she hadn't even known existed. Then, all too soon the moment ended as several men, both young and old, came into the room. Rising to his feet, Sean greeted them, and for the moment at least, Natasha knew she was forgotten.

Retiring to her chamber, Natasha reflected on all she had learned. To her the concept of knowledge and fact was new. Her life had been spent in a perpetual present, her knowledge of the past limited to memories of personal experience or what her elders had told her of the past. Time had little meaning.

On the very rare occasions when news had arrived from the outside, it had been shouted by a crier. She had eaten and slept, spending her long hours on simple, mindless tasks, too busy to realize how monotonous her life had been. The passage of time had merely been marked by memorable events. Her life had been regular, repetitive, and unchanging. Now, however, he had opened up a whole new world. A world of knowledge and learning awaited, a wealth more valuable than gold, which Natasha was determined to master.

Sixteen

The slender tapers flickered as a breath of wind swept through the tiny window of Natasha's room. The flames' slow dance cast eerie shadows against the walls, grotesquely silhouetting the quill she held in her hand as if it were one of the vengeful spirits said to lurk about in the night and plague the world with nightmares.

All was silent in the monastery. All of the monks were abed. The only sound was of her making as she scrawled upon the whisper-thin parchment before her. Because ink and parchment were so expensive, Natasha had taken to practicing on slates of wax tablets, but tonight she indulged herself in the luxury of using a damaged piece of scroll that Sean had thrown out.

Pausing for just a moment, she admired her handiwork, seeing at once how greatly she had improved. She sensed that Sean had given her the scroll just to keep her occupied, as one would a mischievous child, but she also sensed that he would not be amused at her efforts now if he could see them. She was determined not to show him what she taught herself, however—at least not yet. Only after she had mastered the task would she reveal her newfound skill.

Natasha had learned lettering from an alphabet arranged in the form of a cross, a "christcrossrow," as Sean had called it. He had lent her a paddle-shaped hornbook, a piece of parchment protected by a transparent layer of horn wherein lay the letters. It had been, he said, his primer when he was a child. The hornbook, coupled with her determination, had enabled her to learn slowly but very surely how to write the letters of these words Sean had called "Latin." It was, he said, the same language the priests of his religion spoke when they said their Mass. It was "God's tongue."

Natasha had gone further than just copying what Sean had already written, however. She reasoned that if one language could be captured in symbols and sounds, then so could others, even the language the Magyars spoke. If so, then she could create greater magic than the foremost wizard. She could find a way of storing information and passing it on to other people, not only near her but far away in time and in distance. The very thought was exciting, for it was difficult for people to keep all their information in their heads.

Natasha was content the next few days. During the day she watched Sean work from afar and busied herself with her own tasks, treasuring those moments he set aside for her, times of quiet conversation and smiles. It was as if he was growing used to having her around, even welcoming her company. Sometimes she even saw a soft glow come into his eyes when they were together. In those moments his hands were gentle when they touched her, and she found herself hoping that he would desire her, only to know the sting of disappointment when he quickly pulled away.

The pattern of her life had settled into a pleasant routine guided by the many bells of Armagh. At daybreak the bells sounded the first note in a chiming dialogue that went on all day. The bells rang at hourly intervals, dividing Natasha's day. Up early for the morning meal, then simple chores, which varied from day to day according to what needed to be done: making the beds, sweeping the floors and replacing the rushes, filling the inkpots, and various other duties that she had taken upon herself.

In the early afternoon Natasha was free to do as she pleased for an hour or so, which usually meant a leisurely stroll in the garden. Then it was back to her work again. At night, when Sean was abed, she practiced her writing in secret, determined to master it. She wanted to be of value to Sean, wanted to excel in something he held dear. She did not want to be just the girl who dogged his steps like a faithful hound. She wanted to be special to him and felt in her heart that once she was proficient in this task of writing, she would be. Sean and the others would see her far differently then, and she need not be worried about being cast out.

There were times when she could sense Sean's eyes upon her and knew that he watched her, but when she met his eyes he hastily looked away. Natasha was perplexed, wondering just what it was he had been thinking. She knew that she was exceptionally old to be unmarried, particularly when a husband was often chosen for a young woman by her kinsmen in childhood. There were many in the caravan who had given her the eye, hopeful that they might either seduce her or marry her, but Natasha had withered any aspirations they might have had with a frown. She had been too busy looking after Nadia to bother about a lover or husband.

Now, since meeting Sean, everything had changed. She wanted to belong to him, to be loved by him, but wasn't really sure how to go about making her dreams a reality.

Natasha jumped as she heard a sudden though quiet knock. Hurriedly she put her writing materials away, wondering who it could be.

"Natasha . . . !" Sean's voice sounded from beyond the door.

The hour had grown late. Sitting amid a stack of

ledgers, letters, and logs, Sean had felt the sudden urge to see her face. Now he found himself here.

Her face flushed with surprise as she rose to her feet and hurried to the door. When she opened it, however, his appearance startled her. He looked drawn and haggard, as if something of great importance weighed on his mind.

Sean pressed his hands to his throbbing temples. His head ached, his eyes felt as if any moment they would pop out of their sockets. He closed his eyes; then, when he opened them he said, "I saw a light from beneath your door."

"I—I couldn't sleep, that is all." Candles were precious, rationed out among those within, and Natasha moved in the direction of her small table, thinking to snuff the flame. But Sean stayed her, laying a hand on her arm as he entered the room.

"Nor could I." The dim candlelight turned her hair to gold and cast delicate shadows across the hollows of her face and throat. She was a beguiling image, even dressed in her plain gray gown. He was a fool to come here, he thought, for the seclusion of her chamber tested his self-control to the limit.

"You look tired." There was just a hint of shadows beneath his eyes.

He studied her in silence. He had tried to sort everything out in his mind the past few days, only to become more confused than ever. What did he want to do with his life? Why was this woman so important to him? His books and his work here at Armagh had been his whole existence, and yet at the thought of never seeing her again, all that he had done suddenly seemed unimportant. He had to make a decision soon about whether to stay or go and take her with him. Three days had passed. Only four remained.

"I am tired. I have been busy," he said wearily. But not too busy to think of her.

Sean had buried himself in his work, thinking that

perhaps in this way he could cast aside his feelings, but it hadn't worked. Always before, his sense of solitude had been brushed away by deep concentration on his work. Not this time.

There was an aura about her, a glow that made her very alluring and unforgettable even when she was out of sight. More importantly, she was not only beautiful, but she had a keen intelligence as well. An added blessing in a woman. Under different circumstances he knew she would have been the perfect woman for him.

He remembered how she had been so fascinated that words could be recorded for posterity. She had wanted to learn so very much. He had even thought of teaching her. Instead, he had given her quills and an old parchment to experiment with.

"Is there anything I can do to help you?" She would have taken the burden from his shoulders if she could.

"No." His shoulders and arms felt as stiff as stone. Hoping to alleviate some of the stiffness, he moved his shoulders in a circular motion.

"Here . . . let me . . ." When her father had been riding too long in the saddle she often massaged his neck and shoulders. Standing on tiptoe, she did that now to him.

Her hands held the touch of healing as she stroked away the pain. In these moments when they were so close, when he touched her or she bent close to talk with him, he had a difficult time controlling his emotions. It was no different now. Her firm, cool fingers unleashed a maelstrom of sensations.

He turned his head to look at her. The candle cast long shadows on her cheek, outlining her eyelashes, and he fought the urge to reach out and touch her. For a moment it was as if his soul cried out to be with her.

"Does that feel better?"

"Yes." It felt glorious. His senses came vibrantly

alive. He could feel the heat of desire coiling within his loins. "Where did you learn to work such magic?" What spell was she weaving now?

"Sometimes when my father had been in the saddle or had fought in battle I would move my fingers over his muscles to take away the soreness."

Their eyes met and held. A fierce surge of tenderness rose between them. At that moment he wanted nothing more than the solace of her arms, wanted her to hold him tightly against her heart until he blissfully forgot his troubles. What was it he saw when he looked into her eyes?

"Tasha . . ." He wanted to kiss her. Slowly he bent his head and moved closer, remembering how perfectly their bodies had fit together when they had embraced, how soft her lips were beneath his own.

He remembered himself just in time and stepped back. To do such a thing here was unthinkable and unforgivable. If anyone found out, she would be immediately banished from the premises. He had to use his head, not his emotions. He had to make a decision based on what was best for her as well as him.

"I shouldn't have come here. . . ." But the last few nights, she had intruded into his sleep, his dreams.

"Don't go. . . ." She took a step toward him.

She was standing much too close. So close that he could see the perfect texture of her skin, the curve of her mouth. He was becoming uncomfortably aware of the tension simmering in the room and his stirring desire for her. Turning his back, he walked to the door, pausing for just a moment as he looked over his shoulder. He wanted to stay, and that made it all the more important that he go.

"Good night."

"Good night. . . ." She wanted to show him her writing, wanted him to stay so that they could talk, but something about his attitude silenced her.

"Snuff the candles," he croaked. "The abbot doesn't allow anyone to be wasteful."

He welcomed the coolness of the hall as he stepped outside. Still, when he closed his eyes on returning to his chamber, he remembered the wounded look in her eyes and cursed himself for a fool.

"Who am I, Bron?"

"Who are you?" Bron's gentle brown eyes looked worried as Sean came up behind him. It seemed that, like Sean, he couldn't eat, though his needs were far different from Sean's. "You're . . . you're Sean!" Reaching into the apple barrel, he grabbed an overripe piece of fruit, picked out a worm, and took a bite. "You're a student here, a child of God, and . . . and my friend."

Sean's eyes swept over the kindly monk. He was short and stout of frame—one might have called him fat—with a round face and gap-toothed smile. Of all the monks at Armagh, he liked him the most, perhaps because his constant hunger made him so imperfect and therefore all the more human.

"Sean is the name the monks here gave me. But who am I really?" When Bron still looked puzzled he said, "I didn't just fall from the sky. I had a mother and a father. Who were they?" It was more important than ever to find out the truth.

"Cormac and Deidre." Bron took another bite of the apple.

"They were my foster parents, Bron, as well you know." Reaching into the pouch, Sean tugged at the pendant, swinging the amber wolf right in front of Bron's eyes. "What is this? Why was it around my neck?" Somehow, he had to find out. It was important!

Putting his hands upon his bulging waist, Bron looked at Sean in reproachful annoyance. "How am I to know? I'm only a few years older than you! I wasn't in on the conspiracy—" With a gasp he put his hand over his mouth, knowing that with just one word he had said too much.

"Conspiracy . . ." It was more of an admission than Sean had expected. "So there is more to it than I was told."

A shadow of distress clouded Bron's face. "I . . . I don't know. It's just that I remember hearing whispering about it all once, a long time ago."

"Whispering?"

His voice lowered as if he were afraid for others to hear. "I listened to Brother Fionan and Brother Doulagh talking; that is all. . . ." The monk drew a breath in the silence that followed, thinking very carefully what to say next. "It . . . it might not mean anything. Anything at all."

"What did they say?" No amount of practiced patience could quell Sean's rising tide of anger. Somehow, he knew now that he had been lied to, but about what and why, he didn't know. "Tell me what you heard, Bron."

Bron's eyes were drawn to the pendant, and he stared at it with unwavering fascination. "Brother Fionan . . . he—he said that the pendant that you have . . . is—is . . . Viking-made."

Seventeen

The moment Sean's eyes closed in sleep, the nightmare exploded in a red haze. He saw a red ocean, and in that crimson water floated a ship with the leering, scowling, snarling head of a dragon.

Spilling from the ship, wading waist-deep in the water, "they" came in a seemingly never-ending wave of ferocity. Vikings. Sea wolves. Helmeted devils moving forward, axes and swords raised high. Swarming like stinging bees, they seemed to multiply as they touched the shore. One became two; two became four; four became eight, moving steadily, weapons slashing, ripping, tearing . . .

Through it all he could see the face of a woman. A beautiful face. Smiling. Laughing. Dressed all in white, her long blond hair flying about her shoulders, she looked so lovely and unaware of the terrifying tide that was rolling in from the sea. He tried to reach out to her only to be swept away by the tide of men as if by an unseen hand.

"No!" He wanted to scream, but no sound came out. Then he was running. Fleeing from his pursuers down a long, dark tunnel. Suddenly, he couldn't move. His hands were wet. Warm. Blessed God! He reached out to the wall for support, but it wasn't there. The floor was moving downward. Then he was falling. . . . He moved in wild, spasmodic gyrations. It was as if he were going to tumble down, down, down for eternity.

He looked up, envisioning the silhouette of a tall Viking whose hair was blowing in the wind. Who was he? He wanted to see his face, but it was hidden in the shadows—that is, until a huge hand with long fingers grabbed the Viking by the hair, forcing him out of the darkness. Slowly, as the Viking turned around, his face materialized as if through a mist of light, the identity at last revealed.

"No!" It was *his own* face! No, it couldn't be. He wasn't . . .

Sean awoke in a drenching sweat, his heart beating wildly. His body was sore. It was as if he could feel every bump, every rut in the mattress. For a long time he lay on his back, staring up at the ceiling. Shivering. He remembered only bits and pieces of his violent dream, his nightmare. The blood. The panic. The girl. Natasha? What did it mean? Anything? Or was it just that—a nightmare?

His eyes burned, but he couldn't quite close them. Was he perchance afraid his nightmare would return? Was that why he now fought sleep?

Viking. The word reverberated over and over again in his mind.

Looking toward the door, he swallowed again and again until his mouth was dry. Silently he cursed. Nothing in particular and everything in general. He wanted to know the answer to a great many questions but didn't know exactly where to begin. His mind began to spin in whirling colors. A kaleidoscope. But he couldn't make any sense of it.

Had he mumbled in his sleep? Looking over to where Brian, the student who shared the beehive hut, lay snoring, he was relieved that at least he hadn't awakened him. Although he had never longed for privacy before, he longed for it now.

Bolting out of bed, he felt the urge to breathe the cool night air, for he felt as if he were suffocating in the small, cramped beehive hut. Hurriedly he dressed;

then, with a furtive look over his shoulder, he pushed open the door and blended with the darkness.

The candle had burned down to the nub. Flickering and sputtering, at last it died, leaving the room in total darkness. Though she would have continued if there had been enough moonlight by which to work, Natasha knew that she was finished for the night. Tomorrow she would take up where she had left off and continue with her scrawling.

Moving to the bed, she started to undress, but first, out of habit, looked out the window of her small room toward the beehive huts where she knew Sean would be asleep. The last three days it had become a nightly ritual to silently say good night to him before she went to bed and to make certain that he was safe from the vengeful spirit who plagued the world with nightmares.

Sleep and dreams were the playground for *Kikimora* to play her demonic games, but Natasha was prepared to ward her off. Every evening she had stuffed the keyhole to her room and Sean's hut with wax and made certain that her shoes and his were pointed away from the door. One could never be too careful, particularly when surrounded by strangers.

Hastily she stepped back from the window, ducking back into her room as she saw a tall, hooded figure hovering in Sean's doorway. The shadow was acting strangely, and for a moment she feared he was guilty of some misdeed, but as he turned his head the faint moonlight revealed the figure to be Sean. For a long, lingering moment, Natasha watched as he moved toward the stables; then, giving in to the urging of her heart, she followed.

It was quiet; only the nickering and pawing hooves of the horses disturbed the stillness. Sean's ears did not perceive any human sounds. Still, he dared not light even a candle lest he attract unwelcome attention and have to answer a multitude of questions. He didn't want that. All he wanted was a late-night ride and the precious chance to be all alone.

Sean chose the nearest horse he came to. Working in total darkness, he lifted a bridle from its peg on the wall, quickly untangling the reins. Calming the horse with soft words, he slipped the headstall over the ears, then pressed the bit against the animal's mouth. Fumbling about for a saddle and at last locating its bulk, he swung it upon the horse's back. Bending down, he fastened and tightened the saddle girth. Suddenly, he heard the soft sound of footsteps behind him. So much for privacy. Squinting, trying to attune his eyes to the darkness, he recognized her in an instant.

"Natasha!"

They stared at each other for a long while, two quiet shadows in the dusky darkness. A knot squeezed in the pit of her stomach as she asked, "Are you all right? You seem troubled."

"I am!" Though at first he had thought that he wanted to be alone, he knew now that he welcomed *her* presence.

"What's wrong? Tell me."

Though others' chatter could often stretch his taut nerves even tighter, Natasha's voice always soothed him. He was content just being near her. It was as if a delicate thread bound them together.

"Tonight I had a troubling dream."

"A dream?"

Closing his eyes, he remembered bits and pieces. He covered his eyes with his hands as he once again seemed to see the red ocean. An ocean of blood.

"A nightmare."

Natasha pushed inside the door, kicking it shut behind her. For a long moment she merely looked at him; then, moving toward him she stood up on tiptoe, put her arms around his neck, and gathered him into her arms. "Don't worry," she whispered. "I'll protect you."

"You'll protect *me?*" His lips curved up in a smile at the thought of a woman protecting a man, yet strangely at that moment he felt as though he were safe, even from the doubts and worries that now plagued him. "I told you that I don't know who my parents are, that I was found by the monks; but now I think I know. I think I know, Natasha, and it is tearing me apart!" He remembered seeing his own face revealed in his dream, and he shuddered.

"It's all right. . . ." She held him closer, tighter, until his trembling ceased.

"I've been blind and stupid. Perhaps I didn't want to see, but Bron told me that the pendant . . ." The amber wolf was Viking-made, and it had been hanging around his neck the night the monks had found him. Why hadn't he guessed? Or better yet, why hadn't he been told? Why had the monks kept the secret all these years. "I'm one of *them,* Natasha! I know it now. I'm . . . I'm a Viking!"

He waited for her to stiffen, to feel the same revulsion that he had felt upon realizing the truth. But she didn't; instead, she reached out and touched his face, and when she looked at him he saw an aching tenderness.

He reached out and took her by the shoulders. "Didn't you hear what I said? I'm a Viking. A Norseman. I'm one of—"

She silenced his words with a kiss, joining her mouth to his in the way that she remembered he had done. Pressing her body closer to his, she sought the passion of his embrace. She craved his kisses with a warm, sweet desire that fused their bodies together.

"Tasha!" He spoke her name in a breathless whisper as he drew his mouth away. He had tried to stay away from her. He had tried. But he was only flesh and blood. He wanted her now with a fever that stirred his blood beyond all reason, yet that fire was tempered with a gentleness. He felt a warmth in his heart as well as his loins. "I don't want to hurt you. . . ." But he had never wanted anything as much as he wanted her.

The fingers of one hand tangled in his hair as she kissed him with a fierce, sweet fire, silencing him again. Sean gave in without protest. Her hands slid up to lock around his neck, drawing him so close that they seemed to melt into one another. She could feel the heat and strength and growing desire in him, and it warmed her. The feel of him, so hard, so strong, was all she wanted in the world.

The heat of her body warmed him, aroused him, turning his thoughts into chaos. "Oh, Tasha!" he groaned, his mouth roaming freely, stopping briefly at the hollow of her throat, lingering there, then moving slowly downward to the skin of her bare shoulder. Sean held her against him, his hands spanning her narrow waist. Murmuring her name again, he buried his face in the silky strands of her hair, inhaling the delicate fragrance of flowers in the luxurious softness. His fingers parted the fragile fabric of her gown to cup her breast. His fingers brought forth a tingling pleasure.

Sensations tingled inside her, making her body a dizzying maelstrom of need. It seemed his hands were everywhere, touching her, setting her body afire with a pulsating flame of desire. Natasha writhed beneath him, giving herself up to the glorious sensations he was igniting within her.

Taking off his hooded cloak, draping it over a soft pile of straw, Sean hurriedly made a makeshift bed; then, taking her hand, tugged her down to lie beside him. There on the soft bed of hay, he held her cradled in his arms. He would hold her for only a few moments longer, then he would let her go. . . .

Natasha slipped the gown from her shoulders and

let it slide slowly to the ground. He looked at her for a long while, his face flushed with passion, his breath a deep-throated rasp.

"You are so lovely!" he murmured, his hands moving along her back and sending forth shivers of pleasure, his in the touching and hers in being touched. Her waist was small, her breasts perfection, her legs long and shapely. As they lay bathed in the soft glow of moonlight, he let his eyes roam over her body.

"Am I?" Natasha made no effort to hide her curves from his piercing gaze. This was her fate, her destiny: to belong to this man, just as it had been her mother's to belong to her father. She felt that in every bone, every muscle, every sinew of her body. As he touched her she gloried in the thought that her body pleased him, her pulse quickening at the passion that burned in his eyes.

"Natasha . . ." He spoke her name softly, caressingly. Their kisses were tender at first, but the burning spark of their desire burst their love into flames. Desire flooded his mind, obliterating all reason.

Wrapped in each other's arms, they kissed again, his mouth moving upon hers, pressing her lips apart, hers responding, exploring gently the sweet firmness of his. Shifting her weight, she rolled closer into his embrace. There was nothing else as important as being here with him.

Oh, blessed Christ, Sean thought. How could he have ever realized the full effect her nearness would kindle? She fit against him so perfectly, her gentle curves melting against his own hard body. It was as though Natasha had been made for him. Perhaps she had been. Certainly, at this moment it seemed so.

"This is not the place . . ." he whispered against her mouth. He tried to pull away, but she held him tightly to her as she kissed the corners of his lips, tracing the outline with her tongue.

The night was warm for autumn; with a sigh he

relaxed. His hands moved on her body, stroking her lightly: her throat, her breasts, her belly, her thighs. With reverence he positioned his hands to touch her breasts. Gently. Slowly. Until they swelled in his hands. He outlined the rosy-peaked mound with his finger, watching as the velvet flesh hardened. Her responding moan excited him, but he wanted to be gentle. Nevertheless, it took all his self-control to keep his passion in check.

Sean lingered over her, exploring her with hands and mouth, discovering the sweetness of her body. His exploration was like a hundred feathers, everywhere upon her skin arousing a deep, aching longing. Natasha closed her eyes to the rapture.

Wanting to bring him the same sensations that she was feeling, Natasha touched him, one hand sliding down over the muscles of his chest, sensuously stroking the warmth of his flesh in exploration. She heard the audible intake of his breath, and that gave her the courage to continue in her quest.

"Natasha . . ." He held her face in his hands, kissing her eyelids, the curve of her cheekbones, her mouth. "Natasha. Natasha." He repeated her name over and over again, as if to taste it on his lips.

Her fingertips roamed over his shoulders and neck and plunged into his thick hair as he kissed her once again in a fierce joining of mouths that spoke of his passion. Then, after a long, pleasureable moment, he drew away, taking off his leine and tossing it to the side. All the beauty of his masculinity towered over her.

Reaching out, she drew him down beside her. "I like the feel of your skin against me," she breathed. Her hands caressed his chest, her large blue eyes beckoning him, enticing him to enter the world of love that she sensed was awaiting them both.

Natasha was shattered by the all-consuming pleasure of lying naked beside him. Like a willing sacrifice, she entwined her arms around his muscled neck, her body writhing in a slow, delicate dance. A heat arose within her as she arched against him in sensual pleasure. Her breath became heavier, and a hunger for him that was like a pleasant pain went from her breasts down to her loins. The pulsing, tingling sensation increased as his hand ran down the smoothness of her belly to feel the softness nestled between her thighs.

Natasha gave way to wild abandon, moaning softly, joyously as her fingers likewise moved over his body. She felt a strange sensation flood over her and could not deny that, before he left, she wanted their spirits to be joined together. She wanted his erect manhood to fill her with excitement and pleasure. His strong arms were around her, his mouth covering her own. She shivered at the feelings that swept over her.

The moonlight gently illuminated their bodies, hers as smooth as cream, his muscular form of a darker hue. He knelt down beside her and kissed her breasts, running his tongue over their tips until she shuddered with delight. Whispering words of love, he slid his hands between her thighs to explore the soft inner flesh. At his touch, she felt a slow quivering deep inside that became a fierce fire as he moved his fingers against her.

Supporting himself on his forearms, he moved between her legs. Slowly his pelvis caressed her thigh, letting her get accustomed to the hardness of his maleness.

"Love me, Sean," she breathed. Arching up, she was eager to drink fully of that which she had only briefly experienced.

His mouth closed over hers with hard, fierce possession, mingling his breath with hers, probing her mouth with his tongue as he entered her softness with a slow but strong thrust. He pulled her more fully beneath him as he buried his length within the sheath of her softness, allowing her to adjust to his sudden invasion. She was so warm, so tight around him, that he closed his eyes with agonized pleasure.

"My God!" he muttered hoarsely. Closing his eyes, he wondered how he could ever have thought that anything was as important as this. At the moment, the only thing he wanted was to bring her pleasure, to give her his devotion.

As they came together, spasms of feeling wove through Natasha like the threads of her embroidery. She had never realized how incomplete she had felt until this moment. Now, joined with him, she was a whole being. Feverishly she clung to him, her breasts pressed against his chest. Their hearts beat in matching rhythm even as their mouths met, their tongues entwined, and their bodies embraced in the slow, sensuous dance of love. She was consumed by his warmth, his hardness, and tightened her thighs around his waist as she arched up to him, moving in time to his rhythm. He was slow and gentle, taking incredible care of her.

"Sean . . . !" She clutched at him. It was as if he had touched the very core of her being. There was an explosion of rapture as their bodies blended into one. It was an ecstasy too beautiful for words. *Love* . . . Such a simple word, and yet in truth it meant so much. She had never realized before how incomplete she had been without him until this moment. With her hands, her mouth, the movement of her body, she tried to tell him so, declaring her love with every motion.

Sean groaned, giving himself up to the exquisite sensation of her flesh sheathing the entire length of him. Again and again he made her his own, wanting to blend his flesh with hers, to bring her the ultimate pleasure of love, succeeding beyond his wildest expectations. With Natasha he knew the shattering satisfaction of being whole, of being totally one with a woman.

Languidly they came back to reality, lying together in the afterglow of passion, their hearts gradually resuming a normal rate of rhythm. Time drifted past, yet they were reluctant to move and break the spell. Sean gazed down upon her face, gently brushing back the tangled pale-gold hair from her eyes.

"We have to go back. We can't stay together like this." It was an awkward, troubling truth. Though he didn't feel a shred of guilt for what had passed between them, he knew that others would not be of like mind.

"I know."

"But we will be together again, Natasha. And this time it will be forever." There was no turning back now. He had made his decision to leave Armagh and take Natasha with him.

Eighteen

Shadows veiled the moon as Sean escorted Natasha back to her room in the guest quarters. All the buildings were dark, without even one candle to illuminate the windows. For the moment, at least, it seemed as if they were the only two people in the world.

"The next time we make love, it will be in a much better place than a stable, Tasha," he vowed, looking back over his shoulder. His hands lingered on the soft curves of her body. It seemed perfectly natural to drape his arm possessively across her shoulders as they walked. From this moment, she was his!

Natasha paused to look up at the sky, letting her breath out in a long, deep sigh. "I never knew that it was possible to feel like this."

"Nor I." As the moon came from behind the clouds, he gazed intently at her, wanting to engrave every detail of her beauty upon his memory: the arch of her brows, the upward tilt of her mouth, the way the moonlight danced upon her light-blond hair.

Just looking at her brought forth a renewed desire, but they couldn't take the chance of being seen and of Natasha's being targeted for serious rebuke. As for his own punishment, he didn't care. The abbot and the monks had kept the truth from him all these years, which in his eyes was the same as a lie. He had worked for them in the scriptorium all these years to pay them back for having taken him in. He owed them nothing more.

He pulled her to him. "Tasha, I've waited for you all my life." His lips went along her forehead, brushing gently along the heavy brush of thick lashes, teasing the line of her jaw, then caressing her neck. "I don't want to let you go!"

"And I would have you love me again, now that I know what to expect!" Natasha arched against him in sensual pleasure, her hands sliding over the muscles of his arms down to the taut flesh of his stomach.

"You tempt me." His strong fingers stroked and fondled her breast as he struggled with his longing. For an endless moment he held her against him; then, as if fearing to test his resolve, he let her go. "Come. It grows late, and as much as I regret it we must return."

They walked the rest of the way in silence, the looks that passed between them saying far more than words could ever tell. Sean knew that from this moment on Natasha would be branded in his heart, his soul.

They held hands as they opened the thick wooden door and tiptoed in. Sean was determined to protect Natasha's reputation at all costs; therefore, he looked cautiously about the room before he was satisfied that they could enter.

"Deserted. Everyone is still abed."

Natasha paused to listen before following Sean in. As she moved she tried to tread lightly, but each step seemed to explode in the silence.

Sean led her to the stairs. "Sleep well."

Their fingers moved over each other's faces. "Sean . . ." She lifted her arms to encircle his neck. "I will always belong to you now." She clung to him, her breasts pressed against his chest, wishing they didn't have to say good night.

Sean buried his face in the golden cloud of her hair, inhaling the spicy scent she always used. "Tonight as I lie in my bed, I will be thinking of you and how you should be beside me—and will be soon. . . ." Just as soon as he could talk to the abbot and gather up his possessions. And then what? Where was he going from here? At the moment, he didn't want to think about it.

Her body arched against his as he caressed her. His fingers seemed to be everywhere, touching her, setting her body ablaze with desire. But Sean was a man true to his word. "We'll be together soon. . . . I promise."

Sean stood there for several minutes after she had gone; then, with a shrug of his shoulders, he turned away. "Strange how desolate I feel being alone now," he whispered to himself. But he was not alone, nor had their entrance been unobserved.

"So, I see that you have spent a sleepless night, too, Sean," a voice said softly. Waiting in the shadows was the abbot. His silhouette was outlined against the stone wall. "Though for different reasons."

Flushing, Sean tried to control the emotions raging through him, but he was certain that the abbot could read everything that had happened in the glow that suffused his face. If not, then Sean's disheveled hair and torn, dirt-stained garments must surely give him away.

"I saw you with the girl." He breathed in, then out, then in again. When he exhaled, it sounded like growl. "And now you are lovers." It was a statement, not a question.

Sean avoided the abbot's stare as he tried to rearrange his clothes. He wasn't ready to say anything just yet. He had to think, had to be cautious. He didn't want any harm to come to Natasha.

"What wickedness has bedeviled you?" When Sean did not answer, he rasped, "Speak, but remember that the mouth that lies murders the soul!"

"I wouldn't lie."

"Then answer me. Were you *with* her?"

Sean was defiant. "Yes."

The abbot took a couple of steps toward him, then stopped, shaking with incredulity and suppressed rage. "I feared in my heart that it was only a matter of time before you sinned with her."

"To love is not a sin."

"Lust! There is a difference." He nearly choked on his words. "Have you given thought to the turmoil you have unleashed?"

"What turmoil?"

"You have made Armagh a target for vicious slander, Sean. I did not speak with you about it, because I was convinced that I must deal with it in another way, and I was certain that after the girl was gone you would soon forget her. But now I see that I must address the transgression without a moment's hesitation."

"Transgression?" He would hardly have called it that. The moments he had spent with Natasha were the most meaningful of his life. "I'm not a saint. I found out tonight that I am very human."

The abbot's tone was scathing. "Human! Human, you say. Of course I know that, but I never thought you would so lose your head." The abbot lowered his voice, talking to Sean as if addressing a child. "Many of the monks have suspected that you have been fornicating with this pagan girl beneath our very roof."

Fornicating. Such an ugly word for it, Sean thought. "I love Natasha," he said emphatically. "We have done nothing wrong."

"Then I misunderstood you, and you have not touched her in sin." An audible sigh of relief escaped the abbot's throat.

He would not cheapen his love for Natasha with a lie, nor put his soul in jeopardy. "I have consummated my love for her. . . ."

"Then you *have* done wrong." Putting his hands behind his back, the abbot paced up and down, then stopped a foot away from Sean. "She has seduced you. You are not at fault; thus, all can be easily forgiven."

Meeting the abbot's gaze unflinchingly, Sean came to her defense quickly. "Natasha did not seduce me! What happened between us was mutual." His voice was choked with emotion. "I'm not a monk. Why should I deny myself the sweetness she brings me?"

The abbot looked stunned. "It's true you have not taken holy vows, and yet you disappoint me, Sean. I had thought you understood my plan for you."

Folding his long arms across his chest, Sean asked, "And just what is that?"

Putting his hand up, the abbot tugged at his earlobe as he said, "I hoped that one day you would take my place as abbot of Armagh."

"Why me?"

Abbot Righifarch cleared his throat and seemed to be ill at ease. "As I told you once before, you are strong, intelligent, and charismatic, but continuing with this woman will be the ruination of all that you and I have worked for."

"I'm not your puppet!" Sean drew a breath in the silence, thinking very carefully what to say next. He was tired of being on the defensive. It was time for some answers. "Who were my parents, Righifarch? I think that you know. I think that is why you sent me to meet with the Viking Thordis."

The abbot thought carefully. "I sent you on the mission in hopes that seeing evil would inspire you to make the commitment to us that I know has hovered in your heart and mind."

"That is not the reason. Tell me the truth. Tell all that you know about me." Now it was Sean who was angry. "The mouth that lies . . ."

The abbot started to say once again that he didn't know, but thought better of it. "If I told you the truth, it would be your downfall."

"Because I'm at least part Viking?" If Sean had not

been certain of the truth before, he was certain of it now. The expression in the abbot's eyes told the story.

"Who told you? Who betrayed—?"

"It doesn't matter."

"We . . . all of us . . . wanted to protect you."

"From the truth."

The abbot nodded. "From the truth."

Some inner surge of defiance prompted him to pull the wolf pendant out of his pouch and put it around his neck.

"What are you doing?" The abbot crossed himself.

"Someone put this amulet around my neck. Who?" When Righifarch didn't answer, he asked again, Who?"

"Your father gave it to your mother to put around your neck when you were born, so that someday, when the time came, he would be able to find you."

"How do you know this?"

The abbot put his hands up to his face, mumbling, "Your mother was my sister."

The admission seemed to make everything fall into place in Sean's mind. He had not been just some foundling; he was the abbot's illegitimate nephew. "And my father? Who was he?"

"Ragnar Longsword."

Closing his eyes, Sean envisioned the scenario. No doubt his mother had been vilified, raped, and then forsaken by one of the Viking raiders. It was a tragedy that had been repeated over and over in Eire. And bastard children like him were the result.

"What happened to my mother?" Why had she abandoned him?

"With the sisters at Bangor." As if to make atonement for her, the abbot whispered, "She was told that you had died. It was better that way, for then she could go on with her life.

"At Bangor!" What an irony that was. He might very well have passed right by her and never even known. It took all the self-control that he could muster not to give in to his emotions, and he said only, "I'm leaving Armagh in the morning."

"No, Sean. . . . Wait . . . you can't—"

"To the contrary, Abbot Righifarch, I can!"

Without a backward glance, he walked swiftly to his quarters in the small beehive hut. Slowly he moved about the room, gathering up his possessions, taking only what he needed.

Natasha sat on the edge of her bed, reliving over and over in her mind each touch, each embrace, and the way Sean had whispered her name. Though her knowledge of lovemaking was limited to him, she knew instinctively that he had taken her with the greatest tenderness. *Love.* It was an all-powerful emotion, made all the stronger when it was shared.

Yes, she loved him. There could never be any doubt of that. Even now she could feel the whole world whirling and spinning around her when she imagined his hands upon her.

"Tonight as I lie in my bed I will be thinking of you and how you should be beside me and will be soon. . . ." he had said.

How soon?

Although she told herself to be patient, she knew it was impossible. That is why she so quickly bounded to her feet as she heard a soft knocking at the door, certain that it was him.

"Who . . . ?" Five gray-hooded men stood at the door, waiting in the shadows. Taking her by the arm the tallest of the monks let it be known that she was to come with them.

Nineteen

After so many years, it was impossible for Sean to leave without telling the monks good-bye. Though he was angry at the abbot, that anger did not extend to Bron and some of the others. Hastily he said his good-bye, seeking Bron out at the last.

"You're certain that this is what you want to do?" Bron asked, not even bothering to hide the moisture that sprang to his eyes at the thought that he might never see Sean again.

"It's what I have to do. I was never a part of Armagh in the way that you and the others are. Not really. Perhaps I always knew in the back of my mind that I was destined for other things."

"You are taking the . . . the woman with you?" Bron's words revealed that he had heard the whisperings.

"Yes." For a moment he wanted to tell Bron how he felt about Natasha, but he kept his silence.

"But where are you going to go?" Bron had never lived outside the monastery's walls. "What are you going to do?"

Sean had thought about it carefully. "I thought I would seek out Maelsechnaill, prince of the Ui Neill. He has need of me and the knowledge that I have to aid him in his bid to become the Irish high king."

"And if you cannot abide his presence and his arrogance?"

"I'll travel to the court of Charlemagne. I have heard that he has need of scholars to teach at the palace schools."

Bron thought a moment; then, as he looked up he smiled. "I wish you every happiness, Sean. If ever you have need of a friend, remember me." He watched as Sean hefted his satchel over his shoulder and headed toward the guest quarters, then whispered, "Go with God, my friend."

Sean stumbled once or twice in his haste as he took the steps two at a time. It was decided. He had told the abbot that he intended to leave this very morning, to take Natasha with him. Now he was going to make his words come true.

He'd credited the abbot with more understanding and compassion than he had displayed. Righifarch had not even tried to understand what it was like to be in love. Well, a practicing eunuch the abbot might be, but he would not make one out of *him.*

"Natasha . . ." Pushing open the door, Sean was surprised to find the chamber in darkness. Usually at least one candle was lit, but perhaps she was abed. "Natasha?" He moved toward the bed. "Natasha!"

An eerie feeling crept up his spine as he hastened to strike the flint and light one of the candles. The room was too silent. Somehow, even before the flickering flame illuminated the room, he knew she would not be within.

"No!" All sorts of thoughts ran through his head. Fear coursed through him. She was gone. At a glance he could see that she had taken all of her possessions. It gave testimony to the permanency of her absence. Natasha was not coming back.

Like a man demented, Sean flew out into the hall. Uncaring of the scene he created, he shouted out her name, hopeful that she would answer. When she didn't, he searched the anteroom, the garden, the kitchens, the scriptorium, and every nook and cranny he could think of, questioning everyone he met whether they had seen Natasha leave. He even searched the monks' cells, but no one had seen her leave and no one had any idea where she might have gone. That caused Sean to panic. Natasha had *not* left on her own. After the night they had spent together, she would have waited for him, trusted him.

In frustration and helpless anger, he strode up and down, wearing a path with his steps, cursing the abbot beneath his breath, working himself into a frenzy as he headed toward the abbot's quarters.

"She's gone!" Sean's voice was filled with agony.

The abbot did not hide his relief at a problem solved. "Yes, she is. You were ready to throw your life away, give all up for love; thus, I did what needed to be done."

"What?! What did you do?" An idea was forming in Sean's mind, but it was too terrible even to imagine.

"I have sent her back." He moved toward the door, blocking Sean's exit.

"Back . . ." Sean's eyes narrowed.

"Brian, Culdee, Fionan, and two others are escorting her to the Viking settlement, as a sign of good faith."

Sean ran his fingers through his hair until the dark strands stood on end, truly making him look like a wild man. "You didn't send her back to him, to Thordis . . . ?"

The abbot was as expressionless as a statue. "She was an escaped slave, Sean. Her presence here might have goaded Thordis to attack us. I could not take that chance. I will not risk the lives of my monks for the sake of a slave."

"And you call yourself a man of God." Grasping the abbot by the arm, Sean pushed him roughly away from the door, unmindful of all else except finding Natasha. "I will find her. In this you will not have won so easily."

"Leave it be, Sean. You know it was the only way. Thordis is not a man to anger."

"Nor am I!" Sean was tormented by the time he had wasted in the early morning hours. He should have run away with Natasha the moment he realized the abbot's feelings about her. Instead, he had foolishly waited too long and been blindsided. "I won't let you do this! I won't rest until she is once again by my side."

"Search for her, then." The abbot's manner was curt, though he smiled. "You will be back." There was a tone of finality in his voice, an assurance that he was right. "Your future is with me, Sean. You will soon come to your senses." He closed his eyes, as if in prayer that he could avoid the explosive quality of the silence that followed. Then, before Sean could give vent to his vexation, he simply turned and walked away. With an oath, slamming the door behind him, Sean hurried to the stables. There were only so many routes to Larne. If he rode like the wind and attuned his ears and eyes to the roadway, he could find her before the monks delivered her into the clutches of Thordis.

The hills and glens seemed to stretch for leagues and leagues. Natasha was lost, with no hope of finding her way back. Worse yet, she was with strangers with whom she could not communicate. Where were they taking her? And why? She was confused and slowly starting to fear that these men were up to no good.

"How could I have been so foolish?"

When the hooded men had beckoned her to follow after them, she had trusted them, knowing well that they were friends of Sean's. She had no reason to think they meant her any ill. Foolishly she had assumed that perhaps they had come to escort her to some sort of ceremony, or that they were taking her to meet Sean. When they had walked and walked without any sign of him, however, she had grown suspicious. Something was not as it should be.

"Please . . . take me back," she said frantically, trying, in some way, to make the tall monk understand what she was saying. She pointed in the direction they had come, but he only shook his head. The five men surrounded her, prodding her in the back to signal her to continue walking.

She shivered, suddenly feeling cold. That was how life without Sean would be. Dark. Devoid of light. Empty. Cold. It just couldn't be. These men had no reason to dislike her. She didn't understand their ways; that was all. She was jumping to conclusions.

"Oh, Sean!" She paused, turning her head to look for him, hoping to see that he had come after her. But the path was empty.

An overwhelming sense of dread swept over her. No, it couldn't be. Sean wasn't sending her back to the gray place where nobody smiled. He wouldn't betray her that way.

Her head ached; her throat was dry. Her heart was pounding so loudly it shook her chest. How could she ever hope to ease this terrible emptiness that even now was coursing through her heart, her soul, at the very thought of him betraying her?

He wouldn't do that. He loves me. He told me so many times. . . .

She had to trust him. He had told her that they would be together. She had to hang on to that hope; that Sean was waiting for her at the end of this strange journey.

The fresh morning air was invigorating. It lightened her mood as she walked down a steep hill beside the gray-robed men. She could smell water on the breeze and knew that they were headed toward a body of water, most likely a river.

Suddenly, she knew the horrible truth. It was upon

her the moment her eyes touched upon the sails of the Viking ship. "No . . . !" With agonizing clarity, she realized the worst was still to come. In that moment she was suddenly conscious of the greatest sorrow she had ever known.

Twenty

It was alarming how easily one's life could be shattered. Or how quickly one could go from the pinnacle of happiness to the depths of despair. As Sean held the struggling monk with both hands, demanding answers, he learned only too well.

"Where is she?"

The voice was muffled. "Don't harm me. I beg of you. I only did what I was told."

Recognizing Fionan, one of the older monks, he let go of his cloak. "Where is Natasha? What have you done with her?"

With undisguised irritation, the monk brushed at his now-wrinkled brat; then he pointed toward the horizon. In that moment, as he saw the ship, Sean realized that he was too late.

For a long moment, all he could do was to stand thunderstruck as he mentally digested what had occurred; then, losing all control, he gasped, "No-o-o-o-o-o-o-o-o!" Although he had ridden nonstop, he had taken a different path from that the monks had taken, and thus had arrived too late. "I assumed that you were on your way to Larne. . . ." He swallowed, not wanting to give in to the emotions that were welling up inside him.

"We didn't have to go all that way," Culdee said gently, sensing Sean's emotional pain. "The Viking leader intercepted us, for he was eager to regain possession of . . . of *her.*"

"Intercepted . . . but he wouldn't have had time . . . unless . . . !" It took only a moment for Sean to realize the truth. The abbot had to have sent a messenger to Thordis the very day he first arrived with Natasha. No wonder he had agreed to let her stay at Armagh for a few days. "I've been betrayed!" More importantly, so had she.

"What Abbot Righifarch did, he did for the good of us all. You will see, Sean. In time you will understand." Fionan patted him on the shoulder.

With an oath, Sean pulled away. "I will never understand how a man who professed to follow the teachings of Christ and Saint Patrick could be instrumental in bringing another human being the pain that will be that innocent young woman's fate." Remembering Thordis's cruelty, he shuddered. "You have condemned her either to death or to a life so miserable that she will beg for death a thousand times."

"No, Sean. The abbot made the Viking Thordis promise that she will not be harmed." Again, Fionan put a hand on his shoulder. "That was part of the arrangement.

"Arrangement."

As if to try to salvage a bit of Sean's goodwill, Culdee spoke up. "She is on a ship bound for the land of the Russ. Thordis is only too anxious to sell—" An elbow to his ribs silenced the short monk's words.

Sean's eyes touched on each monk with scorn. At the moment they reminded him of coconspirators, not holy men. "How could I have been so blind for so many years? How could I have even imagined for a moment that I could be happy living among you with your warped sense of importance? You don't know the true meaning of what brotherly love really is, nor do you know anything at all about life."

Though the others hung their heads, Brian stepped forward. "How dare you speak—"

"To all of you like this?"

Once, he would have feared the abbot's retribution, be that a whipping, going without food, or banishment to a darkened room to repent his sins. Now, however, he was fearless about such petty punishments.

"I do dare, Brian. Were you not wearing robes to hide behind, I would do much more than that!" He raised his fist, then quickly lowered it. A show of temper and violence would not help Natasha now. He had to hold his emotions in check and think of what to do.

"For such transgression you will be blessed if you are not packed off into exile," Brian threatened. He was taken aback as Sean laughed.

"Exile? You can really believe that I would fear never seeing any of you again after what you have done this day?" To prove to them how little he cared, he turned his back—on them and on the life that he had known. "It cannot be too late. I won't let it be."

Touching the amber wolf around his neck, Sean was reminded of his Viking heritage, and in that instant he thought of a way he could rescue Natasha.

Sean rode nonstop to Bangor, only pausing to rest his horse. At last, when he felt certain he was so tired that he would fall from the saddle, he saw it looming on the horizon. Somehow, though he was totally exhausted, he found the strength to reach the monastery.

As a child, Sean had been given to periods of sleepwalking. Now, as he made his way past the stables and through the garden and courtyard to the nun's quarters to seek out Bridget, he felt as if he were sleepwalking again.

"You came to see me?" Though she tried not to make it obvious, the nun's eyes touched on Sean's pendant again with what he knew to be recognition.

"I came to see my mother. Either you are she, or you know who she is."

She paled. "I thought it must be you! But it was too much to hope for. We were told that you . . . you . . ."

"Had died. I know. Abbot Righifarch revealed some of the story to me." He would never call him his uncle. Never! "Are you . . . ?" He looked searchingly at Bridget, trying to find something of himself in her face. He saw nothing familiar.

"Me?" She shook her head. "No, but she is here. Once her name was Tara. Now she is Sister Erin. Come . . ."

He followed her down the long passageway, only now realizing how nervous he was. His mother! For so many years he had longed to know something about her, longed to feel her arms around him, kissing away his childish tears. Now the moment had come.

Sean's fingers trembled as he opened the door to the library. At first the figure was only a shadow; then, as she turned around and stepped toward him, he could see her face.

"Mother . . . ?"

Though he had envisioned in his mind what must have happened to her and how it had destroyed her life, she showed no trace of remorse in her expression. Instead, she had a look of total peace upon her face, and the smile upon her full lips told him that here in the abbey she had found the calm and tranquility to help her forget any heartache.

"That which was lost will be found again," she whispered, moving toward him.

Despite all the years that had passed, Sean could see that his mother was a beautiful woman. She was of medium height, though her willowy form gave her the appearance of being much taller. Her skin was flawless except for a sprinkling of freckles on her well-formed nose. Her cheekbones were high, but it was the eyes that gave proof of their kinship. Those eyes were misted with tears as she appraised him.

"You're strong, healthy, and handsome. The greatest gift I have ever been given." With a sob, she gathered him into her arms, holding him so tightly that he could hardly move.

"A gift?" He had feared that perhaps she would not have seen him as such, that she would have regrets and would not want to see him and be reminded of what had happened; but now he had no doubt that she welcomed him.

"The most blessed gift that God can bestow . . ." Pulling away for a moment, she ran her fingers over his face. "You look much like me, but there is something of your father in you, too."

"My father!" He spat out the words, despite the fact that in order to rescue Natasha he would need his father's help. "A thief, murderer, and rapist!"

"No!" She shook her head emphatically. "He was none of those. Your father was and is a great man!"

"A great man?" Of all the descriptions he had expected, this was the last he had thought to hear.

"Come, sit down." She led him to a wooden bench and pulled him down to sit beside her. "There are so many years to catch up on. Where shall we begin?"

"With you! Tell me what happened."

It wasn't the story that Sean expected, nor what the abbot had led him to assume. Instead, his mother told him that she had once loved Ragnar Longsword, a Viking jarl of great reknown; that he had wooed her, wedded her in a Viking ceremony, and given her his child, a son.

"We named you Kodran. Kodran Ragnarsson." She

reached out and touched the wolf pendant with familiarity, as if it brought back pleasant memories. "I had everything that I have ever wanted until . . ."

"Until your brother committed the loathsome act of lying to you and stealing your child for his own selfish ends." Sean's anger for the moment was focused on Abbot Righifarch. "Did he force you to come to Bangor, or was that your choice?"

Rising to her feet, she walked over to the small window, gazing out at the ground below. "When I was told that you had died of a fever, I wanted to die, too. I was filled with anger at God, blaming Him for taking you away. I was, I fear, out of my mind for a time, but my faith has healed me."

"Your own brother did this to you. Why?"

"I was going to go to the Northland with my . . . my *pagan* husband and newborn child. I think that in his way, my brother was trying to save my soul at the cost of my happiness."

"Just as he did with me!" Because someone believed differently, the abbot had taken it upon himself to play God, Sean thought bitterly. Not once, but twice.

"You were the bond that held me even closer to Ragnar. My brother realized that, and so . . ." She heaved a sigh.

"What of my father? Why did he desert you?" He had to know the whole story.

"He was told that I had died and that you had survived. Though Ragnar would have taken you with him, his request was denied. You were hidden away until he sailed off." She answered his question before he had a chance to ask it. "I didn't know any of this, Sean, but Bridget did. When she saw you here with the pendant, she at last revealed the truth to me.

"Bridget? Who told her?" Who was it he had to thank?

"Fionan." She paused to take a deep breath.

"Once, before they went their separate ways, they were lovers."

In spite of his mood, Sean smiled. "Surly, pious Fionan gave in to temptation?" All the time he was growing up, it had been Fionan who had been his strictest taskmaster, driving him unmercifully in his studies and in his discipline. "Why was Ragnar told that I was still alive? What did the abbot hope to gain?"

"I don't know. Perhaps he thought that, were the Vikings to gain prominence in Eire, he might have need of you."

Sean winced. "What a tangled web deceit can be." His thoughts turned to Natasha; he could only hope that she was not being treated unkindly.

Sister Erin took his hand in hers. "I can tell by your eyes that you have suffered. For that I am so sorry."

It was strange, but even though he hadn't been raised by her, nor had he seen her in over twenty-five years, Sean felt an instant bond with his mother. Wishing to unburden his heart, he told her all about his boyhood, about his hopes and dreams, and finally about Natasha and the joy he had felt in her arms.

"And now she is gone. For that I can never forgive my abbot uncle," he grumbled, doing little to hide his anger. "I have no way to travel so that I can bring her back. No way unless I call upon my father. But I know nothing about him, nor where I may be able to find him. Can you help me?"

There was no hesitation in her response. "I will and may God go with you."

PART TWO
The Search

Norway and Kiev

Twenty-one

Huge waves wrinkled the horizon as the Viking ship sailed north, its destination Hafrsfjord. Remembering the Norseman Wolfram Olafsson, whom he had met briefly at Larne, Sean had sought him out and convinced him to take him to the Northland aboard his merchant ship. Now Sean was on his way to his father, a man he had never even seen. He could only hope that Ragnar Longsword would give him what he needed: a ship and a crew. At the moment that was the only thing that drove him.

Positioned at the helm, Sean watched as Wolfram piloted the ship from the steerboard. He studied his every move as diligently as he had studied his books. He was determined to learn all there was to know about ships, for he intended to be at the helm when he sailed to the land of the Russ in pursuit of Natasha.

From his vantage point he appraised the ship in great detail, his eyes moving along the full length of the vessel, marveling at the skill of craftsmanship in every detail. Unlike the monks, who viewed the huge and menacing long ship as the embodiment of evil, he viewed it as a work of art. To put it simply, the Vikings knew how to build ships.

While others feared to venture too far out to sea in their clumsy ships, the Vikings seemed to skim over the ocean like water birds over a pond. He suspected that part of their mastery over the sea was found in their ships, which were constructed to be light and flexible. Having built a curragh for the monks, Sean knew that the thinner the planks, the lighter the craft. The lighter the craft, the less water the ship would draw, so that it could be maneuvered in shallow waters, where heavier craft would most certainly run aground. With a light but sturdy shell, a Viking ship could flex in the ocean waves like a slim leaf. This lightweight craft could also be beached easily and could be taken far up shallow rivers.

There were two ways to propel the ship. The first was the large rectangular sail; the second was by oar power. All during the voyage, Sean had taken note of every detail so that he would be prepared. He had learned that when the ship was "running before the wind," as the Vikings called it, the sail was spread by two whisker poles, spars fitted into sockets in a pair of blocks mounted on each bulwark just forward of the mast. When the vessel was sailing across the wind or into it, only one of these whisker poles would be used. Great power could be obtained from these coarse wool sails, but when they were wet in a severe storm they became exceedingly heavy and could be dangerous. He had watched in horror during a storm as one of Wolfram's Vikings had been knocked from his feet and nearly shoved over the side of the long ship.

A single bank of rowers on each side was the other source of power, pulling the ship through the water with steady, even strokes on their long oars. Under each man's bench was a length of rolled-up leather, which was used as a sleeping bag. Beside the bags, each man kept his weapons—spears, swords, and axes—just in case there was trouble. Though it was a merchant ship, it seemed that the Vikings always came prepared.

Slowly Sean moved to the stern, where a muscular

Viking steered the ship by its tiller. The Vikings had devised a remarkable rudder: a stubby, modified steering oar that was fixed to the starboard quarter of the craft on a large block of wood pegged so that the tiller would rotate as a lever rotates on a fulcrum.

"We're nearly there," Wolfram called over his shoulder.

The announcement caused Sean to tense. All during the journey Sean had put his misgivings about this meeting with his father out of his mind, but now they resurfaced. He remembered Thordis and his brutality and drunkenness and felt a sick feeling in the pit of his stomach. Though his mother had insisted that Ragnar was an honorable and just man, unlike some of the other Norsemen, he wasn't so sure. All his life he had been told that they were evil, and somehow that thought echoed again and again in his mind.

"Are you anxious to see your father?" Wolfram's young son, Fenrir, came up behind him and tapped on his shoulder.

"Yes and no," Sean answered truthfully. He was impatient to get the necessary ship and crew to go in search of Natasha, yet uneasy about the coming reunion, undoubtedly because he wasn't sure what to expect.

"Well, if your father is at all like mine you will be glad to see him. I always am, when my father returns from the sea."

Rorik, the other boy, grinned. "But this time he took us with him so that we can learn to be Vikings."

"Merchants," Fenrir corrected. He ran to the side of the ship, pushing past one of the oarsmen. "Look at all the rocks."

"Let me see!" With a childish cry of exuberance, Rorik, who was Fenrir's younger brother, ran to join them, his eyes poised on the horizon. "Those are mountains."

"Mountains. Rocks. Same thing." Fenrir cocked his

head as if trying to figure out how the rocks had risen up from the sea.

"Big rocks rising right out of the ocean, as if one of the giants father told us about put them there."

The two boys, who, like Sean, were half Irish and half Norse, had accompanied their father on his ship. They had entertained Sean on the long journey and plied him with a hundred questions or more. The dark-haired Fenrir had even taken an interest in letters and had sat patiently for hours as Sean taught him writing and how to use numerals to keep track of sums. The boy, who reminded Sean of himself at that age, had insisted that he would use what he had learned to help his father. Rorik, on the other hand, was the more aggressive and adventuresome brother, and scoffed at his brother's fascination with learning such things.

"Rocks and trees. That's the Northland, where father was born," Rorik said, making a sweeping gesture with his hand just in case Sean hadn't noticed.

Sean trained his eyes in that direction as they moved toward the shore, and what he saw made a more than favorable impression. So this was the Northland, he thought, gazing at the cliffs that rose abruptly from steep-sided, long, narrow waterways. The elongated rock formations extended inland for many miles in what appeared from a distance to be a ribbon of water. As they moved closer, the high, straight rock walls suddenly seemed to rise on both sides of the ship.

"Fjords, they are called," Fenrir exclaimed.

"Fjords," Sean repeated, feeling a surge of excitement as the ship sailed through the cliffs. They were actually sailing between these astounding towering rocks as they headed inland.

Sean's eyes were focused on Wolfram as he guided the ship through the rocks with great skill and nerves of iron. Navigation took a great deal of ability considering the magnitude of the rocks that rose right up from the waters. One misjudgment, one mistake, and the ship could crash into the side of the mountain.

Sean watched intently as they sailed, so close to the formations that he could see the very texture of the rocks. He was more determined than ever to learn all that he could about ships and the sea, so that he would be able to master a ship of his own very soon.

"You are going to see your father?" Rorik asked, running his fingers through his blond hair as he mimicked his own father's actions.

"Mmm-hmm." Reaching up, Sean touched the pendant, tracing its contours with his fingers, while at the same time he clutched his rosary with the other hand. "I've come to show him this pendant."

"I like your wolf," Fenrir said, reaching out to touch it. "My name means *wolf* you know."

"Yes, I know," Sean answered, fondly ruffling the boy's hair.

"But do you know who Fenrir was?" the dark-haired young Viking pressed.

Sean shook his head.

"The son of Loki, who is bound by the gods until Ragnarok, the end of the world." Putting his hand up to his mouth, he confided, "My mother and I don't believe that Viking story for a minute. We're Christians, you see. Like you."

"And just how do you know that I'm a Christian?"

The other boy laughed. "Because when Sigurd almost fell overboard, you did this. . . ." Rorik made the sign of the cross with his hand. "And because my mother told us about the monks and priests and how special they are because they can read."

Sean put a hand on Rorik's shoulder as he looked out at the coast, which had changed from rough, barren, rocky cliffs to an area with trees that looked as if it had been hacked out of the mountain. Seemingly, it was a village, for he could see clusters of large longhouses emerging through the clouds, and from the rocky ledges came the bleating of sheep.

As the ship approached a headland, it ran close under its lee and Sean could see ferns in the clefts of the rock. Again, he studied every detail of the land and the inhabitants, determined to keep an open mind as he remembered that his father's people were pagan. That was why he was so startled to see a limestone cross rising up on the summit.

"A Christian symbol," he mumbled, pointing in that direction.

The man at the tiller overheard him and shrugged. "Why not? Ragnar's own daughter and the wife of his son are both Christians. I think perhaps they were responsible for putting it there."

"Ragnar's daughter and son?" Sean had prepared himself to meet with his father, but he was not prepared to find himself face-to-face with sibblings. What else had he not been told? Like bubbles on the water, all his misgivings rose upward, filling his thoughts as he looked out at the Northland.

At a signal from Wolfram, the rowers positioned themselves at the oars. As the shrill notes of a faraway horn sounded from the crest of the rocks, one of Wolfram's men shouted back, then, raising his own horn, tooted out some kind of a signal. The horn's blare was answered by another horn high atop the hill, in what seemed to be a greeting.

Rounding a headland in the high-cliffed fjord, they sailed up to a grassy, gently sloping plain that seemed to have been hacked out of the sheer, towering walls. It extended from the hills in the distance to the water's edge. Sean watched as the Vikings unfurled the sail and then, as if in a salute to those on shore, raised their oars in unison on a signal from the helmsman. Likewise they lowered the oars together, then rowed in steady cadence.

As they approached the settlement, Sean had time

to observe that it was similar to the settlement in Larne except that it was larger, cleaner and grander. He noticed a small wooden house balanced precariously on the bank of the waterside, another nearly touching the mountain slope, and even dwellings perched on ledges high above the water. It was a rugged and coldly beautiful land, just as he had imagined it would be. Avidly he scanned the picturesque scene and committed it to memory.

Wolfram's men sailed the ship all the way up to a planked breakwater and tied up the ship. Once the strong ropes had been secured around the bollards, they wasted no time in unloading the cargo, and Sean wasted no time in inquiring as to the whereabouts of Ragnar Longsword's abode.

"Who are you? You are a stranger here." The gray-haired man squinted as he stared up at Sean, his eyes taking in Sean's gray-hooded cloak with a frown.

"I have business with Ragnar Longsword."

"Business . . ."

"I wish to speak with him about a ship," Sean answered without touching on the subject of his parentage.

"A ship?"

"And a crew."

Mumbling, the old man led Sean on a long hike toward a group of wooden outbuildings, then to a building larger than the others. "Here. He is here. This is the *skaalen.*"

The house was made mainly of wood, with a turf roof and a stone foundation. Around the building was a planked wooden walkway, which led up to one of the two entryways. Sean could see that, like the small huts at the settlement in Larne, this large building had slats to let in the light, and a hole in the roof to allow smoke to escape and the sun's rays to enter. Because of the cold climate, there were no windows.

"Whose house is this?" he asked of the old man as they stepped through the door.

"Ragnar's."

A shiver of anticipation ran through him. What would his father be like. Like Thordis? If so, then he had come all this way for nothing, for he would not compromise all that he held dear for a ship. Nor would he beg. Ragnar was not the only one who had ships.

Putting his hands behind his back, Sean paced up and down, staring at the walls of the large room. Critically his eyes scanned the room, as if by doing so he could glimpse the character of the man who owned it.

Down the center of the hall was a long hearth on a raised platform. Big pots hung over the fire on chains from beams in the ceiling of the gabled roof, much the same as at the settlement. Here, however, there were fewer weapons displayed, less clutter, and more organization. There was also a homier touch. A loom and several spindle whorls for the spinning of wool stood against the far wall. On either side of the long hall, indoor benches lined the walls. They appeared to be used for either sitting or sleeping. Toward the far wall was a chair, much higher than the benches around it. It was heavily carved with geometric and floral designs and forms. Sean crossed himself as he realized they were representations of the Vikings' gods. Several tables, which could be pushed aside to make more room, stood heavily laden with food, a welcome sight after traveling.

"You have brought a visitor with you, Gorm."

The loud voice took him by surprise. Turning, Sean was rendered speechless as he found himself face-to-face with the powerfully built Viking that he knew in an instant had to be Ragnar.

Dressed in a brown tunic bordered with fancy embroidery at the sleeves and hem, a brown leather corselet with shoulder straps fastened at the chest with buckles, dun-colored leggings, and silver and gold bracelets arraying his arms, he looked impressive and every inch the jarl that his mother had told Sean he was.

The Viking's strong features were marred by a scar across his cheek, yet strangely, the blemish was not distracting. There was no denying that he was an imposing man, a fine specimen of manhood with broad shoulders and muscular arms. He had thick tawny hair and a beard that was streaked with gray. Unlike Thordis, his eyes were not beady and filled with malice but were thoughtful, as if he was studying Sean. Despite his being a Viking, he didn't look the least bit terrifying. As to there being a resemblance between them, Sean couldn't see one thing about this man that looked like him, except perhaps when he smiled.

Ragnar studied Sean just as intently as he was studying him, his eyes lingering on the hem of his cloak. He said, "You are dark of hair and obviously not Viking. Have you come to see Gwyneth?"

"No. . . ."

"Who, then?"

Sean clenched and unclenched his hands. He hadn't the time for pleasantries. Time was of the essence. He had to get the ship and crew and rescue Natasha before she got into trouble. "I've come to see you." Brushing aside his cloak, he held the wolf's-head pendant up for Ragnar Longsword to see.

For a moment it was Ragnar who could not think of anything to say, then he blurted, "Where did you get this?"

"It was given to my mother. She gave it to me."

Ragnar hesitated, then asked softly, "Are you my son?"

Sean nodded, feeling suddenly choked up. What did he feel for this man—revulsion, admiration, affection? At the moment he wasn't quite sure.

"I've imagined this moment so many times, but now

that you are here, I don't know what to say." Hurrying forward, Ragnar enclosed his son in a bear hug, overcome by his emotions. "Kodran! Kodran! My son . . . my son . . ." He didn't seem to notice or to care that Sean was not responding to his show of affection. Then, at last he pulled away. "Where is Torin?"

"Torin? Who is Torin?"

Ragnar was taken aback. "Why, the man I sent to find you and bring you back."

Sean shook his head. "No one brought me here. I came on my own."

"Came on your own." First Ragnar grinned; then he chuckled. "So, I think perhaps you are like me after all, despite those skirts that are on your back." He flung his arm over his shoulder. "Come, let's find something much better for you to wear, and then we can talk."

Sean was surrounded by several women carrying bowls of warm water and towels that had been heated over the fire. "For guests and travelers," Ragnar explained. Then, seeing Sean's expression he chided, "We are not, as you have heard, 'unwashed heathens.' "

"I'm sorry; I meant no offense." It was just that he had been remembering that Thordis and his band of Vikings had smelled like swine.

Ragnar moved past the women and, hunkering down, searched through a pile of clothes until he found what he was looking for. "These will have to do until we make you your own garments," he said, draping them over his arm.

Sean dipped his hands in the warm water, then splashed it on his face and hair. He wiped his hands on the towel the women had given him, then dried his face and wrapped the towel around his hair to dry it.

Ragnar shooed the women out of the room. "Here;

put these on." He gave Sean the red woolen tunic decorated with embroidered animal faces, and the plain tan woolen trousers he held clutched in his hand. "They belong to Selig, but they look as if they will fit you."

"Selig?"

"Your brother."

The thought of having a brother was strange, yet not unappealing. All his life, Sean had felt isolated and alone, longing for ties to a real family. But could he accept a Viking as a brother? He wasn't certain.

"Ah, Kodran, Kodran . . . you are a boon to an old man's heart." Ragnar patted him fondly on the shoulder, but Sean did not respond with any sign of affection of his own. He couldn't, at least not yet.

"My name is Sean," he corrected stiffly.

"Bah, a Celtic name. You are Kodran. No matter what anyone else called you, Kodran is your name!"

Sean wasn't in the mood to argue; besides, there was no reason to anger the man. He disrobed and pulled the tunic over his head, then came quickly to the point. "I need a ship."

"A ship?"

"And a crew."

Ragnar pulled at his ear, then leaning his head back, gave in to his laughter. "A ship. A crew. Just like that. And to think that I feared by looking at you that I might have a rough time making a Viking out of you."

"I'm not a Viking. I'll never be a Viking," Sean answered rebelliously, pulling up his trousers and then tying them around his waist.

"You *are* a Viking, and your name *is* Kodran. There can be no argument, for it is the truth." Ragnar stomped his foot as if punctuating his pronouncement. "Now, tell me why you want a ship and a crew, if not to go a-viking."

"I want to sail to Kiev, or wherever I must go, to find Natasha and bring her back with me."

"Natasha." Again Ragnar tugged at his ear. "A woman. You want a ship and a crew to go after some woman. Why?"

"Because I love her." Sean's eyes held steady.

"Because you love her," Ragnar repeated. "Hmmmmm." Bending down, he searched for something, then came up with a pair of leather shoes and a belt. He handed them to Sean. "Tell me the story."

As he finished dressing, Sean told him about having been sent to Larne by the abbot; about his meeting with the Magyar slave; her escape; their fight with Vikings at Bangor; and finally about how he had taken her to Armagh only come up against the abbot's firm resolve.

"An escaped slave. That is not good, Kodran. That is not good at all. She belonged to someone else. What you did was much the same as stealing."

"Stealing! You speak of stealing. You who have pillaged, raped, and burned, and stolen from everyone in your path!" Sean's wrath exploded as he remembered what the abbot had done. Though his anger was not really at Ragnar, he vented his feelings on him nonetheless. "You are no better than he! You don't understand. You don't know how I felt when the abbot betrayed me and sent her back to him. To that brute Thordis!"

"Righifarch sent her back to Thordis?"

"To spite me, to force me to become a veritable eunuch like him. Well, I fooled him. I left the monastery forever and I will never go back. Never." It was unlike Sean to lose his temper, yet unburdening his emotions in this way was strangely soothing. He felt much better. "I thought that you would help me, so I went to Bangor and asked my mother how to find you."

"Your mother?" For a moment, Ragnar's face turned red and he looked as if he might collapse.

"Righifarch wove a web of lies. He told my mother that I died the night I was born, and he told you that she had died. But she is very much alive."

"Alive! Tara. . . ." He grabbed Sean's arm. "Where is she? Is she with you?"

Sean shook his head. "No. She is in Eire, at Bangor. She is a nun. Sister Erin now."

"A nun!" Ragnar's face contorted, and for a moment it looked as if he might cry, but he held back the unmanly tears. "So not only did Righifarch steal your love from you, he stole my love from me." He growled low in his throat. "That cowardly dog!" He motioned for Sean to follow him. "I'll give you your ship and your crew. Righifarch will not win. Not this time."

Twenty-two

In the tranquil waters of an inlet, a dragon ship lay at anchor, it's image reflected in the shimmering blue water. It was the finest ship that Sean had ever seen. As the small knarr rounded the promontory, he wondered whether he dare hope that this was the ship Ragnar was going to give him.

"There she is, Kodran!" Ragnar sailed the small ship as close to the dragon ship as possible. "What do you think?"

Sean let his eyes move appraisingly over the Viking ship from stem to sternpost. It was indeed a powerful and well-crafted vessel. He could imagine the prow sweeping the skies, plowing a path among the stars. "She's beautiful!" His eyes lit upon the strongly curving ship's bow that ended in a wolf's head, and he raised his eyes in question.

"Yes, I had this ship built just for you and had the wolf head carved there."

"I'll call her the *Wolf's Head.*"

"Wolf's Head!" Ragnar smiled his approval. "I hoped that we would soon be reunited. And now, Kodran, we have been."

"Yes, we have. . . ." It was strange, Sean thought, how quickly he was coming to have a sincere affection for Ragnar, perhaps because he seemed to understand him. And now he had gifted him with the one thing that had been his dream since boyhood.

"We've been reunited only to be torn apart again when you sail." Ragnar's voice was choked. "How ironic that it is I who give you the very thing that will take you away."

"I have to find Natasha." Sean's voice was soft, his eyes filled with a special glow as he talked about her. "I have never seen a woman so unafraid, so strong. When even the bravest man would have been afraid of incurring Thordis's ire by escaping, she didn't have a second thought about it. Even if I didn't love her as much as I do, I couldn't bear to have her stay in his power."

"You admire as well as love her."

"She is strong and brave." Remembering how well she rode on horseback, he smiled. "You should see her on a horse! Were I not a Christian I would have thought her to be a goddess."

"You make me anxious to meet her . . . so hurry and find this woman of yours and bring her back to the Northland."

The smell of smoke mingled with the scent of fresh rushes and the appetizing aroma of the beef, onions, and cabbage that was stewing in the soapstone cauldrons over the fire. The table was covered with platters and bowls filled to the top with food: hunks of cheese, barley bread, blackberries mixed with raspberries, and assorted green vegetables.

As Sean returned with Ragnar from their outing to look at the ship, the meal preparation was halted. Everyone in the room stopped and stared. Suddenly, he was surrounded by the small group of people who boisterously welcomed him into the family by talking excitedly, grabbing his hand, or slapping him on the back. A tall woman with red hair was even so bold as to throw her arms around him, hugging him close.

"Now we are all together. All three," she whispered

in his ear. "I canna' tell ye how happy that makes me."

After so many years keeping at arm's length from other people, Sean was uncomfortable with the familiarity and intimacy. First he stiffened; then he pulled away, looking quizzically at the pretty young woman.

"Forgive me. I'm your sister, Erica."

"Sister . . ."

"And I'm Selig, your brother." Sean was face-to-face with a man his same height but as fair of hair as Sean was dark.

"My brother . . ."

The two men were a study in contrasts, though both were tall, broad-shouldered, and strikingly handsome. They eyed each other up and down; then Selig held out his hand, clasping Sean's hand warmly to demonstrate his welcome.

The air exploded with questions from the two siblings and from the other people surrounding him. Amid the confusion, he tried to identify all of them and satisfy their curiosity, but he was lost in the cacophony of names. Which ones were family, which were friends, and which were the unfortunate thralls?

Sensing his anxiety and confusion, the woman named Erica looped her arm through his and slowly made the introductions. The rest of the family members were Gwyneth, a petite dark-haired woman who was wife to Selig, Nissa, wife to Ragnar, and Torin who, although not there in body, was there in spirit.

"While Torin and I were in Staffa we met a priest who mentioned having seen the wolf's-head pendant in Armagh. My husband sailed to Eire in search of you, Kodran."

Kodran. Again and again Sean was pelted with his Viking name. He put his hands up to his ears, fearing for a moment that the man he had been for several years was close to disappearing.

Selig seemed to sense his agitation, for he grabbed

Sean by the arm as he verbally shooed everyone else away. The women returned to the business of preparing the food, and the men to their tankards.

"Our father tells me that you have need of a crew to go after Thordis. I'll help you get the necessary men, and we can go together."

"I would prefer to go alone," Sean said emphatically.

"Alone?" Selig clucked his tongue. "You are overconfident, brother. As fine as yours is, the sea-borne success of a Viking depends as much on skilled seamanship and bravery as it does on ship design and craftsmanship. You think it's easy to sail over the waves, but it is not. There are days spent in the open sea without sight of land, when you have only the sun and the stars to rely on."

"I know. I watched Wolfram Olafsson very carefully as we sailed from Eire to here. Besides, I have seen several maps of the lands near Kiev."

"And so you think that you are ready?"

He nodded. "I do!"

"You're wrong! Even I, as long as I have sailed, I learn something new each time I sail, like how to watch the movements of birds and sea mammals."He crossed his arms across his chest. "You need my help in this rescue you intend, in more ways than one." When Sean hesitated, he said, "Think on it. What I say is true."

Sean stubbornly stared long and hard at Selig. He had wanted the experience of being the master of his own ship, but he couldn't let his own ambitions jeopardize Natasha's future.

Before Sean had a chance to say a word, Selig continued. "I know where Thordis will go. I know his trysting places. I know everything there is to know about the greedy fool. I know how he thinks!"

Squinting his eyes, Sean eyed his new brother suspiciously. "Why do you know him so well?"

"Because once, before I met my Gwyneth, I was just like him. We were friends. . . ."

"Friends?" Sean grimaced as he remembered the brutish Viking. "So, you too were in the business of obtaining slaves."

"I *was* a slave."

"You?" He didn't believe it.

"Look." Holding up his long golden hair at the nape of his neck, Selig exhibited the scar that his slave collar had left, an ugly red welt that had faded but not vanished over the years.

"I'm sorry. . . ." Remembering the brutality with which the slaves were treated, he looked at Selig with new respect. He had not only survived, he had escaped. "How . . . ?"

Selig shrugged. "It's a long story. I'll have plenty of time to tell you all about it as we travel together."

Sean thought the matter over, but only for a moment. "You would sail your ship and I would sail mine?"

Selig smiled. "That's the only way I would have it." He stretched forth his arm, his hand poised for a handshake. "So . . . do you agree?"

Sean suspicions were aroused again. "You are not accompanying me just out of brotherly loyalty. Will there be any raids?"

Selig grinned. "Let us just say that I intend this journey to be profitable." When Sean didn't answer he added, "I'm a Viking. So are you, *Kodran;* whether you want to remember that or not is your concern. You must make up your mind."

Realizing that there were few alternatives open, Sean reached out and took his brother's hand. "We'll sail together."

That same day, the two dragon ships were heading out into a tossing sea. Sean felt the wind tickle his cheek. Leaning over the rail, he watched the green, glassy water slipping and glinting past the ship, nearly hypnotizing him as it curdled with foam where the oars struck the sea. Seagulls rose and drifted over the ship, mewing and shrieking.

The ships skimmed past the promontory. The men sweated at the winch, mounting the mast. And then the sail was up, whipping as gusts of wind caught at it sharply.

Once again she was chained, enslaved, and on a ship. Even so, Natasha wasn't intimidated or depressed. Sean would find her. Somehow. She felt it in her heart. Meanwhile, she had the memory of their lovemaking to calm her troublesome days, and the heated passion of her dreams to sooth the chilly nights.

Standing at the side of the ship, she closed her eyes and thought very hard, hoping that somehow the power that her grandmother had always said was in the mind could transport her thoughts. Mentally she tried to guide Sean into finding her, only to feel a jab of reality intrude upon the images in her mind.

"How is he going to find me in this ocean when he doesn't even have a ship?" The small boat he had rowed down the river would never survive in the sea.

Leaning over the side, looking down at the foamy water, she clenched her hands, feeling uneasiness sweep over her as a wave struck the side of the ship. No. She couldn't allow herself to lose hope. Only by believing could she hang on to her sanity. Sean would come. She must continue to believe that.

"No!" The Viking leader's strong arms reached out to grasp her shoulders.

Natasha had learned that word very well. It was always spoken when the Vikings wanted to vent some displeasure. She realized by the expression on his face that he had feared that she was going to jump overboard. She shook her head, repeating the word.

"No!" She wasn't going to jump, but somehow she couldn't quite make him understand that. She cursed the language barrier, wishing she were able to speak in several languages the way that Sean had done.

Shrugging off Thordis's hands, she moved quickly to the middle of the ship and plopped down on a blanket that had been haphazardly thrown on the deck for warmth and a small measure of comfort against the hard wooden deck.

"Sean . . ." Just saying his name aloud brought her a sense of peace and made it easier for her to regain her composure.

What would have happened if I hadn't followed those gray-hooded men? she wondered. In a mood of reverie she took out the damaged piece of scroll that Sean had once given her, and stared at the letters that she had written there. Chicken scratching, her father would have called it. To her, however, it seemed to be a link to the man that she loved.

"I wanted to learn to read and write like you," she whispered, tracing the letters she had practiced with the tip of her finger. Sean had once told her that the pen and the words that it created were mightier than the sword. Was it true? Somehow, she thought that a definite possibility.

Suddenly, the piece of parchment was yanked from her hand, and though she tried to regain it, it was dangled just out of her reach.

"Please . . . give it back." Though they couldn't understand what she was saying, she knew they understood what it was that she wanted. "Give it to me! It's the only thing I have that belonged to *him*. . . ."

The Viking named Thordis was staring at her, as if he somehow had learned that she was very strange. He was grumbling at her in the harsh, explosive Viking language, raising his brows as if asking her some kind of question.

She nodded her head fiercely. "Yes, it's mine. Give it back to me."

He spewed another stream of verbiage at her. Questioning. Demanding. All the while, he pointed at the piece of parchment. He wiggled his finger, as if mimicking what she had done.

"You're asking me if I wrote this, aren't you? Why? Would it increase my value to you if I said yes?" By the look in his eyes she knew the answer.

Twenty-three

A gusty wind drove the ship and stirred up waves that surged over the shuddering prow. Sean watched as the wind lifted the sail, and for the moment he felt as if he were flying. He brushed his fingers through his wind-ruffled dark hair, knowing that this was where he wanted to be: on a ship with the wind at his back.

"Freedom, ultimate freedom . . ." he said aloud, gazing out at the wide expanse of ocean. Day by day, under his brother's tutelage he was learning new things and becoming as comfortable on the sea as he had been on land.

"That's because the sea is in your blood," Selig had told him. "You are more Viking than you realize."

"Viking!" he murmured. Once he might have been insulted if anyone had called him by that name, but now, after talking with Selig, he felt a sense of fierce pride.

Ragnar was not the heathen that Sean had first supposed. Although it was true that he had first embarked with his men in a fleet of dragon-prowed ships, it had been only the beginning for the Viking leader. Sean now knew that his father was intelligent as well as strong and had proven himself to be an able administrator in the lands that he had subjugated. Ragnar had realized that a man had to be a creator as well as a destroyer and had to reach out to other cultures, to learn from them and absorb outside influences and ideas.

A spark inside Sean had flamed into a determination to do as his father had done. There were new lands, new peoples just waiting to be found. During the times when the two ships had pulled to shore to make camp, Selig had told him stories and fragmented legends that taunted him to explore. He wanted to find new lands that no other Viking had ever set foot upon, at least not until now. He had a deep yearning to sail out and find what lay beyond the well-established trade routes. As a reward, the men who pledged to follow him would all share the profit upon their return. But that was in the future. Now his only thought was finding Natasha as quickly as they could.

Taking in a deep breath of the salty sea air, he thought of her, and his flesh ached as he remembered how it had felt to hold her in his arms. Closing his eyes, he welcomed the memories of the night of his nights. It was almost as if the word *passion* had been created to describe how she had fit so perfectly against him, so warm, so loving.

A rush of blood surged through his veins; an emotional hunger gnawed at him. He missed her. Even now he could remember her strength, feel the pull of her fascination. She was an unusual woman. Passionate, giving herself to him without reserve, she had proved to be the kind of woman a man dreams about.

Under the rigid training of the monks, Sean had learned to hide his loneliness and deep emotional scars, but when he had been with her he had returned her love freely and naturally. He had felt whole. He had known love.

I'll never give her up. Never! he thought, staring wistfully out at the Baltic Sea. No matter what happened, he was determined to find her.

"She is amazing, isn't she?"

Sean whirled around and found himself face-to-face

with Refkel, one of his brother's crewmen, called "Ref" for short. Though so far he had not interfered in the day-to-day managing of the Viking ship, Sean suspected that it was Ref's duty to watch over him and be there in case of sudden trouble.

"She . . ."

Immediately his thoughts turned to Natasha. "Yes . . ."

"She goes on and on, and if you are at all like me, you want to know what is out there and if there really is an end to it all. Or if she just drops off into nothingness like a waterfall . . ."

"The ocean . . ." Sean laughed softly as he realized that Ref was talking about the sea and not a woman. For the moment he put Natasha from his thoughts.

"There are those who are afraid to sail too far in uncharted waters, but I want to sail farther and farther until I know the truth of the quarrel. What about you? Have you ever had an urge to sail so far that you reach the far horizon?"

"I have. Since my first visit to the sea."

"Then perhaps we are more alike than I first supposed." The red-haired, freckle-faced Ref grinned. "I have a confession to make. When your brother first asked me to sail on this ship with you, I was greatly perturbed."

"Perturbed. Why?"

"Because I thought you would be a stone around my neck. I thought because you once spent your time with books you would be inept at sailing and I would be called upon to right all your wrongs. But I must confess, I am pleasantly surprised."

"I haven't made any serious mistakes, at least not yet."

Ref looked at him levelly. "You have made a few mistakes, but you have learned from them and corrected them quickly and with courage. Selig is right. You are a true Viking."

"Thank you." Sean welcomed Ref's show of friendship. "But don't compliment me too soon. We aren't even halfway through our journey yet, and from what Selig tells me, the worst is yet to come."

"Ah, at least you have been forewarned." Ref explained that once they reached the mouth of the Dvina River, they would be traveling through areas where there was no alternative but to portage across land, dragging or carrying the ships until they reached water deep enough for the Viking ships to sail.

"My brother told me what to expect." Sean was prepared for that part of the journey to be exhausting, but it didn't matter. All that mattered was finding Natasha.

"Once we reach Kiev the journey will become easier, but there will be other kinds of dangers."

"From the Slavs?"

"From everyone you meet." Ref cautioned him that in the land of the Rus, Viking often preyed upon Viking, so special care would need to be taken to locate the towns and trading posts were they were safe from easy attack.

Kiev, because of its strategic location on the Dnieper, was the most important of all the towns of the Rus, and at the same time the most dangerous. It was the southernmost fortified point in the forest region. Just below it, in the town of Vitichev, flotillas of boats would assemble before making the run south through the dangerous steppe to the Black Sea.

From what Sean remembered and what Selig and Ref told him, he pieced together the story of Kiev. It seemed that the Vikings had been able to spare men and energy from their assaults upon Alba, Eire, Britain, Germany, France, and Spain to send men to prey upon the communities of Balts, Finns, and Slavs and then return with their booty. To protect their robberies with law and order these Vikings that called themselves Varangians, or followers, of a chieftain, had established fortified posts on their routes and had little by little settled down as a ruling Scandinavian minority of armed merchants among the subject peasantry. Some towns had hired them as guardians of social order and security and paid a tribute. They had now become the masters of their employers and governed Novgorod and had extended their rule as far south as Kiev. The routes and settlements they controlled were loosely bound into a commercial and political empire that was called Rus, derived from *Ruotsi,* the Finnish name for the Swedes, the largest group of Viking that had come to the area.

They still had a long way to go before they reached Kiev. It was already late autumn. Winter was approaching. They had to find Natasha and rescue her quickly before the murderous cold of the winter weather moved in.

Water, as far as the eye could see. It seemed as if she was always going to be on water—first the ocean and now the river, Natasha thought as she stared out at the amber-tinted currents of the Dvina. Her captors were headed toward Kiev, a land filled with her enemies, the Vikings and the Slavs. What was to become of her when they reached their destination?

What does it matter? A slave is a slave is a slave. . . ."

Though her captors had changed their attitude toward her and begun to treat her with deference, she was disheartened just the same. As two days became three, and three days became four and multiplied on and on, she had begun to give in to her fears that she would never see Sean again. Worse yet, the farther they traveled, the less it made sense to escape. Thus, for the first time in her life, she felt a sense of hopelessness and entrapment. And yes, anger. Anger at her captors, anger at the gray-hooded men who had betrayed her, and anger at herself for allowing herself to be betrayed. Worst of all, she felt hollow inside—alone.

No one to talk with, no one who understands my language, no one who cares . . . As the ship bumped along over the river, so roughly that it was all she could do to stay on her feet, she longed anew for Sean's strong arms.

It was a rough journey, made even more so as the river grew narrow, winding through the lowlands, passing by the twisted trunks of pine trees then, past the ferny glades of the forest. When they came to an area of the river that was choked with water growth and they could not sail, the men rowed, pushing the ship past the crumbling banks. Then, in places where the river became too shallow to float upon, the Vikings worked alongside the slaves, hoisting the dragon ship on wooden rollers and dragging it along a forest track for hours until the sluggish water flowed freely again. All the while, the heavy sails hung lifeless. As lifeless as she felt.

The river is endless. . . . A clouded amber stream, winding deeper and deeper into the forest, taking her farther and farther away.

Twenty-four

As if somehow to compensate for the cold climate and the monotonous landscape, the land of the Rus possessed a great natural asset, a magnificent system of interlocking rivers. Slow-moving and meandering, these waterways made it possible to travel in almost any direction across the great plain.

The first river that would take them to their destination was the Dvina. Once they had sailed as far as they could on it, they had to drag the boats overland, using logs as rollers. It was at least a half-day's portage, up the forested slopes of the riverbank, over the ridge, then down the brush trail, through the quagmire and swamp until they came to the great river, the Dnieper.

Sweating and straining, Sean and the others hunched their shoulders under the great bulk of the dragon ship, easing it over the ragged roots in the trail. Ahead of them, some of the other Vikings hacked with axes at the brushwood.

Here the air was dank and oppressive. There was a smell of rotting logs and sunken water growth. "Watch out for hoop snakes," Ref warned.

"Hoop snakes. Poisonous?"

"Deadly."

Sean moved cautiously, all the while reminded of Saint Patrick and how he had driven the snakes out of Eire so many years ago.

At last, both ships were in the water again, sailing

past the twisted trunks of pines, past ferny glades of forest, through tall water reeds that seemed to bow in homage as they passed.

In a land with so many forests, wood was the main building material. Houses were built of logs, much as they were in the Northland. The people that they could see from the ship wore clothes of wood and linen, covered with fur and long boots.

"Who are they?" Sean asked, always interested in learning everything he could.

"Slavs. They occupy much of the forested land from the area of Kiev north and east to Moscow and Novgorod, driving out or absorbing the weaker Lithuanians and Finns in their path."

The abbot had once told him that human sacrifice was known among Slavic pagans. It was said that the land was drenched in human blood, though Sean had the feeling that the abbot had greatly exaggerated.

Ref confirmed what Sean thought and told him that the Slavs were a peaceful people who, like the Vikings, were expert navigators—but on rivers. They were also strong swimmers and were renowned for their ability to hide underwater for long periods by breathing through reeds held in their mouths. The Slavs were peasant farmers who lived close to the earth, on which they relied for daily sustenance.

"They mingle quite peacefully with settled tribes, though they often quarrel amongst themselves, which is how the Varangians got a foothold."

Sean was puzzled by Ref's knowledge both of the Slavs and the Varangians. "You seem very well versed on this area. Have you been here before?"

Ref pointed to his face. "Take a good look at me and you will see the stamp of both Nordic and Slavic parents." When Sean seemed confused, he pointed to his wide cheekbones, the arch of his nostrils, and his dark, piercing eyes that looked out of place with his red hair and ruddy coloring. "I was born here. Like you, I did not see my Viking father until I had grown to manhood."

"Then you know firsthand about all that happened here. Tell me, for I would like to learn everything one can know."

As they traveled, Ref told how the Varangians, his father among them, had proceeded southward along the Volkhov and Dnieper Rivers; they had passed through the heartland of the Slavs and gradually brought it under their domination, either by insinuating themselves into the upper class of wealthy Slavic traders or by outright conquest.

"The Slavs were not militarily organized or well armed, having no weapons to match the heavy two-edged swords and battle axes of the invaders; thus, you can guess the outcome."

"Much the same as in Eire . . ."

"At first the Slavs fought against the Varangian incursions, but then my grandfather, among others, asked the Rus to rule over them and keep the bitter battles they fought among themselves in check."

"And thus they have seemingly flourished. That is a sign of a hardy people."

"Forest life was difficult," Ref continued. "Against the crushing cold the Slavs built pit houses with low walls and roofs rising only a few feet above the ground, mounded over with earth for insulation. Agriculture demanded prodigious labor. Clearings were made with axes, and the felled trees were burned to provide fertilizer. Marriage by capture or purchase was common, as was polygamy. Idols were venerated, and there was widespread belief in Volos, the god of the dead, and Perun, the god of thunder and lightning, who is much like Odin."

Sean grimaced at the mention of the Norse god. The Viking gods were still a sore spot with him. Somehow, when this was all over he wanted to try and convert his father to Christianity.

Ref told Sean that the harsh environment of the cold forests kept the Slavs' agricultural production to the level of their own immediate needs, and so they had resorted to trade, turning to the forest for rich furs, honey, and beeswax.

"I met your brother, Selig, at Kaupang while I was there trading my family's goods, and he convinced me to go to his settlement."

Sean could hear snatches of chatter from the people on the banks of the river. Listening closely, he could tell that long ago they spoke the Slavic tongue with Norse words mixed in. Pure Norse, however, was spoken in Kiev, Ref told him.

As the river curved past a cluster of Slav dwellings, Sean remembered Natasha having talked about these peoples who shared the land with the Magyars farther south. In that moment, his longing to see her again was almost more than he could bear.

"You are thinking about the woman," Ref said softly.

Sean saw no reason to lie. "Yes . . ."

"She must be special for a man like you to come such a long distance and brave such dangers."

"There aren't enough words to explain just how extraordinary she is, nor how I feel about her."

"You don't need to explain. Your eyes tell the story." Ref pounded him on the back. "To feel such love as that, I think perhaps I would risk my life."

That night they made camp along the bank between two huge fires. It was then that Selig and Sean talked about what to expect on the morrow.

"The river will become even narrower and narrower, until it flings itself between high walls of black rock. Here the passage will be treacherous."

Because the Dnieper River was so wide and deep, Sean assumed that the downstream voyage would be easy, but Selig quickly put an end to that notion.

"There is more danger from now on, because the

current is so rapid and there is a succession of treacherous waterfalls that are not safe to navigate."

"The Slavs are fearful of the rapids. They say that the river demands many lives," Ref added.

"A sacrifice?"

Selig nodded. "We will have to stop, unload the ship, and portage around each one." He tensed and Sean sensed there was something his brother was not telling him.

"Tell me what concerns you."

"There are brigands who wait to kill off the unwary and steal their goods while they are engaged in portaging. Thus, there is danger either way."

"Brigands?"

"Thieves." Selig moved closer to the fire to bask in its warmth. "I have braved them before, but you are not used to danger."

"I'll learn. . . ."

"It's more than just the brigands. There are waterfalls—cataracts. We can move around them across the land."

"Portage?" Sean shook his head. "Sailing down the Dnieper—is that the quickest way to get to our destination?"

"It is."

He spoke without a moment's hesitation. "Then I'll brave the danger."

Sean's eyes were riveted on the water as the ship neared the treacherous stretch on the Dnieper. He could understand at a glance why Selig had cautioned him, for here the river narrowed between high, rocky cliffs, its mighty force compressed into a channel of churning waters.

"We will need men in the water to guide the ships," Ref explained, stripping off his garments as if to say that he would be the first to volunteer.

The sound of the rapids roared in his ears. Sean watched as several of the crewmen followed Ref's lead and stripped themselves naked. Other crewmen picked up stout poles and stood poised at the stern near the prow and amidships. Dark-gray rocks up ahead seemed to be drawing them, pulling them. Sean could only guess what would happen if they capsized upon the jagged rocks.

As the ship reached the churning waters, the men who had torn off their clothes went over the side, where they felt their way among the hidden rocks with their feet, their faces mirroring their pain. Bravely they guided the ship through the narrow passage of rock, while those with poles assisted in the maneuvering. Their skills helped Sean keep the ship from smashing against several large boulders and thus being ripped apart.

The ship shuddered and made a crunching sound as it was guided through the hostile waters. All the while, Sean feared that the men in the water would be sucked down into the furious whirlpools or become trapped between the ship and the rocks and crushed to death. Those on board were also in danger of catching their poles beneath a rock and being pulled off the ship and into the water. If that happened, he could only hope that Selig's dog, Baugi, would be able to save them before they were tugged under.

Once or twice the hull of the ship scraped a rock, yet Sean maintained his calm. Though he tasted fear, he was determined not to show it.

Selig had tried to prepare him for the trial they were going to undergo, but no words could describe the noise. He could feel the river's pulsation as if it had a heartbeat. It pounded in his ears. There were times he almost thought that it was as Selig had said: a living being. If so, then it seemed to be angry, and for a moment Sean feared that perhaps this was the way that he was to be punished for turning his back on a monastic life.

But no. He wouldn't feel that way. What he was doing was right. He would brave the dangers and be rewarded when he saw Natasha welcome him with a smile.

The river widened and grew deeper. The men climbed back aboard the ship as they eased into the hissing current. The ship rocked from side to side, jangling his nerves and stretching his courage to its limit. He remembered his brother's advice: "The prow rides high. Traverse the thirteen leagues very rapidly."

As the ship was pulled steadily by the current, the sound of the water deepened into a roar. The water quickened and broke, foaming over the gray-brown rocks. A powerful force took hold of the ship, pulling it faster and faster.

"Be aware of the water. React to it like a living thing with a mind of its own," Ref shouted in his ear.

The water was raging now, yet instead of feeling any fear Sean felt excited, vibrantly alive, as if he were facing a battle. Perhaps he was. A fight for survival and for the chance to prove his courage to those aboard his ship, and, most important, to himself.

On both sides of the ship the treacherous river flung itself in massive crests, the spray whistling into the air. The rumble of the water was so loud, it caused the ship to vibrate. Even so, Sean did not lose his nerve, not even when a white spray of water boiled over the bow.

The ship traversed two rapids without mishap, but Sean realized that each rapid became more treacherous than the last as the river's flow increased. Though he braced his feet and clutched at one of the side beams, he was heaved from side to side. Then, all at once, the current slowed, ending in smooth dark water—water so dark that it was almost black.

After the excitement was over, it seemed to take

forever to reach Kiev, and when they did it wasn't at all what he expected. It wasn't a large town at all, just a port with a forest of ships tied up to the landing. Ref pointed them out: merchant ships, biremes from the Black Sea and Mediterranean, galleys from Rome, smaller dhows from Arabia, and, of course, the long ships and dragon ships that belonged to the Vikings.

Ref noted his expression. "This is not Constantinople. Trade has brought wealth to only a few in Kievan Rus. Most of the people are not merchants but farmers, who survive by growing crops and raising stock animals. They also keep bees for honey, and some go out fishing and hunting. They keep cows, sheep, and pigs; grow wheat, hemp, rye, millet garlic, cabbages, and turnips."

Ref explained that Kiev was built amid an expanse of swamps and forests. The Slav farmers were free men known as *smerdy* or stinking ones, because it was said that they smelled of the manure they used in their fields. Even so, the prosperous Vikings had provided an eager market for luxury goods and for honey and furs. The lucrative trade routes were groups of farmsteads that formed the basis of the first towns.

"As trade has to be protected from bandits, most of these places were fortified by merchant-warriors. . . ."

"The Varangians."

"They formed a new elite focused on protecting their own interests. Towns soon developed into major centers for the surrounding countryside, offering professional craftsmen a secure place to settle and make a living. The Varangians have won control over the lucrative trade routes that run across the region."

Sean remembered learning that the great rivers that traversed the land connected, through canals and short overland hauls, the Baltic and Black Seas, and invited a southward expansion of trade and power. Now these Vikings, or Varangians, were selling their goods or services as far away as Constantinople itself.

Now he could see that there were also Moslem merchants who came up from Baghdad and Constantinople and traded spices, wines, silks, and gems for furs, amber, honey, wax, and slaves. Thus the Scandinavian, Slavic, Moslem, and Byzantine traded freely.

It was a chaotic scene. Buyers and sellers alike swarmed the wooden streets, haggling in at least a dozen languages. While Selig and his crewmen engaged themselves in trading, Sean went toward the center of Kiev, asking everyone he met if they had seen a woman of Natasha's description.

He spent the entire morning searching, questioning everyone he came to, but to no avail. Though many slaves had been put up for sale, no one had seen a woman with Natasha's coloring. All of the women had either had red or dark hair.

"She was not sold here," Selig explained as soon as he was finished trading. "A mutual friend told me that Thordis bragged that he was going to take her to Constantinople."

"Constantinople. Why so far?" All sorts of ominous reasons flitted through his brain.

"Because he thinks that he can get a higher price for her there. Apparently there is something about her: something that makes her different from the other slaves and quite a prize."

"Her beauty?"

Selig shook his head. "Though I do not doubt that she is lovely, Gorm sounded as if there was something else. A skill that few women possess."

Sean made the assumption that it had something to do with her horsemanship. "From my studies I know that the Byzantines have walled their city. Will we have any trouble getting in?"

Again Selig shook his head. "I know the gates by which the ships enter Constantinople. But we must be careful that Thordis doesn't get wind that we are following him. The city is a maze of avenues and twisting streets that would make it easy for him to evade us. Worse yet, he has bribed his way into the favor of those who frequent the bazaars and inhabit the palaces. If we are not careful we can find ourselves the victims of foul play."

Twenty-five

Natasha knew that her captors had arrived at their destination by the way they flitted around the ship like a nest of agitated bugs beneath a rock that has just been disturbed. Their faces were animated, and one of the more loathsome Vikings actually rubbed his fingers with his thumb as if he could already envision the profit that was about to be made on the poor unfortunates they had enslaved.

Although the Viking named Thordis had kept an arm's length away from her during the journey, he now hovered about her anxiously, circling around her again and again, running his fingers through her hair, pinching her cheeks, tracing the contours of her face with his index finger. All the while, she suffered his sudden attentions in silence. When he reached out to cup her breast, however, Natasha growled at him and pushed his hand away. If she was going to be treated like an animal, she would act that way. Angered by her actions, Thordis raised his hand but did not strike her.

During the journey, Natasha had listened carefully as the Vikings had talked among themselves. She had studied their hand gestures, trying to decipher bits and pieces of what they were saying. Now it seemed as if Thordis and two of the other men were discussing what was to be done with her, and the price that should be paid. One name was mentioned over and over—Demetrius—and she could only suppose that whoever that was would be her new owner.

Owner, but not master! Turning her back on Thordis and squaring her shoulders, she was determined to maintain her pride no matter what happened.

The air was filled with mumbled oaths and shouts as Thordis saw to it that the sail was furled and every man had a firm grip on the oars. The serpent ship moved up the shoreline like a huge dragon with oars for wings. Natasha looked toward the land, and her first impression was of one tremendous, unending stone wall, bisected at irregular intervals with gates. Looking at the walls, she wondered if they had been built to keep the people in, or as a precaution to keep unwanted people out. She decided that it must be the latter.

The ship sailed through an arch of a bridge that spanned the harbor, then passed by two fortified gates. When the Viking ship tried to enter, it was turned away and Natasha did not even try to smother her smile. Perhaps Thordis was not as welcome here as he supposed.

The harbor was massed with ships, a vast armada of merchant vessels and fishing boats as well as ships that had more than one sail and small huts on the deck, the likes of which she had never seen. All the vessels seemed to be heading toward another of the gates. This time, after Thordis handed over some of his precious coins, the Viking ship was allowed to enter.

Once the ship was moored inside the gate, Natasha was thrust into a strange, gaudily ornamented wagon and transported along a road that was covered with stones. It seemed that even the pathways were decorated in this large walled town.

Upon entering the city that she heard Thordis call Constantinople, Natasha had been awestruck. As she looked around, she was both fascinated and frightened by the great size of the city. Surrounded by water, with its tall buildings and strange, rounded and pointed roofs reflected in those waters, it was like a fantasy, the kind of place one only dreamed about. Perhaps its beauty was even beyond dreams.

The city teemed with people of every imaginable color, shape, and height—all types of humanity dressed in garments the likes of which she had never seen before. Though most of the people wore linens and furs, a few wore long tunics covered by rectangular coverings that were rich in texture and weave and exhibited a variety of colors that spanned the hues of the rainbow. Patterns of gold and silver made the garments shimmer in the sunlight. Jewels adorned many of the people and were as plentiful as stars in the sky.

It was a beautiful place. The coastline, the buildings, and the people all fascinated her. How she wished Sean were here to see what she was now seeing. He had told her of his longing to see such places. If only she could share her thoughts and the images she was seeing with him!

"Sean . . ." Reaching up, she was not surprised to find that her cheeks were wet. She felt apprehension grip her like a fist. What would be her place here? she wondered. Would this be her final destination?

Surrounded by Thordis and several of his Vikings, Natasha was escorted between massive stone buildings, past small craft shops, and through a colorful open-air bazaar. Sitting up as straight as she could, she stared out at the donkey carts, two-horse chariots, camels with saddles and riders, strange ornamented, curtained boxes that carried people on the shoulders of slaves by means of poles, and the elaborately dressed men on horseback. All the other people were walking, either leisurely or at such a brisk pace that they kept up with the wagon.

Natasha looked down at her own garments and felt self-consciously out of place. She looked as ragged and soiled as the beggers who roamed the cobbled streets, beseeching passersby for food. She eyed these impoverished men and women with pity, for certainly their plight was even greater than hers. How strange, she thought, that some should have so much here while others had so little.

The procession of Vikings traveled a long way before stopping beside yet another gate, this one at the entrance of a building. Natasha was pushed out of the carriage just as a small door was opened. Thordis made a great show of shouting at the youth who manned the gates, before they, too, were opened. A dark-skinned man gestured that the assemblage of Vikings was to wait in a large hall.

Once again Natasha was stunned by her opulent surroundings. She stared in wonder at the marble floors, the brightly colored mosaic walls, and the archways supported by carved and enameled pillars. Taking off one shoe, she touched the marble with her foot, recoiling as she found that, though it was beautiful, it was very uncomfortable to walk upon. Whoever these people were, she couldn't understand why they would want such hard floors, which were not as soft and yielding as earthen floors.

When the dark-skinned man returned, he motioned for them to follow him, then led them down several corridors floored with mosaic tiles, around an open courtyard crowded with colorful flowering shrubs and a bubbling fountain. They passed through a door to a chamber decorated with silken curtains and Arabian carpets. The tall, gaunt man with salt-and-pepper hair and beard who awaited them there was as grandly decorated as his surroundings.

It was the first time she had seen Thordis openly exhibit deference toward anyone, but as she watched. he bowed slightly at the waist and muttered a greeting. Natasha, meanwhile, remained in the shadows gazing at the man, assessing him from afar. Then, when Thordis addressed the man as Demetrius, her scrutiny intensified. Who was he? What kind of man was he? Why had Thordis brought her to him? Her inner questions intensified as the man moved toward her.

At first he appraised her from several feet away, then took a step closer, then another step, talking avidly to Thordis—not in the Viking tongue but in a language she had never heard before. When he was right in front of her, he raised his hands and Natasha cringed as she awaited the indignities of prodding and pinching she knew were to come.

The man did not grope her, however; instead, he took her hands. Saying something to her in a soft voice as if to soothe her, he turned them palms down, then palms up. Slowly he massaged each finger, all the while talking to Thordis. The man named Demetrius snapped his fingers, issued an order to one of his slaves, and then, when a piece of parchment, quill, and ink pot were brought to him, he handed them to Natasha and waited expectantly.

Realizing the importance of the moment, and that her success meant getting free of Thordis, Natasha was determined. For a long moment, she stared at the blank page; then, closing her eyes, Natasha tried to envision the written page that she had copied from so many times. As her eyes flickered open, she picked up the quill, dipping it in the inkpot and carefully transcribing the Latin letters from memory.

Thordis laughed triumphantly, then held out his hand in a gesture that stated that he wanted his payment. Without hesitation, Demetrius complied, and Natasha was shocked to see how many coins exchanged hands. Knowing how to write must truly make a person valuable. A deep respect for Sean's knowledge and skill swept over her, coupled with the love she already felt. Oh, how she missed him!

Demetrius rang a small bell on the table, and several young female slaves appeared. There were girls with blond hair like hers, red hair, black hair, and varying shades of brown. Some were pale, others were golden, and a few had skin the color of ebony. Forming a circle around her, they tugged at her, laughing gaily all the while. It soothed Natasha's apprehension to see that at least they did not appear to be miserable here.

She followed them along more halls, to a room off a small walled garden with flowering shrubs, colorful birds, and a small fountain. Silk hangings covered the walls and completely surrounded the large oval bed.

In a small alcove off the main room was a large sunken marble tub, into which water flowed just as it had in the fountains. Flower petals floated on the surface of the water, and as Natasha came closer she could smell their perfume.

Sighing, only then realizing how exhausted and dirty she was, she didn't protest as they helped her undress. She let her garments slip to the floor and pinned up her golden mass of hair with the combs they gave to her. The water in the bath was cold, but one the girls quickly rectified that by pouring in pitchers of warm water.

The young women helped her bathe, and Natasha laughed softly as she remembered how fearful she had once been of enjoying such luxury due to her fear of water. After so many days on the ocean, she had willfully conquered that fear and was now free just to relax as the women washed her body and then, taking out the combs, washed and perfumed her hair.

It was frustrating, for though each of the young women talked in turn, Natasha couldn't understand a word of what they were saying. Each spoke a different language, their speech as different one from another as their appearance. They did, however, seem to have a language that they all held in common: a language of simple words and hand signals that she was determined to learn.

One of the girls held up a polished silver mirror,

and as she looked at her face, Natasha cringed as she only now realized that the skin on her face was dry, her nose sunburned, and her hair bleached by the sun.

"I'll help you," one of the youngest slaves said softly, procuring some kind of ointment for her face. Though the language was not that of the Magyars or Slavs, the young woman spoke with a similar dialect. She told Natasha she was from a land far to the north and that she was a Finn. If she spoke slowly and distinctly, Natasha was able to communicate with her.

Slowly her feeling of total isolation was melting, and she felt strangely akin to these young women. "What is this place? Who is Demetrius?"

The young woman hesitated, then said, "He is a man who likes to collect beautiful things. Birds, flowering plants . . ."

"And women?"

The girl nodded.

"What if a woman doesn't want to be here. What then?" The girl's silence seemed to tell her that she hadn't any choice. A gilded cage this might be, but it was still a cage.

Reclining in the bath, letting the water wash over her, Natasha tried to sort things out in her mind as she relaxed. Obviously, Thordis and now Demetrius assumed that she knew more about writing than she actually did, but what would happen when Demetrius learned the truth? Would he take out his disappointment on her?

She sat up. "What is your name?"

"Dayna."

"Dayna, is there a way out of here?"

Dayna shook her head. "During the day we are watched by several guards, at night we are all locked in."

"Locked in!" She was a prisoner, then, with little

chance of gaining her freedom. "What about the others? How many are there? Has anyone ever escaped?"

"Escaped . . . ?" The expression on her face seemed to say that no one had even tried. "There are fifty of us now that you have come. Each with something special about her that makes her unique." Dayna blushed. "Demetrius likes the way I massage his neck and arms—a small accomplishment."

"What about the others?" Natasha accepted a small cake that Dayna offered and a goblet of red liquid. Wine.

Dayna pointed to each in turn. "Zoe is skilled at healing; Chantel is graceful when she dances; Eudora has the singing voice of an angel; Odelia can paint pictures; Tanya can play the harp; Pia the flute . . ." As she pointed to the various women, Dayna rattled off their various talents.

Natasha stood up and was immediately covered with linens that would dry her skin. She helped the young women towel her dry and slipped her arms into the soft, shiny tunic Dayna handed her.

"I will not share his bed, Dayna. . . ."

"That is not a choice that is yours to make," she whispered, tying a wide cloth belt around her waist. Leading Natasha to the bed, she turned the covers down and Natasha slipped between the silk sheets.

"I love someone else. I could never . . ." Her eyelids felt so heavy. She felt her head reeling as the room began to spin. *The wine!* Although there were hundreds of questions she wanted to ask, Natasha fell asleep as soon as her head touched the pillow.

Natasha awoke with a start to find Dayna standing by her bed. Quickly her thoughts coalesced in her brain. She remembered her arrival in the city, her meeting with Demetrius, and all that she and Dayna had talked about. "How long have I been asleep?"

"A long time. It's morning."

"Morning!" She hurried to get out of bed, taking the long aqua-colored tunic with long, tight sleeves that Dayna handed her. Quizzically she ran her fingers over the smooth, soft cloth.

"It's called silk. The material is woven by worms." Dayna giggled.

"Worms!" Natasha eyed it with sudden distaste. "Really?"

Dayna laughed again. "Really. It is just another of the Mother goddess's miracles that so lowly a creature could create such beauty."

Natasha slipped the tunic over her head, then took a second tunic from Dayna. This one was shorter and fuller, with wide sleeves that came to just below her elbow. It, too, was aqua, but a lighter shade, with designs running through it that she was certain were of gold.

"Until I came here I had never seen cloth like this, either. It's called brocade. And these are slippers made of velvet."

The garments and shoes felt cool and soft against her skin. Brushing her hair as Dayna held up a silver mirror, Natasha puzzled about this strange city. But not for long. As Dayna hurried her along, she walked through the wide halls to an area that overlooked the first inner court, which was filled with carefully tended flower beds, trees, and shrubs that were fully in bloom despite the fact that it was autumn.

"You must be hungry." The heavy aroma of flowers wafted up to the eating area; the chirping of birds could be heard.

She hadn't even thought about it, yet as she spied the cloth-laden table that was covered with platters and bowls of food, she was overcome with hunger and embarrassed as her stomach growled loudly.

The table was surrounded by young women, some

of whom Natasha had not seen the night before. She hesitated.

"Sit beside me."

Ravenously hungry, Natasha didn't wait. She attacked the food, stuffing bits of sweet bread, sliced fruit, and other morsels in her mouth and chewing loudly. Suddenly, she realized that the others weren't eating; instead, they were watching her eat. Blushing, she dropped a piece of cheese back on her plate.

"Why aren't they eating?"

"Because we must first say a prayer over the food and give thanks that we live in a city where everything is so bountiful."

"Oh . . ." Natasha remembered that Sean and the men and women dressed in gray had likewise mumbled over the table before they ate. She bowed her head accordingly, waiting until it was silent again before she reached for a small fruit-filled cake. She stuffed it in her mouth, savoring its texture and its taste. Certainly, they knew how to please the stomach here.

Dayna held out a cup of steaming hot liquid that smelled sweet and slightly pungent. "Try it. It's tea. It comes all the way from the East. China, May Ling's country." She nodded toward a young woman with black hair and golden skin, whose eyes were long-lashed and slightly slanted. "Some sweeten it. I put milk into it."

Natasha did both and found that she liked the taste. She emptied her cup, then asked for another. Around the table some of the young women burped, then covered their mouths with their hands.

Now that she had finished eating, Natasha gave vent to the questions that had troubled her last night but which she hadn't had time to ask. "Am I a prisoner here, Dayna?"

"A prisoner? No. You are a guest, or so Demetrius would say."

"I'm not a slave?"

Dayna hesitated. "No exactly . . ." She handed Natasha something very sweet to eat. "You are free to come and go from your quarters as you wish. There will be a palanquin and slaves at your disposal."

"A palanquin?"

Dayna explained that it was the curtained box that was carried on poles. Natasha thought of it as a wagon with human legs instead of wheels.

"What if I want to leave? To explore the city?"

Dayna's eyes stared into hers. "You must not leave these walls. Constantinople surpasses all other cities in wealth, but it also surpasses them in vice. You would be in great danger."

"Danger? What kind of danger?"

Dayna looked around her as if fearful of speaking too freely in front of the others. It gave Natasha the impression that perhaps not all the young women could be trusted. Already life in this strange, gilded city was puzzling. She was free to move about within the walls but not outside them. Although to her mind that meant she was a prisoner, she was told that she was a guest. It was much the same as the birds who sang so sweetly in the courtyard. Their wings had been clipped so that they could not escape, and she feared that if she attempted to leave, something similar and just as sinister just might happen to her. But what?

Twenty-six

The two dragon ships skimmed down the great river, and Sean watched as the water changed color from dark to almost white as it tumbled over sunken ledges of limestone and sandstone.

It had been a harrowing journey, with more dangerous cataracts in their path. The last rapids had claimed two men, for as the ship's bow had plunged, so had they. Sean grimaced as he remembered watching the current snatch the two Vikings, dragging them under. Like fearsome masks, their faces had bobbed up to the surface, their mouths gaping open. Though Baugi had made a valiant attempt to rescue them, it had been too late; the big black dog's eerie howls of grief had sent shivers up his spine.

After the mishap and tragedy and the exhausting experience of trekking across land dragging his ship, he was thankful that the channel was broad and deep and that a brisk wind made for good sailing.

But the danger wasn't over. By the time they reached the entrance to the Black Sea, the weather had grown stormy and the sea turbulent, and the wind, which had just recently been their friend, turned suddenly to a hazardous foe. Sean could hear Selig shouting out his commands as his crew hustled about with poles and ropes, rigging and tacking the spar as the ship rolled and pitched. Sean likewise yelled out commands to his men.

Suddenly, the deck plunged and dipped beneath Sean's feet with a fury that snapped the rigging and tore at the sail. As the huge Viking ship dipped dangerously low, the crewmen struggled to keep it afloat. Foaming spray sprang high in the air, splashing into the ship. Giant waves lashed out like hands, and the entire ship's company was faced with a desperate struggle to keep the ship afloat, some even using buckets to clear the water that flooded the deck.

Sean took his place at the stern, heaving on the tiller to keep the ship from broaching to in the fearsome waves. Then the rains came, pouring down upon the ship like water from a barrel. Those aboard the *Wolf's Head* fought for their very survival as the ocean threatened to turn the ship facedown in the churning waters.

"Look out, Kodran, the mast is beginning to creak," his brother called out just as the mast spun around, nearly hitting Sean in the back. The force of such a blow would have sent him over the side into the swirling dark water.

"A timely warning, brother." He turned toward Selig to vent his appreciation, then looked at his brother in horror as a giant wave lashed out like a hand, crushing another beam and sending it tumbling. "Selig, watch out!"

This warning was too late. With a resounding crash, a beam swerved, landing with full impact upon Selig's skull with a force that sent him hurtling over the edge.

"Selig!" Quickly, without thought to his own safety, Sean stripped off his leather corselet and stout, ornamented belt and dove into the swirling waters.

The ice-cold sea took Sean's breath away as he hit the waters. He heard a roaring in his ears as the ocean closed about his head. He felt as if his lungs would burst. The burning in his chest was unbearable. *Don't let the seawater fill your lungs,* he thought. If he did, he wouldn't have any hope of surviving.

Ignoring the icy-cold waves, using all the strength in his arms and legs, he fought to stay above water, but though he struggled, he felt the strong currents of the ocean carrying him farther and farther away from his ship. It was a helpless feeling. He thought about Natasha's fear of water and in that moment felt that same fear himself.

"God help me!"

Pushing with all his might against the fierce ocean water, Sean broke the surface. Air filled his lungs. Though the saltwater stung his eyes, he opened them wide, scanning the surface. *Blessed God, where is my brother?* The question was a torment to him. There was no sign of Selig—no trace of him at all. It was as if the ocean had swallowed him.

He was exhausted. Breathless. His battle with the currents had taken their toll on his strength, but he felt a renewed surge of energy as he saw a human form several feet away. With strong strokes he swam toward the shadow and was relieved to see that it was Selig. He was guided in his efforts by Baugi, who was also trying desperately to save his master.

Grabbing Selig by the arm, Sean pulled him toward the *Wolf's Head*, coughing as he swallowed some of the water. With Baugi in between the two brothers, they made it to the ship, where they were pulled out of the water by means of ropes.

"What were you doing out in that water?" Selig scolded as he dragged his hands through his wet hair.

For a long moment, Sean was too busy choking to talk, but then he said, "What was I doing? I was saving you!"

"Saving me? I didn't need saving. I've fallen overboard a dozen times or more and made it back to the boat." Selig glowered. "It looked to me as if *you* needed rescuing!"

"I wouldn't have needed help if that beam hadn't knocked you on the head and pushed you overboard."

Sean hurriedly took off his wet garments, replacing them with dry ones from his wooden sea trunk. "I jumped in to keep you from drowning!"

"And you would have been the one who would have drowned if not for Baugi." Taking off his clothing, Selig toweled himself dry, then slipped a dry tunic over his head. "He saved you."

"He saved *you*, or at least he helped me save you. I saved myself!" Suddenly, the two brothers started to laugh as they realized the foolishness of their quarreling.

"It doesn't matter who saved who, only that we are both safe and sound." Selig patted his brother on the back. "I wouldn't want to lose you, little brother."

"Nor I you, especially when I'm the one who is responsible for your being here."

Selig shook his head. "I came for two reasons: to help you find your woman, and for more selfish purposes. Riches! Kiev and Constantinople offer goods beyond your wildest dreams. . . ."

Having made peace, the two brothers fought the storm side by side; then, when at last the gale had subsided, they stood together near the prow of the ship looking out to sea as they talked about many things: their early years, their father, the women they loved, and what they were going to do once they reached Constantinople, the "queen of cities."

Sean was weary from the many days of traveling. His skin was burned from sun, wind, and salt air. Those times when the wind was weak and they had to row, he had joined in, the muscles in his arms, legs, and back straining to pull the heavy oars. Still, as the ship sailed into the narrow strait between the Black Sea and the Sea of Marmara, known as the Bosporus, he felt more alive than ever before, with the exception of those moments he had spent with Natasha.

Constantinople, located on the site of the ancient Greek colonial port of Byzantium, was built on an easily defended small triangular bit of land on the European shore of the Bosporus Strait. Directly to its north was the crescent shaped mouth of a small river emptying into the Bosporus, known as the Golden Horn, which formed the only natural harbor in the area. To its south stretched the Sea of Marmara, which emptied into the Mediterranean through the Dardanelles Strait.

Sean had heard stories about Constantinople. It had always been the city of his dreams, a place he had longed to see one day. Now as they sailed closer, he saw that it was everything he had envisioned and much more.

With its sea walls and the Golden Horn, Constantinople dominated traffic on a crucial seaway. Moreover, the city was located on the most direct overland pathway between Europe and West Asia. Through fortifications of this land triangle and the Golden Horn, Constantinople had been transformed into an impregnable fortress-city that controlled all the important lines of communication between the European and Asian worlds.

Sean knew it to be the largest, strongest, wealthiest, and most culturally developed city in all of Europe. It symbolized the Orthodox Christian Roman imperial order. With its massive triple land walls and encircling seawalls, it was considered the God-protected capital for all of His chosen Christian people, home to the supreme Christian emperor, and site of the patriarchal Cathedral of Hagia Sophia, the heart of Orthodox Christianity.

As they sailed through the arch of a bridge, Selig described Constantinople as a city of magnificent palaces, broad avenues lined with trees, open-air bazaars, and blocks of arcades filled with craftsmen. At the same time there were three- and four-story pestholes of poverty, and narrow alleys heaped with refuse.

Sean knew from his studies that it was a city of contradictions, the center of a great Christian empire, and yet its wealth had been generated by heathen trading practices. It was a place where godliness went hand in hand with intrigue and evil. It was a mysterious, exotic city of beauty and mystery. Somewhere within its depths was Natasha, and Sean knew that he would not rest, nor take comfort for himself until she was found and safely in his arms again.

The harbor was filled with merchant vessels and fishing boats. As they sailed past them, Sean scrutinized each ship, searching for the one ship that was important to him. At last he saw the huge serpent's head and the red-and-white sails.

"Thordis is here! There is his ship."

Having found it, Sean was frustrated that it was deserted. Apparently, Thordis was somewhere in the city, but wherever he was they would find him, and when they did, if they had to beat it out of him they would find out where he had taken Natasha.

Leaving the *Wolf's Head* behind to intercept Thordis should he try to leave the city, Sean sailed with Selig to the Plateia Gate, where they moored the ship. They walked along broad avenues, past the church of St. Savior Pantocrater and beneath the great viaduct of Valens. Sean wanted to take the lead but knew he had to follow Selig. He had only been to Constantinople in his dreams; Selig had been here before in reality.

Behind the walls Sean could at last view what he had only read about: the impressive civic structures, including palace complexes, the huge circus arena of the Hippodrome, where events such as chariot races, hunts, mystery plays, and acrobatics were staged by the imperial government.

Just as there had been in ancient Rome, there were aqueducts and water cisterns. The municipal government and the Orthodox Church ministered to the social and health needs of the inhabitants.

Even though it was not the height of the trading season, buyers and sellers alike swarmed the streets, haggling in at least a dozen languages. By their clothing and speech, Sean could tell that there were Greeks, Armenians, Bulgars, Jews, Turks, Khazars, Syrians, Slavs, Egyptians, Italians, and others drawn from the corners of the Empire, blended with a colorful infusion of merchants and soldiers from Scandinavia, the Rus, Italy and Arabia. One of the monks who had resided in a monastery in this imperial city had told Sean that residents benefited from organized fire brigades, plumbing and sewage systems, free hospitals, and another amenity unknown in the rest of Europe: public baths. Open-air markets nurtured commerce. Numerous monasteries provided food, shelter, and health care to the homeless and destitute. It was a city based on glories of the past, yet a city way ahead of its time.

"If you truly want to find Thordis, then follow me, Kodran," Selig ordered. He led Sean to the slave mart.

Just watching the unfortunate captives being paraded about in the nude so that they could be inspected by prospective buyers made Sean feel sick. "It's a hateful business. And Thordis is a hateful man."

"As well I know!"

"Was he the one who sold you into slavery?" Sean inquired.

"No! To the contrary, he helped me after I had escaped. We became friends, but our friendship ended when he insulted my wife." It was a long story that Selig related as they watched the human merchandise being pinched, prodded, and examined as thoroughly as if they were horses, goats, or cows.

"Thordis captured the man who had enslaved me. He brought him to the settlement to give to me as a gift." Selig kicked at a loose stone in the cobbled street. "To make a long story brief, the man Thordis had enslaved was kin to Gwyneth, my wife. When he escaped, Thordis insisted that she had set him free and demanded that she be punished. For a time I locked her in a storage shed, but when she told me that she was not guilty I set her free. Thordis and I fought a battle so that by Viking custom I could clear her name."

"Once friends, now foes."

Selig didn't answer. He was too intent on staring at the procession that was just entering the area. "It's he!"

Sean whirled around, and in that instant his heart pounded and his anger rose to a boiling point. But where was Natasha? What had he done with her?

In a fit of rage he pushed past the others in the crowd and flung himself upon Thordis. "Where is she?"

At first Thordis didn't recognize him, then as he did, he grinned. "I sold her! If you wanted to bid on her, you are too late."

Anger exploded behind Sean's eyes. Maybe once he wouldn't have been a match for Thordis, but after weeks of rowing and dragging the ship through the mud, he was stronger than he had ever been before.

A fierce fight ensued. Sean and Thordis rolled over and over on the ground, but there was no doubt about the outcome. Sean's fury seemed to give him superhuman strength. Closing his fingers around Thordis's throat, he squeezed tightly, watching as the sparkle of fear came to his eyes.

"Where is she?" When Thordis didn't answer he squeezed tighter. "I ask you again, where is she? Who did you sell her to?"

The answer came out in a hiss. "Demetrius!"

Twenty-seven

The garden was quiet. Natasha stood at the entrance for a long, lingering moment, then moved toward the white stone fountain. Letting the morning sun strike her bare shoulders, she listened to the cool voice of the water that gurgled from the sculptured dolphin's mouth as it spilled to the basin below.

Although she enjoyed the hours she spent with the other women, there were times when she felt the need to be alone so that she could think and remember who and what she was before she came here. She didn't want to become vain and spoiled or forget the people who had mattered so very much in her life, though she realized that such a thing was possible in this luxurious house with its terraced gardens, gabled roofs, and tiled floors and walls.

I'm still the same inside. The same courage, strength, and tenacity.

On the outside, however, she was slowly undergoing a change. Something had been used on her hair to lighten it to a shade that was nearly white. Instead of falling to her shoulders, it was curled and often piled high atop her head in the Greek style. Sometimes they even sprinkled powder in her hair, mixed with gold dust so that it would sparkle, or wove gold wire into it so that it would stay piled high on her head.

Paste of palm oil mixed with dregs of wine for reddening the lips was oftentimes applied to her mouth.

She used powdered chalk for the throat and the curve of the breasts. Though she would not give in to the pastes that were applied to the skin, she did let Dayna put dark brown around her eyes, and an aqua powder on her eyelids. Holes had been pierced in her ears so that she could wear earrings.

Natasha remembered how Dayna had laughed at her when she had thought the ear bobs would stick to her ears on their own. After watching her fumble around helplessly, grumbling as they fell on the ground, Dayna had shown her how the ear jewelry was slipped through the tiny hole in her ear. She had made the decision that she wanted to be able to wear earrings, too.

The sight of Dayna heating a long needle in a candle flame was unnerving, yet as the other women stared at her, she made up her mind to face the procedure bravely. Gritting her teeth to keep from crying out when the needle went through her earlobe, she sighed when the ordeal was over. It had been her sacrifice to vanity.

Vanity . . . On the steppes, and then with Sean, she had been much too busy to pay much attention to her appearance. Here, however, it seemed that a woman's favorite way to while away the time was sitting in front of gilded mirrors looking at herself while changing her hair or artfully applying paint to her face.

Natasha had stood watching the other women as they dipped their fingers from jar to jar and color to color, then touched their faces. With black kohl they outlined their eyes and darkened their lashes. Their nipples were stained with henna. Henna for fingernails as well. They also adhered to a strange habit of reddening the palms of the hands to show up the whiteness of the skin.

"If Sean saw me now he wouldn't recognize me," she whispered. Though her garments were of different colors, they were always made of either brocade or silk. Tunics and dalmatics, they were called. The tunic had wide sleeves coming just to her elbows. Both the hem and the sleeves were edged with a wide border of embroidery and gold braid. The long white pellium fell in a train carried over her left arm and was embroidered with gold thread. On her feet were velvet slippers. She wore a necklace and earrings in her newly pierced ears.

Everything was beautiful here, but although she was completely surrounded by physical perfection and splendor, it was a beauty that disturbed her. Something sinister seemed to be hovering over her. Worse yet, her inactivity troubled her. She wanted to be outside in the open air, not locked inside.

As each day passed, Natasha thought more and more of Sean. Although she was relatively content, there were times when she lay between the silk sheets and could not sleep. The bed was much too large for one person, and she wished with all her heart that she could somehow share it with him. Her whole body ached to feel his arms around her, his chest pressed against her breasts.

"Natasha, what are you doing all by yourself? Come and join us. The others are very interested in you."

Natasha had begun to learn the language the other young women used to communicate—a unique multilingual dialect comprised of equal amounts of Greek, Norse, and Arabic and embellished with words and expressions from a variety of languages. First she learned the names for specific objects, then learned to express herself in complete sentences.

She followed the young woman through the carved wooden doors to the eating area. The table was spread with baskets of grapes and pomegranates, wheat bread, and coarse white cheese.

Several of the women were seated around the table. They wore long, loose tunics of white or light colors.

Some were barefoot, others wore light sandals. Two or three wore full trousers and small jackets. One had her hair and face swathed in veils. All were adorned with gold or silver bracelets, finger rings and earrings. Their whispers and laughter hummed in the air. They quickly grew silent as she sat on a pillow closest to the doorway.

Natasha ate quickly, though once she was finished, she wondered why she had hurried. Aside from sitting or lying around on cushions, gossiping or telling stories, there was very little for the women to do.

"Has Demetrius sent for you?" Dayna asked, mumbling as she let a grape roll around on her tongue.

"No. . . ."

So far, Demetrius hadn't made any innuendoes nor tried to seduce her in any way but by the way that he looked at her whenever he passed by, she knew that the time was coming soon. The very idea unnerved her, and she prepared herself to fend off any advances. She wanted only Sean beside her in bed. She would not let her loneliness goad her into allowing her to seek a substitute for the man she truly loved.

Besides, even if she hadn't loved Sean, she would never have picked a man like Demetrius. He was too old for her, among other things. She was physically repulsed by him. There was something about his eyes and the touch of his cold hands that made her shiver. Even so, she doubted that he would be satisfied just watching her practice writing with her parchment and quill.

"He will . . ." Dayna informed her that there was to be a feast in her honor. "A haunch of roast goat wrapped in vine leaves with almonds in the sauce will be served."

Natasha remembered that her father had always said that goat on a spit was a dish fit for a king. That was why she was taken aback when Dayna said something to the other young women and they laughed. Somehow, Natasha got the impression that they were laughing at her.

Natasha had soon learned that there was fierce jealousy and rivalry among some of the women—petty quarrels and tattlings. A few of the women carried small jeweled scissors with them, and she had begun to wonder whether it was for protection or so that they could do some mischief to any woman they thought to be a serious rival. One thing was certain: a swift stab with the point could be as fatal as a knife wound.

"The feast would have been held sooner, but Demetrius had to be cautious."

"Cautious?" Natasha wondered why.

Dayna cocked one kohl-darkened brow. "It seems that there was a confrontation at the slave mart. A terrible scuffle, so I'm told."

"A confrontation?"

"A fight, and the man who caused the trouble was asking about you!"

"Me!" Her heart palpitated, then seemed to swell in her chest until she couldn't breathe. Could it have been Sean? Her hands started shaking as if she were suffering from a sudden chill at the very thought.

Demetrius. The name resonated in Sean's ears and pounded in his brain. "Why couldn't he have been a merchant or a tradesman? Why did he have to be a man with an imperial rank?" It would make him a more powerful enemy and make it all the more difficult to get Natasha away from him, Sean thought as he stood in the doorway to his small room.

The palace was the political center of the empire. Byzantines flocked to the imperial court in search of rank an office. They wanted this because imperial rank was the only recognized mark of status in their society.

Imperial office brought wealth. The man named Demetrius held a senior title. He was a *patrikios.* Though holders of such title held no particular office, he was nonetheless an important figure at court.

Sean listened to the deep, rumbling snore of the guardsman who shared the room with him. He was now a guard, hired by Demetrius himself to be the protector of his palatial house and the gates that imprisoned his collection of women, one of whom was Natasha.

Although Sean had hoped to buy her from her new owner, he had soon learned by way of the grapevine that it was out of the question. Once Demetrius bought a young woman, she was his for life. Having learned this, he had thought of a plan to enable him to keep an eye on her from a safe distance and had been able to hire himself out as a guard.

Many of the guardsmen in the city were Norse, Rus, Slav, Turk, or Greek. Sean had wanted to keep his heritage a secret just in case Thordis had given warning that he might try to rescue Natasha; thus, he had taken on the name, clothes, and appearance of a Turk. Luckily, his dark hair and sun-tanned skin enabled him to disguise himself as such.

In his role as a guard, Sean wore knee-high brown leather boots, full crimson pants that were gathered at the knee, and a knee-length tunic of brownish pin wool that reached to midthigh. He also wore a leather corselet molded to the shape of his body, and a wide-brimmed helmet with a metal crest. Whenever he was on duty, he wore the helmet to hide his face, just in case he should be recognized as the man who had caused all the havoc at the slave market.

"Natasha . . . !" The thought of finding and rescuing her obsessed him.

Selig, Ref, and Sean had discussed a plan for rescuing her. The people of the city used palanquins to travel about the city. These vehicles had curtains that could be closed for privacy. If they could smuggle Natasha out of the manor and somehow get her into one of these palanquins, then they could hurry to the ships and immediately set sail. He was impatient, anxious, determined.

Sean had quickly familiarized himself with the palatial home of Demetrius. It consisted of three attached buildings, each successively smaller as one proceeded from the street to the high rear wall.

The first two were three stories high, built around inner courtyards and gardens; the third was a single-story rectangle facing a walled garden. The lowest level of the first building contained Demetrius's offices, reception rooms, a large dining hall, four small dining rooms, and other rooms for entertaining guests. The floors above contained his personal living quarters as well as those for his sons, male guests, and male slaves.

Natasha was living in the third, or smallest section. All entrances to where the women were kept were carefully guarded by huge, menacing armed eunuchs, who looked as if they were prepared to kill if given provocation.

Pretending to be engaging in morning exercise with sword and javelin, Sean had spent five hours in the sun early this morning. He paced along the catwalk, then entered the courtyard.

The terraced enclosure had been deserted, but as he looked toward the fountain, he had seen Natasha from a distance. Her blond hair had been pinned atop her head, and she had been dressed in the tunics and drapings of the Byzantines, but he had recognized her. As she gazed at the stone dolphin that spewed water into a stone basin—water brought down to the city by a huge aqueduct left over from the great age of the Romans—she had looked reflective but not unhappy.

Seeing her had totally unnerved him, so much so that it had taken a moment to regain his composure.

It had been so long since he had held her in his arms that his first impulse was to run to her, but a show of emotions wouldn't do either of them any good.

Guardsmen were allowed to fill their canteens and drink from the fountain; thus, he had an excuse to be in the garden, but not to talk with her. He had urged himself to use caution, moving slowly. Too slowly. Before he could attract her attention, she had been wisked away by one of the other women. It had been like losing her all over again. Sean had been so sick at heart that he couldn't do anything but look toward the doorway where she had disappeared, staring after her for a long, long time. Then he had returned to his quarters.

The sound of snoring was disturbing. Leaving the room, Sean soothed his anxiety by walking, scrutinizing his surroundings as he strolled. He walked beside the wall, then stood atop the parapet. From there he could look down on the landing stage paved with white marble. It was guarded by statues, both heroic and grotesque, each in its pool of shadow. He moved down a craggy flight of steps that led down to a place used only by guardsmen. For a moment he hesitated as he saw one of the statues below him move.

He crouched behind the parapet, ready to pounce. Before he had a chance to lunge, however, he heard a familiar voice. "Kodran . . ."

It was Selig. He grabbed his arm and drew him out of the sunlight and into the shadows.

"Tomorrow night. That is when we'll make our move. It's all arranged."

Twenty-eight

Once when Natasha was a little girl, her brothers had caught a colorful singing bird in a net and put it in a wooden cage for her pleasure. She had loved it immediately and had made it her duty to care for it and tend it, giving it seeds and berries every day. To her childish mind, the pretty bird had everything it needed, and she had enjoyed watching it, waiting for it to sing and fill the air with music. But once caged, the bird had never trilled cheerily again. It had sickened and died. Tearfully she had asked her father why.

"The bird was a wild thing, Tasha. It needed to be free."

"But Papa, I gave him treats and loved him in my heart. Wasn't that enough?"

She remembered the look on his face as he shook his head. "No, Tasha. Freedom . . . freedom is the most precious thing of all."

Now, as she sat in the garden she fully realized how true her father's words were. *Freedom.* How she longed for it now! She wasn't like Dayna, Eudora, Tanya, Zoe, or Pia. She would never be content here.

Freedom . . .

Seeking refuge and solitude from the others in the garden, she sat on a carved bench of marble and watched a pair of green-and-blue songbirds flit from tree to tree, singing their hearts out. They were happy.

For a moment as she watched them, so was she. At least in the garden she felt a semblance of freedom, and the fresh air and smell of the flowers revived her and gave her hope.

It was always pleasant in the garden. She could feel the sun on her face, feel the breeze ruffle her hair, and listen to the sound of spraying water from the fountain. Whenever she was in the garden, she felt a new awareness of life surging through her, a renewal of dreams and the optimism to realize what a beautiful world it was.

She turned her head and looked toward another tree, where a small yellow bird and its mate were building a nest. Even when they dropped the twigs or grass from their beaks, they didn't give up but seemed to work together to create their tiny home.

Strange, how the sight of those two little birds should once again make her think of Sean. It was strange, but although they hadn't spent much time together, he was and always would be in her heart.

Closing her eyes, she envisioned him in her daydreams, remembering how close to him she had felt. It was as if he were there with her, as if his presence sat beside her. She had an eerie feeling that if she but opened her eyes she would see him. It was a sentiment that both comforted and haunted her.

"Natasha . . ."

She smiled as she imagined his voice calling out to her.

"Tasha . . ."

She seemed to hear it again. Opening her eyes, she thought she saw someone—a man—watching her from behind a tree. Squinting her eyes against the sun, she tried to see his face, but then he darted away and seemingly vanished.

"Natasha!" The voice that called to her now was not the same voice.

She turned her head and saw that Dayna had come

out to the garden to join her, but this time there wasn't the usual smile upon her face.

"What's the matter?"

"It's . . . it's Eudora. She angered me just now."

The birds in the garden, although uncaged, were nearly tame. Natasha watched as a green-and-blue bird lit on a branch just above Dayna's head, trilling right in her ear.

Natasha gasped as Dayna reached up and caught it in her hand, crushing the bird with a malice Natasha had never seen exhibited by her before. Then she threw the dead body to the ground.

"Why did you do that? How could you?" Natasha's heart ached for the bird. She felt sick at heart and at her stomach.

"It reminded me of Eudora. How I wish it had been her just now!" Just as quickly as she had displayed her anger, Dayna smiled again. "Come . . . let's go to the pool." The pool was the center of activity where the women sat or lay on cushions, gossiping or swimming and often splashing each other. Though Natasha was not in the mood, she followed Dayna, fearing that she might take out her strange mood on another poor creature.

As she walked, Natasha was filled with foreboding, fearful that if she didn't get away from this strange place she would either die or be destroyed like the bird.

Sean was discouraged. He had come so close to Natasha just now, so close that he had been able to attract her attention when he had whispered her name, only to be chased away once again by one of the women. He had to be careful; still, he was determined to find a way to talk with Natasha.

Returning to his room, he picked up his helmet and plopped it on his head. He had better return to his post at the wall before his absence was noted. Critically he eyed his quarters. It was a small room, nearly as small as the beehive hut he had shared at the monastery. His bed was a strip of gray canvas stretched taut between two X-shaped posts. On the white plaster walls were black and white mosaic tiles, an attempt at elegance to go with the surroundings. Against the wall was a chest of olive wood, inlaid with ebony in patterns of twisting laurel leaves.

"Omar . . . what are you doing in here? Omar!"

At first he didn't respond; then as he remembered that Omar was the name he had been given, he turned around to see his bunk mate looking at him from the doorway, his arms across his chest.

"I forgot something. My helmet," he answered in Greek, the language used at court.

The other man grinned. "Well, snatch it up and then hurry. I'm envious and you are one lucky fellow."

"Me? Why?" For a moment, he feared that perhaps he had been seen out in the garden and that the luck spoken of was Natasha.

"Your duty today is to go with Demetrius's wife to the Hippodrome."

"The Hippodrome?" Why him?

"Aye, the Hippodrome. Some men have all the luck." Moving past Sean to the small table, he reached into a vase and pulled out several coins. "While you are there, place a bet on the horses for me, will you?"

Sean nodded, thankful that so far his disguise had not been detected.

"Now you had better hurry. Sibyl, Demetrius's wife, is not known for patience."

Sean hurried to the courtyard just in time to take Sibyl's hand and escort her to the waiting cart, an opulent, well-upholstered conveyance that displayed the family's stature and wealth. Sean walked beside it as the vehicle moved along the tree-bordered avenues to the Mese, which led through several forums to the

Hippodrome next to the imperial palace. He watched as myrtle and rosemary were sprinkled on the cobblestones in order to mask the normal street odors. Even so, it seemed that there was always the strong smell of horses and the stench of camel dung.

As they walked, beggers jostled the cart, thrusting their bony arms and skinny fingers through the openings, all the while wailing in high, shrieking cries. Sean tried to push them back, but that only seemed to make them all the more violent in their demands. They clawed at Sibyl's tunic and stretched their hands right up into her face. Sean felt pity for these poor people whose bodies were only barely covered with shreds of cloth. Some were crippled and maimed. Some were diseased, their skin covered with sores.

"What is the matter with you, Omar? Strike them down if need be. Keep them away!"

Though it deeply troubled him to have to do so, Sean did as he was told, pushing them to the ground or threatening them with his sword. Still, as unnerving as this duty was, it gave him a chance to see part of Constantinople.

Constantinople was an enigma to him. It was at the height of its glory, surpassing ancient Rome and Alexandria, Baghdad, and Cordova in trade, wealth, luxury, beauty, refinement, and art. It's architecture consisted of stone palaces and houses that were gabled, terraced, and domed, with balconies, loggias, gardens, pavilions, and gazebos. The use of stone and marble was as common as the use of mud and wood elsewhere. Physically it was everything he had imagined it to be.

Churches seemed to be everywhere, glowing with candles and lamps and smelling of incense. It was said that there were as many churches as there were days in the year, and many of them were jewels with altars enshrining the most revered and precious relics in all of Christendom. Monasteries, too, were unashamedly magnificent. Unlike in Eire, where faith was judged by good works and dedication, here it was seemingly judged by the amount of incense, finery, and pageantry.

Markets were filled with goods from all over the world. There were thousands of shops and bazaars. Every luxury available could be found, from silks to marble, from doors inlaid with silver to plates made of silver or gold. It was easy to be impressed until you looked closely, for if Constantinople surpassed all other cities in wealth, it also surpassed them in vice; thus, although he had dreamed about it, fantasized about it, spiritually the city deeply disappointed him.

All the sins of a wealthy city could be found there. Sin and poverty. For every rich man there were fifty who were poor, like the poor unfortunates dressed in rags he had to shove to the cobbled streets. And there were the slaves, as plentiful as leaves on a tree, awaiting their masters' commands.

Many of the citizens believed in magic, astrology, sorcery, and witchcraft. Houses of vice, where men could buy sexual favors, could be found on nearly every street. Sean had heard the talk among the guards, who smirked about their exploits and the bribery that went on at court. Though he had been a guard for just a few days, he had seen worse things with his own eyes: first the blinding of a political rival, then the assassination of an ambitious foe. Brutality, greed, and piety seemed to go hand in hand. The populace could be bloodthirsty, turbulent, and eager to participate in beast baitings, pagentry, gambling, horse races, and womanizing six days a week, and then atone for their vices at church on the seventh day.

Demetrius's wife was given a cushioned seat in a pillared box near the emperor's loge. Because it was on the upper level, it offered an excellent view of the entire arena. Though there was a slave to attend Sibyl, she nonetheless seemed to call upon Sean for every little thing that concerned her comfort, to such a point that he feared she might have eyes for him.

"Omar . . . a pillow for my back."

He hurried to comply, cringing as the tips of her fingers caressed his hand.

"Are you thirsty?" Holding up her glass, she offered him a sip of her chilled wine. "How long have you been in Constantinople, Omar?"

"Not long," he answered evasively, fearful that her questioning might somehow unmask his disguise.

"You must be enchanted by our city. It's built on seven hills, just like Rome."

"It's impressive and beautiful."

"Much different from where you come from, or so I would suppose."

Sean answered truthfully. "Very different." Suddenly he longed for the lush greenery of Eire.

"Are you a Moslem?"

He was startled by the directness of her question. "Yes," he lied.

"Mmmmm. Well, you might change your mind once you see the beauty of Hagia Sophia. It means Holy Wisdom." She told him about the mosaics which depicted scenes from the Bible, the life of Christ, and the lives of saints and martyrs. "Every picture was created from thousands of tiny pieces of stone, all almost identical in size."

"So I have heard."

She startled him with another bold question. "Are you married? And if so, how many wives do you have?"

He stiffened. "Just one." Then he smiled. "That is enough for some men."

She started to say something else, then concentrated on the action in front of her, and Sean was more grateful to the horsemen down below than he could ever express.

The Hippodrome was an elongated oval several thousand feet long and about six hundred feet wide.

Down the center ran the *spina,* a low stone barrier around which the races were run. Along the top of the spina were sculptures in bronze and stone, some of which Sibyl told him had been brought all the way from Egypt.

"There will be nine chariot races today, each one more exciting than the last, or so I hope. . . ." She told him that the first two in each set of three were called heats.

Sean could not only see the horses as they came into the arena; he could feel their thundering hooves shaking the ground. Four chariots hurtled into the arena to the cheers and urging of the spectators. The small, lightweight chariots were pulled each by a single horse.

Clouds of dust and the cedar shavings on the ground filled the air as the drivers raced their chariots around the course four times. Two winners from each of the heats met in a final third race to determine the final winner.

"Have you ever seen such horsemanship?" Sibyl asked, eliciting a laugh from Sean. He had seen the best. He had seen Natasha on a horse, and that amazing sight made these other horsemen pale by comparison. "Do you find something amusing?"

"I was just wondering if you were going to place any bets. One of the other guards wanted me to place a bet for him. Perhaps you can give me some advice."

"Place your money on the black horse!"

The air was suddenly filled with shouting as the onlookers engaged themselves in heavy betting. Taking a chance, Sean put the guard's money on the black horse, just as she advised. As the race got underway, he joined in as the audience cheered their favorite horses on. The black horse was the winner.

"You see? I told you."

Sean placed another wager on the next race and the next, again taking her advice. Again he won. It was easy to see how such gambling could become a habit.

As the races continued, Sean found that he was enjoying himself, particularly when the second set of races was run by larger, two-horse chariots. Then the third set, which consisted of huge chariots pulled by four horses, began.

Excitement pounded through his veins as the four contestants pulled close together in their chariots, their horses panting and snorting, hooves pounding. Around and around the chariots moved, seeming to head toward the wall at the end of the arena, but always at the last moment swerving around the tip of the *spina*.

A feeling of anticipation moved through the crowd as there was a pause before the final race. Acrobats and jugglers had entertained after each set of races, and Sean laughed along with the crowd. Laughter turned to boos, however, as the time before the final race grew much longer than the audience would stand for.

"Why not be daring? Place all of the money you have won on this last race?" Sibyl's smile was challenging, a challenge that Sean accepted. "Bet on the Magyar!"

"The Magyar?" Sean's couldn't hide his surprise.

"His name is Osip the Tall. He is from the steppes. He was brought here as a slave, but he proved to be so able at handling horses that his master trained him as a chariot racer. He is always the winner."

Osip. The name sounded strangely familiar, and he wondered whether it could possibly be the same Osip that Natasha had spoken of, the man who had taken her father's place as leader of the caravan. Quickly he placed a bet on him.

This time when the race started, he was doubly fascinated, watching Osip whip and curse at the horses as they circled the arena, so close to the other chariots that there was only the length of a thumb between them. Suddenly, when it came time for the drivers and horses to swing the curve, Osip cut in front of his nearest rival, ramming his chariot into another. The horses went down as the chariots crashed. The drivers were thrown backward, and though the other chariots swerved, trying to get to the outside of the ring and around the fallen horses and drivers, they misjudged the distance. Sean watched in horror as the two fallen men were trampled.

"You won! See, I told you." Sibyl stood up and brushed at her gown, unaffected by the tragedy.

At first Sean gave her the benefit of the doubt, but in the conversation that ensued with some of the other onlookers, it became apparent that not only had they seen the bloodied men on the ground, they had reveled in the excitement.

"Omar, you forgot your winnings!" Sybil held the money out to him.

Blood money, Sean thought. "Keep it. I don't want it or need it." He looked on in disgust as the dead and mutilated bodies were carried away. He felt disgust at these people and their way of life.

During the journey back to Demetrius's home, Sean opened his eyes fully to the reality of Constantinople. Though he tried to tell himself that there were hundreds of men who gave themselves to the tasks of administration and statesmanship and had somehow saved the city from total ruination, he was nonetheless disheartened. Though once he would have given anything he owned to live in a city such as this, he was now interested in only one thing, finding Natasha and then leaving Constantinople behind in the mists that often blew in from the sea.

Twenty-nine

Night came like a dark stranger, quickly and silently cloaking the earth with darkness. Sean paced alone along the catwalk. Leaning on the parapet, he could look down. Far below him against the dark stone walls, the waters of the Marmara, the Marble Sea, lapped softly. He leaned his elbows on the wall, trying to maintain his calm and losing the battle.

Where within these walls is she? Even though he had seen her just this morning, he had no idea where her quarters were, but he had to find out. They were going to make their escape, but first he had to find her and let her in on the plan.

Sean had tried to find time earlier in the day to search for her, but his job as guard had taken up all his time. Now, however, he decided to risk his safety and look for her. His starting point for the search was the courtyard and the dolphin fountain.

He was in luck. Hiding in the shadows, he could see the silhouettes of the women through the wall hangings as they relaxed after their supper. The air still held the scents of the food they had partaken of, and Sean fought against his hunger. He hadn't had time to eat. Cupping his hands, he tried to quell his aching stomach with the fountain's cool water.

Suddenly, he heard the soft sounds of music. He stepped back, fearful that he might have been seen lurking about, but no one came to scare him away, so he stayed to listen as a strong, clear, melodic singing voice filled the air. Whoever she was, she sang so sweetly that for a moment he was certain that she could charm the stone dolphin down from its pedestal. For a long, soothing moment, the lovely voice enchanted him.

All too soon the singing stopped, and he watched as the women dispersed to go to their own quarters. Squinting against the darkness, he followed the young women, taking extra precautions that he would not be seen.

Down long corridors, through double doors, past wall hangings and through gardens he walked, searching all the while for that one special face and then having the luck to find her. Natasha's quarters were at the far end of the hall. Sean waited until all the other women were in bed; then, using the tip of his sword, he opened the lock.

She didn't hear him enter until he called out her name. "Tasha!"

Slowly she turned, afraid to believe; then, as she caught sight of his face she felt joy, elation, and passion roil within her like a frantic whirlpool.

In the blinking of an eye she ran toward him; then she was safe within the circle of his arms, kissing him, whispering his name. "I wanted you to find me, but I feared they had taken me so far away that I would be lost to you. How . . . ?"

He silenced her question with a kiss, such a fierce joining of mouths that she gasped when at last they pulled free of each other to breathe. Then no words needed to be said. They were moaning with relief, agony, and passion.

"Do we dare . . . ?" If they were caught, it might well mean her death, his, or possibly both. Still, it had been so long.

The faint rays of moonlight that streamed through a tiny window in the roof were the only source of light.

Still, he could see her beauty as he looked at her. She was a vision. The blue of her tunic set off her wide blue eyes and fine complexion; her golden hair made her look like a queen.

Natasha could see how greatly Sean had also changed. His skin was tanned a red-brown hue, making his eyes seem all the more blue. His lithe body was muscular and hard. His dark brown hair was streaked from the sun.

"You're even more beautiful than I remember," he whispered. "I have missed you more than you know."

The sight and smell and touch of her was intoxicating. His eyes feasted on her beauty. "I preferred your hair flying about your shoulders," he said softly, reaching out to pull out the pins. In an instant, her blond hair cascaded like a silken waterfall across her shoulders.

Natasha could read the desire in his eyes—desire that matched her own. A warm tingling swept over her as she reached up and held him close.

"We don't dare. . . ." he sighed, but as he spoke he moved closer, brushing her breasts lightly with his hands. The heat from his body enveloped her.

It was a sultry night, a lovers' eve. From a distance they could hear the crickets in the courtyard serenading them as if they knew that her life, her heart, was entwined with Sean's. Warmly, sensuously, her body, too entwined with his.

"Natasha . . ." Sean was unable to take his eyes away from her loveliness.

The air crackled with anticipation, pulsated with expectancy, surged with promise. A shiver danced up and down her spine as he picked her up and carried her to the bed. For a timeless moment they stared at each other; then he took a step closer.

Slowly his hands closed around her shoulders, pulling her to him. At first he simply held her, his hands exerting a gentle pressure to draw her into the warmth of his embrace. Then, before Natasha could make a sound, her lips were caught by his in a gentle kiss, but one completely devastating to her senses. Opening her lips under his, she gave herself up to the passionate sensations that flowed through her.

Sean's tongue moved against hers, savoring the warm softness. His hands moved lower to encompass her small waist, then slide over the curve of her hips in sensuous fascination. Natasha put her arms around Sean's neck, her fingers tangling in his thick hair. Their bodies touched, intensifying the emotions churning within them. Breathless, her head whirling, she allowed herself to be drawn up into the mists of the spell. She was engulfed in a whirlpool of sensations. Leaning against him, Natasha savored the feel of his strength; dreamily she gave herself up to the fierce sweetness of his mouth.

Sean's lips parted the soft, yielding flesh beneath his, searching out the honey of her mouth. With a low moan he thrust his fingers within the soft, silken waterfall of her hair, drawing her ever closer. Desire choked him, all the hungry promptings of his fantasies warring with his reason. His lips grew demanding, changing from gentleness to passion as his hands moved down her shoulders and began to roam at will with increasing familiarity. More than anything in the world, he wanted to make love to her. Still, they had to be careful.

Putting his finger to his lips, he cautioned her to silence. He paused, listening, then expelling his breath in a grateful sigh as he realized it was totally silent beyond the door.

"Once I'm in bed, no one disturbs me," she said, quelling his fears.

Like a spark, his lovemaking ignited a fire in her blood. Her heart skipped a beat as he brought his head down and traced the bare curve of her neck with his lips. Then he was tugging at her garments nearly as frantically as she was pulling at his. Naked, they lay together. For a long while he didn't say anything, he just stared at her.

Natasha tensed, fearing something was wrong. With a sudden sense of modesty she started to cover herself, but he clasped her by the wrists and drew her hands away.

"You're even more beautiful than I remembered." He let his eyes wander for a long moment, then reached out to caress her, sliding his hand over her stomach.

"Sean . . ." She ached for him, longed for him to make love to her as he had that time before.

He seemed to read her mind. "It was dangerous then; it's even more dangerous now. If we are caught, Demetrius will do more than send you away. He might kill you!"

"I don't even want to think about what he might do to you." She didn't have to think. She knew. He would punish Sean by turning him into a eunuch. He had done such a thing once before, or so Dayna had told her.

"I can run very fast. He would have to catch me. . . ." He felt daring and invincible, perhaps because of his success on the seas.

Bending his head, he worshipped her with his mouth, his lips traveling from one breast to the other in tender fascination. His tongue curled around the taut peaks, his teeth lightly grazing until she writhed beneath him. He savored the expressions that chased across her face, forcing himself to push away the question that now plagued him. Had any other man touched her?

"Demetrius . . . ?"

She shook her head. "No."

"Even if he had, it wouldn't matter to me. I love you, Tasha. . . ."

A sudden tidal wave swept over them, intensifying

the passion that flowed between them. They were like two pagan lovers in the moonlight, their skin glistening with moisture. Sean crushed her against the wet sleekness of his chest, shivering as he felt her nipples harden against his skin. Their bodies were crushed together as both simultaneously reveled in the delight of the texture and pressure of the other.

He kissed her again, his tongue searching and demanding as it explored. His fingers moved freely, leaving no part of her free of his touch—caressing her, loving her, learning her body as well as he knew his own.

"Once we get away from here, we'll never be parted again, I swear it," he whispered. Burying his face in the soft, silky strands of her hair he breathed in the fragrant scent of her hair, and was lost.

Natasha's arms entwined around Sean's neck, her fingers tangling in his thick dark hair. Fascinated, she let her hands explore his body as his had done to hers. He uttered a moan as her hands moved over the smoothly corded muscles of his shoulders.

"Ah, how I love you to touch me. . . ."

"I've heard the women talk. There are so many different ways to make love. . . ."

He smiled against her kiss. "We'll have time to try them all. . . ."

She laughed; then, closing her eyes, Natasha awaited another kiss, her mouth opening to him like the soft petals of a flower as he caressed her lips with all the passionate hunger they both yearned for. Natasha loved the taste of him, the tender urgency of his mouth. Her lips opened to him for a seemingly endless passionate onslaught of kisses. It was if they were breathing one breath, living at that moment just for each other. Mutual hunger brought their lips back together time after time. She craved his kisses and returned them with trembling pleasure, exploring the inner softness of his mouth.

Desire that had been coiling within Natasha for so long only to be unfulfilled sparked to renewed fire, and she could feel his passion likewise building, searing her with its heat. They shared a joy of touching and caressing, arms against arms, legs touching legs, fingers entwining and wandering to explore.

Natasha was lost in a sensual dream, a dream that intensified her daring. She remembered Dayna telling her how sensual it was to make love with the woman on top and the man beneath her. Giving in to her imagination, she slowly rolled over on top of him, sliding her body sensuously up and down. As his muscled body strained so hungrily against hers, she put the hardening length of his manhood inside her, sighing as she felt him shudder.

Sean felt the shock of raw desire as she undulated her body back and forth, stroking him erotically. He moaned aloud as he was gripped by the most powerful desire he had ever experienced in all his life. All coherent thought fled quickly from his mind.

Looking down at his face, she saw that his eyes were closed. How strange that his expression made him look as if he were nearly suffering, yet he was smiling all the while as if in sweet torment. Then he was reaching down, grasping her hips firmly yet gently, moving her body upward, then down. She could feel the insistent pressure of his swollen manhood moving within her.

Sean's size made her ache, but Natasha was conscious only of the hard length of him creating unbearable sensations within her as she began to move, her rhythmic plunges arousing a tingling fire. Arching herself up to him, she fully expressed her emotions with passion and with love.

Sean groaned softly, the blood pounding thickly in his head. She was so warm, so tight, that he closed his eyes with agonized pleasure. His hold on her hips tightened as the throbbing shaft of his maleness possessed her again and again.

He smiled. "How could I ever have thought that I could become a monk?"

Instinctively Natasha tightened her legs around him, certain she could never withstand the ecstasy that was engulfing her body. It was as if the night shattered into a thousand stars, bursting within her. Arching her hips she rode the storm with him. As spasms overtook her, she dug her nails into the skin of his back. Wave after wave lashed through them as they came close to mutual fulfillment.

"Tasha!" A sweet shaft of ecstasy shot through Sean, and he closed his eyes, whispering her name again and again. He wanted to make love to her all night. Again and again. Wanted to taste her, touch her, feeling her tight softness sheathing him.

Natasha felt for a moment as if her heart had stopped, as if she had stopped breathing. She was shattered by the pulsating explosion, the wondrous feelings that surged through her. Even when the intensity of their passion was spent, she still clung to him, unable to let this magical moment end. She touched him gently, wonderingly.

"I love you. . . ." Sean placed soft kisses on her forehead. She mumbled and stretched lazily, her soft thighs brushing against his hair-roughened ones in a motion that stirred him again. "That was pure heaven. Shall we try it again?" he breathed mischievously.

Suddenly, she tensed. She had the feeling that someone was right outside the door. Spying? Rising up from the bed, she cast a worried look in the direction of the door.

"Natasha?" It was Dayna.

"What is it?" Natasha did her best to sound sleepy.

"Demetrius is asking for you. I have come to take you to him!"

"No!" Sean rasped. It appeared that he couldn't wait until tomorrow to rescue her, for if he did he might have to share her with another man.

Thirty

Natasha knew that if she refused or insisted that Dayna go away there would be trouble, nor did she dare trust the young woman. Once she might have, but the episode with the bird in the garden had shown that Dayna had a dangerous side to her nature.

"I don't have any clothes on," she called out, afraid that Dayna might open the door any moment. She had not bolted it.

Sean exchanged worried looks with her, then hurried from the bed and gathered up his clothing. There was only one door. No windows. He was trapped. There was no way out without being seen.

"Natasha, I've seen you without clothes on before," Dayna laughed. "Now, open the door."

Hastily Sean searched for a hiding place. The bedroom was sparsely furnished with only a small table, one chair, and the large oval bed. The only place able to accommodate Sean's well-muscled frame was underneath the wooden bed frame. Taking a deep breath, he managed to squeeze under the bed and lay there as silently and unmoving as possible while Natasha shrugged into her undergown and tunic, then padded across the marble floor to let Dayna in.

"Natasha!"

She waited until Sean was safely hidden before she opened the door. She was flustered and out of breath. She could only hope that Dayna would not guess what had kept her. "I'm sorry. I must have had too much wine. I was so sleepy. . . ." She looked away to avert Dayna's piercing gaze.

"Are you certain that you are telling me the truth?" Stepping inside the room, Dayna looked around.

"Of course I'm telling the truth." Natasha's whole body tensed. She took a deep breath. "Why would I lie?"

Natasha was nervous as Dayna approached the bed, wondering if there were any telltale signs of the amorous activities that had occurred during the night. Certainly the coverlets were in disarray.

"You must have had a nightmare. The bed sheets are all tangled up." Reaching down, Dayna tugged at one of the sheets and nearly brushed Sean's knee with her hand as she pulled it up.

"A nightmare. Yes . . ." She could tell that Dayna was suspicious. Would she betray her?

"Poor, poor Natasha."

Dayna plopped down on the pillows scattered near the bed, nervously tapping her toes against the bed frame. She was obviously agitated, and that sparked Natasha's own agitation. She didn't know if she could trust her with the truth. Although Dayna had offered her friendship, she had also verbally stabbed one or two of the other young women in the back.

"You seem troubled. I have herbs that will calm you. Herbs that you can eat, drink, or put in a pipe and smoke. It will relax you and intensify the colors around you."

"Herbs." Natasha saw a way out of the predicament. "Could you get them for me? Now?"

Dayna paused and looked toward the door, but then she shook her head. "I'll give them to you after your meeting with Demetrius. You might need them doubly then." She laughed suggestively.

Beneath the bed Sean cursed softly. How was he going to get Natasha out of the manor? And when he did, how was he going to find Selig? Tomorrow was still a long way off. Would they still be able to put their escape plan into action?

Natasha's hands were trembling as she slipped on her garments and tried to repair her tousled hair. "I'm a bundle of nerves. I don't know what to expect. I don't know anything about Demetrius. Nothing at all." She stabbed herself with a hair pin and winced. "How am I going to talk with him? I won't understand him and he won't understand me."

Dayna laughed. "You won't need to say a word." She stood up, helping Natasha pin up her hair. "Your lip paint is smudged, but it can be repaired."

Visually she searched the room, looking for the tiny paint pots that were so important to a woman's beauty. Suddenly, her eyes darted to the spot on the floor where Sean's boots were flung haphazardly, left behind in his hurry to hide. Cocking her head, she raised her brows. For a moment, she was deep in contemplation as if deciding what to do. A myriad of expressions flitted over her face. When she spoke, her words exploded in the room.

"You fool!"

Natasha turned deathly pale but didn't say a word.

The time for pretense had ended. Quickly Sean crawled out from beneath the bed. "No, I'm the fool for coming here. Natasha is completely innocent of anything."

Dayna slowly looked him up and down, starting at his feet, lingering on his manhood, then staring him boldly in the eye. "Who are you?"

"Natasha belongs to me. I'm going to make her my wife."

Dayna threw back her head and laughed. "I doubt that you will live that long, and even if you do there is every possibility that you will not be able to celebrate your wedding night." Her meaning was obvious.

"So you would betray me." Somehow that knowledge bothered Natasha, for once she had considered Dayna to be a friend.

"I don't want to; you must believe me." She sounded sincere. "But if I do not, then I will be deemed as guilty as you." She turned toward the door, but Sean was on her in an instant, stifling her cries with his hand.

"I'm sorry. . . ." He needed to knock her unconscious, but the thought of striking a woman bothered him. Sensing why he hesitated, Natasha hurried forward. Picking up a vase, she raised it high and knocked Dayna over the head.

"I'm sorry, too," she said. The die had been cast. There was no turning back.

"Hurry, help me tie her up!" Sean used his belt to bind her hands and feet, and Natasha's sash to gag her. Gently he placed her on the bed, covering her over so that it would look as if it were Natasha, asleep.

Sean opened the door, and seeing that there was no one there, he motioned for her to follow him. Hand in hand they fled down the corridor, conscious of the danger of running into slaves or guards. When they were out of breath and feared they could run no farther, they came to a broad marble staircase.

"Wait!" Sean heard footsteps below. He pushed her against the wall, where they froze against the balustrade until the footsteps faded.

They hurried down the stairs, through the arches that led to a large room. "We have to go through here. It's the only way to reach the courtyard," Natasha whispered.

They stepped into the room, preparing to cross it, when a huge shadow spread across the floor. Though the features were obscured, Natasha feared that it was either one of the guards or a eunuch. Either would be just as dangerous.

The shadow moved faster than Sean realized was possible and threw him aside. He landed on the hard marble floor, looking up into savage eyes that glared at him from the ugliest, most menacing face he had ever beheld. The man was a dark-skinned giant who was bald as an egg. With a roar of outrage, this dangerous colossus came at Sean brandishing a thick, curving sword. Sean saw the weapon raised above his head and pulled away just as the blade descended.

"Sean!" Natasha's shout distracted the eunuch for just a heartbeat. Rushing up, Natasha pushed the mammoth man from behind with a body block, just in time to assist Sean in keeping his head. By dodging the sword, Sean suffered only a minor shoulder wound instead of decapitation. Still, the battle was far from over.

With a grunt of anger the bald giant swung around, this time aiming for Sean's head. The swish of the sword reverberated again and again. He knew that he could only keep up his acrobatics for so long, for he was no match for the eunuch's strength, nor was his sword any use against the giant's curved blade.

Suddenly, one well-placed blow caused the sword to fly from Sean's hand. "Dear God, he will kill us both!"

Sword upraised, eyes wild, the eunuch gave an ear-shattering yell and lunged again at Sean, who was scarcely able to dodge the blow. He was tiring. The next blow might well hit its mark.

"Run, Natasha! Save yourself!"

"No!" She was determined that they would get out of this place. Coming up behind the eunuch, she quickly picked up Sean's sword and, remembering how her father had slain his enemies, stabbed the eunuch in the side. Pulling out the sword, she looked down at the blood in shock, watching numbly as the man fell to the ground with a grunt. She had never killed anyone before, although she had witnessed a great deal of killing. She hated the feeling that overcame her, the compassion and the grief. She started trembling.

"You saved my life!" Tenderly Sean gathered her into his arms, staining her gown with his blood.

They couldn't stay together for very long. Total pandemonium broke out. Doors opened, flooding the hallway with men and women who were in the employ of Demetrius. Fingers pointed. Voices shouted. Sean and Natasha were trapped in the middle.

"The guards!" The six men coming toward him were the ones that Sean feared. He was outnumbered. Surrender or fight. He had no choice but to do battle, for he wisely judged what their fate would be if they surrendered. He picked up the eunuch's sword.

Natasha looked around frantically. Spying several rounded urns, she hurriedly sent them all hurtling at their attackers, then said sharply, "Come!"

He followed her as she headed for the stairs; then they were running so fast they were nearly tumbling to the bottom. There was a door at the ground floor, the door to one of the manor's gates. Sliding the bolt, she pulled it open, and together they dashed out.

It was dark. The moon had passed behind a cloud, so the street outside was in total darkness. Taking Sean's hand, she moved swiftly from one narrow alleyway to another. She looked in vain, trying to remember any landmark from her journey to the manor, but her mind was a blank.

"I know the way." Perhaps his duty today as Sibyl's guard would turn out to be a blessing.

"They're following! I don't think we can lose them for long. . . ." Her lungs were bursting; she needed to rest, but they didn't dare.

Sean led her through cavernous alleys between three- and four-story buildings that reeked of stale urine and rotting food. It was the poorer section of the city, the dangerous part of Constantinople. And yet, how could anything be more dangerous than the guardsmen who were after them?

Natasha looked over her shoulder. Their pursuers

were getting farther and farther behind, but they might easily catch up if she and Sean went down the wrong passageway. She remembered Dayna telling her that the city was a tangled maze of alleys where one could get lost forever. Were she and Sean to be united only to die amid the city's garbage?

"Hurry!" Searching desperately for a place to hide, Sean pulled her with him behind one of the thick doors of a great stone church. He closed the door firmly behind them.

Trembling, her chest heaving, she tried to catch her breath, fearful that anyone passing by would be able to hear her ragged breath. She had an idea of how to escape without being detected. There were beggers in this part of the city. If they could only exchange their clothes for rags and pose as beggers, they might be able to get away.

She whispered her plan in Sean's ear, watching as he smiled.

"Wonderful!"

Meanwhile, they would have to remain in this hiding place until the tumult outside quieted and their pursuers passed by.

Sean's eyes rested on the statue of a woman holding a child, a statue more detailed than any he had ever seen before. "Mary . . . !" He was struck by the kindness on her face.

"The earth mother . . ." Natasha whispered, reaching out to touch the cold stone. "We are safe here."

Sean stared at the statue, then moved to another statue of a man in a robe reaching out as if to touch him. Recognition flooded through him. He breathed a sigh. He felt at peace. "Yes, Natasha, we are safe. . . ."

Thirty-one

The waters of the Bosporus Strait looked like hammered silver. The ocean was calm, which was a welcome boon after the tumultuous time Natasha and Sean had gone through to get to the Viking ship.

Having pilfered some tattered and patched garments from the church's poor box, leaving their own garments behind, they had wound their way through muddy alleyways, found their way through several of the desserted bazaars, only to realize they were going the wrong way in the dark, when they spied the silhouetted dome of the Hagia Sophia. Changing direction, they had both run and walked in the direction of the harbor, only to be turned away by the man at the gate, who had been loath to let them through, particularly since they were "coinless."

Sean had stared at the wall, wondering if it was possible to climb over and drop to the other side. In that moment, Natasha's pierced ears saved the day, however, for she had forgotten to remove her silver earrings. Taking them out of her ear, she had handed them to the gatekeeper, laughing at his look of amazement. Now powerful hands were lifting her up, then dropping her ever so gently to the deck of the ship. Even so, as her legs collapsed from beneath her she fell, with a thud.

"Odin pluck out my eyes, I'm sorry! I didn't mean you any harm."

Looking up, Natasha saw a dark pair of eyes staring at her from a ruddy face. The man had spoken to her in Slavic. She was puzzled. "Who are you?"

"My name is Ref, and you must be the woman who rivals Freja in beauty."

"Freja?" The name was unknown to her.

"One of our Norse goddesses." He took his thumb and wiped a smudge of dirt—or perhaps it was eye kohl—from the tip of her nose, then brushed the hair out of her eyes with the tip of his finger. "There, now I can see you better." He clucked his tongue. "Having never seen Freja, I can't make any real comparison, but I would think I can safely say that you must surely surpass her in beauty. Kodran didn't lie. He told me you were pretty enough to die for, and so here we are. . . ."

"Kodran?" Natasha looked at Sean, doing little to hide her confusion. "First one strange name and now another. Is Kodran another of your gods?"

"Not mine," Sean replied.

"Then who . . . ?"

He reached into his sea chest and pulled out a blue woolen tunic and a beige pair of trousers, anxious to be out of the begger's garments before he got fleas. When he was fully dressed, he explained. "Kodran is my Viking name, and you are standing on the deck of my Viking ship."

"Kodran . . . !" To her he would always be Sean, yet she somehow liked the name. "I think there is a great deal you need to tell me."

"And I will, just as soon as we are safely away from here." Though the harbor seemed quiet, he had the uncomfortable feeling that something unforetold still might happen.

Natasha tugged at her tattered clothes. "Is there anything that I can wear?"

"We don't have any silk or brocade," Sean teased, "though I do have an extra tunic I can lend you until we reach Kiev." He reached into the chest again and handed her a red woolen tunic that reached to his knees but hit Natasha at midcalf. She belted it with one of Ref's metal necklaces that fit around her waist.

"Dayna and the others would criticize my apparel, but I would rather wear this tunic than all the silks in the world." Taking her hair down from its curls, she let it blow free in the wind.

"Does that mean that you will become a Viking bride?" Sweeping her into his arms, he didn't give her a chance to answer, for his lips were moving against hers with such ferocity that she cried out.

"Kodran! Kodran . . ."

Ref tried to get his attention, and when he could not, he physically separated the pair of lovers, pointing toward the seawall. Three ships were sailing their way, and their green-and-white banners proclaimed them to be Byzantine.

"We're being followed."

"Oh, no!" Natasha ran to the rail, looking out in dismay. "I don't want any harm to come to you, Sean. If it means going back to Demetrius, I will if it will save you."

"Save me for what? To live alone without you? No. Whatever happens, we will be together."

"They say that the Byzantines cannot be defeated, that the Virgin, whose special province it is, will protect them—but I have my goddesses too, both Norse and Slavic. Do you want me to call upon them for help, Kodran?" Ref asked.

"No!"

"Shall I call upon the gods?"

Again he shook his head. "We will have to save ourselves. I have found that gods seldom interfere in the fate of man despite what we have all been told." Hastily Sean gave orders to row with all their might.

"Then we are doomed, for I do not think we can

win, even with Selig's aid. We can't outrun them, nor do we stand a chance if we fight."

Not only did the Byzantines have every available luxury, they were also equiped to wage battle. They had the battle engines that they had inherited from Rome: the catapult and the ballista, the testudo and the battering ram.

"If we were trying to invade them I would be worried, but those weapons are of no concern to us here."

"No but they have something even more dangerous: Greek fire!"

Though Sean knew many things, he had never heard of this. "Greek fire, what is that?"

"It is a highly ignitable substance which, when projected through syphons or thrown in earthenware pots, shatters on impact and causes great damage." Ref tried to demonstrate with his hands but realized he wasn't communicating the danger to Sean. "It catches everything in its way on fire. A fire that burns on water."

"Impossible."

"No. The Greeks bring in oil from the desert. They call it naphtha. It is a fierce-flaming oil such as we do not have in the North. By molding it into balls and stuffing it into giant copper tubes, they lay down a wall of fire upon the sea or splatter it on the decks in masses of flame. Water will not put it out."

"And it is two ships against three." Sean looked over at Selig's ship. His brother was unaware of the danger and was cheerily waving back at him. Sean jabbed his finger in the direction of the Byzantine ships, then made the gesture to mimic rowing. "Row, Selig, row! Your life depends on it!" he cried out.

"It's my fault. If you hadn't come after me . . ."

He silenced her with a quick kiss on the lips. "We won't talk of blame, for I am the one who bungled this." He looked at Ref. "If this Greek fire hits the ships, is there any way to put it out?"

Ref nodded. "Urine."

"What?" He thought Ref was making a joke. "Tell me!"

"Ships that sail in the Black Sea or Sea of Marmara who fear the Byzantines carry vats of urine on board to quench the flames. It is collected from the men on board."

"Then quickly, empty some barrels and see that the men make their contribution just in case it is needed." Looking toward Natasha, he added, "And be discreet about it—we have a woman on board."

"Discreet?" Ref didn't know the word.

"Don't be oafish about the deed." He crossed himself, despite what he had said about gods interfering with men. "If we are hit, Natasha, I want you to jump overboard even if you can't swim."

"But I can. Dayna taught me. There was a pool. . . ." She thought of Dayna and wondered if it was her tattling that had gotten them in this trouble, or if it was the men who had chased them through the city. "I don't want to leave you."

"If you must, I want you to promise me that you will save yourself." He wouldn't take no for an answer.

"All right. I will. . . ."

Sean issued orders, hiding his own fears behind a calm exterior. All the while, his crew would never know how violently his insides were churning. He had to be an inspiration to his men. They had to win, for the alternative was too terrible to imagine.

"Get your battle axes ready—and the barrel. Be prepared to fight, but make use of the sails and the wind to get away." He wasn't too proud to retreat, nor should they be.

Sean watched as his skilled Viking sailors maneuvered the sails of the *Wolf's Head*, allowing the ship to take advantage of the wind. Speeding upon the sea like a sailfish, it outdistanced the three ships coming from Constantinople.

"There's another ship following us. A ship with a sail the color of blood."

"Thordis!" So he had joined in for the kill. It irked Sean that a man such as he might be victorious, and he wondered what profit he would make if he brought Sean's head to Demetrius.

Thordis made use of his knowledge of sailing and his years of experience to catch up with the *Wolf's Head.* The serpent ship rammed them at full speed at the bow end. The impact knocked Natasha off her feet, and she crawled along the deck until she could find something sturdy to hang on to.

"The Viking ship! It has the Greek fire!"

The air was filled with the turbid smoke of the enemy's strange fire, but that fire was quickly extinguished. "God bless the men." Sean laughed, saying, "Save some in the barrel for Thordis."

The water beyond the ship was streaked with patches of fire. The *Wolf's Head* quickly sailed away from the danger, only to be pursued by the ship with red sails and one of the Byzantine ships.

"They are gaining on us," Ref declared.

"Will they ram us again, do you think?"

Ref was sure that they would. "And worse."

Sean's stomach tightened into knots. Was a man ever really prepared to die? For a long moment, there was no sound at all from the men. It was as if they were preparing themselves for the worst, holding their swords aloft so that they could go to Valhalla.

"The ships—Thordis and the others. They are turning around." Ref was as amazed as Sean was when he told him.

"Why?"

As he looked out at the horizon, Ref saw the answer. The swiftly flowing Dnieper had carried two ships into the Black Sea. From a distance Ref recognized the sails: red and white with a dragon's head, and a purple sail with a black raven.

"It's Torin and Ragnar."

"My father?"

"Thordis is not so foolish as to brave your father's anger. Besides, four ships have a greater chance of winning than two or three."

Ragnar soon had Thordis on the run, though he tangled once or twice with the Byzantines, to their disadvantage. Perhaps when all was said and done, Greek fire wasn't as treacherous as first had been assumed. Certainly valor and skill had turned the tide of battle today, Sean thought.

Once the fighting was over and they were safely away from Byzantine territory, the ships pulled into shore. Sean found himself face-to-face with another family member, the tall, blond Viking named Torin who was married to his sister, Erica. At the steerboard of the lead vessel was his father, Ragnar.

"I have some trading to do at Kiev. I just thought I'd make certain that you had found your woman," he called out as the deck of his ship pulled parallel to Sean's.

"I did." Proudly and possessively he put his arm around Natasha's waist. "This is Tasha."

Ragnar heartily approved of Sean's choice and boldly told him so out loud. "Where are you headed now, Kodran?"

"Kiev!" Sean had a surprise for Natasha. Selig had learned from Thordis that Nadia had been sold to a farmer in Kiev. Now they were on their way to buy her freedom.

Thirty-two

Slicing through the waves, four Viking ships, their colorful sails unfurled, headed north, leaving the Black Sea and sailing toward the entrance to the Dneiper River. As they headed up the river, the ships moved through the waters in tight formation, led by the ship with the raven's head, captained by Sean's father. Natasha sensed at once that he was no ordinary Viking. The ship was longer than the others, the carved head intricately detailed.

Natasha watched Sean from afar, marveling at his strength and his love of the sea. He had assumed a domineering pose, a wide-legged stance to brace himself against the rolling of the ship. With his hands on his hips, his dark hair blowing in the wind, he looked determined and decisive. He was jubilant, full of life as he strode about issuing orders.

For a moment she felt her heart lurch. For better or for worse, he was not the same. He had changed in many ways. They had been apart so long that they needed to become reacquainted.

"Kodran, do we need to man the oars?" she heard one of the Vikings ask.

Kodran! Even his name had changed. Kodran, a Viking name. A name that she wasn't sure she liked, perhaps because it emphasized the differences in him.

He changed because of you, she thought. *Do not be unfair to him.* He had gone all the way to the land of the

Vikings so that he could procure a ship to aid him in his rescue of *her.* What greater proof of love could there be than that? But would he give it up? She doubted it. Sailing seemed to get in a man's blood. It had a hold on men that was only rivaled by their lust for a woman. She wasn't at all certain that she liked the idea of his being a Viking, for up until now the only Vikings she had known were those who had sailed with Thordis—brutal men.

But Sean is not like that. . . . As she watched him, she was touched by his feelings for his ship. He was strong, capable, and determined, yet, he was still a sensitive man whose capacity for love was staggering.

Reeling as a wave hit the ship, she grabbed for an edge of the prow but tumbled by mistake into Sean's arms. Well, perhaps it was not a mistake, for as their warm bodies tightly embraced, he bent his head and kissed her.

"It takes a while to get used to the rolling of the ship, but I'll soon make a sailor out of you!" He grinned, tugging playfully at her hair.

She reveled in the glory of being with him, but the respite from his duties was short-lived. The men needed him, and for a moment Natasha felt a flash of resentment toward these Vikings. She wanted to be alone with him, to bask in the warmth of his undivided attention. They had to make up for so much time. . . . They had been apart so long. Couldn't they let him have at least a few moments away from the prow?

The sun was warm on her face, but the early morning wind was chilly. She shivered the moment he left her arms. Sensitive to her needs, Sean quickly found a woolen cape and draped it over her shoulders.

"Once we get to Kiev, I am going to buy you garments the likes of which you have never seen before, in more colors than the rainbow." He smiled mysteriously. "And once we get there, I have another surprise for you." Ragnar had promised him as much money as was needed to buy Nadia's freedom. It was to be a wedding present to his soon to be daughter-in-law.

"A surprise?" She had heard Sean, his father, and his brothers whispering and had been puzzled. "What kind of surprise?"

"A gift from the heart." He smiled at her, and in that moment she thought that in matters of the heart he had not really changed at all.

Nadia looked toward the shore, recognizing the rock formations from the time before. She gritted her teeth, remembering what a difficult journey awaited her, for the River had been much harder to navigate than the sea, and the rocks had posed a constant danger.

Natasha moved to the cargo hold of the ship and sat under a makeshift tent Sean and Ref had put up for her. It had a dual purpose: to shield her from the sun's scorching rays and to protect her from the rain. She suspected that it also got her out from under the feet of the men as they worked, but Sean would never have wanted to hurt her feelings by telling her that.

As she watched him work at the oars with the others, she ached with memories, remembering how it felt to have her bare breasts pressed against the hair of his bare chest. He had opened up a whole new world of beauty and emotions to her. She wanted to experience those feelings again, to sleep against his chest, but how was that possible when they were surrounded by all these other men? Oh, how she longed for privacy! Without his arms around her she felt so lonely.

As if sensing this, Sean found the time to seek her out, gently kissing her brow, but then left her to return to his duties aboard the ship. She heard his voice rise above the others as he issued orders in the Nordic tongue.

Oh, how she hated the language the Vikings spoke. It was harsh and explosive, not soft like the words of her people's tongue. Nevertheless, she was determined to learn the meaning of every word. Until she did, she would be isolated and unaware of what was going on. Therefore, she listened carefully when they spoke, mimicking the words she heard, trying to understand their meaning.

Staring out at the sea, Natasha wondered what Nadia was thinking, what she was doing. Despite what had happened to her, being taken to Sean's land of Eire and then to Constantinople, she had been the fortunate one. She hoped with all her heart that Nadia was still alive and that somehow, despite her enslavement, she was happy.

Three days later, after a harrowing journey of braving rapids, portaging, and winding their way through the rocks, the entourage of ships sailed into Kiev. Easing into the port where a multitude of boats stood moored, they tied up at a landing. The four ships joined the others, and Natasha watched as they were unloaded, undoubtedly so that the Vikings could see to making a profit from their journey. While she and Sean had been running for their lives, it seemed that the other Vikings had been taking the time to accumulate all of the treasures Constantinople had to give.

Sean led her ashore, but while the others made their way to the marketplace, he found a spot by the river where they could be alone. Together they sat in the shade beneath a willow. The sun was bright upon her hair, and as he looked at her he was as struck by her beauty, as if he had never seen her before.

"Ships take a lot out of a man, but even though I didn't get much of a chance to be with you, I was thinking about you all the time."

She laughed softly. "Were you?"

His heart seemed to rise like a stone in his throat as he took her in his arms, holding her close. For a long moment, he did not kiss her but instead traced each curve of her face with his finger. "Yes, I was. Even at night, your face haunted my dreams and I cried out for you. Each time I mumbled your name, I woke poor Ref up and he would poke me in the ribs." He lifted up his tunic, exposing several black-and-blue marks on his waist as if he needed proof.

Reaching up, she touched his face, bringing it down to hers, then kissed him. When she drew away she said, "What a waste of precious time—all that time that we have spent not kissing."

They sat together, totally contented, watching the light of the sun cast an amber glow on the river.

"I wish that I had had time to bring you jewels from Constantinople, and silks—blues and greens to match your eyes. And an ivory comb to wear in your hair . . ." He looked toward the marketplace in the distance. "I hope that they save at least some of the treasures. . . ."

"Even if they don't, all I want is you."

As if he felt the need to tell her again, he said, "I love you. . . ."

"And I, you." She leaned against him and put her head on his shoulder. "So many people crave love, but so few people truly find it."

"We are so lucky, Tasha."

She was silent; then she said, "You've found another love, too, haven't you. One that you didn't have before."

He tensed. "It was always my dream to sail. Now that dream is a reality, and yet I would give up the sea if you wished it."

Part of her wanted to make that request of him, for she knew that the ocean and being a Viking was fraught with dangers, yet she couldn't do that to him. She had learned that part of love was putting the other person's needs above one's own.

"I would never ask that of you. How could I?"

He stroked her hair. "Then sail with me, Tasha. There are so many lands waiting to be explored. Lands farther to the north and to the west."

"Come with you?" She had never thought that he would ask her that, and she smiled at the idea.

"We'll marry here. It is the closest place we can find to your beloved steppes. Then we'll go to my father's land and stay through the winter. But in the spring . . ."

"Our wedding . . . I know that you are a Christian, and that as such you would marry in a church. But I . . . I . . ."

"I would marry you under a tree, in a cave, or standing knee-deep in a river. Whatever would make you happy."

She looked up at him. "Perhaps we can compromise. . . ."

Wrapped in each other's arms, they drew contentment in just being together for a long, long time. Then reluctantly Sean stood up, drawing her with him. "We should join the others."

Slowly they walked, listening to the rumbling noise of the crowd. As they neared the marketplace, the fresh smell of the open air was replaced by the unpleasant odors of unwashed human flesh and animal waste. Animals and humans surged through the narrow streets: donkeys, sheep, cows, pigs, dogs, and cats—even ducks and geese. Voices blended with grunts, bleats, and other animal sounds and the clatter of feet over the wooden walkway. It was a jolting difference from the marble streets of Constantinople.

They passed by the area where slaves were being traded. Two dozen slaves were being readied for the auction block. As was the custom, the women stood on one side and the men on the other. Remembering the indignities she had suffered, Natasha shuddered, trying to push away the unpleasant memories of her own servitude.

"You will never have to suffer such treatment again, Tasha," Sean said, putting his hand on her shoulder.

"I know. . . ."

He hurried to take her mind off of the past, making a sweeping gesture with his hand. "Pick whatever you want and I will buy it for you." He handed her a bag filled with coins from Constantinople.

Natasha bought fruit to eat as she walked along, exploring the goods in the open stands, wagons, and stalls. She wasn't certain just what she wanted to buy for her wedding; thus, in the meantime she purchased a silver necklace, a bracelet made from amber stones, and three pairs of earrings—silver, bronze, and jade—to replace the ones she gave to the guard at the gate in Constantinople. Then she saw it: a sheepskin cloak exactly like the one she had been wearing the day she was captured. On closer examination, she realized that it *was* the cloak she had been wearing.

Sean draped it over his arm as they went to another of the booths, then another and another. They purchased several gowns, tunics, and dresses; two pairs of boots, one black and one brown; a silver brooch; hair ribbons; and last, the skirt and overdress of white and red that Natasha decided on for her wedding ceremony. Sean chose the gown for their wedding night—something so sheer that Natasha blushed at the sight of it.

"It looks as if it were made out of spiderwebs," she whispered.

"Mmmm-hmmm. And all I can say is, God bless those spiders." He nuzzled her ear. "Are you as impatient as I?"

"Oh, yes." Leading the way, she decided to begin her wifely duties by choosing his garments for him: a dark-blue overtunic, knee-high black boots, and pants that were full, gathered around the knee. Like the red trousers he had worn that day he rescued her.

With their arms full of packages, they returned to

the landing to meet with the others at the appointed time of sunset. The river was still, and the sky was streaked with rose. Holding up some of her gifts from Sean, she looked at her reflection in the river. She was so distracted by her vanity that she didn't notice the young woman standing behind her until she heard a soft cough.

Turning around, Natasha saw a young woman with dark-blond hair standing beside Ref. The face was familiar—a very pretty face, though the woman's eyes seemed old, as if she had seen a great deal of suffering and pain.

Natasha stiffened; she blinked, afraid to believe her eyes. "Nadia?"

"It's me . . . oh, Tasha . . . !"

They laughed until they cried, then cried until they could laugh again, all the while locked in each other's arms.

"I thought I'd never see you again! How . . . ?" Natasha turned her eyes toward Ref in gratitude, thinking that it was he who had given her this wonderful gift, her beloved friend.

"It wasn't me. It was Kodran . . . and Ragnar." There was something about the look in Ref's eyes as he looked at Nadia that told Natasha he was smitten with her friend.

"How can I ever thank you? All of you . . ." She wondered if Nadia was likewise attracted to Ref, and decided that she wasn't just yet; but given time and a nudge in that direction, anything was possible. . . .

Thirty-three

Natasha's people had always celebrated weddings in autumn and winter, when their workload and traveling was lightest, for they believed that even in the dying of the year the spirit could be renewed. As the first heavy clouds of autumn came rolling in across the plain, and the earth began to harden in the early freezes, the people would have time and hopefully food to spare, and thoughts could turn to the elaborate ceremonies of love. Weddings were a time for a robust celebration thus it seemed very fitting that her wedding to Sean should be in the final days of autumn.

It seemed like old times, having Nadia nearby. It was she who came to Natasha's room in the small timbered house that Sean and his brothers had built in their temporary Kievan village. First, she heated water over a small fire, then helped her to bathe. Before the ceremony, a young Magyar bride-to-be was ritually cleansed. Nadia stood by as Natasha washed her hair in heated rainwater. Once her hair was dry with the help of the fire and rough towels, Nadia braided it carefully, from one plait into two as was their custom, signifying that she would go from being alone to living with a husband.

"Maybe one of these days I will be doing this for you," she said softly, hopefully.

"No, not for me. Never for me!" Nadia's eyes held a glow of pain.

"How can you be so sure?"

Nadia touched her leg. "This!" She tugged roughly at Natasha's hair, then hastily apologized. "Besides . . . my—my master coupled with me and I did not like it at all!"

"Oh, Nadia, I'm sorry!" Nadia had been strangely quiet about her ordeal and the details of her enslavement. Now Natasha understood and wished with all her heart that she had been there to help her, as she had been when they were children. "Was he rough with you?" Nadia didn't have to answer; the truth was written clearly on her face.

"It doesn't matter—really. I'm free now, thanks to Ref and your soon-to-be husband."

"Ah, yes, Ref. He is handsome, don't you think?"

Nadia's face turned a soft shade of crimson. "Very."

"And he is a pleasant fellow"—Natasha wrinkled her nose mischievously—"for a Slav with Viking blood, that is."

"There is nothing wrong with Slavs or Vikings. Ref is very proud of his mixed heritage, and . . ." Suddenly, Nadia realized that Natasha was trying to trick her into defending Ref and thus revealing her feelings. "He is as you say: a pleasant fellow."

Remembering Magyar customs, Natasha had embroidered intricate patterns on the soft linen of her wedding dress and also on the linens that would be used for their wedding night. Because the wedding was to be so soon, Nadia had helped her. Now, after putting on her chemise, Natasha slipped the longsleeved, knee-length white bridal gown over her chemise. Beneath the gown was an ankle-length embroidered red skirt that would purposely be revealed. Around her small waist was a tight belt of red, decorated with multicolored beads. Gold earrings and a matching bracelet completed her ensemble.

Natasha tugged on the knee-length brown boots that Sean had bought for her. Nadia slipped the bridal crown of leaves laced with multicolored ribbons on her head. The ribbons fell to either side of her face and looked somewhat like the bridal veil that Christian women always wore.

Natasha felt Sean's eyes upon her, sensed his presence with every fibre of her being, heard the sound of his footsteps as he entered the *skaalen,* but she didn't turn around for fear that she might succumb to her emotions. No one wanted to see a bride with tears, even if they were tears of happiness.

Silently, his fingers trembling, Sean pinned on her a brooch with a golden chain from which several keys hung. "A Viking custom, Ragnar tells me. The keys are the badge of honorable wifehood." Three other chains were hung upon her wedding dress, with a knife, scissors, and a container of needles dangling respectively from the chains.

She cast a sideways glance at him. He was wearing the full blue trousers that were gathered at the knee and a wine-colored tunic embroidered with gold. A finely wrought belt was wrapped around the tunic at the waist. On his feet, he too wore knee-high boots, though his were black. Around his neck he wore the amber wolf pendant, which caught the light of the sun.

Together they walked from the house in solemn procession, carrying sheaves of rye. They were followed by Ragnar. Those who followed held branches of evergreen. Although a Viking ceremony would have been held in a grove of trees and a Magyar ceremony in an open field, Sean had wanted the ceremony to take place outside the door of the only church in Kiev.

The ceremony itself was filled with a mixture of customs representative of bride and groom. Sean and Natasha stood before Ragnar, who recited the vows, as was his right as Viking chieftain. Sean repeated after him, translating the words into her language so that she could repeat her portion of the vows. The thought ran through Sean's mind that in some ways this ceremony was not all that different from Christian rites. They drank from a single goblet while uttering a melodic chant, but in deference to Natasha's belief, it was water not wine.

Sean was offered the goblet first; then, with trembling hands Natasha took it and raised it to her lips, feeling the cool water trickle down her throat.

According to Magyar custom, Ragnar bound their wrists together with three knots, to symbolize unity, fertility, and a long life. "For as long as time rules us, you can never be divided." He held forth a piece of bread and a lump of salt crystal for them to eat. "May Thor and Odin smile upon you always and bring many children to your hearth."

A crash startled them both. Looking over his shoulder, Sean saw Nadia standing there, the earthenware jug that had held the sacred water in pieces at her feet. Sean thought it an accident, but as he noted the grin that she exchanged with Natasha, he knew it was part of the ceremony.

Ragnar was prepared for the shattering of the pottery. Bending down, he picked up two of the pieces and held one out to each of them. "Keep these and take care. If you lose them, misery and loneliness will surely come upon you."

Sean reached out his hand very slowly. It sparked of superstition. Abbot Righifarch would say that partaking of this ceremony reeked of heresy. And yet, he was suddenly loath to part with the earthenware shard. He tucked it into the pouch that he wore hanging from his belt, for safekeeping. His eyes shone with love as he bent to kiss her before the small throng of family and friends.

"May you have a lifetime of good fortune and love,"

Nadia exclaimed, not realizing that she was looking at Ref until he turned his head and smiled at her. Hastily she turned away.

Ragnar had arranged for a wedding feast. Though there was a chill in the air, the mead and barley beer soon warmed the assembled guests. He walked about the hall, slapping the other Vikings on the back and refilling their drinking horns. The horns were elaborately ornamented, and more than one brawny man soon found that the first trickle could often become a sudden tidal wave of brew.

As was tradition, Natasha took off her new husband's boots at this feast. The exchange of vows, the passing of her hand from that of one male to another, all signified the male's guardianship and authority, her acceptance of the protected and subordinate position as wife.

In the long hall of the newly constructed hall, Sean and Natasha sat in two large chairs to receive the congratulations and best wishes of family and friends. Since it was all men except for Nadia and Natasha, the food was good but simple fare: roast meat and vegetables cooked in a pot, and berries for dessert. The men were more interested in drinking and telling tall tales than eating. It had been a long time since there was a wedding.

The men gambled, laying bets as to who could hurl an ax, spear, or knife the farthest. The bets turned to matters that touched upon the newlyweds as to the sex of their firstborn child, when it would be born, and the color of its hair.

"A boy, nine months from today, dark hair."

"A girl, eight months and three weeks from now, red hair."

"Twins, one of each sex, eight months three weeks five days, yellow hair . . ." The bets went on and on.

Sean nervously tapped his foot. He was anxious to be alone with his new wife.

"I can see that you are in a hurry to leave." Ragnar was all smiles. He waited expectantly; then, realizing that Sean didn't know Viking customs, he whispered, "Kodran, pick her up in your arms. That is the sign that you have claimed her as your mate."

Sean swooped her up. Ragnar had told him that in order for the marriage to be considered legally binding, the couple had to be seen going to bed by a minimum of six witnesses. He motioned to his father, Selig, Torin, Ref, Nadia, and one of his crewmen. As they watched, he carried her into the sleeping chamber, then turned on the six in mock anger.

"Out—everybody out!" As soon as they had left, he gathered Natasha into his arms. "At last we are alone."

Worshipping her with his hands, Sean slowly stripped off her dress and the red skirt. There was a languid quality to his movements, as if he wanted to savor this magical moment. Her chemise followed. When she was completely naked, he let his eyes roam over her, caressing the flat stomach and rounded hips, the graceful curve of her waist, and the full softness of her breasts.

"I feel as if this were our first time together. How strange!" she whispered.

Proudly she stood before him like some pagan goddess, basking in the warmth of his heated gaze. When he reached out to touch her again, she could feel the tremor of his hands. Nervous. He was nervous. Why? Her eyes questioned him, knowing the answer long before he answered.

"You have unleashed emotions in me that I did not know I had, and I suppose I'm trembling because there is a part of me that fears I might lose you. I don't think I could ever bear that."

"I'll never leave—and I won't let you leave me. You

asked me if I would travel the world with you. I will. . . ."

Pulling her gently down upon the bed, he explored Natasha's body with the moist fire of his lips, intoxicating her with sensuous tenderness until she was writhing against him, wanting him with a blazing longing. For just a moment, he left her to divest himself of his tunic, boots, and trousers, and she watched him silhouetted by moonlight. What a magnificent man he was, all grace and strength, she thought. Her Sean. Hers. Sleek and powerful, with wide shoulders that tapered to narrow hips and long, powerful legs—the very sight of him stirred her.

Sean was not unaware of her eyes caressing him, and it pleased him. Joining her on the bed, he took her hand and guided it to the strength of his manhood.

Her body arched up to his, seeking closer contact with his strength. Reaching out with impatient hands, she let her fingers explore him with as much wonder as she had that very first time.

"Love me . . . now. . . ."

The frantic desire for him was nearly unbearable as he covered her body with his own, stroking her, kissing her. His bare chest brushed the tips of her breasts, searing her with the heat of his passion. Warm, damp, and inviting, she welcomed him and he entered gently. Natasha locked her long, slender thighs about him, arching and surging against his thrust.

"Tasha!" His cry was like a benediction as he buried himself deep within her. She was tight and hot, like a sheath around him, and he closed his eyes to the delirious bursts of pleasure that rippled through him. It was heaven here in her arms, as if she had been sent to earth just to him. She was all things to him at this moment—nymph, temptress, angel—as fragile as a flower with the fire of a star.

Natasha had never felt so loved. She would remember this moment forever. It was what she had always imagined her wedding night would be like, and she knew in her heart that Sean was truly her husband for as long as they both breathed the air of life.

Thirty-four

The evening mist had gathered; the Dneiper River was still. It was near sunset, the hour of shadows. Sean was tired from loading and unloading the ships of the goods the Vikings had bartered for in Kiev, but not too tired to spend the night making love to his new wife.

It was the third day after their wedding, yet he still felt a special glow from his wedding night and the nights that had followed. How was it possible that every night of lovemaking had been better than the first? Though he supposed that Natasha had retired to their sleeping chambers an hour ago, he knew that, were he to wake her, she would be just as amorous as he. With that thought in mind, he moved toward their chamber, but Ragnar blocked his way.

"Sit. With Selig, Torin, and I. There are so many years we need to make up for, let us talk for just a little while before you go to your wife. . . ."

They built a large fire on the riverbank, drank their evening ale, and sat in a circular formation on tree stumps. Their love of the sea was a bond among them as fierce as family ties; thus, they talked first about ships and the ocean.

Ragnar swilled great draughts of mead and seemed to be in a riotously good mood. "You have done well, Kodran, far beyond my mere imaginings. You have all done well."

"I have a lot still to learn: how to use the figurehead as a direction guide against more distant landmarks; how to steer by the stars, and to know instinctively which ones can be relied upon to keep the same positions from night to night." He turned to Selig. "You know the stars as well as you know the rivers and streams. I want to know what you know. I want to go way beyond the boundaries of our maps, to those places where men only dream they can go."

"What if that takes you to the end of the world?" Ragnar asked.

"I'll go as far as I can possibly go, and then if I must, I'll turn around and come back," Sean replied, his voice strong with determination. "And take solace in the fact that I was the first to try."

Torin remained silent. Part of his wisdom lay in keeping silent while other men revealed their every thought. Now he broke his silence. "There is no end to the world; it just goes on and on. Selig knows that, and I think that you do, too."

"Follow the birds," Selig said.

"The birds?"

"When we explore unknown waters we take a crate of ravens," he explained again. "If there is no land in any direction, the raven will return to the ship. If he doesn't return, then you know that land is not far off. That is when you lead your ship in the direction that the bird has taken."

"What if the birds keep returning?"

"You either keep sailing or give up and go home. It is as simple as that."

They drank in silence, taking measure of each other. As twilight deepened, the mead warmed them and the four men fell to talking about other things: trading, drinking, lovemaking, and war.

Ragnar told Sean about his own life: his conquests, his successes, and his failures. He spoke about his brother, Herlaug, and his brother's betrayal. "He tried to kill Selig and captured Erica with mischief in mind. I had to banish him, though it broke my heart to do so."

Selig made a sour face, though Sean didn't know if that had to do with sour mead or because he did not like Ragnar's brother.

"Our dear uncle had it in mind to become the next jarl, no matter who he had to wound to gain that honor," Torin explained, turning to Ragnar. "He was slowly poisoning him. Had his villainy not been discovered . . ."

"But it was." Ragnar touched each of them with his eyes. "And some good came about because of Herlaug's perfidy. I started my search for my progeny, and now I have found you, every one of you! What's more, my search has somehow prodded each of you to find a woman who suits you. Now you are all married." He turned to Torin. "You to my dear daughter, and Selig to a spirited dark-haired wench." He looked at Sean. "And now you, Kodran, to your brave Tasha." He pounded the table. "But I want more. I want grandchildren to hold in my arms before I die."

"Your wish is soon to be fulfilled," Torin said softly.

"Did I hear you right?" Ragnar was silent, watching as Torin nodded. *"Ahh-ehhhhh-yahhhh!"* His loud cry of joy pierced the air. "A baby. A grandchild." He was reflective for a moment. "This time I will not be away. I may have missed the births of my children, but I will not miss the births of my grandchildren!"

Selig and Sean wore their amulets, the dragon and the wolf. Ragnar stared at them in contemplative silence for a long moment; then, with the slow movements of a ceremony, he took the amulet from around his neck. It was like the others, but the stone was green. The amulet had the carving of the "gripping beast." The gripping beast was a fantastic composite creature: a mixture of a bear, lion, and dog rolled into one. It was a carving full of vigor and animation that seemed never to be still. Its paws were always clutching either itself, a neighboring animal, or the edge or corners of the frame. Its head was large, its eyes round and solemn as if to suggest deep thinking. It suited Torin.

"Restless energy, regeneration, mobility, and power . . ." He placed it around Torin's neck. "You have always been like a son to me. Wear this for good luck and protection."

Sean could tell that Torin was obviously very touched by the gesture. Ragnar must have meant a great deal to him and been much more than just the father of his wife.

"No, I can't take it. . . ."

"You can and you will!" Once Ragnar had spoken, he expected his whims to be obeyed.

"But what about you? What amulet will protect you?"

Ragnar laughed and pointed first to one and then the other, making a sweeping gesture with his hand. "All of you. You will protect me. And Odin." He leaned back. "Ah, but I am a happy man. Were I to die today, I would die contented."

"Don't say that!" Though he had never been superstitious, Sean felt a chill edge up his spine. "Let us not talk of dying but of life."

"Agreed."

The last days of autumn were quickly approaching. Winter was coming. It was a time when the river northward was swept by sudden squalls, so it was not surprising that the conversation turned to the subject of winter.

"We must not wait too long before going north, or the river will be frozen," Torin advised. He explained to Sean that if the river became hardened they would have to take the time to put ice runners on the dragon ships. These could help them penetrate deeply into the river when it was slick with ice.

"Do you have skis in Eire?" Selig asked. When Sean shook his head, he told him that these boards attached to the feet were like shadows over the snow. "You can sail down a mountain like the ships sail downstream."

"Or walk on the snow." Torin explained that the Slavs were able to walk along the riverbank on strange snowshoes of thongs and bent willows.

Putting his arms around himself, Ragnar shivered. "All this talk of winter could make a weaker man cold." But not him, his sons decided. Weak was a word that would never apply to Ragnar. He stood now like a pillar of iron, silent and strong. "We have stayed here but a few days, but it seems like a year. Let's go home!"

PART THREE
Land of the Frost Giants

Norway, Winter

Thirty-five

The raw, icy wind ruffled the sails of the Viking ships as they made their way up the fjord. Natasha could sense a change in the air. The wind tickling her face was much colder than it had been. The skies seemed cloudier. Shadows crept along the deck. In that moment, she was far less enthused than Sean about coming to the Northland.

He saw her shiver and quickly covered her with his cloak. "Is it colder here than where you come from?"

"No. In winter it was cold and the wind howled. Sometimes it became so cold that the rivers froze completely. So cold that wolves came out of the woods in droves just so that they could get close to our fires." She puckered her mouth in a frown. "One winter it was so cold that you could cast water into the air and it would freeze before touching the ground. That was the winter my mother's uncle was found out in the grasses, frozen stiff."

As the ship sailed toward the land, she was, however, apprehensive about the steep and solid cliffs that rose on both sides of the ship like rock walls and were covered by snow and ice. The mountains rose abruptly from steep-sided, long, narrow waterways that extended inland for many miles. It was as if a friendly giant had taken his finger and gouged out a place for ships to sail.

"Fjords," Sean called them.

Natasha assessed the Northland with a critical eye. It was as if frost giants had painted their pictures with ice and snow. The ground was blanketed in a white shroud, and ice hung from the roofs of faraway houses like large needles.

Sean put his arms around her and nuzzled her ear. "I'm not used to the cold. You'll have to keep me warm on cold, cold nights. . . ."

Silently Natasha leaned against his warmth.

From Ragnar's ship the sound of a horn could be heard blasting three notes into the freezing silence. The sound was echoed from the land.

"They are welcoming us," Sean exclaimed.

"Welcoming . . ." Natasha stiffened, remembering just how welcome she had been the last time she had reached a Viking settlement. Taking a deep breath, she was determined to put all of that behind her. This time she was a Viking wife, not a slave. Besides, she had come to like Ref, Ragnar, and Sean's brothers. Not all Vikings were bad!

The ship reached the shore at midday and the helmsman guided it to its mooring. Men, women, and children ran down to the landing to greet them, several dogs nipping at their heels as they ran. It was obvious that all those assembled had come to greet a loved one.

The ship sailed up a long, quarter-circle arc constructed of tree trunks and planks that jutted out from the bank. Then, when the ship was safely secured, the men began to unload their cargo of furs, chattering as they did about what they would trade for them. Ref wanted the prize coveted most by the Norsemen—silver; Torin, silks and spices. Selig was determined to barter for weapons to replace the ones he had lost on their journey. Sean wanted to keep the rarest of all treasures: books, purloined from the monasteries in Ireland several years ago, he said.

Natasha smiled. Perhaps he had not changed so much after all.

"Someday I'll return these," he whispered, touching them with reverence. "They took so much work. Believe me, I know."

Natasha watched as the ship was emptied of its bundles. It was different here from in Kiev, though both places were noisy, crowded, and filthy, with the smell of fish heavy in the air. Kiev had seemed to be filled with transients. Here in the Northland, it seemed as if the people had made a permanent home.

Even from far away she could see that several of the inhabitants were looking in their direction; one woman with red hair was waving frantically. "That's Erica. My sister. Perhaps she can take you under her wing."

"Her wing?"

Natasha was staring so intently that Sean laughed. "It's an expression they use in Eire. It means befriend someone, like a sister or mother and . . . and make them feel welcome until they get used to customs and . . . and ways in a new land."

"Oh . . . I see. Take under the wing, like a mother hen with chicks." As she had done all these years with Nadia. She started to follow Sean, but Nadia stopped her.

"No! Please, let me stay here on the ship." Suddenly, Nadia was terrified.

"But you cannot stay. . . ." Natasha looked toward Sean, then Nadia, then Sean again. In the end it was Ref who solved the problem.

"I'll carry her to shore. She is the most valuable cargo of all!" Coming up behind her, Ref lifted Nadia up and carried her in his arms.

Nadia buried her face in Ref's shoulder. "I'm heavy."

"No, you are light as a feather."

All eyes were upon Ref as he carried his precious

bundle to the shore. Natasha could hear the sound of Nadia's laughter. It was a welcome sound because Nadia had been so solemn and seemingly troubled on the journey.

"Ref likes her," Sean whispered in her ear.

"And she adores him. How are we going to get them together?"

"Give them time. Somehow, I have a feeling that they were meant to be together. Like us." Affectionately he brushed her golden locks from her face and reached out to hold her arm as they walked.

Natasha could see Selig being greeted by a petite dark-haired woman who clung to him joyously. The red-haired woman, Sean's sister, greeted Torin with a lusty kiss that revealed how much she had missed him. Then, putting her arms around Ragnar, she was talking excitedly.

"My sister is going to make Ragnar a grandfather," Sean explained. "Torin gave him the news while we were in Kiev, though now that I see how rounded she is, I am surprised that Ragnar did not notice that for himself."

"Men never notice such 'woman' things. They are much too busy with 'man' things, like ships and exploring."

Reaching down, Sean swept Natasha up in his arms as Ref had done with Nadia. "I'd notice. I'll know the moment you are carrying my child. I'll see that special glow."

As Sean transported her in his arms, Natasha looked about her at the cluster of houses huddled together. Here and there were houses balancing precariously on the waterside, another nearly touching the mountain slope. What amazed her, however, were the houses perched on ledges high above the water. It seemed that the Vikings were not only good builders, they were very ingenious.

Ragnar, Selig, and Torin headed toward a large

wooden house with a turf roof and stone foundation. Likewise, Sean took Natasha to the house that he told her was the central dwelling house, where cooking, eating, feasting, and gaming were done. Once they stepped inside, she could see that there were slats to let in the light, and a hole in the roof to allow smoke to escape and the sun's rays to enter. Because of the cold climate, there were no windows.

Sean took off his heavy woolen cloak, stomped his boots, then helped Natasha off with her cloak. They joined the others, who had already divested themselves of their cloaks, in the large hall

"Kodran! I'm so happy that ye came back to us safe and sound." Sean's sister greeted him affectionately, then turned to Natasha and held out her hand, clasping Natasha's warmly to demonstrate her welcome. "She is lovely, Kodran. No wonder you traveled so far away to bring her back."

Natasha listened carefully as Erica talked, feeling very proud of herself. On the journey Sean had helped her learn the Nordic language. His excellent teaching, coupled with her own determination, made it possible for her to understand and converse in their language.

"Thank you for your nice words . . . your compliment," Natasha said slowly. "I hope we can be . . . be . . . friends."

"I wish us to be more than that. I want us to be like sisters."

"Sisters?" Natasha nodded eagerly. "Sisters. Yes."

Erica took her by the arm, leading her over to where the dark-haired woman who was Selig's wife stood. At first the woman named Gwyneth was a bit stiff and haughty, but she soon warmed to Natasha, extending her hand cordially to welcome her to the family and introducing her to Nissa, Ragnar's wife and, as such, "queen" of the household, as Gwyneth and Erica said with a wink and a smile.

Natasha had lived among the Vikings briefly in Kiev, so she was familiar with the indoor benches that lined the walls, the big pots that hung over the fire on chains from the ceiling, the looms and other implements used for making cloth, and the cooking utensils. That knowledge was quickly made use of as Nissa handed her a knife and a small bag of onions.

"Here. In this household we must all earn our keep," she said by way of greeting.

"You'll get used to her," Gwyneth whispered in her ear. "Erica and I did."

Natasha noted that Ragnar had several slaves, who were busily darting to and fro bringing loaves of flat bread from their baking spot upon the rocks of the fire to the table. She hated slavery, but at least here they seemed to be healthy and treated fairly. Even so, she wondered where each of them had come from and how they had been captured. Had they left loved ones behind to mourn their loss?

Nadia gravitated toward the slaves, helping them with the bread and setting out the plates and eating knives and spoons. Natasha hurried to her side, whispering, "You are not a slave anymore, Nadia. Come, over here with the others."

Erica and Gwyneth helped Natasha to chop the onions and put them in a large pot, then chopped up other vegetables while Nadia diced pieces of meat. Nissa sat in a chair and gave instructions. Natasha raised her eyes quizzically, wondering why Nissa didn't help them do any of the cooking.

"Where I come from everybody does things. They . . . they help unless they have slaves to do the work." She grimaced as she remembered her former status. "Is there something that . . . that is wrong with this woman? Is she . . . is she. . . ." She searched for the appropriate word. "Is she ill?"

"She is as healthy as a horse," Gwyneth sneered. "What afflicts Nissa is something called *lazy.*"

"Lazy?" Natasha didn't quite understand the meaning of the word.

Erica explained. "She does not like to participate in anything with her hands. She doesn't like to do women's work. Instead, she sits around while others do the work for her."

"Oh!" Natasha nodded, remembering that a few of the women at Demetrius's house in Constantinople had been like that. What she could not understand was why Ragnar, who was always so helpful to the other Vikings despite being jarl, allowed such a thing. Bluntly she asked that question.

Erica made a gesture with her hand like lips moving up and down. "Dear Nissa is a nag. I suppose my poor father doesn't want to be the target of her scolding; thus, he has learned to turn his head and ignore all her faults."

A thick cloud of smoke hung over the hall from the large hearth fire as the women prepared the evening meal. They chattered away about all that they had done to prepare for the winter. Listening to Nissa, it would have seemed that she alone had been responsible for drying and salting the food, pickling the herring, and storing the grain in the big barns. But as Natasha listened, she soon learned to do as Erica advised and "turn a deaf ear" to Nissa's chatter.

Soon there was another topic of conversation, Erica's coming child. Nissa calculated from the Scottish woman's symptoms that the child would be born in the dead of winter.

"When do you think the child was conceived?" Gerda, another of the Viking women, asked. "I always say that a woman knows."

"On a boat in the sea off the isle of Staffa," Erica said softly, smiling mysteriously, then closed her eyes as if remembering. She looked toward Torin, who was sitting by the fire playing a board game with Sean called *hnefatafl*.

She quickly explained to Natasha that the game involved a set of glass game pieces being moved across the wooden board in the manner of a Viking jarl and his men. Each player had to defend his men from attacking forces. Catching Torin's eye, she smiled, and he grinned back as if to tell her that he was winning.

"I say it will be a girl," Nissa stated, continuing the talk of babies. "You can see how she swells in the belly, carrying the child high in her womb. It is the sign of a female child." She smirked as if somehow a female child were less than a male.

"What would you know about it?" Gerda's gaze was scornful, causing Nissa to flush. Natasha rightly assumed that Nissa was barren. "It will be a male child, a grandson for Ragnar. Erica's belly is big, to be sure, but that is because the baby will be a big, strong boy!"

Nissa and Gerda argued back and forth, but Erica seemed to ignore the banter with a contented smile.

"I don't care what sex the child is. I will love it because it is part of Torin." She laughed softly. "Besides, for all their talk of having sons, I know that a female child can do anything that a male child can do. Sometimes better!"

"Daughters soon find a way to wrap their fathers around their little fingers," Gwyneth added, smiling as if to say that she had quickly learned that skill.

Natasha remembered her father and the close bond they had had. "It's true. Despite the fact that my father had three sons, I know in my heart that I was his favorite!"

At last, when the food had cooked and Natasha was certain that her grumbling stomach could be heard all the way across the room, Ragnar took his seat at the table, motioning the others to join. He rapped sharply with his knife.

"To signal that the meal has officially begun," Gwyneth whispered, nodding toward Nissa, who had hurried to take her place at the table while the other women scooped and ladled the food onto plates and into bowls.

Erica fixed a plate and bowl for Natasha, urging her likewise to take a seat. "You have had a long journey. Gwyneth and I and the others can finish up."

Just as in Kiev, mealtime was a happy and noisy event with laughter, boasting, and storytelling. Natasha noted how easily Sean fit in, relating to Erica, Gwyneth, and the others how he and Natasha had escaped from the walled house in Constantinople and run through the streets and alleyways. Far from giving himself all the credit, however, he spoke of her as the bravest woman he had ever known.

"I've promised to take her with me the next time I go exploring," he exclaimed.

"Take her?" Nissa was aghast. "But why?"

"Because I do not want to be away from her even for a moment." The look in his eyes seemed to say that he was just as anxious as she to be together in a warm, soft bed. Though they had been together on the ship, they had been unable to give in fully to their desires, because Natasha had been afraid that their moaning would be heard by the others.

Once the evening meal was finished, however, and they had quickly retired to their room, they made up for lost time in an explosion of passion and pleasure as he cried out her name again and again.

With a satisfied sigh she snuggled against him. His hands still held her tightly, as if afraid to let her go, afraid that she might somehow disappear. Smiling, Natasha held on to him, too, drifting off into a contented slumber in the afterglow of their lovemaking as words of love were whispered softly in her ear.

Thirty-six

Winter's stiff, cold fingers gripped the Northland. The rocky terrain seemed to stretch out in unending jagged formations of white. If Natasha was used to the cold, Sean wasn't. Never had he felt such cold. No matter how many fires stirred in the household, the chill seemed to go right through him.

The Northland was often called the "land of fire and ice," but Sean thought of it as the land of the frost giants. There was snow, ice, and frost everywhere. So decisive a factor was winter in the life of the Vikings that they counted time not in years but in winters.

One winter storm was so severe that it froze the water in the soapstone bowls within the hall. He thought how appropriate it was that the Vikings conceived of the realm of the dead as cold, rather than the flaming hell of the Christians.

Sean remembered Ragnar's explanation of Niflheim, that icy place where the dead went when they were in disfavor. It was ruled over by the goddess of death, Hel. "In Norway we say the gateway is through a hollow mountain, the mound where men lie buried. It is a region veiled in mist, a land of nothingness. The land of punishment lies beyond and is a realm of endless night, of eternal cold, where the wind stings like a serpent's strike."

"To Christians, hell is a fiery land ruled by Satan and his fallen angels. We also call him the devil. But

I have found that hell is really up here"—Sean had tapped his temple—"in the mind."

Now he tried to tell himself that cold was also in the mind and that if he refused to think about it he wouldn't feel the cold, but that wasn't true. He felt it in his bones, flesh, and muscles.

Sean had heard that in the summer there had been seemingly endless light; now in winter it seemed as if there was endless darkness. Darkness and cold. The men spent the long, dark hours working at tasks that still had to be done despite the winter. They also hunted and fished to add to the ever dwindling food supply. A long, cold winter would mean that the provisions put away in the fall might run out while the weather was still too severe to replenish them. Thus, Viking men were no different from other men now that they had changed their attentions from ships and sailing to the land and matters of survival.

When ice formed on the ponds, men and women alike were called upon to assist the slaves in chipping it away so that the animals could drink. The barns, storehouses, and byres had to be kept weather-tight with new layers of sod on walls and roofs. Protection of the animals and food took precedence in winter, when one's life depended on food for survival during the long, cold months.

The same was done for the longhouse, though there were times when, no matter what they did, it was so cold that they all had to stay as close to the fire as they could. Sometimes Sean worked so hard that by the end of the day his arms and legs were almost paralyzed from hard work and the cold. Lovingly Natasha would rub him down with soothing oils, which were not only warm but erotic. Was it any wonder how many hours he spent cuddling with her under the eiderdown in their bed? He could have stayed in bed with her for eternity.

Though the slaves and others of the household

slept on bed shelves, ledges divided by upright planks into compartments and covered with piles of furs and located in the main hall, Ragnar, Erica, Selig, Sean, and their spouses had small rooms with doors and bolts. In the middle of the room was a bed with eiderdown coverlets and a fur spread. In addition there were large chests for their possessions, and pegs on the wall for hanging clothes. More importantly, the room offered privacy, a chance to be alone so that they could talk, make love, and just enjoy those moments of being together.

Despite the privilege of having a room, however, it did not keep out the banging and clanking sounds as the household arose and everyone got out of bed. Though Sean held Natasha tightly in his arms, she struggled to pull away.

"Stay!"

"I can't. A woman's work is never ended," she whispered in his ear. "I have to help the others prepare the food for *davre.*" Natasha said the word with a heavy accent. "Davre. Breakfast."

Sean nibbled on her neck. "I'd rather eat you! Oh, why is it, woman, that you taste so good."

Natasha hesitated, tempted to stay in the nice, soft bed with Sean lying beside her, but as she heard the clanking of pots, she pushed him gently away and rose from the bed.

"There are meals to be cooked, dishes and pots to be cleaned, and housework to be done. The slaves can't possibly do it all." She looked at him accusingly. "The halls have to be cleaned more often now that you men spend so much time inside and—"

"The men! You are blaming us?"

"Mmm-hmm. You are all used to wives picking up after you," she said with mock anger. "But I suppose we will still keep you." Playfully she blew him a kiss.

He rolled over on his side to face her, rising up at an angle so that he could pat her on her rounded behind, then lying back down as he watched her dress in the woolen gown, tunic, and apron he had gifted her with. When she was half finished dressing, he opened the trunk and took out his heaviest woolen tunic, cape, and trousers.

Sean accompanied her to the hall. In the center of the floor was a deep pit that was lined and rimmed with stones. There a fire burned, not only to heat the long room but to be used for cooking. Natasha gravitated toward that area and bent over to pick up one of the large cauldrons to clean it.

"That is too heavy." Sean immediately aided her with his strong arm. Their fingers touched as they grabbed the handle, and he was pleased to see by her expression that she was feeling just as stirred by the contact of skin upon skin as he was. Somehow, he thought it would always be that way and they would never grow tired of each other. "Where do you want it?"

Though she knew she would have huffed and puffed, he lifted it up as if it weighed nothing at all. "Over there." She pointed toward the area where there were large buckets of water, then followed after him. "What would I do without you?"

He grinned at her. Though she was very independent, he was needed and she was never afraid to let him know it. That soothed his pride as he picked up a dried plum from a plate on the table. Though there were only two meals in a Viking household, there were fresh fruits in the summer and dried fruits in the wintertime to nibble on between meals.

The hall was bustling with activity as the slaves stoked the fire, brought wood in from outside, and saw to the menial tasks, while the women stirred the porridge that bubbled in the pots, and gathered honey from the honeycombs. Two slaves had been given the duty of making sure the fire was kept going. Day and night, one or the other of the thralls sat by it, leaving only to get more wood.

In addition to Selig's dog, Baugi, there were two other dogs who bounded up to greet Sean as he walked toward the fire. Trying not to show partiality, he petted them each in turn.

Erica saw Sean from across the room and called out his name. So did Selig and Gwyneth. Torin was already at work out by the barn, replenishing feed, he was told. Selig was going out to repair the storage shed after the morning meal.

"Good morning, Kodran." Ragnar patted him on the shoulder, exhibiting his robust mood. "I want you to help me fix the roof after we eat. And then I have a surprise for Tasha and Nadia: a ride in a wagon without wheels."

"A sleigh!" Sean had heard Torin talk about the various ways they traveled over the snow and ice, and he thought how clever the Vikings could be.

When snow covered the rugged terrain, freezing lakes and rivers, the people got around on sleighs, sledges, skis, and skates. Like the Slavs, they also used snowshoes. Since the large sleighs were pulled by horses, they had even devised a method to keep the horses from slipping on the ice, by nailing studs or iron crampons to their hooves.

"Can you show me how to build one?" Sean could foresee the need to learn so that he could use such skills in any unchartered lands in the north where his crew might have to wait out the winter.

"We'll build one together, you and I." Taking a piece of charcoal out of the fire, Ragnar busied himself by drawing the design of a sleigh on a flat stone he pulled from the cooking fire.

No matter how cold it was outside, Sean was warmed by the love that existed within the walls of his father's household. Whenever there was something to do, they all cooperated and did it together. He was slowly getting to know his father, sister, and brothers. He had a family. He felt loved. Sean knew that was more important than anything else in life. And soon there would be an addition to the family. He looked across the room toward Erica, who was standing close to the fire as she tended to the poached gulls' eggs.

"Are you cold, Erica?" Ragnar asked from his place across the fire. "I thought I saw you shiver. I don't want you to catch a chill. The baby will soon be coming."

Ragnar had been so concerned with his daughter's welfare the past few weeks that it was obvious to Sean how much the gentle giant of a man really loved her. It was also obvious that she was touched by that love.

"I'm fine, Father. . . ."

"Are you sure?"

"I'm sure."

"And how is my grandson?" Sean saw him wink at her.

"*She* is fine," she answered, standing firm in her opinion that she was going to have a girl no matter who said otherwise.

Ragnar assessed the skaalen with a critical eye. "Much too small. We are soon going to outgrow it here."

In order to accommodate the needs of his growing family, Ragnar was planning to erect a second large skaalen at right angles to the long hall, ignoring his sons' insistence that they wanted longhouses of their own. Moreover, they would be traveling, Selig to his settlement in Britain, Torin on his merchant routes, and Sean on voyages to the north. Ragnar told them that he wanted to keep the family all together during those times when they were all in one place.

"We have all been apart for so long, and time is so short, particularly when a man is getting long in the tooth."

"You're not old," Sean said quickly. "I've seen you

work circles around Selig and me." Though Torin had told him that Ragnar's ill health had been the catalyst for him to search for his sons, his father was not showing any outward signs of ill health now that Herlaug had been sent away.

"Ah, but I feel old in my bones, and I know a man does not live forever, at least in the flesh." He held up his hand when it appeared that Sean and Selig were going to protest. "I am mortal, and though I hang on to the hope that I will go to Valhalla, I have to make certain that all that I have created here is in order. I have to decide who is going to take my place."

Erica shivered. "Please, Father, do not talk about death before breakfast. It is a bad omen."

"I have to talk about something when it is fresh on my mind." He took a deep breath and let it out in a sigh.

"You have two sons, a daughter, a coming grandchild, and Torin, Natasha and I," Gwyneth said. "And undoubtedly there will be more to add to your family." She looked at Selig and blushed. "Your seed will be secure, but you must be patient."

"A man's children and grandchildren are his immortality—that and a man's good name," Ragnar replied. "I know that. But I also feel that time is running out. Last night I had a dream that I was sailing off to the west, going on forever. I was peaceful and content, until I looked behind me and saw the chaos that was shattering the peace I had created here." Ragnar paused as Torin entered the room, stamping the snow off his boots, then shaking himself dry. "One of you must be prepared to take my place, for only then will I be able to sleep easily."

"No one can ever really take your place, Ragnar," Torin said dryly.

"Perhaps no *one* should try," Selig stated. "There are three of us."

Ragnar shook his head. "No. I won't have you fighting among yourself for supremacy!"

Sean quickly protested. "We wouldn't."

Ragnar was realistic. "Ah, but you would. I have seen such things put brothers at odds before. Once Herlaug and I were as close as two brothers could possibly be, but he was tempted by the thought of power." He paused to sniff the appetizing aroma of food that was wafting in the air. "No, it is time for me to make a decision. One of you will be named my successor in seven days' time, and the others will take a blood oath to follow, protect, and be loyal to that successor until the day of Ragnarok."

"Until the end of the world?" Selig asked incredulously.

"It is the only way."

Sean looked at Selig, Selig at Sean. One of them was going to be given the honor. But who?

Thirty-seven

The morning meal was over. The dishes had been cleared from the table, washed, and dried. A few of the slaves were busy boiling seawater to collect salt for the food while others were gutting the fresh fish the men had caught so that it could be pickled. The smell of fresh bread baking wafted through the room.

Natasha looked over her shoulder to where Nissa and Gerda sat at the loom, weaving wool into a blanket. Spinning and weaving were year-round tasks of Viking women, she had soon learned. They needed cloth for garments as well as to make sails for the ships, which would be seaworthy again in the spring. When she had told Sean that a woman's work was never done, she had not lied.

Men ploughed, hunted, fished, traded, and fought. Crafts were also the preserve of men. Women's lives were confined to the home. They ground flour and baked bread, brewed ale, spun woolen thread, wove cloth, made and mended clothes, milked the cows, churned butter, nursed the sick, and looked after the children. There weren't enough hours in the day. Even so, every day Natasha desperately fought to find the time to practice with the piece of parchment Sean had recently given to her.

It just didn't make sense to her that reading and writing be confined to certain languages such as Latin and Greek. Why couldn't other languages be written down as well? From what she had learned about writing, it was merely a collection of sounds, all put down on paper like a code.

"Tasha!" She turned to see Ragnar standing behind her.

Feeling self-conscious when in his presence, Natasha hid the parchment behind her.

"You . . . and . . . Gwyneth . . . get your fur capes and put on your warmest woolens and come with me. I have a surprise for you!"

"A surprise?" Ragnar rarely talked with either Gwyneth or her, so she was taken aback. What was on his mind? Surely he was not going to cajole them with his desire to have grandchildren.

Ragnar smiled mysteriously. "The winds have stopped howling, the snow has died down, and I fear I have a wanderlust. What about you?"

"Wanderlust?" Immediately a ship came into her mind, and she shivered.

"I have watched you. You have worked long and hard without once uttering a word of complaint. Tell me the truth. Aren't you tired of being cooped up?"

"Yes." She was. Why not admit it? "My people were wanderers. We seldom stayed in one place, even when it was cold."

"Then come!" He saw her looking toward Nadia. "Ah, yes, the little one. She can come too."

The three women hurriedly changed to their warmest woolens, grabbed their fur capes, and followed Ragnar outside. There they saw a sleigh harnessed to a pair of black horses. The sleigh was carved and had two runners instead of wheels.

Gwyneth raised her eyebrows in bewilderment. "How does this move upon the ground without wheels?"

Ragnar threw back his head and laughed. "Ah, Gwyn, I see that you do not have much snow in your land, uh?" He explained. "It skims the top of the snow as the ship skims the waters." He picked up each young woman one my one and placed them onto the seat, where they huddled together. "I'll show you what fun this can be. . . ."

Ragnar jumped up on the seat and took the reins while Natasha, Nadia, and Gwyneth buried themselves in the furs he had piled on the seat. Then, just as they made themselves comfortable, he pulled at the reins and the sleigh took off with a jerk. The runners skimmed over the snow like magic. They rode across fields covered with several feet of snow and topped with a hard crust, and Natasha thrilled at the sights around her. It was a fantasy kingdom of ice and snow.

The sleigh passed by the area where the ships were riding at anchor. Even from a distance, Natasha could see that Ref was among those making repairs. His red hair against the snow was like a beacon.

"Ref!" Nadia's hands twisted nervously in her lap, just as they did when he was around. Natasha noticed how her friend's eyes suddenly softened as the sleigh came closer.

"We haven't seen much of Ref this winter." Natasha wondered why.

"I know." Nadia was strangely quiet. Did Natasha imagine it, or were there tears in Nadia's eyes?

Something was very wrong between the two of them, something that words alone could not erase. She wanted to ask Nadia so many questions, but now was not the time. She would wait until they were alone.

"Look there!" Gwyneth gasped, seeing several people gliding about upon the frozen waters.

"They are skating," Nadia said. "Tasha and I have seen many people skate."

"They have animal bones attached to their feet much the same as we have runners attached to this sledge," Natasha explained.

"I've heard that it is fun! Someday I would like . . ." Nadia halted in midsentence as she remembered her leg. For the rest of the sleigh ride she was strangely quiet.

"Won't they fall through the water?" Gwyneth asked.

"If the ice is thin there is a chance for such a thing to happen," Ragnar said.

"You have to be very careful," Natasha cut in, remembering how she had been fearful of skating because she was afraid of water. That fear was behind her, however, and the daring in her made her wish that Ragnar would stop the sledge so that she could give skating a try.

It felt so good to be out of the hall! The air was cold and her cheeks and nose were half frozen, yet she was enjoying herself. Everything looked so different when it snowed. So fresh and clean. For a long while the whole world was silent except for the *thunk* of the horses' hooves and the hissing of the runners slipping across the hardened snow.

Ragnar broke the silence. "One of you may well be a jarl's wife one day after I am gone. With that honor comes a great deal of responsibility."

"I know. . . ." Natasha was reflective.

Though women had no formal role in public life or legal procedures she knew that a strong-minded woman could enjoy a great deal of practical influence and authority. She had quickly learned that when the Viking husband was away from home, a wife had full responsibility for running the household and surrounding lands until he returned. If she was widowed, a woman had to take her husband's place unless she decided to remarry. Women were no less zealous in defending family honor than men, whether in Viking lands or those of the Magyar.

"I know all about such responsibilities," Gwyneth said softly. "Despite the fact that my father would not admit it, my mother was my father's right-hand man."

Ragnar laughed, then looked first at one daughter-in-law and then the other. "I love all of my children equally. The past few weeks I have studied them with a loving though critical eye, trying to judge their strengths and their faults. I need to weigh my decision very carefully."

"You intend to choose between Sean and Selig?" Gwyneth asked. "In Wessex a man's lands and honors are transferred to the eldest son." She looked at Ragnar as if to remind him that Selig had been born to him first.

"First, middle, or last does not matter to me," Ragnar answered, dashing Gwyneth's hopes. "I want to choose the successor who understands and loves the Northland the way that I do. Someone strong, yet at the same time a peacemaker." He laid the whip to the horses and turned the sleigh around. "As to choosing between Sean and Selig, you forget that there is a third choice."

"A third?" Gwyneth was stunned. "Another son? Who?"

"A daughter."

They were showered with snow as one of the runners hit a large clump. The women brushed the snow from their hair and eyes, then Natasha leaned over and did the same to Ragnar, whose hands were holding tightly to the reins.

"Erica is married to a man who has been like my own son in every way. Torin has been my silent strength for all these years. . . ."

"Of course . . . Torin. . . ." Erica and Torin. They would make a perfect pair to step into Ragnar's boots. Natasha couldn't hide her sense of relief. It was as if a mountain had suddenly been lifted from her shoulders. Sean had told her over and over again how he wanted to sail to unexplored lands. It had always been his dream. A dream that would be shattered if he were suddenly under that burden of responsibilities that being a jarl would bring.

The crystalline white world seemed suddenly brighter, as if the sun was suddenly shining; then, all too soon the sleigh ride came to an end and they found themselves back in front of the large building that housed the family.

Helping the women off the wooden seats, Ragnar acted as if he, too, felt lighter of heart. Because he had come to a decision? Natasha was certain that he had. Or perhaps he had always known in his heart who was destined to follow him.

Ragnar led the horses back to the barn and gave them over to one of the thralls; then he returned to where the young women stood. Together they walked back into the hall.

The moment they pushed through the door, Natasha knew that something was wrong. Her eyes sought out Sean. He was hovering over Erica, holding her hand, trying to comfort her.

Natasha had no need to ask what was happening. She read it in Erica's eyes, woman to woman. "It's the baby!"

"The baby!" Ragnar paled. "Frigg, Earth Mother, Wife of Odin, be with my daughter. . . ."

"Frigg is the goddess invoked by women in labor," Nissa explained, pushing Sean aside. Always proficient at issuing orders, Nissa soon had the women of the household bustling about, gathering up the necessary items to help in delivering the baby.

Erica, meanwhile, slowly moved toward her bedchamber, where she would have some privacy to have her child. It took all her courage to move about, for by the look on her face it was very apparent that the pains of labor were cutting through her. Even so, it wasn't like Erica to utter so much as a sigh.

"Quickly, boil the water!" Natasha had seen enough babies born on the steppes to know that should be done.

The whole household was on edge, watching as

Erica doubled over in pain. For just a moment Natasha empathized and could nearly feel that pain herself. She watched as Torin pushed through the door, gently picked his wife up in his arms, and strode through the door to their chamber and laid Erica on the bed.

"Squeeze my hand when the pain becomes unbearable," he whispered, determined to stay by her side. Gerda and Nissa, however, would have none of that. Telling him that men had no place in the room when a baby was being born, they shooed him away.

Gerda placed a cup of herb tea in Gwyneth's hands and told her to take it to Erica. "She must drink it all. The liquid will relax the muscles needed for the birth and at the same time soothe the pain." When Gwyneth hesitated she said, "It is a secret Ragnar brought back from the East."

Hurrying to the chamber, Natasha held Erica's head up while Gwyneth administered the tea. "Drink it slowly."

Though Natasha had been anxious to have Sean's child, she now had second thoughts as she watched the expressions that contorted Erica's face. Expressions that told of her pain despite Erica's silence.

The hours dragged on. Erica's labor was long, her pain severe. Nissa and Gerda kept her upon her feet, walking as long as it was possible, telling her all the while that it would make the birthing easier. Then, at last they laid her back down on the bed.

Natasha remembered watching while one of her cousins was born. She openly disagreed with Nissa despite the consequences of her anger. "She should be crouching, squatting, not lying down." She had seen Slavic women deliver their babies out in a field, then resume their harvesting.

"What do you know about it?" Nissa scolded, pushing Natasha toward the door.

"Wait . . . listen . . . listen to her. I think she is right. It makes sense. . . ." Erica motioned for

Natasha to come back in the room. Slowly maneuvering herself into a crouching position, Erica pushed with all her might.

"That's right, bear down," Natasha urged, watching as Erica writhed in agony, bearing down in an effort to push the child out of her womb.

"She's thin in the hips and small boned. The birth is much easier when a woman is big!" Nissa insisted.

"That's it; push down," Gwyneth breathed, ignoring Nissa's interruption.

"The head is about to come!" Gerda picked up a towel. "Scream if you want to; it may help."

"No. . . ." Erica was resolved not to cry out. To her a show of strength was important. "I won't. . . . I am a Viking now!"

Natasha reached out, clasping Erica's hand to give her comfort while Gerda held her hands out to catch the baby. It was quiet in the room as all eyes watched the baby's delivery. Only when they heard the cry of the newborn child did they break the silence.

"It's a boy!" Gerda intoned with a note of pride. "A handsome son with red-gold hair."

"A boy . . ." Erica sighed. "Father was right."

Natasha watched as Gerda cut and tied the long, gray cord, then wiped the baby off. "He is strong!"

"Let me hold him!"

Gerda placed the baby in his mother's arms. In that moment, seeing Erica with her baby, all Natasha's former apprehension about having her own baby melted away. There couldn't possibly be anything more wonderful than bringing a new life into the world, a blending of mother and father.

Ragnar looked down at his daughter. Her gown was soaked with sweat; her hair was mattered around her face. He knew she must have suffered pain, yet she had not uttered one scream.

Gerda held the infant high in the air. "It is a male child, a son!"

"Aha!" Looking upon the infant, at the proof of maleness, Ragnar's eyes flashing with pride, he cried aloud for all to hear, "I have a grandson."

Gerda handed him the tiny bundle wrapped in swaddling cloth. "He looks like Torin. The same strong chin and well-formed nose, but the eyes are mine and the hair is yours, Erica!"

Natasha and Gwyneth peered at the baby, marveling at the tiny toes and fingers. So perfect, yet so small. Looking in Sean's direction, she made a wish that she would have a child of her own soon.

Taking the baby from his mother's arms, placing it at the patriarch's feet for the ceremonial act of acceptance, Gerda asked, "Do you accept this child?"

Ragnar took the child from Gerda's arms and poured water over the infant.

"It is to show that he has been admitted into the family," Erica whispered.

"He is baptizing him," Gwyneth exclaimed. "But the Vikings do not worship the Lord. . . ."

Gwyneth had confided to Natasha that the difference in their religions had been a source of contention between her and Selig. Now Gwyneth was the first to admit that the ceremony, though pagan, was beautiful.

"He shall be called Roland, after the father I took from Torin so long ago. Perhaps in this way I can make up for some of the pain he suffered as a boy. Roland Torinsson! Grandson of Ragnar Longsword!"

"Father . . ." Erica was touched. Though Natasha had never seen her cry, she witnessed tears rolling down her cheeks now.

"Thank you!" Taking his place by his wife's side, Torin took his turn to cradle the newborn infant.

"Perhaps my child can erase the stain to my father's name. . . ." Lying beside Erica on the bed, he put the baby between them, then held her close with such special tenderness that everyone within the room felt a sudden surge of love and warmth.

Thirty-eight

The days following the birth of Sean's nephew remained dark and cold. There was one winter storm after another. Even so, the week passed with happiness for Sean, Natasha, and the rest of the family. An air of harmony surrounded them as they waited for spring. There were, of course, a few scuffles from time to time; being cooped up in such close proximity for so long was sure to be trying, but basically there was more brotherhood among them than Sean had witnessed even among the monks.

There was more and more work to be done as spring approached, but in the evenings Sean relaxed with Natasha as they both sat by the fire, listening to Ragnar tell stories of his early days at sea, spent both in raiding and in establishing trading settlements. He had traveled to all the major ports in the Western world, and as he told about the different customs of the people, Sean felt more and more impatient for spring to come so that he could explore such places.

Ragnar was happy and content, more so than Sean had ever seen him. His world centered now on his grandson, as if making up for all the time he had missed with his own children. Natasha and Sean would often find him bouncing the baby upon his knee, holding the precious bundle in his large hands.

"He has the strong chin of a jarl," he would say to all those around him. "And see how he clings to my finger. He will have a mighty sword arm, this grandson of mine. Roland the Bold, Roland the Strong Arm, that's what he shall be called. He'll make all my exploits seem like nothing."

It seemed that everyone in the household loved the child, everyone except Nissa. The baby reminded her of her own failing, her barrenness.

"You spoil the babe," Nissa chided.

"Of course I do. I won't deny it!" Ragnar had dipped his finger in honey, and he watched with a smile as the baby licked at the sweet confection. "He is my greatest treasure." His eyes were filled with pride. "I would give my very life to make certain that he is safe and happy. He is the hope of the family, first in a new generation of Vikings."

"You should not give a child sweets, husband."

"Bah! It is right for the grandson of a jarl to be at least a little coddled."

"A little . . ." Nissa shrugged her shoulders.

Ragnar turned to Sean. "What about you? Do you think I spoil my grandson?"

Sean echoed Nissa's words. "A little . . . but I see no harm done."

Oblivious to the argument concerning him, Roland uttered a lusty wail. Ragnar rocked the child, looking strangely clumsy with a baby so small. When Roland didn't quiet right away, Ragnar handed him back to his mother.

"Ah, he is going to be a Viking, all right. Just listen to that war cry," Ragnar said. He brightened as he had an idea. "Let's have a feast."

"A feast?" Natasha frowned, imaging all the work the preparations would create. Not to mention the snow and the mud that would be tracked in by all of the guests. And where were they going to put all the cloaks and capes of those who had come in from the cold?

"Yes, a feast. Right now. Today. This very minute. I

am the most fortunate of men! I feel like being generous."

Later that night there was a feast, with everyone from miles around in attendance. While the men and women ate there was entertainment—a skald strumming his harp and singing about Ragnar's exploits, and a juggler who, although he dropped as many colored balls as he caught, was applauded.

Seeing Ref, Natasha gravitated to his side, sensing a feeling of loneliness and isolation about him. Putting a hand on his shoulder, she whispered, "I've missed seeing you."

"Nadia doesn't want me anywhere near."

"Did she say that?"

He shook his head. "Not in so many words, but each time she sees me she goes the other way. What am I supposed to think?"

Natasha started to tell him the truth, then said only, "Nadia is lonely. I think she pines for you."

Ref looked down at the toes of his boots as if afraid to show the depth of his feelings. "She has you and the others around her. How can she be lonely?"

"A woman can be lonely amid a whole crowd if the man she loves is not with her. And on the other hand, if she is without her loved ones and with the man she loves, then her world is full."

"You sound as if you speak from experience."

She looked toward the table where Sean sat talking with his father. The men were loudly applauding Ragnar and drinking to his good fortune. "I do!"

"But Nadia does not love me."

"She does!"

"Then why does she always pull away? When I ask her to come away with me she stiffens. How can I think otherwise than that she doesn't care for me as I care for her?"

Natasha didn't want to betray a confidence or her friendship to Nadia, yet she felt Ref had a right to know why Nadia was scorning him. With a sigh she told him about Nadia's accident and how it had left her with a twisted leg and a limp.

"She thinks I would care about that?"

Natasha didn't have a chance to answer. Gwyneth was motioning for her to come and join the rest of the family. The high point of the celebration was to be the distribution of gifts by Ragnar: tools for the men, trinkets for the women, silver coins for each of his slaves.

Gifts of new swords were given to Selig, Sean, and Torin, all with the same carving as their amulet carved on the handle of the sword. To Erica he gave a golden box that had a compartment to keep tiny valuables; to the baby he gave a golden cup. Natasha and Gwyneth received silver arm rings, Natasha's with matching earrings for her pierced ears, Gwyneth's with a matching brooch. To Nadia, however, he gave the greatest gift of all: he made the promise that were she to marry he would give her a dowry.

"How could you have so completely looked into my heart and known my greatest wish?"

"I've seen you hover over the little one like a mother hen, and Sean has told me the story of how you were enslaved because you stayed behind with her and thus were captured and enslaved. In a way I am rewarding you for your bravery."

Natasha hugged him tightly. "Oh, Ragnar, I love you like a father. Thank you."

Taking Nadia aside, Natasha was determined that now she would not take no for an answer. "You care for Ref; I have seen the way you look at him. Oh, Nadia, Ragnar is giving you a chance for happiness. How can you do anything else but grasp it?"

"I must . . ."

Angered by Nadia's stubbornness, refusing to leave anything to chance, Natasha took her by the hand, pulling her to where Selig and Ref stood. She could feel Nadia try to pull away, but being the stronger of the two, she managed to draw her to a spot in front of Ref. With a knowing wink at Selig, she led him away, leaving Ref and Nadia alone—but not so far away that she could not listen to hear if her matchmaking was going to work.

"I'm glad that you . . . you could come to the feast," Nadia said somewhat stiffly, as if she felt awkward to have been so obviously foisted upon Ref.

Ref grinned at her. "It seems there is matchmaking afoot, but I don't mind, for I cannot imagine a woman I would rather have at my side."

Nadia smiled, a radiant smile that emphasized her fragile loveliness. "Do you remember in Kiev, the celebration we had there? You bought me ribbons for my hair."

"I remember. You looked beautiful then and you look beautiful now."

She flushed. "I am not a beauty."

"I think that you are. Your hair is the color of burnished gold; your eyes sparkle like stars. . . ." Suddenly embarrassed by this effusive emotion, he said a little awkwardly, "I care for you, Nadia. Why have you avoided me? Why do you push me away?"

"I think you . . ."

Suddenly Ref was kissing her, a soft, gentle kind of kiss. When he pulled away he said, "I have wanted to do that since the first time I saw you. I love you, Nadia."

She stiffened. "How could you?"

"Because you are everything I have ever wanted." He cupped her face in his hands. "What is it?"

"Are you sure that what you feel for me isn't pity?"

"Pity?" He was incredulous. "Why would I pity you?"

"My . . . my leg. It's twisted and ugly from my accident."

Pulling her into a corner where they would have

privacy, he bent down and lifted the hem of her gown, touched her knee with his large hands, and kneeling before her, kissed and caressed that part of her that Nadia had always been self-conscious about.

"You are beautiful in every way, Nadia."

"My owner . . . he . . . he . . ."

He kissed her again and again, his hands caressing the curve of her waist, the thrust of her breasts. He might have done even more had Natasha not protectively moved between them.

Ref blushed. "It's all right. I want to make Nadia my wife."

"You've asked her?" Natasha was triumphant with her successful matchmaking.

"Not yet, but I am asking her now. Will you, Nadia?"

Natasha waited nervously for the answer which came in a whisper.

"Yes."

Ref's eyes looked down upon Nadia, and the tenderness written there could leave no doubt of his love.

Natasha pushed Ref toward the table where Ragnar sat. "Hurry. Talk with him, before he changes his mind about the dowry."

Watching as Ref strode toward Ragnar, she felt very pleased with herself. If only everything else in life could be as easy. Seeking Sean out, she leaned her head on his shoulder as she told him about the young lovers.

Out of the corner of his eye, Sean saw Selig move toward his bedroom and knew that he was going to join Gwyneth, who was already abed. Selig had offered Sean a brotherly, competitive challenge, that he and Gwyneth would have Ragnar's second grandchild before Sean and Natasha. It was a bet that he was more than happy to accept, he thought as he swept Natasha up in his arms.

Thirty-nine

Sean awoke with a start. There was something wrong; he sensed it. That eerie noise: was it the howl of a dog, or something more ominous?

Mumbling in her sleep, Natasha reached out to touch him, smiling as her soft hand met the firmness of his chest.

I must have been dreaming, he thought.

Willing himself to relax, he let his eyes feast on the beauty of his wife as she lay cradled in his arms. Her long lashes fanned out from her closed eyelids, her thick mane of golden hair was spread out like a silken cloak over his chest and shoulders. He felt an aching tenderness.

"I love you, Tasha!"

As if she could hear his words, she smiled, then turned over on her side. Her back was molded against him, and he felt his pulse quicken as he remembered the passion they had shared during the night. They had spent the whole night making love.

Reaching out now, he stroked her hair, contenting himself just to lie there with her without moving even a muscle or saying a word. Then, when she shivered in her sleep, he gathered her into his arms, the heat of his body warming hers until her slight trembling subsided.

Suddenly, he heard the sound again, louder this time. Certainly not the wind. A wolf? He listened more closely. It was a mournful sound. Though he was comfortable and didn't want to leave the bed, some gut feeling goaded him into investigating. If it was a wolf, he knew that they roamed in packs and that they could put the animals in jeopardy and affect the food supply.

He remembered how afraid the Slavs were of the creatures, insisting that they preyed upon men. But the Vikings shared no such fear. Even so, he had to be cautious.

Gently disengaging his arms and legs from his wife's sleeping form, he rose from the bed and hurriedly got dressed. Everything had been going so smoothly. He had the sinking feeling that one gets just before a storm breaks.

Pushing through the door, he stumbled once or twice over the inert forms of the revelers who had imbibed too freely of the abundant mead. The hall was strewn with the bodies of Ragnar's drunken guests, who were either sprawled on the hard floor or slumped in chairs. The room had the unpleasant smell of sweat, stale mead, and vomit. He had soon learned that such celebrations were the Viking way.

Gathering up his woolen cloak, he hurried outside, where a breath of the fresh morning air acted as a potion to revive him. Breathing in and out, Sean closed his eyes. Though he would never have admitted it to Natasha, he had partaken far too freely of the wine and mead that had been flowing abundantly last night. His temples throbbed, and his stomach was queasy.

Abstinence from now on, or at least until the next celebration . . .

He stiffened and grew still. He heard the yowl again; it was growing louder. It was coming from the direction of the storehouses!

The food . . . Guarding the food supply from wild

animals, spoilage, and thieves was an imperative at all times.

Arming himself, prepared to fend off ravening wild dogs or wolves if need be, Sean ran to the storehouse, bumping headlong into Selig, who had likewise heard the sound and made the assumption that all was not as it should be.

"That howl. Must be wolves."

"No. I recognize that yowl. It's Baugi."

"Your dog?" He sighed with relief.

"It's the same one that he makes when he jumps overboard to save a drowning man only to find that the man is well past saving."

"A death yowl."

Selig nodded.

Gripping their swords tightly, they ran past the barns and byres, stopping at the top of the hill to look around. They could not see any sign that there was anything amiss, though they could see footsteps in the snow. Two sets of tracks. When they reached the storehouse they pushed through the door.

Selig lit a torch. Holding it high, he visually searched the room. There was nothing unusual. All the barrels, boxes, bags, and crates were in their proper places. They went inside. It was then that they saw signs of a struggle and a trail of blood. Was it animal or human?

"Look!" Sean spotted what looked like a large sack. Beside it, Baugi was curled up, howling. Sean ran forward. It wasn't a sack; it was a person. Kneeling down, he made a gruesome discovery. "Father!"

"Is he dead?"

Sean bent his ear to Ragnar's chest. There was a faint flutter, a heartbeat. He was alive, but for how long? He picked him up in his arms. "Let's take him back to the hall."

Selig was staring. "Your hands . . ."

Sean looked down. They were covered with blood.

"He's been fighting with someone. Look. There's his sword!" The once mighty weapon had been haphazardly discarded, but not by Ragnar. A Viking would have hung on to his own sword for dear life. He picked it up, noting at once that it, too, was stained with red.

"Let's get him back to the hall, where the women can minister to him," Sean said, trying to keep control over his emotions. It was difficult, for over the past few weeks he had come to know and love Ragnar. Already he could feel the pain of the possible sudden loss.

"Let's take him home. . . ."

It took both of them to carry him, but at last they half dragged, half carried Ragnar inside and put him on his bed. The sight of the mighty Viking covered in blood caused a flutter of anxiety and tears among the women, yet after their initial reaction of shock they hurried to get bandages and other healing supplies.

Ragnar's eyes flickered open for only a moment and he moaned, but his eyes remained shut.

"What happened? Who did this to you?" Selig's voice trembled with anger.

"Her . . . her . . . laug!"

"Herlaug!" Sean breathed, remembering the name of Ragnar's ambitious brother. At the sound of the name, the flutter of activity ceased and everyone was silent.

"But he was banished!"

Ragnar's breathing was ragged yet he struggled to tell them what had happened. He had gone out to the storeroom for another barrel of mead and had surprised Herlaug in the act of setting fire to all the food in the storehouse. There had been a battle between them, but although Ragnar had frightened his brother off before he could do any damage, he had been wounded in the scuffle.

"Is he . . . is he going to . . . to die?" Gwyneth asked.

Sean had seen wounds such as these after the Viking attacks on the monastery. Some survived, others died. "I don't know," he answered truthfully.

"It depends on the severity of the wound and whether it gets putrid," Selig said solemnly, ripping Ragnar's tunic so that he could look at the injury. "He must have been lying there for a long time, so we have that to worry about, too."

Pushing his way to Ragnar's side, Torin assigned each woman a task: Erica, to see to the linen for bandages; Gwyneth, to fetch poultices; Natasha, to heat water over the fire for a hot broth that would warm Ragnar. As his wife, Nissa was to supervise and issue necessary orders to the slaves.

"He's lost a lot of blood, but at least the bleeding has stopped," Torin said, only narrowly maintaining his calm. "I don't think it necessary to cauterize him."

"Find Herlaug. Bring him back to me!" Selig thundered, motioning to the men hanging around the hall who were standing around gawking. "He must be punished for what he has done!"

There was a flurry of activity as the men armed themselves, then poured through the door, hurrying to obey.

Gwyneth, Erica, and Natasha took turns keeping a constant vigil over Ragnar. Meanwhile, the men searched everywhere they could think of for any sign of Herlaug, but could not find him. It was as if he had come just long enough to do his mischief and then vanished into thin air.

Natasha bent over Ragnar, putting her hand against his brow. She was worried, for despite the fact that they had cleaned the wound and applied a healing ointment, he was feverish. Natasha remembered her mother telling her that often it was not the wound itself that was the cause of death, but the pus that often invaded afterward.

"We must make certain that he has fresh water and that he drinks frequently," Erica advised. "My mother nursed many a wounded Scot and that was her secret."

"My mother used mud," Gwyneth insisted. Taking matters into her own hands, she went outside to get the necessary dirt, then mixed it with water. "It draws out the poison."

"No. Mud will infect the wound." Pushing Gwyneth and the others away, Nissa took charge once again of her husband. "If given enough time, the wound will heal itself."

"You're wrong. Gwyneth is right. Mud and moss are healing." Erica held out a small bowl of the concoction she had made.

"I am his wife."

"And I am his daughter."

It was a battle of wills that Erica soon won. Taking off the bandage, she applied the poultice, then replaced the linen.

"We must do everything we can . . . try anything . . ." Erica insisted.

Natasha took Erica aside. "I'm worried. There is something about the color of the wound." Though she did not want to cause panic, she had to reveal anything she knew that might help Ragnar to recover. "In Constantinople I remember the women telling me about a poison that is sometimes put on the blade of a knife or sword to cause a poisoning of the blood."

"Poison? What kind of poison?"

"I don't know. All I know is that the flesh around Ragnar's wound has a yellowish tinge that is spreading, not lessening."

"Is there an antidote?"

Natasha shook her head. "I don't know. I don't think so."

"Then let's hope that even Herlaug would not be so foul as to stoop to such a trick." Sitting on the bed, Erica rechecked the wound, then kissed Ragnar's brow. "I love ye, Father. Please don't die. We have so many years ahead of us. . . ."

Suddenly, it was as if a dam had burst. The usually resilient Erica, who had braved childbirth without crying in pain, now gave vent to the strain on her emotions.

"I don't want to lose him. . . ."

"Nor do I," Torin whispered, coming quickly to her side to gather her into his arms.

Sean looked on, feeling a sense of helplessness. Worse than that, he had somehow lost the strong spark of faith that had been with him through so many years. Why was it that evil had such a strong hold on the earth? How could God turn his head away and ignore all the prayers spoken so fervently to him?

Looking down at his father, he wanted to believe that even if Ragnar died he would go to a better place, a place where they would all be reunited—but for the first time in his life he wasn't sure. It was a devastating feeling.

Despite the fact that Nissa seldom showed her feelings, she did so now. Her face was a mask of grief. Erica's eyes were red with weeping. Gwyneth and Natasha hurriedly dashed away their tears.

The hours passed slowly, transforming day into night. Ragnar's face was pale, his once strong body getting thinner and thinner. Natasha feared for his life. He was so still. And pale. Almost a ghostly white.

"He's . . . he's not dead, is he?" Gwyneth breathed.

Putting her head down to his chest, she listened for a heartbeat. "He's alive." For a long, lingering moment she stayed curled up by his side, and Natasha had the feeling she knew in her heart that the time he had left on the earth was limited and that she was saying good-bye.

As Ragnar's wound festered and he grew more pale by the minute, Selig, Sean, and Torin also said their good-byes to him in turn. There was no denying it. Ragnar Longsword, the most venerated Viking of his age, was dying.

"No. . . ." Sean said softly.

Erica was too choked with sobs to speak. It was obvious that her father had been the person she loved most in the world next to Torin.

"May Odin in his wrath strike Herlaug down!" Selig hissed.

Gritting his teeth to keep from showing his emotions, Selig put a sword in his father's hand. "May the maidens take you quickly to Valhalla. . . ."

Natasha was certain that she must be imagining it, but she could have sworn she saw Ragnar's lips move, thought she heard him whisper, "Odin . . ."

Taking Gwyneth and Erica aside, Sean whispered a soft prayer for the man who had given them life and whose love had bound them together.

Forty

As in life, also in death, Ragnar was given the greatest respect. The women of the household bathed his body and clothed him in all his bracelets and best garments; his sword was placed in his hand. Looking as regal as he had in life, he was laid upon his large bed as the members of the household, including the thralls, and his friends and companions filed past to give their last respects to this great jarl who had now gone to his glory in the realm of Valhalla.

Seeing him lying there so peacefully in his eternal sleep was nearly more than Sean could take. He wanted to hear him laugh, see him smile; wanted to watch him bounce little Roland upon his knee again. But that would never be. A man named Herlaug, his brother, had killed him and robbed them all of all those special moments. Though Sean had always loathed the thought of taking human life, he hungered for it now. They would find Herlaug; they would make him pay, and the words of the scripture would come to pass: *an eye for an eye and a tooth for a tooth.*

"And a life for a life!" Listening to the wailing, keening cries of the women as was the Viking custom, Sean fought against an unmanly display of his own grief, but he felt it.

"We'll find Herlaug and he will die for this!" Selig growled. "After the funeral I am going to search every waterway and under every rock if I must, but I will find him."

"You will not be alone!" Torin rasped. "I will be right behind you."

"And I," Sean added, hastily crossing himself. What he was going to do was against everything he had ever been taught, everything he had once held dear, and yet for the sake of his father, he would give in to the blood lust that tore at him like a claw.

The mourners walked in a stately procession, the women following the men as was the custom, until they reached Ragnar's ship. Because Ragnar was a man of renown, a man of status, mourners flocked to his burial. Sean had quickly learned that, contrary to what he had been taught by the monks about being rewarded for a lifetime of peace, for the Vikings, death after a lifetime of combat was thought to be the beginning of a glorious hereafter of feasting and fighting in Valhalla. His father's body was placed in a long ship, the same ship he had commanded during the days of his youth, the ship that would carry his soul to the Vikings' idea of eternal glory.

Sean watched in silence as his father's possessions were put aboard the ship. Everything that he would need in the next world was taken on board: a wagon, chest, buckets, a sledge, even food for his long journey. Ragnar's treasures were also piled upon his ship, including his favorite swords and battle-ax. Even a horse was killed and placed on board so that Ragnar would have the animal in the next life. Then Ragnar was placed on a narrow bed within an open pavilion erected in the center of the ship.

Sean was proud of his father and proud of Natasha, who was dressed in her finest garments. All the others at the funeral were also wearing their finest clothing: thick woolen tunics and trousers of bright colors, furs, and metal armbands. The women wore woolen gowns, brooches, braided armbands, hair ornaments, and breast chains. All of the jewelry was of gold or silver. Torin and Selig were even carrying their swords, though Sean had laid his aside.

After bidding his last good-bye to his father, Sean watched as friends and warriors carried the rest of his personal belongings aboard the ship. Watching made him feel like an outsider, for the traditions were so foreign from his own Christian teachings. The abbot had told him over and over that a man had to leave behind his worldly possessions to enter the kingdom of God. Was he right? Sean had begun to doubt for the first time in his life, for although the abbot had been so certain, who really knew what happened when death gave its kiss of eternal sleep?

A neighboring chieftain, who was acting as priest, walked slowly around the ship, intoning a repetitive chant as he sprinkled dried herbs and small plants from a basket. As he sang a chant, the men in the crowd sang along with him.

Sean watched as torches from a bonfire set the ship ablaze. The ship was towed to the center of the river and sent floating downstream amid wild yells to Odin and Thor to send him quickly to Valhalla.

"He died with a sword in his hand, doing battle—the greatest boon to a Viking," Selig whispered in his ear.

His brother's words eased the tension in Sean's breast, and he felt a sense of relief. The Christian teachings were against cremation, and for a moment he had feared, but no. In his way, Ragnar had lived a good life. He was a good man who, in his last years, had tried to bring about peace in the Northland. Whichever land existed in the hereafter, he knew his father would be there.

The wooden ship burned quickly; its timbers blackened and fell off in the water as the flames cascaded into the water like a waterfall of fire. Sparks from the pitch leapt skyward, carrying prayers to Odin and Thor. Sean, Erica, and Gwyneth said their own prayers as well. Ragnar's immortality would be assured.

At last, as the serpent ship burned itself out, hissing like a live serpent beneath the waves, Sean said his last good-bye to his father.

Forty-one

Sean and his brothers did not have to find Herlaug. After Ragnar's funeral, Herlaug made it a point to find them and taunt them. Einar Magnusson told them that word was quickly spreading throughout the entire area surrounding Hafrsfjord that Herlaug had openly claimed the lands that had belonged to his brother and had proclaimed himself the new jarl.

"He's a murderer! He will never take our father's place," Selig seethed, taking great pleasure in sharpening his sword as he stood by the fire.

"But who will?" Einar asked.

The two brothers looked at each other. Though Ragnar had been planning on naming his successor the very night of his death, he had not been given the chance.

"According to Herlaug, his brother named *him* as successor before he died."

"Before Herlaug killed him, you mean," Sean corrected. He spoke sternly but did not raise his voice to the angered pitch of Selig's.

Einar held up one boney hand. "You cannot prove that. There were no eyewitnesses."

Setting down his sword, Selig strode forward, purposefully standing as tall as he could before the little man to intimidate him. "There was Ragnar. He told us before he died who killed him."

"Ah, but Ragnar is dead." Einar took a step backward, trying to distance himself from the muscular Viking. He took another, then another, but with each step he took, Selig took one step forward. "He can—cannot bear witness at the *thing.*"

"But we can, my brother and I." Sean came to stand beside Selig, as if to emphasize that they were united, at least on this matter.

"There are only two of you. Herlaug is cunning enough to produce several men who will make your words sound like lies."

Sean's patience was wearing thin, and Selig had no patience at all. "Then we will have to forget diplomacy and depose that murderer by fighting him."

"War?"

"We have no other choice," Selig replied. "Besides, I want revenge."

Sean clenched and unclenched his fists. "My uncle has much to answer for. He has tried to do harm to all of us at one time or another."

"But many men will die. Is revenge on one man really worth the price?"

Selig gritted his teeth. "Revenge can be sweet."

"Revenge is a selfish reason for war!" Einar responded, stepping behind Sean as if to find a human shield.

"It's not just for revenge," Sean answered. "Under my father's guidance the people in Hafrsfjord prospered. There was peace. Herlaug will destroy that. For the good of the people, Herlaug must die, for he will always be a threat to the peace and security of the Northland."

Sean had heard his father talk about the Vikings' system of justice. Treachery could not go unpunished and had to be arbitrated either by *thing* law or in hand-to-hand combat.

"So you are saying that this goes far beyond vengeance and ambition."

"Far beyond."

Selig listened intently, but his body remained tense as he continued to scowl. "Let me challenge Herlaug to a fight. I will win and all the blood spilled will be his."

"And then what? The people need a strong, experienced leader, one they will listen to, someone who can bring them together as Ragnar did. Who will take Ragner's place?" Einar looked first at one brother and then the other again. "Which of you?"

Sean answered without hesitation. "Torin!"

Selig was stunned. "Torin?" It was obvious by his expression that he had assumed that as the eldest child of Ragnar he would be the choice. "But . . ."

Despite his brother's disappointment and the bruise to his pride, Sean held fast. "If you will look into your heart, you will know that it is the right thing to do, what Father wanted. Remember when he took his own amulet off and gave it to Tor?"

Selig bit his lip as if to keep from saying something that might ruin his newfound relationship with his brother, but it was obvious that he was upset. He nodded grimly.

"I think that Ragnar had made up his mind then that Torin should follow him. Torin was the man he always depended on, the man he sent to find us."

Selig shrugged. "*I* found *him!*"

Sean ignored the retort, saying, "He gave us another sign when he named his first grandson after Torin's father." He paused, looking pointedly at his sister gently cuddling her child. "And do not forget Erica."

"Erica . . ." At the thought of his sister and what she had gone through to bring Ragnar's grandson into the world, Selig's whole body relaxed. "Had she been born a male she would have been Father's first choice."

"Just think of what strength and wisdom Torin and Erica will bring."

Selig knew when he had lost an argument. "With you and me to give them our loyalty and our strength." He looked at Einar. "We are united. All of us. Torin will succeed my father, and you can let it be known that my brother and I will give him our full support."

The decision had been made, and Sean knew that if Ragnar could see them now he would smile. Before Torin could take over as jarl, however, there was one thing standing in the way: Herlaug.

Sean stared out at the harbor. Already three ships had provisioned to follow him and Selig when they attacked. The days of preparation began quickly, for timing was vital. Torin made the decision that instead of going after Herlaug, they would wait until he came to them.

Torin, Selig, and Sean would each take command of their own ships, but Torin would be in the lead, making all the critical decisions.

"I want to go!" Erica was insistent.

"No." Torin was unwavering. "There will be no women on board the ships."

"He was my father!"

"We go as a fighting force. I will not take the chance of anything happening to you!"

Putting her hands over her ears, Erica refused to listen.

Torin's expression softened. Taking her wrists, he gently pulled her hands away and held them in his own. "You have our son to think about now. I would not want him to be without his parents. Besides, you would be a distraction."

"I don't want to lose you!" Her eyes touched on Selig and Sean. "I don't want to lose any of you!"

Sean stepped forward. "In this life there can be no assurances, but I can only promise you one thing: that we will protect each other and thereby be a force the likes of which Herlaug has never seen before."

Forty-two

If Natasha had not known what it meant to be a Viking wife before, she did now. It meant waiting. It meant preparing herself to lose everything she loved and held dear at the slash of a sword. It meant watching as her husband practiced throwing axes at a target and ducking just in time to keep his head on his shoulders, knowing that, unlike his brother, an enemy would not give him a second chance. It meant being forgotten while her husband gave everything he had to training for the combat to come. It meant sleeping alone, hoping that this nightmare would end and she would wake up and hear the familiar sound of his voice whispering in her ear, "It's over. I've come back to you forever. . . ."

Natasha sat with Gwyneth and Erica in the great hall, listening to the sounds of the men outside as they yelled and roared at each other like men gone mad. Over and over they repeated exercises to hone their skills and those of their men as well.

"Say what ye will about Herlaug, he is a fighting mon. Torin knows they have to be prepared," Erica declared, her own arm swinging back and forth as if she were out in the yard practicing with them.

"Ha, if you ask me, there is more danger of their killing each other than dying from Herlaug's prowess," Gwyneth mumbled, tangling the yarn on the loom. "Well, I don't want my child to grow up without his father."

"Your child?" Natasha rose from the chair and knelt beside her.

"Gwyneth!"

Gwyneth blushed and was suddenly flustered. "I—I mean . . . well . . . I . . . don't say a word. I don't want Selig to know until this is over. He might not put his full attentions on the battle because he would be worrying overmuch about me!"

Natasha squeezed Gwyneth's hand. "So you and Selig won the contest. Ragnar's second grandchild is on the way. . . ."

For a long time there was silence. "If only he were here to know. He would be pleased."

Erica looked toward the ceiling. "Perhaps he does know."

Natasha, too, had a confession. "I may be wrong, but I think . . . that . . . because I missed my monthly time and . . ."

If the men had their bond of the sea, the women had their bond of life—creating it, nurturing it, and securing the future so that their husbands' seed would continue. Sitting together, unified by the love they felt for the men in their lives, they had never felt closer or more appreciative that they had been given the blessing to create life.

The precious moment was interrupted, however, as the men came bounding back into the hall to celebrate the end of the day's training. Downing flagons of mead and ale, they yelled wildly as they romped through the hall. Remembering the loving men they had once known, Natasha and the others exchanged glances. It was as if Selig, Sean, and Torin had been transformed into men they didn't even know—at least not at the moment.

Even their way of dressing was different, for they wore their "war" clothes: a thick, protective leather jerkin, woolen trousers tightly wrapped to their legs with leather thongs, and bronze helmets. Seeing Sean dressed that way made Natasha remember Thordis, and a part of her mourned the changes in him. Though she loved him no matter what, a part of her longed for the gentle Sean she had first met, whose love was for writing and not fighting.

Later that night, however, as she was wrapped in his arms, she caught a glimpse of the Sean that used to be. "Once this is over I want to travel, Tasha. One of my father's men knows of a land west of here where few men have gone. Some have called it the land of ice, though in truth it is really green."

"Iceland?"

He nuzzled her ear. "We'll take Ref and Nadia with us and make it the kind of land I've always envisioned. Like in days of old. And I'll write down a saga of the journey so that those who come after us will know what it is like to be the first in Eden."

"Eden?"

He smiled. "It's a garden, a place the monks wrote about, a place mentioned in the scriptures. We'll create our own."

It was a beautiful dream, a dream that was shattered as she thought about what might happen in the next few days. Anytime there was fighting, a man's life was at risk, and she shuddered to think of spending even one moment without Sean's love.

"Hold me close, Sean. Promise me that you will not die!"

Stroking his fingers through her hair, he said, "I cannot make such a promise; you know that. But I can promise you that I will love you for eternity."

"I'm afraid for you. The others have spent their whole lives being Vikings. They are used to fighting, but you . . ."

"Hush. . . . I will not die, for I could not bear to

leave you." He enveloped her in his arms, holding her so close that their hearts seemed to beat as one.

The day Natasha had dreaded came much too soon. At dawn the next day, the dragon heads and red-and-white sails with Herlaug's insignia of a bear were spotted sailing up the fjord. Hearing the news, Sean, Selig, Erica, and Torin stood in a circle together. Holding up their amulets, they joined the raven, the wolf, the dragon, and the gripping beast together as if to unleash a powerful force.

"It has begun!" Erica whispered.

One by one the men put on their helmets and armed themselves. Gathering together their crew, they walked shoulder to shoulder to the ships. Erica led the women to a hill overlooking the waters, where they could watch safely from a distance. She pointed to the largest ship, and Natasha knew without a word being spoken that it was Herlaug's vessel. Like a bully it pushed up the fjord, ramming two of the ships that were favorable to Torin's cause.

Natasha watched in horror as the men on those two ships were vanquished and the ships soon put to the torch, flaming as Ragnar's burial ship had done. Worse yet, Herlaug had quickly maneuvered it so that there was one fire ship at one end of the fjord and one at the other, the flaming ships being used as a weapon against Torin to trap him in between and keep him isolated from the others.

"I've seen the same thing done with wagons," Natasha whispered. What she did not want to say was that the maneuver was treacherous and aided in the defeat of all those trapped in between.

They were haunted by the roar of the flames, the screams of the wounded, the smell of the smoke, and the hissing sound of the burning wood as it hit the waterline. It was as if the sea had turned to a raging inferno, as if the hell Sean had told her about had come to earth. Even so, as they watched they could see Torin standing courageously at the prow, leading his men in the fighting.

Then suddenly, Torin's ship was also aflame. With each puff of smoke and fallen timber Natasha's heart sank. Poor Erica! How terrible for her to see such a thing.

"Torin!" The air reverberated as she called out to him.

Like seals the men dove overboard, and for a moment it seemed as if the end had come—at least for one of their husbands.

Suddenly, Natasha and Erica noticed that the men were swimming toward another ship that had entered the melee.

"Selig!" Gwyneth breathed. Next came Sean's ship, then one commanded by Ref, followed by Einar's vessel and thirty others.

"They used Torin's ship as a diversion. . . ."

"A sacrifice!"

The fighting was fierce and erratic, the clanging sound of ax upon ax and sword upon sword ringing in the air, but it was soon obvious that Herlaug was outnumbered two to one. Even more importantly, it seemed that all the days of training had been well worth it. They could see the silhouetted forms of their men thrusting forward, fighting in the midst of the holocaust Herlaug had created. Though Herlaug pulled back to regroup and plan a new strategy, he was clearly losing.

There was a price to pay for victory, however. The ocean had a pink hue from all the blood that was spilled in the fighting. Bodies floated in the water. Ravens and other scavenger birds hovered in the air, waiting to pick the bones. It was a morbid scene, one

Natasha had seen on the steppes all too often. Whispering to her gods, she made the wish that the battle would be over before more had to suffer and die. But the battle raged on until suddenly Herlaug fell, his sword raised aloft as if in a final challenge.

"Is it over?" Erica squinted her eyes to see who had struck the mortal blow to Herlaug, but the sun's glare off the ocean made it difficult to see.

"Not yet." A few stubborn men continued the fighting, but then, as they fell, a horn sounded. The fighting was over. Torin, Sean, and Selig had managed a victory, the kind that would be remembered by the skalds in years to come.

Herlaug, the murderer of Ragnar, was dead. Ragnar's honor had been avenged. Now a new jarl would take his place. Torin Rolandsson would now wear the circlet and carry the sword of his father-in-law. Among much pomp, ceremony, and feasting, he would be proclaimed the leader of his people with his wife beside him and the strong arms of his brothers-in-law by his side, Selig at the right and Sean taking up the left. Ragnar's final wish had come true.

The next moments that passed seemed like an eternity, but at last Natasha looked up and saw that he was there, the one face above all others that she wanted to see. His face was smudged with charcoal from the fire; his face was lined with fatigue; his garments were torn and dirty; his cape was hanging by a thread; but he was alive and he was there. Picking up her skirts, she ran to him.

"Shall we go home?" he whispered against her hair. It was a question asked by Selig and Torin also as they made their way up the hill.

"Home. . . ." No matter what the language was, that word was the most glorious word ever spoken, except for *love.*

"I love you," Sean murmured. "I always will."

"Forever." She said softly.

"All my life I dreamed of discovering new lands. Now I realize that love is the greatest discovery of all." And it was. As he walked with his wife back to the hall, Sean knew that without a doubt.